TESTAMENT

Shaun Hutson

Fiction to die for…

Published by Caffeine Nights Publishing 2019

Published in Great Britain by
Caffeine Nights Publishing
4 Eton Close
Walderslade
Chatham
Kent
ME5 9AT

www.caffeinenights.com

British Library Cataloguing in Publication Data.
A CIP catalogue record for this book is available from the British Library
ISBN: 978-1-910720-99-8

Cover design by
Ria Fend

Everything else by
Default, Luck and Accident

Acknowledgements for TESTAMENT

No one writes a book and then has it published without a bit of help.

Either during the actual physical and mental process of writing it or in what follows after its finished. The only help I usually need during the writing process is a bit of moral support (maybe the odd comment to tell me that I am indeed a great writer and that all should tremble before me!) and the occasional reminder that I haven't actually forgotten how to do what I've been doing for most of my adult life. Apart from that, I usually sail through without too much trouble. The book is my baby after all and has been from its inception so, if there are any problems, it's me who has to solve them.

Once it's completed, that's when the help really begins so I'll start there. Huge thanks as always to my publisher, Darren Laws at Caffeine Nights for his continued faith and support, Charlotte Garvey for her proof reading and Ria Fend for bringing the covers to life and thanks also to anyone else there who actually does the hard work and gets the book ready for readers to buy. This part of the ordeal also needs me to thank my agent Meg Davis for her efforts.

The other people I thank here have probably provided something but I'm not always sure what it is. Inspiration. Support. Something like that. They should know what they've done even if I can't always remember. So, on that count I'd like to thank Matt Shaw, Graeme Sayer, Michael Knight and Emma Dark.

Everyone at the Broadway cinema in Letchworth and Cineworld in Milton Keynes.

Dani, Claire, Leah, Bruce, Steve, Dave, Adrian, Janick and Nicko. Rod Smallwood, Gary Farrow.

My daughter, Kelly, Belinda and my mum.

And of course, the most important people I know. You lot.

The people who actually buy my books. This one has been a long time coming so we won't wait around any longer.

Let's go.

Shaun Hutson

Dedication

For my daughter.
No words are enough
to tell her how much
I love her.

"I fear to turn on the light,
For the darkness won't go away..."
Metallica

PROLOGUE

SOCIAL MEDIA
Posted on YouTube; 09.47; November 9th; 2017;

T he man walking across the baking sand was dressed in a bright orange boiler suit, open to the sternum.

Through the widespread garment it was possible to see the wounds on his torso. Some were the marks made by cigarettes, stubbed out on his flesh. Held there until they formed oozing blisters. Others had been put there by knives. Cuts up to eight inches long, opened in the flesh with blades of devastating sharpness. Sliced deeply enough to cause massive blood loss but not death.

The hand of a torturer had to be light sometimes.

The man stumbled once, almost fell, but regained his footing as one of those escorting him moved towards him.

The five men marching along on either side of him and behind him were clad from head to foot in black.

Four of them carried automatic weapons. AK-47s, the Russian made assault rifles otherwise known as the Kalashnikov after their designer, slung across them by the leather straps. They walked stiffly, careful not to overbalance on the shifting sand as their prisoner had almost done.

Not that he needed an escort. If he chose to run, where was he going to go? The desert stretched for miles in all directions and the sun was beating down so mercilessly from the cloudless sky that anyone out in these temperatures would succumb to heat stroke and dehydration faster than they could say 'dying of thirst'. Temperatures at midday had been known to reach well over 120 degrees.

The man in the orange suit stumbled again and, this time, he dropped to his knees. Unable or unwilling to go on he waited there, his head bowed slightly until one of the black-clad men ran towards him and dragged him to his feet, grabbing handfuls of his boiler suit, pushing him ahead.

The man moved on, his steps faltering now.

The fear that was coursing through his veins, as surely as drugs through an addict, was making it difficult for him to even co-ordinate his steps now. There was a mound ahead, rising from the sand like a blister from scorched flesh, and the man was sure that was where they were taking him.

When he hesitated again one of the black-clad escorts drove the butt of the Kalashnikov into the small of his back with such force it caused the man to wet himself. A dark stain spread rapidly across the front of the orange boiler suit and the man looked down at it. Along with fear he now felt shame and anger. He didn't want the others to see that he was afraid but what was he to do? Would any man who was walking to his death truly have the heart to show no fear?

As the man rose to his feet again, he could feel urine trickling down his leg. But that didn't seem to matter any more. Nothing did if he was honest.

The little procession reached the mound of sand he'd been looking at and they started up it. When they had reached the pinnacle the fifth man in the group stepped forward and barked something the orange suited man could not make out. Seconds later he was grabbed by both shoulders and forced to his knees, the tallest individual now standing behind him.

One of the other black-clad men ambled across in front of him, digging inside his jacket for something.

The orange suited man began to breathe more quickly, his heart hammering harder against his chest as he wondered what the figure before him was going to produce. It turned out to be a camcorder which the black-clad man checked over quickly, ensuring that no sand had got into the device during the march across the desert. Satisfied, he removed the lens cap and peered through the viewfinder, checking focus and anything else he felt he should attend to. When he had the camcorder ready, he raised one hand as a signal.

The figure behind the orange suited man now stepped forward, speaking as he did.

"This is for all Kaffir watching," he said, his voice loud. "For all those who would set foot in our beloved homeland. In the land of the Prophet, all praise be to him."

The other black-clad men added their own words of affirmation as the figure went on.

"We did not ask you to come here," he continued. "We did not want you here. You thought you could conquer us. You kill our families. You rape our children and you expect us to allow this." He raised his voice. "You will pay for this. All of you. We will carry this jihad deep into all your homelands. Into your lives. Into your lands."

More words of agreement and encouragement from the other black-clad men. They rose on the desert wind and were carried away.

"And now," the figure went on. "You will see how we treat all invaders. All defilers. All enemies. All Kaffir."

Barely had the last word left his lips than he opened his tunic and pulled a hunting knife from his belt. It was fully ten inches long. Wickedly sharp on one side and serrated on the other. The blazing sun glinted on the oiled steel momentarily, the flash flickering across the man in the orange jumpsuit who was now murmuring something unintelligible under his breath.

His eyes were closed, and he was hunched further over, his shoulders drawn up as if to try and protect himself from what he knew was coming even though he knew the gesture was pointless.

He felt hands on his shoulders, on his hair, pulling him upright. And now he began to shake uncontrollably. To hell with bravery. To hell with dignity. He was going to die. Nothing had prepared him for that, not even the unshakable realisation of that fact since his capture. All through his time in captivity he had clung to the tiny shred of hope, that he knew he was foolish to entertain, but it was all he'd had.

That minuscule fragment of optimism he had managed to retain was now being blown away as surely as grains of desert sand in a storm. He had tried to imagine being with his wife and child again. He had clung to that like a drowning man clings to a lifebelt. The thought that he might actually be rescued. Might actually get out of this place alive. Might...

There was nothing left now but terror.

He felt strong hands dragging him upright and he tried to struggle but they just held him more tightly, holding him upright, stopping him from rocking back and forth as he waited there on his knees.

He thought about begging for mercy but realised it would do no good. There was nothing he could do. These men did not acknowledge mercy. They did not acquaint themselves with forgiveness. They wanted only one thing. His death.

And now he felt the knife against his neck, the honed edge gliding gently over his flesh as the man behind him adjusted his stance, ensuring that he had maximum leverage for when he began to cut and hack.

The man in the orange boiler suit wet himself again. His stomach somersaulted and he thought he was going to be sick as the fear gripped him as surely as the hands holding him upright. He wanted to scream. He wanted to cry. He wanted to live.

But these men would not allow that.

He shrieked madly as he felt the blade cut into the flesh of his neck, dragged back and forth with such force that it sliced muscles easily.

The man holding the camera tried to zoom in but the picture became blurred and he could not correct the fault.

He called to his companion with the knife to wait while he adjusted the camcorder and the figure agreed, irritated by the screams of agony coming from the orange suited man.

When the cameraman was ready again the blade once again began cutting through the flesh of the kneeling man's neck and the screams began once more. Louder this time. Screams of pain. Of fear. Of desperation.

All lost on the rising desert wind.

PART ONE

"Time chasing time creeps up behind
I can't run forever, and time waits for no one."
Megadeth

ONE

BAGHDAD; JADRIYA DISTRICT; CENTRAL IRAQ;

S ean Doyle lit his cigarette, took a couple of drags, and propped one booted foot on the dashboard of the jeep as it swept along.

The motion of the vehicle at least created a cooling breeze that helped to dispel the sweltering mid-afternoon heat a little but, despite that, Doyle could feel the sweat soaking into the T-shirt beneath his Kevlar body armour.

He glanced at the driver, but the man seemed unworried by the blistering temperatures or by the dust that was filling the jeep as they drove further and further out of Baghdad itself. During the summer, the city was often troubled by sand and dust storms that were relatively easy to avoid by sheltering inside but those same storms became more problematic in the open areas beyond the suburbs and it was into one of these areas that the jeep was now heading. Doyle had often wondered if a westerner ever became used to the heat and the conditions here and, having already been present in this particular part of the Middle East for over a year, he was beginning to think that even the most basic assimilation into this place was impossible.

He took another drag on his cigarette and blew out the smoke, noticing that the jeep was taking him further and further from the confines of the city. The built-up areas he had become accustomed to were now being replaced by the flat, arid and featureless expanse of desert that one found eventually upon leaving the city.

"Why did they call me?" he grunted, nudging the driver. "Someone else should have been able to take care of this."

"They are frightened. Two men have been attacked already," the driver told him. "They not come this way if it is dangerous."

"Right."

"They need someone with gun," the driver went on.

Doyle nodded.

"I'm not the only security operative here, you know," he murmured.

"Others not good with guns," the driver told him.

Doyle shrugged.

"How many of them?" he wanted to know.

"Five or six they think. Maybe more. Fucking dogs."

"Fucking dogs," Doyle repeated, nodding sagely.

Wild dogs had been a problem in and around the city for years. Nearly 60,000 of them had been exterminated during the last twelve months, shot on the streets of Baghdad itself, but those that had survived had moved out of the confines of the city and into the surrounding areas. Here they scavenged food if they could and, if that wasn't possible, the packs that had become completely feral hunted prey like any other hungry predator. There had been attacks on locals and several had been killed and eaten. A kill made these packs even more dangerous because it gave them a taste for human flesh, Doyle knew only too well the trouble he would face if confronted by one of these feral packs. He pulled the Beretta from its holster and slid the magazine from the butt, checking it was full. Satisfied that it was he slammed the slim metal clip back into the weapon and re-holstered it.

The sound made the driver look around and Doyle simply met the man's gaze.

The jeep came to a halt and Doyle glanced out across the landscape before him.

There were several small, flat roofed dwellings ahead of them close to the road. Beyond those, Doyle could see that the ground sloped away sharply, making it almost impossible to see what lay over the sand ridge ahead.

"Over there," the driver urged, gesturing towards the ridge.

"Take me closer," Doyle said, preparing to climb back into the jeep.

"No. You go," the man said, nervously. "I wait here."

"Thanks a lot," Doyle muttered, setting out across the sand, looking around him to see if he could see any movement in or around the houses. They remained silent.

He was halfway up the incline when he heard the growling.

Doyle slid a hand inside his jacket and flipped open one of the shoulder holsters he wore, ensuring that he could reach the Beretta easily when the time came.

The sound seemed to grow louder for a moment then it ceased as Doyle reached the top of the ridge. He looked down and saw that, where the ground sloped away, it led to several deep cracks in the earth. To call them caves was probably incorrect but, at this precise moment, he couldn't think what else to call them. They were more like crevices in the sand, wide enough to drive a car into and with sand all around them, apparently blown into high mounds by the wind.

Doyle advanced a little further.

Again, he heard growling.

As he drew closer to the first of the openings, he heard the sound growing in volume and drew the pistol from its holster, hefting it before him.

"Oh, shit," he murmured under his breath.

Even he had not been prepared for what he saw now.

TWO

The first of the dogs emerged, lips drawn back from yellowed teeth, the growl rattling in its throat as it advanced slowly.

It was a big animal and Doyle took an involuntary step backwards.

Its ribs were clearly visible beneath its mangy fur and, when it moved forward, it hobbled slightly due to the injury it had sustained to one of its front paws. Nevertheless, it was still a ferocious looking creature, and, to Doyle's eyes, it looked hungry like so many of its species in this area. This made it doubly dangerous. He swung the 9mm up, drawing a bead on the dog, watching for any signs of movement.

As it took two or three steps towards him, he saw another animal emerge from behind it.

This one was bigger. No, actually he thought, revising his initial opinion, it was fucking big. Fully four feet high at the shoulder and it reminded Doyle of a Great Dane or a mastiff of some kind. Like the first dog, it was thin and badly undernourished, and, like the first animal, it was growling agitatedly. Those low rumbling growls very quickly became deep guttural barks and, when it opened its considerable jaws, Doyle could see thick white saliva flying from its lips. He had one thought when he saw that.

The animal was very probably rabid.

Without hesitation, Doyle shot it.

The bullet hit the animal squarely in the forehead, blowing most of its head off. It dropped like a stone, blood spouting into the sand around what remained of its skull.

However, despite the thunderous retort of the pistol, the first dog actually advanced a few feet, its eyes now fixed on Doyle.

It was joined by another. And another.

Big, powerful looking animals all dripping thick saliva from their muzzles. They began to bark in unison and Doyle took a step backwards, steadying himself.

As if a switch had been thrown, the dogs came hurtling towards him.

Doyle fired twice and managed to hit the first animal in the chest, the second one in the eye. Both of them went down heavily, the first one still breathing but unable to move any further because of its wound. The third dog, however, came rushing towards him, teeth bared.

Doyle dropped to one knee to steady his aim, squeezing off two shots.

The first nicked the dog's rear right leg, the second smashed into its mouth, driving several teeth backwards as it ploughed on, erupting from the back of its head along with gouts of blood and sprays of brain matter.

As he stood up more dogs came sprinting from the second of the caves.

Rather than being frightened off by the sound of the gunshots and the fate of their companions, the dogs seemed hell-bent on reaching him. Doyle shot the first one but missed the second. It was a fast animal, some kind of lurcher he guessed. Much skinnier now because of hunger but it still possessed frightening speed, it rushed towards him and Doyle fired twice, unable to sight the weapon properly. Both shots missed, drilling into the ground in front of the dog.

It launched itself at Doyle, slamming into him and knocking him off his feet. He saw the jaws only inches from his face, trying to bite him, spattering him with saliva but he had managed to grab the animal by the throat and, as it barked and yelped madly, he managed to roll on top of it, gripping its windpipe, trying to throttle it before it could bite him. As it struggled it scratched against his stomach and thighs with its paws, but Doyle ignored that discomfort, using the Beretta like a club at such close range. He slammed the butt against the dog's head hard enough to stun it then hauled himself up onto his knees where he levelled the pistol and fired twice, both shots powering into the animal's upper body.

As blood spread across the sand around it, Doyle stepped backwards, spinning around as quickly as he could to see if any more of the dogs were coming towards him. He was relieved to see that they weren't.

As he glanced up towards the crest of the sand ridge, he saw the jeep driver looking down at him, surveying the dead dogs impassively.

"Fucking dogs," the driver said.

"Yeah," Doyle agreed, wiping spittle from his face. "Fucking dogs."

THREE

The explosion startled him.

He'd been expecting it, but the ferocity of the blast still made him wince involuntarily.

Sean Doyle looked around in the direction of the eruption, watched the smoke and dust billowing into the cloudless blue sky for a second then walked on, the ground still quivering beneath his feet. A few clouds might have been nice, he thought. They would have sheltered the parched land from the blistering rays of the sun. It was like a blowtorch, suspended in the clear blue firmament.

Sean Doyle hated the heat.

He didn't like warm weather at the best of times, but this was approaching the limit of his tolerance.

He could feel the sweat pouring down his face as he walked and, beneath the Kevlar, his T-shirt was already sticking to his torso. The waistband of his trousers was drenched, and Doyle was beginning to think that he had more than the regulation number of sweat glands in his body. He knew the human body had millions of them, but he was beginning to think that his entire body was composed solely of sweat glands. It wasn't normal to lose this much fluid, was it? He puffed out his cheeks and continued walking, occasionally wiping droplets of moisture from his face when it trickled into his eyes.

He took off his helmet, wiped his forehead with one sleeve and exhaled wearily glancing around as he paused momentarily, reaching into a pocket of the trousers he wore. He pulled out a bottle of water and sipped it, wincing as he tasted that it was already warm. He'd filled it less than thirty minutes ago from one of the many stop-taps dotted around but still the liquid had heated inexorably, just like the land itself beneath the unremitting glare of the sun.

Doyle had never been able to understand why people loved the heat so much. To him, it meant being uncomfortable, it meant people with body odour and it meant flies. The only creatures who got justifiably excited about heat like this were fucking reptiles as far as he was concerned.

Away to his right two bulldozers were trundling across the landscape with their buckets lowered, pushing mounds of rubble before them. Cranes, towering above the desolate landscape swung back and forth. Dust particles billowed around the debris and filled the air like millions of insects. They clogged your nostrils and your ears, and they stung your eyes, Doyle noted. And of course, there were insects galore to add to the discomfort. Flies were the worst. They landed on you even while you were moving. Doyle watched a bloated black fly as it crawled over his knuckles before taking to the air once again. He wondered where it had been. Crawling over dog shit or camel shit probably. He wiped his hand on his trousers and walked on.

The city, the dust choked shithole where he had been for the last fourteen months, had three temperatures as far as Doyle was concerned. Hot, very hot and for fuck sake. It was a for fuck sake day today.

Even the locals were nowhere to be seen. Like any sensible person, they retreated to their homes or to any welcoming shade when the sun reached its zenith. Doyle glanced at his watch and noticed that it was just past noon. What was that old song about 'Mad Dogs and Englishmen' going out in the midday sun? He shook his head and almost managed a smile.

Almost.

It seemed that was right. Mad dogs, Englishmen and any locals engaged in the building of a railway from Baghdad to Karbala, he reasoned. He sipped more water and glanced up at the cloudless sky and the searing sun. For the next two hours you'd be able to fry an egg on any metallic surface if that was your wish. Doyle's only wish was to be out of the fucking sunshine.

There were several Portakabins on the far side of the site

24

and it was towards these that he headed. Trekking like some deranged hiker over the landscape that resembled a cross between a First World War battlefield and the surface of the moon.

He ducked involuntarily when he heard the explosion.

The ground shook beneath him and he glanced in the direction of the blast to see a funnel of dirt and dust rising into the sky. It rolled away in all directions and Doyle saw another bulldozer rumble towards the site of the blast, ready to push away the debris it had created.

Several dozen workers in orange jackets and yellow safety helmets scurried around the site, like fluorescent ants eager to repair a rent in their nest wall, and Doyle glanced impassively at them as he headed towards the nearest of the Portakabins. Most of those workers would be stopping their labours soon, he thought to himself, called to prayer by the voices of their imāms as they echoed over the city. It was a sound that Doyle had come to accept as easily as the roar of machinery and the buzz of blowflies. He took off his own safety helmet again, wiped more sweat from his face and ducked into the Portakabin.

It was cooler inside the temporary structure. Not that much cooler, not much of an improvement, not welcomingly chilled compared to the intolerable heat outside but it was a fair few degrees chillier than the inferno beyond, and for that small mercy Doyle was grateful. A small generator in one corner of the building powered what passed for air-conditioning. There were several water coolers inside too and Doyle crossed to the closest and gulped down three cupfuls of water in quick succession then he sat down at one of a dozen tables in the makeshift building.

He had barely settled himself when the door opened again.

FOUR

A heavyset man in his forties entered, his pudgy face red from the heat and also covered by a thin sheen of sweat. He smiled in Doyle's direction then filled one of the cups below the water cooler, sipped from it and seated himself opposite Doyle.

Doyle was about to ask why, when the whole room was empty, he'd decided to sit at the same table, but he decided not to and merely hoped the man would go away quickly. Hopefully without beginning some pointless conversation.

"This heat is unbelievable isn't it?" the newcomer observed.

Doyle nodded.

"I would say you get used to it," he began. "But you don't."

The man raised his eyebrows and sipped his water.

"My name's Phillip Robinson," the man informed him, extending his right hand, which Doyle shook firmly.

"Sean Doyle," he announced.

"I've only been out here a week," Robinson told him. "What about you?"

"In Baghdad, fourteen months. Before that I was in Karbala. I've been with them since they started building this railway."

"Security?" Robinson noted, and Doyle nodded.

"And you?"

"I'm a structural engineer," the other man informed him.

"Good luck." Doyle drained what was left in his cup and refilled it.

"I heard there are more private security operatives in Iraq than there are soldiers," Robinson said. "Do you work for an agency?"

"Freelance," Doyle told him.

"Has there been much trouble?"

"On and off," Doyle shrugged. "A few attacks on workers. A couple of kidnappings of westerners. That's big business out here." As he sat back, his jacket gaped open and, he noticed Robinson swallow hard as he saw the two automatic pistols Doyle wore in shoulder holsters, one beneath each arm.

"Are those real?" Robinson asked, attempting a smile.

"They wouldn't be much use if they were replicas, would they?"

"I've never seen a gun up close before."

"Why would you? Not much call for them in the engineering business I wouldn't have thought."

"What are they? What make?"

"You know anything about guns?"

"Not really. Only what I've seen in films." He shrugged.

"What you see in films is usually bullshit," Doyle told him. "People running around firing guns with one hand, no recoil. Four-hundred-round magazines that they never reload." He smiled thinly and shook his head. "People think it looks great on screen but it's not realistic."

"You sound as if you've had plenty of experience."

"A little bit. I know which end is the dangerous end."

"What kind of guns are they?" the man wanted to know, nodding in the direction of the firearms.

"That's a 15RDS," Doyle said, patting the weapon beneath his right arm. "The other one's a 92F. Both 9mm. I've got a Px4 in an ankle holster on my left boot. Happy now?"

"Have you had to use them since you got here?"

"Once or twice."

"But these extremists who are attacking westerners out here are not scared of dying. They blow themselves to pieces in suicide attacks. What makes you think they're going to be scared of getting shot?"

"These guys believe that if they die in the service of Allah, they'll enter paradise, right? Well, if they thought that they weren't going to get into paradise then they might think twice. I make them think twice."

"How?"

"My bullets are covered with pig fat."

"How do they know that?"

"Word gets around, even in a shithole like this. It's the same game I've been playing all my life. They just changed the rules a bit."

"You've done this kind of thing before?"

"I was in the Counter Terrorist Unit when I was younger," Doyle smiled thinly. "A lot younger." He rubbed one hand over his closely cropped grey hair and now, for the first time, he was aware of Robinson's gaze on the scars that marked his face and neck. There were half a dozen. Nothing disfiguring but they were visible nonetheless, some of the more prominent ones looking bleached against the sun darkened colour of his skin. "That was a long time ago."

Another time. A better time. A long time before you hit your fifties, eh, old man?

Robinson frowned, his forehead wrinkling.

"You must have seen some horrible things," he murmured.

"Shit happens doesn't it?" Doyle told him, dismissively.

They sat in silence for a moment longer then Robinson cleared his throat.

"You said there'd been a couple of kidnappings," he said. "Were the people who were taken found again?"

"One was," Doyle said, flatly. "Minus four of his fingers, his nose and one of his ears. Not the other one. If you have a look on YouTube, he's on there. All the private security operatives were shown his execution and told we had to be more vigilant in case it happened to other people under our protection. Like we can do fuck all to stop that kind of thing."

"What did they do to him?" Robinson wanted to know.

"They cut his head off."

"Why?"

"Because the ransom wasn't paid that they asked for."

"Did you know him?"

"I met him a couple of times."

"So, you knew him?"

"No. I said I met him a couple of times. I didn't know him."

Doyle got to his feet, tossed his paper cup into a waste bin and moved towards the door of the Portakabin. He turned and smiled at Robinson. "He was an engineer too. Welcome to Baghdad."

FIVE

BANDON; COUNTY CORK;
THE REPUBLIC OF IRELAND;

The house stood in its own grounds, surrounded by a twelve-foot-high stone wall. It was approachable only by a narrow and poorly tarmacked thoroughfare that was barely a cars width wide and led off from the main Bandon to Kinsale road.

Once the narrow route had been negotiated, any visitors had to pass through a set of large metal gates and traverse the long driveway that led to the front of the house itself. However, those gates had been padlocked for many years now. The chain that hung from them was rusted with the passing of time and the rigours of the weather. In fact, some thought that the chain was so inadequate now that a strong tug would shatter it and allow any who wished to make their way up to the house easy access.

Not that anyone wanted to go near the house and certainly not inside it. The firm of estate agents in Bandon who had taken on the selling of the house had hired a team of gardeners and cleaners to keep the property respectable, but even they had now neglected the maintenance and the grounds had overgrown as the inside of the place gathered dust. There had just been no interest in the house even at the greatly reduced selling price the agents had been prepared to accept.

No one had been past those gates for more than fifteen years now. A family had lived there for a time. A man, his wife and their two teenage children had occupied the impressive structure for just over three years, but their stay had been troubled, and the house had remained empty since their departure fifteen years ago.

Troubled was how the locals described the family's time there. People would nod sagely and then change the subject. No one wanted to speak too much about what had supposedly gone on there. Stories had filtered out and circulated among the few locals who lived near the house but what had happened there, both recently and more pointedly over thirty years ago, was a subject spoken of in hushed tones by those who knew.

If truth be told, locals would have been happier if the house had merely been demolished. At least that way there was a chance that both it and the events that had transpired within its walls, could simply be wiped away.

There were a couple of farms and a handful of houses dotted around the rolling landscape surrounding the estate and the residents of those dwellings often met up at a pub called The Standing Stones situated just off the Bandon to Kinsale road. Within the confines of that public house they had spoken of the family who lived at the big house and the troubles they had experienced. The family themselves had been visitors to The Standing Stones during their tenancy of the house. The pub served mountainous and extremely delicious lunches especially on a Sunday and the family had often taken advantage of that.

It was during those visits that others had learned of their predicament.

They had heard noises inside and outside the house. Strange noises that they had been unable to identify. Noises that had unsettled them and caused the teenage girl to have nightmares. They had been aware of the history of the house before they bought it and that had never bothered them but, just two weeks after moving in they had heard the noises for the first time. And there had been the smells too. Rank and putrid smells that had resisted all attempts to cleanse them. As if one of the sewer pipes that ran beneath the house had ruptured but inspection had revealed that wasn't the case. The source of the stench remained undiscovered.

The cold had come upon them gradually. 'As if a refrigerator door had been left open,' was how they described it at the beginning, but gradually it got worse until they could barely tolerate it, even with the thermostat on, their central heating turned to maximum.

The fact that no birds would nest anywhere near the house or even in the grounds seemed to strike them almost as an afterthought. By that time the daughter was suffering from nightmares so severe that they were forced to seek medical help. When the son also began to endure these night-time ordeals, they began to think about leaving the house. Exactly what the nightmares consisted of, no one ever discovered. Whether any of the family ever offered a possible explanation for the phenomena that drove them out of the house, none of the locals ever said. They had their own ideas about what had caused the disturbances, but few ever voiced those suspicions.

Not in public anyway.

So, the house stood empty.

Waiting.

SIX

BAGHDAD; JADRIYA DISTRICT; CENTRAL IRAQ;

Doyle was always in the last of the trucks to leave the city.

Every evening, just after seven, the foreign workers on the site would gather together then clamber into the small convoy of minibuses and lorries that would transport them out of the heart of Baghdad.

This evening Doyle stood as he always did, watching as the engineers, the plumbers, the builders and everyone else climbed into their transports, all of them slicked with sweat from the unrelenting heat they'd been subjected to all day. Some perspired for other reasons and Doyle watched many of the men looking around nervously. Many of them nodded in his direction and Doyle returned the gesture. He knew their faces but was familiar with only a handful by their names.

No point in getting too friendly with them, Doyle reasoned, they could be dead the following day.

Not if you do your job properly.

He smiled to himself as another of the men clambered into the lorry.

But I can't spot IEDs at the roadside, can I? I can't anticipate some mad bastard strapped up with C-4 running at a lorry.

Doyle knew he could only do so much to help the men and women in his charge. If there was anything at all he could do to protect them then he would. If it involved shooting someone then he wouldn't hesitate. Christ alone knew he'd never hesitated before so why start now. He'd found it was best to trust his own instincts, he always had done and if he was wrong then fuck it. Everyone made mistakes, didn't they? It's just that when you were dealing with people's lives it didn't pay to make too many fuckups. It smacked of carelessness and unprofessionalism, and if there was one thing Doyle prided himself on it was his professionalism. That combined with his efficiency, and some would say ruthlessness, had put him at the top of his profession.

But that's all in the past isn't it? All gone. You're not at the top any more. Not even within fucking sight of it.

Doyle watched the last man climb into the Scania then he banged on the side twice and hauled himself up into the rear of the large transport. The lorry pulled away, its huge wheels spinning momentarily on the dusty ground before gaining purchase and it finally trundled off a few yards behind one of the minibuses. Doyle seated himself as comfortably as he could on one of the wooden benches on either side of the lorry's interior, glancing out at the city as the vehicle built up speed.

He didn't look at the other occupants of the truck and he certainly didn't speak to any of them. Not because he was unsociable (although he'd been accused of that often enough in his life) but because he had nothing to say. Why strike up a conversation if it had no point? Why talk if silence was preferable? Besides, he reasoned, what could he talk to these people about anyway? What had he got in common with any of them except that they were all in this godforsaken country for one reason or another? Money mostly. The danger that these people in the convoy with him were prepared to risk was more than balanced by the financial reward. Six months working out here was better than a year's salary to most. They were mercenaries, pure and simple. There was no altruistic motive behind their presence here. They weren't concerned about the living standards and tribulations of the average Iraqi. They were here to make money and improve their own lives back in England, Ireland, France, Germany or wherever the hell else they lived.

Doyle didn't have the same reasons for being in Iraq. He was there for one reason and one only. He had nowhere else to go. That was another reason he didn't strike up conversations with the others who worked here. They would want to talk about their wives, their girlfriends, their families, their homes and their aspirations.

Doyle had none of those.

When he'd been younger it hadn't mattered. His work had been the only thing important to him.

But even that's gone now isn't it? What the fuck have you got? Absolutely nothing.

He reached into his pocket and pulled out a packet of cigarettes, cupping his hand around the lighter flame as he lit up. Smoke billowed back into the lorry and the man sitting next to him coughed a little exaggeratedly and glanced disapprovingly at Doyle's cigarette. Doyle merely took another drag and looked at the array of buildings on either side of the road. Shops, blocks of flats and office buildings vied for space with mosques. Many were damaged. All were covered by a thin film of dust and sand. Palm trees stood like bizarrely placed road signs in a number of places. Locals wandered around in groups or on their own, some glancing towards the convoy of foreign workers as it passed. Doyle watched two women as they crossed the street chattering animatedly, both of them encased from head to foot in traditional burkas.

A boy, no more than ten, was leading five or six sheep along the pavement, jabbing the animals with sticks when they strayed from the direction, he wanted them to follow. There was rubble on both walkways and also on the road. It lay there like concrete confetti after some long-forgotten wedding. Cars, some that worked, some that didn't, were parked on either side of the main street leading out of the Jadriya district. A number had the wheels missing. Half a dozen, Doyle noted, were nothing more than rusted metal chassis.

The man sitting beside Doyle coughed again as more cigarette smoke drifted back into the lorry.

"That's a bad cough you've got," Doyle observed, without looking at him. "You should cut down. I smoke forty a day and I don't fucking cough like that."

The man thought about saying something but the look in Doyle's grey eyes told him that it might be more prudent to remain quiet. He didn't cough again for the duration of the journey.

As the convoy began to leave the confines of the city, the roads it travelled along became both wider and less well tarmacked. There were potholes in a number of places that the drivers of the vehicles did their best to avoid. Some were so deep they could have damaged tyres or axles. The worst of these holes had been caused by explosions. Several badly damaged cars had been removed from the thoroughfares and stood on the parched verges that bordered them.

There were half a dozen kids playing around one of these wrecks, running around or scrambling over the twisted and charred remains like scavengers over a carcass.

A group of men stood motionless at the roadside watching the convoy as it passed. Doyle kept his eyes fixed on them, a hand sliding inside his jacket to touch the butt of one of the automatics.

Be prepared.

Only when the convoy had left the men well behind did he withdraw his hand.

You could never be sure if an attack was on the way. Trust your instincts.

More kids were kicking a battered old football around on a stretch of open ground. One or two of them stopped and waved at the small convoy as it passed. Doyle wondered if any of the occupants of the minibuses were waving back. He took another drag on his cigarette and wiped sweat from his face with one hand. The temperature didn't drop too dramatically in the evenings. The dying sun still pumped out enough heat to make any one but the locals sweat. By the time it was dark, in about two hours, it would grow chillier but there would be no lasting respite from the savage heat that bathed the land during the hours of daylight. He couldn't remember the last time it had rained.

The leading truck turned right and headed along a narrower track that led towards the compound where Doyle and all the foreign workers were housed. Functional was about the kindest word he could find to describe it. But each small dwelling had a bed, a bathroom and a tiny living area. Doyle had brought himself a portable TV when he'd first arrived. Not one of the flat screen modern types but an old-fashioned model that lost its picture if someone walked in front of the twisted aerial, he propped on the top of it. But Doyle didn't care, it gave him a bit of company and that was all that mattered. When he got fed up with listening to music, or when he couldn't be bothered to wander to the large NAAFI that served the compound, he could always sit in his quarters with his TV on.

He felt like some pensioner whose only company was the flickering images on the twelve-inch screen.

Something else that's changed. You never needed the company of others when you were younger did you? Did you even know what loneliness was back then?

As the truck pulled up Doyle clambered out and jumped down, watching as his fellow passengers also climbed out. The other trucks and minibuses were disgorging their cargos too and Doyle saw another security man watching as those who had ridden with him left their transports. Doyle saw the man glance in his direction and nodded curtly by way of acknowledgement. The driver of the Scania also clambered down from the cab and Doyle raised a hand to him before turning and setting off across the compound towards his quarters.

He fumbled for his keys and pushed the one he wanted into the door lock, easing the door open and stepping into his quarters.

The bloody air-conditioning, such as it was, seemed to be on the blink again because it felt only marginally cooler inside than it did out. Doyle closed the door, crossed to the TV and switched it on. He left it on MTV for a moment then tired rapidly of the barrage of vacuous pop music and switched it off again, turning instead to the small CD player propped on a cabinet nearby.

He selected a Megadeth album and turned up the volume.

A shower. Something to eat and bed, Doyle decided. He might read a bit before he dropped off. He had trouble sleeping these days and reading seemed to help a little.

Another night in paradise.

He smiled to himself and shook his head.

So, this is what it's come to?

In the background the music thundered out, filling his ears.

"Peace sells...but who's buying?..."

He slipped off his shoulder holsters one at a time, laying them on the table, looking down at the pistols housed there. He poured himself a drink, swallowed it in one gulp and refilled his glass, his gaze still fixed on the automatics displayed on the table.

Sean Doyle felt like killing someone.

SEVEN

It was a simple process to transform a normal bullet, be it 9mm, .357 or larger, into a dumdum.

A cross shaped cut deep into the head of the bullet, deep enough to open two grooves in the lead, would ensure that small modification was effective. Once done, this would mean that the bullet would explode on impact. Hollow tips had the same effect and they came already prepared but performing this little piece of surgery on shells he may well be firing just felt like a finishing touch to Sean Doyle.

He smiled and rolled one of the 9mm shells between his thumb and forefinger, inspecting the two cuts on the tip of the bullet.

To him it was like a trademark. A personal touch.

Doyle sat at the table with several boxes of ammunition around him, many of them already having been transformed in such a way. Most weapons manufacturers made hollow tips available for their products, but Doyle preferred to carry out the modifications himself.

If you want something done, do it yourself.

It was something to do as well. A task to fill the time, and time seemed to be endless here. Too much time and so little to fill it. Too much time alone gave him far too much opportunity to think, to consider his situation. And that was something he didn't particularly want to do.

He reached for the remote control that lay close to him, easing up the volume on the sound system by a couple of levels.

"We're so fucked...shit outta luck...hardwired to self-destruct..."

The words and music seemed to fill the room, but he knew he couldn't raise the volume too high for fear of disturbing those around him. They were trying to sleep in preparation

39

for the next day's work. Doyle would like to have slept but it seemed that simple respite was being denied to him as it was on so many other nights. Instead of laying restlessly in his bed he got up and he found something to do. He read or he watched TV for as long as he could stand it or he gave himself some task to perform (like turning the bullets into dumdums) and he hoped that the effort would bring sleep.

And he drank.

More heavily than he should have done sometimes but what the fuck. He wouldn't take sleeping pills, they left him sluggish the following day. Enough alcohol and he slept.

But so far tonight, he hadn't drunk enough.

He slid the newly modified bullets back into their boxes, placed the boxes in the small safe in his bedroom then he wandered back into the living area, his eyelids feeling heavier already.

She was sitting at the table when he walked back in.

"Not again," Doyle breathed, reaching for a chair to steady himself.

She merely smiled at him, flicking her long blonde hair away from her face.

She was barefoot, wearing nothing but a pair of tight-fitting jeans and a T-shirt.

"Aren't you pleased to see me?" she purred.

Doyle held her gaze.

"Why now?" he murmured. "Why here?"

"You'll hurt my feelings," she told him. "You could at least tell me I look nice."

"Fuck off."

"Charming as usual."

She got to her feet, but Doyle shook his head.

"Stay there," he grunted. "Don't come near me."

"But I'm cold. I want you to warm me up."

"Stay away from me."

"You don't mean that."

She crossed to him and stood above him, looking down at

him, aware that he was gazing at her body. She could see him appraising her slowly, taking in every inch of her slim form, pausing at the area of her belly that was exposed by the shortness of her T-shirt, knowing that he would have seen her nipples pressing urgently against the material.

"Don't push me away," she said, softly, gently sitting on his lap and settling herself. "I miss you." She ground herself against him, her breathing becoming a little heavier. Doyle could feel the exhalations on his cheek as she moved closer to him.

"Why are you doing this?" he said, the words escaping him with something that sounded like pain. As if each sound was being forced from his lungs under protest.

"You never used to complain," she purred, putting one index finger under his chin and raising his head slightly so he was looking at her. "You used to tell me I was beautiful. Aren't I beautiful any more?"

Doyle looked at her face, into her eyes.

"Please leave me alone," he said, his voice little more than a whisper.

"You don't mean that," she insisted and leaned forward, closer to him, her lips brushing his.

He felt the exquisite softness glide against his lips then her tongue was probing gently, pushing deeper into his mouth, and with one hand she took his right hand and moved it so that it was beneath her T-shirt. Doyle felt the almost impossible smoothness of her skin beneath his fingertips and he closed his eyes, wanting so badly to surrender to the feelings that were beginning to build within him. When she finally broke the kiss, she pulled her head away slightly and a long strand of glistening saliva momentarily linked them like some kind of silvery umbilicus.

He pushed his hand higher up inside her T-shirt and she arched her back and ground more insistently against him while she kissed him once more. More deeply this time. She reached down and undid her jeans, feeling his hands gripping her more

41

insistently now, his left-hand gliding inside the garment and cupping one of her buttocks, his fingers digging into the firm flesh.

And now he tasted the blood in his mouth.

As she sat back slightly, he looked at her face and he saw the smile there.

Blood was running freely from both sides of her mouth and, as she grinned more broadly, he saw that the crimson fluid had stained and coated her teeth as well.

Beneath the fingers of his right hand he felt something other than the softness of her skin. He could feel ragged pieces of flesh and something slippery, something wet. As she pulled up the T-shirt, he saw that two of his fingers were buried up to the knuckles in a wound that was leaking blood and reeking fluid.

She remained on his lap, still smiling, still grinding gently against him as he fought to pull his fingers from the wound in her back.

There was another just below her left breast. Much larger. It was choked with congealed blood that was almost black. The fluid that was dripping from it now was foul smelling and tinged with what looked like pus. As Doyle sat transfixed, she peeled back both sides of the wound so that it was gaping and more of the stinking discharge spilled forth, most of it soaking into the waistband of her jeans after it had coursed down her body.

She pulled his head forward now, forcing his mouth against another laceration just above her heart, one so severe that the organ beneath her shattered ribs was clearly visible. Doyle could see the thick mass of dark muscle and blood-drenched tissue that he knew only too well was her heart. She gripped his right hand again and dragged it towards that gaping maw, towards that cluster of muscle and fibre that had once pumped her life fluid around her body.

But not now.

Doyle actually felt the sharp ends of splintered ribs cutting into his flesh as he reached into her chest and closed his fingers around her heart.

She was laughing softly now, more of the dark and fetid discharge oozing from every wound as she rocked back and forth on his lap.

Doyle closed his eyes.

EIGHT

BANDON; COUNTY CORK;
THE REPUBLIC OF IRELAND.

Michael Coogan brought the car to a halt at the main gates of the house, leaving the car engine idling as he climbed out, expecting the man to follow him.

When he didn't follow, Coogan turned and made his way back to the car, plastering on his best professional grin.

"I wondered if you might want to walk up to the house from here," Coogan said. "Get a better idea of what the grounds look like."

The man seated in the back of the car merely shook his head, his gaze fixed on the high wall that surrounded the grounds.

Coogan had been an estate agent for eighteen of his forty-three years and, during that time, he had met all manner of people, but this guy was something different. He'd barely said fifty words since entering the office the first time around and, with each subsequent visit, it seemed he grew more distant rather than more open.

Coogan knew that estate agents, as a breed, were not exactly top of most people's popularity lists but this guy seemed to have a genuine dislike of them. He had quite pointedly sat in the rear of the car every time he'd visited the house, preferring to keep himself to himself and rarely engage in conversation even when Coogan tried his hardest to inject some levity into proceedings. He merely sat in the back seat, attention fixed on his mobile phone or apparently enraptured by the countryside leading up to the house and the wall that surrounded it.

Coogan had been trying to work out whether the man was rude or whether there was some other reason for his reserved

44

attitude. Yes, that was it, he told himself. The man was reserved. Not withdrawn. Not ignorant. He was just shy. Awkward with others. He wouldn't be the only one, would he? Making small talk with complete strangers was something that not everyone found easy or suited to them. This man who now sat in the back seat of the estate agent's car in his expensive charcoal grey suit, white shirt and blue tie, was just shy. Simple as that.

The estate agent clambered back into the Peugeot and guided the vehicle through the open gates, along the long driveway that led to the house itself.

As he drove, Coogan could hear the man behind him breathing and, for reasons he could not understand, it irritated him. As did the man's habit of sitting directly behind the driver's seat. Coogan could only see him when he glanced into the rear-view mirror and, even then, he couldn't see all of the passenger's reflection. It made him feel uneasy and he didn't know why.

Possibly, he reasoned, because it seemed like another attempt to distance himself. Most clients sat in the front seat, next to him, so they could chat about the house they were viewing. Most people talked happily about their business and their hopes and dreams or even the weather. Not this man in his expensive suit and his highly polished shoes. He was making notes now, scribbling something on a piece of paper with what looked like a Montblanc pen but Coogan thought it was probably even more exclusive than that.

Only when the Peugeot came to a halt outside the house did the man stop scribbling. Before Coogan could even haul himself out of the car, the man was out and walking across the gravelled drive towards the front of the building. He took several pictures of the imposing facade, checking them on his phone before walking on.

"Do you know this part of the country at all?" Coogan asked.

The man merely shook his head.

"It's beautiful," the estate agent went on. "Some people think it's a little too laid back for them, but you can't beat some peace and quiet, can you?"

The man smiled thinly then moved closer to the house, looking up at the windows as if he were gazing into sightless eyes.

"What attracted you to this property to begin with?" Coogan asked, trying to keep up with him as he made his way around the side of the house, taking more photos.

"My client has been aware of it for some time," the man said, flatly.

"Your client? You're not going to be the occupant then?"

The man shook his head.

"Is your client aware of the details of the house and..."

"He knows everything he needs to know," the man said, cutting him short.

"Will he be viewing the property himself at some stage?"

"I have no idea," the man exclaimed. "I'm not privy to all his movements."

"Is your client familiar with this part of the country?" Coogan went on.

"Is that important?"

"Well, if he's thinking of buying this property then..."

Again, the man interrupted.

"My client is aware of the details," he said, tonelessly. "Just as he's aware of the price."

"I should hope so because this isn't a cheap property and..."

"That isn't your concern. All that should matter to you is that your company stands to collect approximately twenty-five per cent of the price this property is sold for. That should be the only thing in your mind."

"My company likes to ensure that our customers are satisfied."

The man nodded.

"I wouldn't trouble yourself," he said, taking more pictures. "Now, if we could look at the inside of the property and I would appreciate the opportunity to do that alone."

He held out his hand for the keys.

NINE

CENTRAL IRAQ;

Doyle must have drunk more the previous night than he'd thought because it took the alarm to wake him the following morning.

Normally he woke up an hour or more before the sound lanced through the room but now, he shot out a hand to silence the strident electronic tone, muttering to himself and irritated that his day had begun so abruptly.

"Fuck it," he grunted, shaking his head as if to dislodge the last vestiges of the dream that had plagued him the previous night. He swung his legs out of the bed, sat on the edge for a moment, then swung himself out and headed for the small bathroom. He showered beneath a spray that was barely powerful enough to cover him with lukewarm water.

His morning ablutions didn't take long and it was less than half an hour later that he stepped out into the compound, gazing around to see who else was up at this ungodly hour.

The answer was the same people who were always up at this hour. Other security men were wandering around, some checking the lorries and minibuses that would transport the workers back into Baghdad. Doyle would let them do the initial inspections then he himself would double-check. Not that there was much chance of any devices being attached to the vehicles while they were in the compound, but Doyle insisted on checking anyway.

Better safe than sorry.

When complacency set in that was the time to worry. He'd learned that over the years. That was one of the ways he'd stayed alive so long.

Despite the early hour, the sun was still beating down. Offering a small warning of the intolerable heat to come when it finally rose to its zenith. Doyle was determined to be inside if possible when that happened.

He nodded affably to those he recognised as people emerged from their quarters and clambered aboard the transports then, after his own checks had been completed, he hauled himself up into the back of a Scania and waited for the convoy to pull away.

The journey into the city took less than thirty minutes. Doyle walked up and down the line of vehicles, watching as the occupants clambered out and set off for their day's work, his eyes constantly moving over the landscape. Ever alert.

He set off on his first tour of the day. It consisted of a slow stroll around the building works, a considerable area now. On this particular day he also had a meeting planned with a captain from the local police force. Doyle had no idea what the meeting was about but, he decided, sitting in an air-conditioned room talking to someone for an hour would be preferable to stalking about in the unbearable heat. He checked his watch and walked on.

The first of the explosions came moments later.

Doyle ducked involuntarily, realising the sound came from one of the crews who were still trying to remove some rubble in the next street. If Doyle was honest, he thought the whole fucking city resembled little more than rubble, but he kept his opinions to himself on that subject as he did on most things.

He stopped momentarily to light a cigarette.

As he did, he saw two men running in his direction. Both were wearing the high-visibility jackets sported by the workers on the site and both of them should know better than to be running in temperatures like this, Doyle thought, affording himself a slight grin.

When the men reached him, they were both covered with sweat but neither of them seemed to be unduly out of breath.

"Can you come with us now?" the first man asked, sweat glistening on his thick beard.

"What's the problem?" Doyle wanted to know.

"You come now," the second man urged, putting his hand on Doyle's shoulder.

"All right. Let's see what you've got," Doyle murmured.

He walked briskly with the two men, the first of whom looked about to break into a run again at any moment.

"Slow down," Doyle told him. "We'll get there. No rush."

"Important," the second man insisted. "You see."

"I believe you," Doyle echoed.

He walked with the men down a narrow alleyway between two high buildings that managed to blot out the sun for a moment or two. It was a welcome respite and Doyle slowed his pace slightly, much to the chagrin of the second man.

"I used to be like you when I was your age," Doyle said to him. "Wanted to do everything at top speed."

The man looked at him with puzzlement on his face.

"What's your name?" Doyle continued.

"Yousef," the man told him.

"You're new, aren't you?" Doyle went on. "I know most of the guys who work here. I don't recognise you."

"He started two days ago," the first man interjected. "He's a hard worker."

"I'm sure he is," mused Doyle. "I just get nervous when I see new faces. People I don't know."

They rounded a corner and the two men gestured excitedly towards what looked like a huge pile of rubble.

There were more workmen standing around, close to the front of this midden of shattered masonry and pulverised rock, and two bulldozers had come to a halt within yards of the destruction. So too had several lorries, the drivers standing close to their vehicles peering towards the rubble.

"Inside, inside," Yousef said, agitatedly, pointing at the huge mound. "Police are coming too."

Doyle took a last drag on his cigarette, dropped the butt and moved towards the area being indicated.

As far as he could see, he was inside what had once been an office block of some kind. Demolished walls stretched upwards on all sides of him, some of them looking as if the only thing holding them up was the mass of debris at their bases. Concrete beams and broken metal pillars thrust upwards towards the sky that was itself barely visible inside the shell of the building he now found himself in. Doyle couldn't help but wonder if the entire structure was about to collapse upon him, but he continued onwards through the devastation, something just ahead of him catching his eye.

As he drew nearer, he could see that a flight of broad stone steps led downwards.

They were covered with dust and rubble but, as Doyle advanced, he could see that there was another door at the bottom of the stairs.

He hesitated for a moment, squinting into the gloom, waving a hand before him in an effort to banish the thick dust that was swirling around like noxious fog within the remains of the building.

Exactly what made him reach inside his jacket and touch the butt of the Beretta 92F he was carrying he had no idea, but he allowed his fingers to play over the automatic briefly, as if that would bring him some kind of comfort.

He glanced around again then prepared to descend the wide steps before him.

Doyle had barely begun his descent when he heard footsteps behind him.

TEN

D oyle turned slowly, aware that the footsteps were getting closer.

The man he saw approaching him was dressed in the blue camouflage uniform of the Iraqi police and Doyle could see from the two stars on his epaulettes that he was a captain. The man was in his early thirties. The body armour he was wearing made him look larger than he was and, as Doyle ran appraising eyes over the newcomer, he wondered how this man managed to keep his boots so clean in such a dust shrouded environment. They were positively sparkling.

"What are you doing in here?" the man asked.

"Security. I work for the company building the railway," Doyle explained. "I've got ID."

The man stood motionless as Doyle dug in his pocket, finally pulling out the necessary papers which he handed to the policeman.

The captain took them, nodded and glanced at the photo ID and then at Doyle himself.

"I'm not very photogenic," Doyle murmured. "But it is me. The permits for my guns are in there too."

"Mr Doyle," the man exclaimed, nodding and returning the papers to him. "We were meant to have a meeting later today. I am Captain Akram Farid. Iraqi Police."

Doyle smiled thinly and shook the man's outstretched hand.

"Good to meet you, Captain," he said.

The two-way radio on Farid's belt crackled.

"Excuse me," he said, holding up a hand and snatching it off, answering the call and then replacing the radio.

"I was about to see what's at the bottom of those steps," Doyle told the man, motioning towards the broad flight that lay before them. He began to descend, the stairwell plenty big enough for the two men to walk side by side.

"The building above had been empty for years," Farid told him, looking around at the rubble. "No one would go near it after the bodies were found."

"What bodies?"

"Thirty-seven of them. All Shia. All tortured and murdered on Saddam's orders."

"He was Sunni, wasn't he?"

"Do you know much about this part of the world, Mr Doyle?"

"Not as much as I should but I've seen what religious differences can do to a country."

"Really? Where?"

"In Ireland. You're too young to know anything about that, Captain. I won't bore you with it."

Farid looked quizzically at him.

"Tell me more about the murders," Doyle went on as the two men continued down the steps.

"The building had been a Shia mosque," the captain informed him. "Saddam's men knew that by defiling it they would make it unholy. Unusable to those who had worshiped in it. No one has been inside it for years. Even the ground it stands on is thought to be tainted now. No one will go inside."

"What about you?" Doyle wanted to know as the two men reached the bottom of the steps.

"Sometimes the demands of my job outweigh those of my religion," Farid told him. "Unfortunately, most of my men don't think the same way."

Doyle reached out and put one hand on the large, dark wooden door that faced them, surprised when it opened a couple of inches, accompanied by a loud protesting creak from the hinges.

He pushed a little harder, opening a gap wide enough for himself and Farid to pass through. Doyle looked at the policeman who hesitated a second then nodded. Doyle stepped across the threshold into the room beyond.

He felt suddenly light-headed and shot out a hand to

support himself against the nearest wall.

Doyle gritted his teeth hard, hoping that the feeling would pass as rapidly as it had come.

What the fuck is this?

He let out a long, quivering breath and blinked hard, relieved that the feeling was leaving him. His heart was beating fast, but he could feel it slowing down a little and wondered again what had caused this feeling. He sucked in a deep breath and held it, pushing himself away from the wall.

"There is nothing to fear in here except memories, Mr Doyle," Farid exclaimed as they moved further into the gloom, the policeman reaching for the powerful torch on his belt.

Doyle didn't answer but merely glanced in the direction of the policeman, wondering why he'd chosen to say something like that. He shook his head, satisfied now that he had banished the feeling that had enveloped him upon entering the room.

The captain switched on the torch, the beam cutting through the blackness, illuminating the devastation within. Pieces of concrete had fallen from above and Doyle could see motes of dust turning lazily in the torch beam as Farid swept it back and forth over the interior.

"The victims were nailed to the walls, had their genitals cut off and were then disembowelled," the captain murmured. "There were rumours of cannibalism too."

"No wonder no one will come in here," Doyle offered, glancing around at the inside of the large room. "Why wasn't the place sealed or destroyed?"

"I don't know," Farid confessed, aiming the torch at the far wall. "There are many stories like that in this country, Mr Doyle. Secrets that came out after it was all over, when Saddam was gone."

"You must have been pleased to see the back of him," Doyle mused, still peering around the cavernous room.

Farid nodded almost imperceptibly, his own gaze moving slowly around the inside of the subterranean chamber, following the passage of the torch beam as he moved it slowly about the place.

"Are your men carrying explosives with them, Mr Doyle?" the policeman enquired. "This room could be sealed now."

"They're not my men, Captain," said Doyle, smiling. "I'm only security, remember? Just a cog in the wheel."

"A cog?"

"Never mind."

Doyle glanced around one last time and then turned back towards the door through which they had both entered.

"Let's get out of here," he offered. "Get this place shut off once and for all."

Again, Farid nodded, also making his way back towards the door.

"Some people believe that to pass through a gateway like this," he pointed at the door. "Is to give up hope," the policeman said. "Metaphorically speaking." He smiled.

"They could be right," Doyle told him.

"In this country, hope seems to be all we have left now."

Doyle nodded.

"What about you, Mr Doyle? Do you still have hope?" Farid went on.

Doyle smiled humourlessly. "I haven't had any of that for a long time," he said, flatly.

ELEVEN

THE BRITISH MUSEUM; LONDON;

A s he sat down at his table in the Court Cafe, Jonathan Sellers let out a long slow breath and smiled.

The cafe didn't officially open for another twenty minutes and he intended taking advantage of the relative peace and quiet before the public finally flooded into both the museum itself and also into this particular eatery within it. It was, he told himself, a perk of working at the British Museum. The ability to mooch about (although mooch was a word that most of his colleagues would probably frown upon) in parts of the building, either before or after the public had entered or left, and also the sheer joy of enjoying a quiet cup of tea before the rigours of the day began, was something Sellers savoured.

He'd worked at a number of museums since leaving university eighteen years earlier, but the British Museum had always felt like his spiritual home and he had experienced feelings of contentment since beginning his employment here that he'd never felt anywhere else.

He felt appreciated for the first time in his career. Something he hadn't experienced during his time at the Imperial War Museum or the Victoria and Albert. But now things were different. Sellers had only been at the British Museum for just under two years and yet already he felt that he was a valuable member of their considerable staff. His colleagues had helped this transition and he felt blessed to have such reliable and competent people working with him.

He had enough to worry about in his private life without adding to the pressure with professional burdens.

His father had died eleven months earlier and the loss had taken an unexpectedly cruel toll on his mother. Already in her late sixties, she was visibly failing since the death of Seller's father. A fall had caused her to suffer a broken hip which had led to a prolonged spell in hospital and, upon leaving it, she had found coping with the daily chores of running a home too much for her. Sellers popped in to see her as often as he could and she had vigilant neighbours, but she was still alone. He'd discussed hiring a nurse or a housekeeper for her, someone who could be present or at least on call twenty-four hours a day, but the prices had been prohibitive. He and his wife both had good jobs but not good enough that they could afford to spend the kinds of money that would be needed to ensure twenty-four-hour care for his mother.

Was it time to consider a home of some description? He had hardly dared contemplate that option. He knew it would kill his mother. She'd voiced her fears often enough about being 'shut away' somewhere. Sellers could not bring himself to even enquire about care homes. Not yet.

He sipped his tea and glanced at the open newspaper, occasionally taking a bite of the toast and jam he'd also brought to the table. He was munching his way through the second slice when he heard footsteps approaching his table.

"I thought I'd find you in here," Caroline Bradley told him, sitting down opposite him.

"Am I that predictable?" Sellers said, smiling.

Caroline reached across the table, picked up a slice of toast and bit a piece off.

"That's my breakfast," Sellers said, feigning anger.

"I'll buy you lunch, how's that?" Caroline promised, chewing the toast.

"Were you only looking for me so you could steal my breakfast?"

"You know me so well." She giggled and, as usual, it was a musical sound.

Sellers looked at her for a moment and tried to suppress the thoughts he was having for her and had for her every time he saw her. She was eight or nine years younger than he was, with the most beautiful eyes he had ever seen. The fact that she also happened to be an incredibly intelligent woman who would not have looked out of place on a catwalk seemed almost irrelevant. Her hair was short, barely reaching the collar of the beige cowl neck sweater she wore, but the style suited her perfectly.

"Actually, I did come for something more than just toast," Caroline told him, grinning. "There were several e-mails from France about the delivery. I was just confirming arrival times, things like that."

"And?" Sellers wanted to know.

"Some of the exhibits are coming by plane, others by road as we agreed," she told him.

"Have they left France yet?"

"That's what I came to tell you."

"Oh, Christ, what's the problem now?"

"No problem, Jonathan. Calm down." She chewed more toast. "They want to fly from Orly, that's all."

"Why go all the way to Paris when they could fly out of Lorient? That's closer to the site."

"The Louvre want to inspect the exhibits before they leave France."

"What do they think we're going to do with them? Vandalise them? If it hadn't been for us no one would have found the bloody things anyway."

"I can sort of see their point, Jonathan. If we were transporting loads of stuff about Nelson or Richard the Lionheart or any other national hero then we'd want to make sure it was well looked after wouldn't we?"

"I wouldn't call Gilles de Rais a national hero, would you?"

"He is to the French. He did fight alongside Joan of Arc."

"He also murdered 200 children. Does that still qualify?"

Caroline smiled and took another bite of toast.

Sellers refilled his mug from the small metal teapot and took a sip.

"What about the book?" he wanted to know. "Is that coming

by air or road?"

"By air, they know how important it is," Caroline told him. "They were even talking about sending someone with it to make sure it got here safely. The Louvre have requested it as soon as we're finished."

"Just the book, none of the other exhibits?"

"Just the book. They know how important it is." Caroline paused for a moment then looked directly at Sellers. "How much do they know about it?"

"As much as they need to know at the moment," Sellers told her.

He took another sip of his tea and, as he did, he noticed that his hand was shaking slightly.

TWELVE

BAGHDAD; JADRIYA DISTRICT; CENTRAL IRAQ;

"How long have you been in the police force?" Doyle took a sip of his coffee and looked across the table at Captain Farid.

They were the only two sitting outside the cafe, sipping their drinks as if they'd been at some pavement cafe on the Champs-Élysées. There was a surreal feeling to the entire scenario, Doyle thought, and he couldn't help but smile thinly to himself as he glanced around, shaded from the blistering sun by the bright red awning that protected the entrance of The Ice House cafe.

The Iraqi raised his eyebrows.

"I joined as soon as I left the army," the policeman told him. "So, that would be six years this year."

"You've done well," Doyle told him. "Reaching your rank so fast."

"What about you, Mr Doyle? What made you come to my country?" Farid enquired, taking a swig of his own coffee.

"I was looking for work," Doyle told him.

"Security work?"

"Something like that."

He took another sip of his coffee.

"You're married, right?" Doyle said, nodding towards the thick gold band on Farid's left hand.

"Yes," the captain said. "My wife is a nurse."

"Any kids?"

"Two. Boys. What about you?"

Doyle shook his head.

"No wife. No kids," he said, flatly.

"Did you never find the right woman?" Farid grinned.

"I did once, but..." Doyle allowed the sentence to trail off.

He lowered his head slightly for a second then took a deep breath. "Fuck it," he grunted. "The past doesn't matter. It's gone."

Farid regarded him silently for a moment then glanced down into his coffee cup.

"There have been rumours about some kind of action being taken against the company building the railway you are guarding," the captain said, finally.

"What kind of action?" Doyle wanted to know.

"As I said, it is only rumours but, here, rumours have a habit of becoming truth."

"Threats have been made?"

"As I said, it is only hearsay, rumours, but it might be wise to listen to them."

"So, what have you heard?"

"It could be an attack on the railway itself, a bomb possibly, or it could be an attack on those working upon it. Kidnappings possibly."

"It wouldn't be the first time."

"I am aware of that, Mr Doyle."

"How reliable is your intelligence?"

"I just wanted to warn you, so that you can be at your guard. That is the right expression isn't it?" The policeman smiled.

"That's close enough," Doyle told him, also grinning.

"I think it's in everyone's interests that we work more closely together, Mr Doyle."

"Fair enough. Anything I can do to help, I will."

"How long are you in this country for?"

"Until this job is finished."

"And then what?"

"Look for something else like it. At my age it's difficult trying to launch a new career." Doyle smiled, humourlessly.

"You're not old, Mr Doyle," Farid told him.

"Old enough. It's a young man's world, Captain. When you get to fifty you turn invisible. Trust me. It's all downhill from there."

"Everyone longs for their youth again, Mr Doyle."

"I agree. Like the man said 'we all dream of being a child again, even the worst of us. Perhaps the worst most of all.'"

"Do you think you are a bad man, Mr Doyle?"

"Who's to judge?"

"God?"

"Fuck him," Doyle said, smiling.

Farid looked a little taken aback by the remark.

"Don't you believe in God, Mr Doyle?" he enquired.

"As someone once said, 'I don't believe in God but I'm afraid of him.'" Doyle announced. "What about you?"

"My beliefs are important to me. I think everyone should believe in something."

"I agree. I just haven't found anything I can believe in yet." He took a sip of his coffee. "But I'll keep looking."

The two men sat in silence for a moment then Doyle spoke again.

"I wonder what those poor bastards believed in who were taken by extremists last time," he murmured. "The ones who they decapitated. The ones they filmed and put on YouTube. What were they thinking about when those mad fuckers started cutting through their necks with knives? Do you think they were waiting for God to save them?"

"Who do you call on when you're in trouble, Mr Doyle?" Farid wanted to know.

"I don't think anyone listens to me any more, Captain." Doyle smiled and opened his jacket, revealing the pistols he wore beneath each armpit.

"The only ones I can trust," he said, flatly. "Mr Smith and Mr Wesson. Maybe Mr Beretta too."

Both men laughed.

"You guys carry Glocks don't you?" Doyle went on, motioning towards the pistol that Farid was carrying on his hip.

The policeman nodded, glancing down at the 9mm weapon.

"Have you ever had to use it?" Doyle wanted to know.

"Three times," Farid informed him.

"How did it make you feel? Having to shoot someone?"

"I hope I never have to do it again."

"What about you?" Farid enquired. "Have you ever shot a man?"

Doyle nodded.

"How did you feel?" Farid wanted to know.

"It goes with the territory, with the job. It's either you or them or some other poor bastard who gets in the way."

"Is that how you justify it to yourself, Mr Doyle?"

"I don't justify it any more, Captain. Why bother? If someone comes after me with a gun, then I'm going to make sure they're the one who ends up in the ground. It's all about survival. Nothing else."

THIRTEEN

BANDON; COUNTY CORK;
THE REPUBLIC OF IRELAND;

It felt as if the entire town was shaking.

Windows rattled in their frames, and more than one inhabitant of Bandon wondered if the glass would indeed shatter, as more and more heavy vehicles passed through on the narrow road through the town.

There was no one left alive in Bandon who had fought in World War Two but, if there had been, they might have been forgiven for thinking that a division of Tiger tanks had descended, seeking revenge.

While most inhabitants were content to stand at their shaking windows and watch the procession of massive construction vehicles as it rolled through, others decided to inspect the juggernauts at closer quarters. People stood by the road watching the huge vehicles pass by. Excavators, bulldozers, trucks, cranes and smaller vehicles all rolled through Bandon, looking like a herd of mechanical dinosaurs in search of the nearest water hole.

Some of the larger vehicles weighed in excess of nine tons and it seemed impossible that they would all manage to negotiate the narrow streets of Bandon without causing damage of some sort. However, despite some stress cracks on the tarmac of the high street, little damage was caused by the procession and, as it left the town and continued on to its proper destination, the people of the town more-or-less forgot about it.

In the days that followed, work on the grounds of the house that stood just off the Bandon to Kinsale road began and the excavators, bulldozers and other construction vehicles weren't seen again in the town.

No one knew who the new owner of the house was. Theories ranged from an English rock star to an American film director and, even more fancifully, someone had suggested that the entire area had been bought by a film company and was going to be transformed into studios where all kinds of films were to be shot. This idea was disregarded as swiftly as the one which proffered that the house and its grounds were to be used as a refuge for battered women and their children.

Even the estate agents who had sold the property weren't one hundred per cent sure who the real owner was.

All negotiations had been carried out by representatives or appointees of the true owner. Minions charged with the task of ensuring that the property was successfully purchased and managed. Rumours had abounded too about what had been paid for the house and its very substantial grounds. Estimates ranged from three to ten million pounds, but the final figure was closer to fifteen million. A huge sum and one that once again caused wagging of tongues as the people of Bandon tried to figure out exactly who their extremely rich new neighbour was going to be.

There was a persistent and convincing rumour that the property had been acquired by a huge multi-national intent on turning it into a vast hotel complex similar to that of Dromoland Castle in County Clare or Waterford Castle. But this theory too was eventually discarded.

In time, the house itself was forgotten too. Surrounded by the bulldozers, cranes and excavators, it looked like an afterthought as the grounds were ravaged by the construction equipment.

At weekends some people would drive out to see what alterations were being made to the house and its surrounding estate but, apart from what they could glimpse through the tall metal gates, they could see very little.

The men who drove and operated the massive vehicles lived elsewhere and, at weekends particularly, the bulldozers and their ilk were left motionless in the grounds, as still as the trees that grew so thickly within the confines of the twelve-foot wall surrounding the estate. The roots of those trees ran deep in the dark earth, stretching down through the soil, like fingers reaching for the very centre of the planet. Some had been where they stood for hundreds of years, looking on impassively as the world changed all around them.

It was about to change again.

FOURTEEN

BAGHDAD; JADRIYA DISTRICT; CENTRAL IRAQ;

Doyle sat back in his seat, glancing at Captain Farid and then at the city beyond him.

There was a vaguely surrealistic feel to the surroundings and circumstances, he thought, sitting in a pavement cafe in Baghdad watching the world go by. However, Doyle couldn't shake the feeling that if you put chairs and tables on a pavement in Paris you got a pavement cafe, if you put chairs and tables on the pavement in Baghdad you got chairs and tables on the pavement and not much else. He smiled to himself and took another sip of his coffee, knowing that this interlude couldn't last for too much longer. He had work to do and he was sure Farid must have as well but, at the moment, the policeman seemed more than happy to pass a leisurely hour or so just seated here, talking. It was as if they were on the Champs-Élysées, not in the middle of what had, until recently, been a war zone.

But the programme of reconstruction and rebuilding that had been undertaken in this battered city and all over the country in fact, was coming along apace and Doyle had to admit he was impressed by the work that had been done. All too often he didn't take enough notice of his surroundings unless it was in connection with his work but, on Farid's prompting, he regarded the centre of the city with an impassive but appreciative eye.

"You didn't learn to use a gun watching TV, Mr Doyle," the captain said. "Where did you acquire your expertise? If you don't mind me asking."

"I was in the CTU.," Doyle told him, expanding his answer a little when Farid looked blank. "Counter Terrorist Unit. It was a long time ago. Before you were born, probably."

"What kind of terrorists?" the policeman asked.

"All terrorists are the same, aren't they?" Doyle mused. "Freedom fighters under a different name? That's what the IRA used to call themselves and that's probably what Isis think of themselves as."

"Do you think any of the people they kidnap and execute would think of them as freedom fighters, Mr Doyle?"

"I didn't say I agreed with them. It's just a matter of perspective isn't it? Which side you're on. The names change according to your viewpoint. To us, Isis are terrorists and murderers but to the people who support them they're heroic freedom fighters."

"Is that what you think?"

"Captain, I couldn't give a fuck one way or the other. All I know is that as long as they're active out here then people are in danger and, as long as there are people in danger, I can make a living keeping them safe."

"Is it all about the money for you, Mr Doyle?"

"You can't pay your rent with ideals. You can't buy a new car with your social conscience."

"Have you always thought that way?"

"Pretty much. I enjoyed my work, but I wouldn't have done it for nothing."

"Times change, Mr Doyle."

"Only for the worst," Doyle murmured.

"You must have something to look forward to. We all have to look ahead."

"I learned to take each day as it comes. If you're climbing into bed at the end of each day then you've done all right."

"And all the while, times are changing."

"Times do, but not me. That's the problem." He smiled and sipped more of his coffee. "I might be old but, in here," he tapped his temple with one index finger. "I'm still in my twenties. The way I used to be."

Farid smiled.

"You're not old, Mr Doyle," the captain told him.

"No, I'm not old, I'm experienced. Or 'well-seasoned' as someone once told me."

Both men laughed.

"Don't you ever want to do a desk job, Mr Doyle?" Farid enquired. "Something where you can just sit around all day?"

Doyle shook his head.

"That's not for me," he confessed.

"It would be less dangerous," the captain reminded him.

Doyle nodded.

"This is all I know," he confessed. "A man has to know his limitations as they say. I know mine."

"Is it the danger that attracts you?" Farid mused. "Some men seek it out."

"I've never analysed why I do anything, Captain. I'm not going to start now."

"You're a very private man, Mr Doyle."

"If you say so, Captain."

"You don't like to talk about yourself. What are you hiding?"

Doyle smiled.

"There's a lot less to me than meets the eye, Captain," he mused. "I wouldn't bother looking too deeply for anything."

"Men don't look back because they're afraid of what might be gaining on them," Farid said, flatly.

"Very philosophical," Doyle grunted.

"What's gaining on you, Mr Doyle?" the policeman went on.

"That's my business isn't it?" Doyle said, draining what was left in his cup.

"Another?" Farid asked.

Doyle shook his head.

"No, thanks," he said. "I've got shit to do and I'm sure you have." He extended his right-hand which Farid shook firmly.

"It was good to meet you, Mr Doyle," the captain said. "I enjoyed our little talk."

"If you need me, you know where to find me," Doyle told him.

He patted Farid on the shoulder and set off away from the

cafe, glancing up briefly at the cloudless sky in which the blazing sun hung unchallenged. The temperature was already nudging one hundred and ten. Doyle blew out his cheeks and continued walking.

FIFTEEN

BANDON; COUNTY CORK;
THE REPUBLIC OF IRELAND;

Rain had been falling steadily for the last seven or eight hours and some areas of the grounds already looked like a Flanders battlefield in the middle of World War One.

The constant coming and going of some many heavy vehicles (many fitted with tracks rather than wheels) had churned the increasingly soggy ground into a quagmire. It was impossible to walk across it in places and men who had tried had been seen to sink as deep as their calves in the sucking ooze.

Michael Brady had seen his foreman do just that earlier in the day and it had made him laugh as uproariously as he had for some time. It wasn't just the fact that he couldn't stand the man (hated him was probably just a little bit too strong) but also that nearly everything, even vaguely amusing, that seemed to happen around him now provoked similar outbursts of merriment. It was as if some kind of chain had been removed from around his neck and shoulders and now, he was prone to burst into fits of giggles at the slightest provocation.

Brady jammed the excavator into the next gear and guided the vehicle across the mud towards his next target.

He pressed the necessary buttons and manoeuvred the long boom arm of the excavator into position, watching as it hovered in the air for a second before slamming down and gouging a deep hole in the ground below.

Even that made him smile. But then again, he reasoned, surely any man who had just been told he'd beaten cancer was entitled to smile. He'd learned of the wonderful development the previous week, having undergone a final series of tests and

X-rays which had confirmed, once and for all, that he was cancer-free. The tumour that had been removed from his left lung had been eradicated completely and Brady had received the news in stages. Firstly, by weeping uncontrollably with relief and then by dissolving into a fit of giggles when the doctor had repeated the prognosis. Brady had apologised more profusely for the giggling than he had for the tears, but the doctor took it all in good heart and told him not to worry about whichever reaction he might experience.

The news was great, and the doctor said it was almost as pleasurable for him to relay the information to his patient as it had been for Brady to receive it. All too often he'd had to be the bearer of tragic news. To inform a man that he was fit and well and had beaten one of the most savage and uncompromising diseases of modern times was indeed a cause for celebration.

Celebrating was what Brady had done for most of the remainder of that day. He'd got the news late on a Friday afternoon and had been delighted to realise that he now had the entire weekend to rejoice. His wife and two daughters had also cried uncontrollably when they'd heard the news (his wife in the doctor's office, his daughters later that day when Brady had relayed the information). But all three of them had been only too eager to join him in banishing the kind of thoughts they'd harboured for too long, driving the darkness away with everything from champagne to Guinness.

It was indeed like escaping a death sentence, Brady thought. He didn't know who to be more grateful to. The surgeon who had removed the growth from his lung, the GP who had first sent him for tests to determine the source and cause of the cough Brady hadn't been able to shift or to his family, who had been unfailingly upbeat (to his face anyway) and supportive ever since he was first diagnosed. Or, he wondered, should he be grateful to God?

Brady was what people, and he himself, liked to call a lapsed Catholic. He didn't go to church. He didn't slavishly follow the rules of the religion that he'd been raised in but, when he'd first discovered he was ill, he had prayed to God that he didn't die. He'd prayed before the first X-rays, before the operation and before receiving his results. Had there been a little divine intervention, he wondered? If there had, he was suitably grateful. Perhaps, he reasoned, he might even start going to church again. The thought made him smile but then, as he reasoned, most things did these days.

He even smiled when the bucket of the digger slammed into something solid about six feet below the surface of the ground.

Brady glanced ahead and saw that he was very close to some ancient trees and he wondered for a second if he might have struck some particularly recalcitrant branches. It had happened before, during the excavation work in the grounds.

He guided the bucket down again, the metal gouging into the earth, dragging up mud, grass and stones.

And something else.

"Jesus Christ," Brady gasped, noticing the dark shape amidst the soil.

He shut off the engine of the excavator immediately.

In the ensuing silence, Brady pushed open the door of the cab, clambered down onto the tracks and then jumped the last couple of feet onto the wet earth.

As he walked towards the base of the trees where he'd already dug a deep hole in the ground, he kept his eyes fixed on the object that he'd first seen. He wondered if he might have been mistaken but, as he drew closer, he realised that he wasn't.

Lying on its side, propped on the pile of excavated dirt, was a coffin.

SIXTEEN

ORLY AIRPORT; PARIS

The flight to Heathrow would take just over an hour, the pilot of the Beechcraft 90 thought as the plane rose into the air.

It was a small cargo plane, powered by twin propellers, which made it something of an oddity among the other planes that had been arranged on the runways of Orly that morning. But it was a reliable aircraft and perfect for short range runs such as the one he had been instructed to complete.

The pilot checked his watch against the clock on the instrument panel and took the aircraft higher, through the low-lying cloud that had been hanging all morning like grubby curtains. The forecast was for fine weather and for that the pilot was grateful, but he had been flying for more than thirty years now, experiencing all manner of meteorological conditions. A simple hop across the Channel to London was a pleasurable enough way to pass the time, he mused.

The two representatives from the Louvre who had checked and rechecked his cargo had reminded him of nervous parents about to let their offspring fly for the first time. The pilot was well aware of the value of his cargo and had tried to reassure the two men that it would be safe until he touched down in England, but they seemed unduly concerned about it. The pilot had listened to them both inside the terminal and also on the runway itself, where they had watched the handlers loading the cargo with a combination of fear and disdain. More than once they had stepped forward to reprimand the men for being unduly heavy handed with the small crates they were packing into the hold of the plane. To the pilot's eye, the handlers had completed their task with the usual level of

74

efficiency and care but to the men from the Louvre it was not enough. If he was honest, he was glad to be in the air and away from their incessant questions and doubts.

He had, he assured them, done this kind of run dozens of times. They had nothing to worry about.

The pilot reached his cruising height and glanced once more at the instrument panel, satisfied that everything was as it should be.

He was under strict instructions to notify the men from the Louvre when he landed at Heathrow. There had also been an insistence that he should tell them when the cargo was unloaded and also when it was successfully transferred to the care of the representatives of the British Museum who were waiting for it. To the pilot, this seemed

overzealous to say the least but he was more than happy to comply with their wishes. It was, as he was only too aware, part of the job.

As the plane reached the Channel, the pilot glanced down at the choppy water below. The sun was blazing brightly in the clear sky and it reflected off the surface of the water. The pilot shielded his eyes for a moment, dazzled by the glare. He reached for the sunglasses in his top pocket and put them on.

The darkness was almost total.

For a second he thought he'd gone blind.

The sky was as black as pitch, the Channel a seething torrent of oil.

He tore off the glasses, blinking frantically.

The sunshine was as bright as it had been before, the Channel below still glinting like burnished steel beneath the dazzling rays.

The pilot let out a gasp, rubbed his eyes with one hand and looked at the sunglasses warily. This time he raised them slowly to his face, pushing them into position more cautiously.

The blackness returned. More total and all enveloping than it had been before.

This time he left them in place, trying to control his

breathing, attempting to understand what he was seeing.

As he squinted through the glasses, he could again see that the sky was a heaving black maw around him and, below, the Channel still flowed and churned like rancid, dark congealed blood. His heart began to thump faster against his ribs, but he kept the sunglasses on for a second longer, staring disbelievingly at the blackness around him.

When he took the glasses off again, he was sweating, the breath rasping in his throat.

He blinked hard.

The sunshine flooded back into the cabin. The sky was bright and blue once more.

The pilot examined the dark glasses carefully for a second, running his fingers over the lenses, wondering what had caused the visual disturbances. The lenses were clear apart from their tint, there was nothing unusual about them.

Until he put them on.

The pilot hesitated a moment then gently slid the glasses back into his top pocket.

Had he imagined what just happened? He shook his head. He was, he told himself, a logical, rational man. What had just happened defied all laws of logic and reason, didn't it? He tried to force the thoughts from his mind, concentrating instead on the objects in the sky ahead of him. Birds he thought. Lots of them. Best to take the aircraft up to avoid them. Even large planes could be troubled by the creatures, so he was anxious to avoid any contact with what looked like a large flock of them.

It was only as he drew nearer to the dense cloud of winged creatures that he realised something that made the hairs rise on the back of his neck.

The dark shapes that were filling the sky, hurtling towards the plane, were larger than any bird he'd ever seen. They flew on leathery wings not feathered ones.

The creatures heading towards him were not birds.

And there were hundreds of them.

Large enough in their flock to blot out the sun, they came on towards him.

The pilot gasped, was this another optical illusion? Some trick his eyes were playing on him? Instead of darkness through the sunglasses he was now seeing something else that he couldn't explain. He rubbed both eyes, wanting the oncoming flock to be something he had imagined and not something real. Something that was going to slam into his plane in a matter of seconds.

He dragged on the controls and sent the Beechcraft 90 rising, nose pushing upwards to escape the onrushing winged horde.

But now the first of them were upon him, slamming into the hull of the plane with impacts that made it shudder.

As if fired from a gun they smashed into the metal chassis, some unable to avoid the spinning propellers. The metal blades sliced them apart easily, blood spraying over the hull and spattering the windscreen. One hit the windscreen, the entire upper body and head dissolving into crimson sludge.

Another followed it, cracking the glass such was the impact. Several shattered teeth sprayed outwards from the open mouth, propelled on gouts of dark blood. The stench was noticeable even inside the cockpit. A thick cloying odour of decay and corruption that was almost palpable.

The pilot kept the plane on its ascent, desperate to escape the onslaught, praying that his eyes were deceiving him again. He hoped that what he was witnessing was simply his mind and his eyes playing tricks on him because otherwise he feared that he was losing a grip on sanity.

The creatures that were still flowing across the sky towards his plane were indeed soaring on leathery wings. Long emaciated arms outstretched from bodies that looked shrunken and lacerated, those bodies topped by contorted and pained faces.

And it was that image the pilot prayed was the product of his imagination because he would have sworn that the faces leering in at him, bloodied, twisted and in pain, were the faces of children.

SEVENTEEN

CENTRAL IRAQ;

D oyle stood beneath the shower spray, his eyes closed, the water coursing down his body.
He felt a weariness this particular night that he experienced only periodically.

It's your age.

Not the kind of tiredness or exhaustion that comes after a hard day's work but something deeper. He felt as if his very soul was tired.

Very philosophical.

Doyle grinned to himself, surprised at his own train of thought but putting it down to the boredom that usually descended on him during the hours of darkness. When he got out of the shower, he told himself, he'd watch TV for a while, have a few drinks and do whatever else it took to help him sleep.

Many nights he drifted off to the sound of music playing into his room. Despite the ferocity of the rock music that Doyle favoured, he found that it had an almost soothing effect on him when it reached the small hours. He would lay in bed with the sound little more than an afterthought and, with luck, he would drift off into dreamless sleep, not waking until the morning when the whole routine began again.

Dreamless.

That would be welcome after the last week or so. He didn't know whether or not to call the subconscious excursions dreams, nightmares or whatever. All he knew was he didn't welcome them. Considering some of the things he'd seen during his life, Doyle had never been plagued by nightmares or bad dreams and that made this latest onslaught even more incomprehensible. Not just their severity but their content.

They always featured the same woman.

Always her.

He swallowed hard.

Her.

"You can say her name you know," Doyle murmured to himself.

Talking to yourself. First sign of madness.

But why her. Why now? It had been more than twenty-five years since her death. More than a quarter of a century since he'd held her bullet riddled, shattered body and looked down at her face as life left her.

"Fuck it," Doyle snarled. He shook his head as if hoping that simple action would somehow dislodge and banish the thoughts he was harbouring.

He switched off the shower and stood motionless for a second, looking down at his own body as if appraising the battered frame, his eyes focussing on the scars and the parts of that body that were no longer sleek and firm but flabby. He could, he supposed, be in much worse shape for a man of his age and he took a little comfort from that thought.

He didn't have much of a belly and he'd retained some of his muscular build, mainly in his upper body, despite his abhorrence of exercise. Doyle had always thought there was something morbidly narcissistic about lifting weights at a gym in front of mirrored walls and surrounded by other would-be fitness fanatics.

Lazy and homophobic eh?

Doyle smiled thinly to himself and allowed the water to splash his face again. He looked down at his own body once more. He couldn't help but feel that he was looking down at the body of a man who was past the best years of his life.

Doyle shook his head, trying to force the thoughts from his mind. Self-analysis had never been his way, so why start now? You had to deal with things as they happened, he told himself, and getting old was just another of those things to be handled.

He stepped from the shower cubicle, realising he needed a

drink. Badly.

As he entered the other room he switched on some music, this time not caring if the volume disturbed anyone in one of the other dwellings nearby. Sound erupted from the small speakers.

"I stand alone in this desolate space; in death they are truly alive..."

Doyle poured himself a large measure of vodka and swallowed half of it in one gulp.

"Massacred innocents, evil took place, the angels were burning inside..."

He turned up the volume, gazing blankly ahead.

"Centuries later, I wonder why, what secret they took to their grave..."

Doyle sucked in a deep breath, finished the vodka and poured himself another.

He crossed to the small table in the centre of the room where his guns were laid out. He'd cleaned them earlier, checking that the mechanisms hadn't been fouled by the dust or sand that was perpetually in the air. It was a ritual with him. Every single night, he cleaned them even if they hadn't been used. They were the tools of his trade and they had to be in perfect condition at all times.

Doyle picked up the Beretta 92F and slammed in one of the magazines, working the slide. If the clip had been full it would have chambered a round but the 9mm rounds were stored elsewhere until the next day. Doyle looked at the weapon, studying its sleek lines and gleaming metalwork. He held it up, sighted it and gently squeezed the trigger, the loud crack echoing around the room as the hammer slammed down on an empty chamber.

He replaced the Beretta on the table and picked up the .357 instead, flipping the cylinder free and spinning it.

"One bullet in one of the chambers, that's all you need."

He heard the voice and barely raised his head to look at its source.

EIGHTEEN

"I was just thinking about you," he said, quietly.

Only now did he look up.

She was sitting on the bed opposite him, her slender legs crossed.

"I told you before to leave me alone," Doyle murmured.

"But you don't want me to leave you alone," she said, brushing strands of blonde hair from her face.

"You're dead," he said, dismissively. "I saw you die."

"And you couldn't help me."

"No one could help you."

"You don't have to feel guilty about it."

Doyle swallowed more vodka.

"Guilt is my middle name," he said, grunting.

"You weren't to blame," she assured him.

Doyle let out a long, almost painful sigh.

"Am I asleep or awake or what?" he chuckled. "You're not even real."

"Do you want me to be real?"

She got up and padded slowly towards him on bare feet.

"Fuck off," Doyle told her.

"You don't mean that," she purred.

"Don't I?"

She was close to him now and he felt her hands brush against his arms.

"Look at me," she said, softly.

Doyle looked at her face.

She smiled.

"God, you were beautiful," he said, quietly.

She moved closer, trying to kiss him. When he moved his head back slightly, she reached instead for his right hand, which still gripped the .357.

"One bullet in one chamber," she breathed, reaching for one

of the powerful heavy grain slugs on the table.

Doyle watched as she slid the bullet into the chamber then snapped the cylinder shut. She raised the weapon slowly until the barrel was touching the underside of his chin.

"Put your finger on the trigger," she told him, kissing him lightly on the cheek.

Doyle turned his head slightly and their lips met.

"Close your eyes," she whispered.

They kissed deeply, passionately and almost despite himself, Doyle snaked his free hand around her slim waist and pulled her closer to him.

"I know you miss me," she said, her breath coming in gasps. "I know you want me."

His hand rose higher beneath her T-shirt, his fingertips gliding over her arched back, enjoying the feel of her smooth skin. She let out a low breath. The sound was one of pure longing and she moved her head closer to him again, her lips brushing his.

"Did you love me?" she breathed.

Doyle nodded almost imperceptibly.

"Then join me," she gasped.

"You're dead," he breathed.

He looked at her, fixing his gaze on her green eyes. They looked as lustrous now as they had when he'd last looked into them.

"Why the fuck don't you leave me alone?" Doyle said, his voice barely audible.

"I never wanted to leave you."

"But why are you here? Why now? After all these years?"

"Is this the first time you've thought about me since it happened?"

"No but I never had to go through...this before."

He felt her hand close around his, realised she was raising the barrel of the .357 until it was pressing against the underside of his chin.

"What's left for you now?" she asked, her breath warm on

his cheek. "What life have you got now?"

Doyle didn't answer.

"Is it worth staying alive for?" she continued.

He let out another sigh.

"What have you got in your life that's so important?" she intoned. "Anything at all worth staying alive for?"

Doyle could only shake his head.

She pushed the barrel of the .357 harder against his chin, a slight smile on her lips now.

Doyle pulled the trigger.

NINETEEN

D oyle sat bolt upright in his bed, his breath coming in
gasps.
"Fuck," he murmured, looking around the room,
blinking myopically as he tried to force the last
vestiges of the nightmare from his mind.

As he swung himself out of bed, he realised that his hands
were shaking. He sat on the edge of the mattress for a
moment, sucking in breaths and trying to compose himself. It
was still pitch black, so he knew he hadn't been asleep very
long.

"Shit," he groaned. If it had been dawn, he could have got
dressed, knowing that the daylight hours would banish the
nightmares at least until darkness descended once again. Now,
Doyle glanced at his watch and saw that it was only just 3.15
am. There was another two hours until light clawed its way
across the horizon.

Doyle could still hear music.

"Now that we're dead, my dear, we can be together..."

And he realised that he had, indeed, fallen asleep with the
sound of rock music blasting from the speakers.

He hurried across the room and hit the OFF button.

Silence dropped like a blanket.

Doyle looked around the room again.

What are you looking for?

He looked at the table where he'd laid his guns and
ammunition out, crossing to the weapons. He reached for the
.357, his hand still shaking slightly.

Doyle flipped open the cylinder.

There was one single bullet inside, wedged snugly into one
of the six chambers.

Doyle took the slug out and put it back in the box with the
other heavy grain rounds.

How the fuck did that get in there? Have you started sleep walking too?

He closed his eyes for a second, images he'd seen in his dream still clearly visible behind his lids.

The guns. The bullets.

And her.

Her. Say her name.

"Georgie," Doyle murmured, the sound deep in his throat.

He sat down, reaching for the vodka bottle he'd left there earlier. Doyle poured himself a large measure and swallowed it with one gulp, feeling the liquor burn its way to his stomach. He wondered how many more he'd have to drink to knock himself out. To insulate himself against more of those dreams. To stop her coming back to him again.

He drank a drop more vodka and glanced at his watch again, realising that even if he did fall asleep again, he would only have a couple of hours of oblivion to enjoy before his alarm woke him to signal the beginning of another day.

Another day just like every other one.

Doyle rubbed his face with both hands, glancing at his right hand. The one that had held the gun. The one she had enveloped in her much softer and smaller hand.

But she didn't, did she? Because you imagined it. You dreamed it.

Again, he looked at the .357, remembering the single bullet in the cylinder.

If the hammer had fallen on that round it would have blown his head off.

But it couldn't because it was only a dream. Only a dream.

Doyle snatched up the .357 and flipped out the cylinder, his teeth gritted. He reached for the box of ammunition and selected one shell. This he pushed into the first chamber then he spun the cylinder and snapped it back into place.

His entire body was quivering slightly as he pushed the barrel against his temple.

"Is this what you really fucking want?" he gasped under his

breath. "Is it?"

He looked around the dimly lit room, feeling the cold metal of the weapon against his flesh.

Doyle pushed harder, thumbing back the hammer.

In the stillness of the room the sound was thunderous.

Doyle closed his eyes, his index finger hovering over the trigger and then closing gently on it, almost caressing the curved piece of steel.

Do it. Pull the trigger.

He clenched his teeth until his jaws ached, his finger still lightly poised on the trigger.

She was right. What have you got left? Do it.

Doyle closed his eyes more tightly.

He roared loudly and hurled the pistol across the room where it slammed into the far wall with a thud.

Doyle could see it lying there, the hammer now resting against an empty chamber.

He clenched his fists and stood there for what seemed like an eternity before retrieving the gun, then he removed the single bullet and put both it and the .357 on the table again before clambering back into bed.

He was still awake two hours later.

TWENTY

BANDON; COUNTY CORK;
THE REPUBLIC OF IRELAND;

At first, Brady thought he was seeing things.

What the hell would a coffin be doing here? In the grounds of this house? Beneath this tree?

As he moved closer to the hole, he himself had made with the excavator, he kept his gaze fixed on the wooden box.

It was polished oak or mahogany, or it had been at one time. It had obviously been in the earth for some time because any gleam the wood used to have had long since gone. The brass handles on its sides were tarnished and darkened by the passage of time.

Brady moved closer to the hole, glancing again at the coffin. He felt suddenly very guilty. Who's resting place had he disturbed? Why had no one mentioned that someone had been buried in the grounds? Brady wondered who was inside the box.

He was still wondering when he reached the lip of the deep hole and peered down.

"Oh, shit," he murmured.

There was another coffin at the bottom of the cavity. Dark wood like the first one.

Brady put his hand to his mouth. What the hell was going on here? Was there a cemetery in the grounds that they didn't know about? Would more digging uncover yet more resting places? He sucked in a deep breath, questions tumbling through his mind now.

The first coffin had been about six feet down. The regulation depth as far as Brady knew, but this second one was deeper. Twelve feet or more.

Brady turned towards the first casket and glanced at it quickly to see if there were any nameplates on it or anything else that might help to identify the occupant. He could see nothing. The wood didn't appear to be unduly damaged, he thought with relief. When he accidentally dug it up, he certainly hadn't caused too much destruction. The wood was scored in a couple of places, obviously caught by the teeth of the bucket when it had torn through the earth but, apart from that, there was no noticeable damage to the wood of either box.

Again, Brady looked at the first box, running his fingers gently over the smooth surface. Two of the screws that held the lid in place had come free but, fortunately, the impact from the digger hadn't forced the lid open. Brady shuddered at that particular possibility, grateful that it hadn't happened. He'd been to a funeral once, many years before, when, by some appalling mishap, the pall bearers managed to drop the coffin while unloading it from the hearse. The box had broken open and the deceased had toppled out onto the gravel drive of the church in full view of the mourners. That particular mishap had given Brady nightmares for months afterwards when he'd been younger, and he was grateful he hadn't disturbed the bodies inside their coffins any more than he could help.

He reached for the two-way radio on his belt, wondering what others reactions would be to his unexpected discovery. Maybe the work would be stopped for a couple of days while the occupants of the boxes were identified and reinterred somewhere else, he thought. That was a pleasing prospect. He smiled to himself and prepared to make the call to his superior.

"Frank," he said into the two-way. "Come in. It's Brady here. We've got a problem."

The handset crackled, static rasping from it.

"Frank," Brady went on. "Can you hear me?"

More static.

Brady sighed and tried adjusting the two-way, changing the

frequency to banish the annoying rasps of static.

"Frank," he continued. "If you're there, answer me."

"Yes, I can hear you, Mike," the voice from the other end of the line finally responded. "What's the problem?"

"You need to come and have a look."

"Can't you deal with it?"

"No. You need to see it."

There was another harsh crackle of static and then the voice came again from the other end of the line.

"I'm on my way," the owner of the voice told him.

Brady nodded; his eyes still fixed on the coffin at the bottom of the hole.

TWENTY-ONE

Why was the coffin buried so deep?

Brady dropped to his haunches, looking down into the hole he'd made, wondering who the hell buried bodies in the grounds of a country house. He shook his head.

Then he heard the sound.

A low wail that reminded him of the wind rushing through a cracked window pane, seemed to be drifting up from the hole. From the coffin itself. But Brady knew that was impossible. He listened more intently but heard nothing except the softly falling rain.

He straightened up, preparing to move away from the deep rift in the earth, but as he did the sound came again. More insistent this time. Louder. Brady turned back towards it, glancing into the pit again.

When the sound came for a third time, Brady barely hesitated. He could see that the sides of the hole were uneven and decided that, if he was careful, he could actually climb down to the second coffin quite easily. There might be some kind of marking or nameplate on this other box that would make identification of the unfortunate occupants easier. He stepped down onto a ledge of mud, relieved that it took his weight.

Below him, several thick tree roots also poked out from the soil and Brady used one of these as a stepping stone, gripping another with his hand as he lowered himself down into the deepest part of the hole. The smell of earth was strong in his nostrils now and he shuddered involuntarily as he saw several thick, bloated earthworms writhing around in the churned-up soil. He wondered if they had been feeding on the bodies inside the coffins and the thought made him wince.

He was now at the bottom of the crater, his feet sinking

several inches into the sucking mud there.

A quick inspection of the coffin revealed that there were no markings anywhere on it. Like the one above, it offered no clue to the identity of the poor soul inside it.

What Brady did see however, something he hadn't been able to discern from his loftier perch on the edge of the hole, was considerable damage to the lid of this second box.

The wood was splintered in two places, one of the panels partially torn away, gouged and battered by the teeth of the bucket when it tore through the earth. Brady felt something akin to shame to think that he'd already disturbed someone's resting place but, now, knowing he'd damaged the coffin too caused him to shake his head apologetically.

He swallowed hard when he realised that he could actually see a portion of the corpse through the lid.

Despite himself, he looked more closely.

He could see dark material which he guessed was a suit and there was a hint of something lighter between the lapels that he took to be a shirt. It was fairly obvious that the occupant of this second box was male.

Brady leaned a little closer, trying to pick out more details of the body within.

The hand that grabbed him exploded through the damaged lid of the coffin, powerful fingers gripping his throat and slamming him down onto the cold wood.

Brady tried to scream but the hand clasped around his throat prevented that. His head was swimming and he could feel a growing tightness in his chest caused by the shock of the attack.

The fingers of the hand bore sharp nails, and these dug into the soft flesh of his neck, gouging skin away and opening several small cuts, one of which caused blood to flow freely.

Brady struck at the hand, his mind spinning, not able to grasp what was happening to him.

Pain was beginning to clutch his heart in a vice like grip, tightening as surely as the fingers that seemed intent on tearing his windpipe free of his throat. The tip of one powerful index finger did actually penetrate skin, gouging through the soft flesh while crimson spurted wildly onto the lid of the coffin. Brady tried to scream but the hand seemed to have sealed his throat and the pain that was spreading through his upper body now made even that impossible.

He heard a loud roar of rage and pain from inside the wooden box and then his head was slammed down onto the lid. Once. Twice. Three times. Each impact seemingly more powerful than the last. He felt consciousness slipping from him, felt his body beginning to shake uncontrollably. And still that clawed hand gripped his throat with the tenacity of a terrier holding a rat.

Brady felt his knees buckle. Darkness raced in around him. Pain filled him.

The hand slammed his head down yet again onto the coffin lid but, by that time, he was past caring.

TWENTY-TWO

HEATHROW AIRPORT; LONDON;

"What the fuck happened?"

Danny Roberts looked blankly at the Beechcraft 90; his gaze drawn to the deep indentations on the fuselage. He reached out his hand slowly and ran it over the dents.

His companion merely shook his head.

Maurice Betts was also studying the numerous marks on the plane. He was in his late forties, perhaps twenty years older than Roberts, but, in all his time as a handler at Heathrow, he had never seen damage like this to a small aircraft.

"What did the pilot say?" Roberts wanted to know.

"He didn't say much of anything," Betts told him. "I was talking to one of the paramedics who took him away and he said the guy looked terrified. They had to sedate him before they got him in the ambulance. He nearly hit two planes on the way in."

Roberts walked slowly around the plane, running his inquisitive gaze over every inch of it.

As he came to the first propeller, he looked more closely at the metal blades. They were spattered with crimson fluid, some of it congealed.

"He must have hit some birds," Roberts murmured.

Betts joined him.

"Birds wouldn't have made dents like that in the fuselage," he mused. "Not unless they were swans or something like that. Those are big marks. They must have hit him going at a hell of a speed."

"What's he carrying?" Roberts enquired.

"Historical artefacts," Betts told him. "Something from France. People from the British Museum are coming to check

94

it before we can unload it."

"Why can't we take it off the plane?"

"I haven't got a clue. I'm just telling you what I know."

"It must be top secret or something," Roberts murmured, looking once more at the indentations in the plane's fuselage.

The two men were still gazing at the Beechcraft 90 when they heard the sound of a rapidly approaching engine behind them. Roberts turned to see a car speeding across the open runway towards them. When it pulled up, he saw that the driver was a man in his early forties who hurried towards the plane without looking at the two handlers.

"Has anything inside been touched?" Jonathan Sellers asked.

"No," Betts told him. "We were told not to unload anything until the people from the British Museum arrived."

Sellers fumbled in his pocket and pulled out some ID which he pushed towards Betts.

"My colleague and I will take the cargo now," Sellers announced, the passenger door of the car opening to reveal Caroline Bradley. She glanced at Roberts and Betts and nodded briskly.

"It's still on-board," Sellers told her.

"What was he carrying?" Roberts wanted to know.

"Something valuable," Sellers said, flatly. He and Caroline walked to the fuselage door and Sellers opened it cautiously before clambering up into the belly of the aircraft.

He turned and glanced at Caroline. "We'll open it when we get it back to the museum."

She nodded.

"What caused the damage to the plane?" Caroline asked, pointing to the dents.

"We were just trying to work that out," Roberts told her.

"Whatever collided with it was big," Betts added. "He's lucky he didn't crash."

"Can you put the cargo in the back of the car please?" Sellers said, brusquely. "We're in a hurry."

Roberts looked at the older man then moved towards the

door of the plane.

"And be careful," Sellers snapped.

Roberts hesitated for a moment, thought about saying something then thought better of it. He was, after all, paid to hump things around. He didn't expect anything approaching good manners from those he was humping it for.

"It's just one crate," Sellers told him.

"We know," Roberts called, moving towards the rear of the small plane.

"Should we talk to the pilot?" Caroline asked, lowering her voice conspiratorially.

"Why?" Sellers wanted to know.

"To find out what happened up there," she insisted.

"There's no damage to the cargo as far as we can see. That's all that matters."

"What do you think happened?"

"I have absolutely no idea, Caroline. My only concern is with the cargo. Thank God it arrived safely. We need to get it back to the museum now."

TWENTY-THREE

BAGHDAD; CENTRAL IRAQ;

D oyle knew he was being watched.

He didn't know how he knew. He just knew.

Call it instinct, intuition, a sixth sense acquired over the years. Call it what the fuck you like, but he knew he was being watched.

It was a feeling. Something that made him uneasy and unsettled. A feeling that caused him to be even more edgy than usual. Doyle didn't like surprises and this new feeling that crept over him hinted at a surprise to come and he did not want that. Surprises meant trouble in his line of work because they meant that you weren't prepared, and preparation was of the utmost importance to Doyle because it meant that no one could sneak up on him either literally or metaphorically.

He sipped water from the bottle he carried and looked out over the landscape before him, glancing behind him every now and then.

He yawned and wondered if this new found feeling of uncertainty was caused, not by someone following him, but by tiredness. Having barely slept the previous night, he was finding it difficult to keep his focus as he wandered around in the searing heat wanting nothing more than to curl up somewhere comfortable for an hour or so and catch up on some of the sleep he'd lost.

Fat chance of that.

Thoughts of the sleep he'd lost made him ponder why exactly he'd lost it. The thought made him shake his head, but Doyle hoped that every night wasn't to be plagued with the kind of dreams that had troubled him so much lately. He didn't want to begin dreading the night as much as he'd begun to dread the daylight.

Sleep was the only escape he had. The welcome oblivion was the only time he wasn't continually confronted by thoughts he would rather not have. Forced, over and over again, to consider his situation and how much he hated it. Life had become an endurance test for him. He didn't live any more, he existed.

Doyle reached for his cigarettes and lit one, glancing around him once more.

If someone was watching him, what was the reason for their surveillance?

In the past he would have known. Anyone watching him or following him for any length of time had just one reason for doing it. They wanted him dead.

Happy days.

Doyle smiled to himself.

You're getting much too old for that kind of shit anyway. Life is meant to be more sedate as you get older. Fuck the excitement.

He blew out a long stream of smoke and waved a greeting to one of the other security operatives who was clambering down from a Scania lorry.

The man nodded in Doyle's direction then set off towards him.

He was in his thirties. Tall, powerfully built. That much was obvious even

though his body was obscured by the shirt and the Kevlar he wore. As far as Doyle could remember, he was American. A Texan. They'd spoken a couple of times before (Doyle had listened at any rate). He'd been invalided out of the American Army because of psychological problems.

Something like that.

Doyle didn't remember. Or, more to the point, he didn't really give a fuck.

"Hey, man," the younger newcomer said, moving closer to him. "How's it going?"

"Yeah, all right," Doyle told him, noticing that the younger man had earpieces in.

Doyle pointed to them, watching as the American pulled one free.

"Listening to music, man," the newcomer told him.

"What is it?" Doyle enquired.

"Eminem. That dude kicks ass."

Doyle sighed.

"Yeah, I'm sure he does," he said, wearily, the sarcasm in his tone lost on his new-found companion.

Doyle pointed again at the other man's earpieces.

"You should leave them out," he observed. "You can't hear what's going on around you with them in."

"No way. I ain't listening to these goddam towel heads talking shit all day long," the American laughed.

"Up to you," Doyle murmured. "But just watch yourself."

"Something going down?" There was concern in the American's tone.

"You never know. Just keep your eyes open."

Doyle thought it best not to mention his completely unsubstantiated feeling of unease.

"I was on a patrol near Kandahar once, can't remember the name of the village. Some towel head shithole. The shit just went off without anyone expecting it."

Oh, fuck, here we go, Doyle thought, hoping the newcomer hadn't seen the look on his face.

"I was in the 82nd Airborne," the newcomer continued.

"You mentioned it when we spoke last time," Doyle said, flatly.

"They'd had some bombings in that area where we were and the locals caught one guy but he managed to detonate the shit that was strapped to him." The American laughed loudly. "Man, what a fucking mess. Me and a couple of buddies, we posed for a picture next to his arms and legs." He laughed again. "But some asshole calls CNN or something like that and they start calling us fucking war criminals and shit."

"Even war is different these days," Doyle said, raising his eyebrows.

"You bet your ass," the American said, laughing again. The sound was a whooping caterwaul of noise that seemed to echo around them.

"Local police said they'd had intelligence indicating there might be a kidnap," Doyle informed the younger man. "So just keep your eyes open, right?"

"Sure thing, man."

Doyle glanced around again, that inexplicable feeling of being watched closing around him once more. He felt the hairs on the back of his neck rise.

"Nearly quitting time," the other man observed, glancing at his watch. "Another day, another dollar."

Doyle nodded.

"Hey, man, we should get a drink or something when we get back to the compound tonight," the American suggested. "You know, shoot the shit for a few hours." He laughed that raucous whooping laugh again. "Nothing else to do here."

"I'll bear that in mind, Texas," Doyle murmured, quietly.

The other man slapped him on the back, a blow that might have floored Doyle if he hadn't been expecting it, then he headed back the way he'd come.

Doyle looked around him once more, still uneasy. Still not knowing why. The breeze that had just sprung up whipped sand and dust into the air. They swirled around like forgotten memories.

TWENTY-FOUR

BANDON; COUNTY CORK;
THE REPUBLIC OF IRELAND;

"Oh Christ," murmured Frank Carey as he approached the abandoned digger and the pile of earth before it.

He'd seen something as soon as he'd pulled up, leaving the keys in the car ignition as he walked across the large open area leading towards the trees.

They rattled and waved in the strong wind, the sound of the breeze whistling through their leaves and branches like discordant whistles as Carey moved closer to the area he'd been called to inspect.

He saw the coffin immediately, propped on the mound of mud next to the hole and he shook his head in bewilderment. No wonder Brady had called him. And speaking of Brady, where the hell was he?

Carey walked around the excavator, glancing up into the cab but there was no sign of Brady. He looked towards the earth again, his attention drawn towards the coffin once more.

It was only when he got to the edge of the hole that he peered down and saw the second box.

"What the fuck?" he murmured.

But there was something else. Not just the uncovered coffins. There was something dark and wet all over the lid of the box in the hole and Carey didn't have to get any closer to see that it was blood.

"Mike," he called, his eyes still riveted to the contents of the hole. When there was no reply from Brady, the other man walked around the hole, pausing briefly beside the first coffin, seeing that there was very little damage to the dark wooden box. The one in the hole had been battered by the bucket of the excavator but, apart from some gouges in the wood of the lid, the destruction wrought had been negligible and for that he was relieved. He didn't relish the task of explaining this situation to grieving relatives and friends.

The blood was another matter.

Carey knelt beside the hole, looking down at the crimson fluid that had spread darkly all over the lid. He remained in that position for a moment, wondering who he should inform of this discovery. Work would have to be stopped, there was no question of that. Who knew what else was hiding in the grounds of the house? Carey reached for his two-way radio.

He was about to switch it on when he was struck.

The blow was thunderous.

Even if he'd been aware it was coming there would have been little he could have done to avoid it.

He was lucky that the impact was so devastating he didn't have to worry about the second or third blow. Delivered with a thick tree branch, the first blow caught him on the nape of the neck and sent him sprawling in the mud. The second slammed down onto the top of his skull, cracking bone. The third actually split the cranium. Small pieces of bone fell into the sucking ooze to be joined a second later by thick slops of brain matter as a final blow tore through the cranial bones and exposed the reddish-grey matter beneath.

Carey's attacker didn't check to see if he was dead. It was hardly necessary.

Instead, the figure moved swiftly towards the car he'd arrived in and slid behind the steering wheel, starting the engine and swinging the car around, guiding it towards the driveway that cut through the grounds and led to the house itself.

But it was the other end of the narrow thoroughfare that the driver now sought. The gates and the road that ran beyond them.

It was the road into Bandon itself that was wanted. The town was less than ten minutes away.

The driver gripped the wheel tightly and drove on.

TWENTY-FIVE

CENTRAL IRAQ;

As the truck rumbled along, Doyle glanced out of the rear of the vehicle, watching the city fall away behind them.

He hadn't been able to shake his feeling of being watched and it irritated him more than anything else. Peering out at the landscape beyond the truck, he allowed his gaze to move back and forth across the parched terrain for a second before reaching for a cigarette that he lit and drew hard on.

The man sitting next to him looked at him but chose not to say anything, and for that Doyle was grateful. He didn't fancy ending his working day by telling someone who objected to him smoking to fuck themselves. Unless he had to of course.

Doyle yawned, remembering how badly he'd slept the night before and hoping that he wouldn't have the same problems again tonight. He took a drag on his cigarette and tried to banish those thoughts.

When he felt the truck slowing down, Doyle sat forward. Other heads in the rear of the Scania also turned, curious as to why they were almost at a halt. They were certainly nowhere near their compound. Why was the driver stopping?

When the vehicle rolled to a standstill, Doyle turned to the other occupants of the truck, one hand raised.

"Stay here," he said, clambering over the tail flap of the truck and jumping down to the dusty ground.

Up ahead, the other vehicles in the convoy were also stationary. Other security men had disembarked. Some were standing at the road side, as puzzled as Doyle himself with why the convoy had come to a stop.

Doyle saw the American he'd spoken to earlier walking towards the top of a dune, one hand resting on the 9mm

Glock he carried in a holster on his right hip.

Doyle looked ahead, gazing further up the road, then he headed to the cab of the leading Scania and tapped on the driver's door, peering up at the open window. When the driver poked his head out, Doyle shrugged in his direction.

"Why have you stopped?" he wanted to know.

"There was something in the road," the driver told him.

Doyle looked at the sand blasted expanse of tarmac but saw nothing.

"There's nothing there now," he said, motioning ahead to where the road snaked away between sand dunes.

The driver looked at Doyle then at the road ahead.

"What did you see?" Doyle wanted to know.

"I don't know," the driver told him.

"What do you mean? You must have seen something, or you wouldn't have stopped."

"What's happening, man?"

The shout came from behind him.

Doyle turned to see the American security operative striding back across the sand.

"Trying to find out why he stopped, Texas," Doyle replied. "What were you doing?"

"Checking the perimeter, man. You never know who might be around."

Doyle nodded.

"What's this fucking towel head say then?" the American went on. "Why'd he stop?"

"He says he saw something. But he can't say what."

"Well, whatever he saw, it ain't there now."

The American banged on the door of the Scania, gesturing towards the driver.

"Hey, Ahmed," he sneered. "What did you see?"

"My name is not Ahmed," the driver said, irritably.

"Well, whatever the fuck it is, what did you see?" the Texan went on. "Why did you stop the truck?"

"I see something on the road. A man. Not sure."

104

The Texan shook his head.

"I thought they didn't touch alcohol here," he said, grinning. "But this boy sounds like he's been hitting the sauce." He laughed his loud whooping laugh.

Doyle nodded again, wheeling away from the truck and heading up the road. The American joined him, striding along briskly.

"I don't trust these guys, man," the American said. "He could be one of them."

"One of who?" Doyle asked, without looking at his companion.

"One of them. One of the terrorists. Insurgents. Whatever the fuck you want to call them. He could be IS, man."

"Take it easy, Texas. Let's just have a look around, see what we can find. He must have seen something. He wouldn't just have stopped for no reason."

"It could be a fucking ambush."

"You checked both sides of the road, right?"

"No one there."

"Then it's not an ambush is it?"

Doyle strode on.

"This is how they do it, man," the American insisted. "They set you up like this and then they fuck you up."

Doyle kept walking, peering around him, shielding his eyes occasionally from the sand grains that peppered him, propelled by the increasingly strong wind. Again, he felt that tightness at the back of his neck and the rear of his skull.

Intuition? Sixth sense?

Doyle reached inside his jacket and unclipped the leather strap secured over the butt of the Beretta automatic.

Just in case.

The sand dunes ahead rose higher, creating a narrow valley that the road passed through. Doyle glanced at the crest of each one.

"Texas," he called, motioning to the American who hurried over.

"What is it, man?" the younger man wanted to know. "You see something?"

"No," Doyle murmured, his eyes never leaving the sand dunes ahead. "Whatever he saw it's gone now. Tell them to move the convoy on."

The Texan hesitated a moment and then nodded, spun on his heel and headed back to the leading truck.

Doyle stepped back off the road, his boots sinking into the soft sand there and he watched as the leading truck trundled past him, glancing at its driver briefly when the man met his gaze.

As the last truck approached, Doyle flagged it down, hauled himself up into the back of it and settled himself on the wooden seat there. As the truck drove on, Doyle looked up into the sky, feeling the wind blowing more powerfully now. Clouds were gathering. Sand grains whipped through the air like tiny pieces of shrapnel, stinging the flesh where they struck.

There was a storm on the way.

TWENTY-SIX

COUNTY CORK;
THE REPUBLIC OF IRELAND;

The clinic was on the outskirts of the town.

Three red brick buildings overlooking a narrow river and surrounded by immaculately manicured lawns and perfectly kept flower beds.

Four doctors had set up their practice there three years earlier when it first opened.

To begin with, it hadn't been a popular addition to health care in the area. There was another practice in the centre of the town itself and older residents had feared that this new place would attract too many of the younger professional people who lived in and around the area. If that happened, then the central practice would close and it would be more difficult to reach the clinic. That at least had been the thinking. As it transpired, there had been no cause for concern and the two practices had thrived.

The clinic in particular had flourished. The facilities there were almost on a par with a hospital and attracted patients from miles around.

This particular evening, the last of them had gone home and the building stood more-or-less silent with just a handful of lights burning within.

No one noticed the car that pulled up on the edge of a virtually deserted car park, hidden by trees from the main building.

No eyes saw the driver slide from behind the wheel and disappear into the enveloping darkness.

Doctor Paul Brennan certainly saw none of this. He glanced up at the window of his office and wondered if he should draw the curtains to shut out the night but, he decided instead to finish his work and go home.

Brennan sat back on his chair and shrugged his shoulders, groaning as he felt the stiffness there. He nodded and closed the file he'd been working on. Definitely time to go home, he mused and rose to his feet.

The drive would take him less than twenty minutes and for that he was thankful. It had been a busy day and he wanted nothing more now than to relax. He'd called his wife earlier to inform her he'd be late. He'd do so again once he got into his car.

Brennan switched off his computer, took a final sip of coffee from his mug and got to his feet. He stretched, hearing and feeling his shoulders crack. He massaged his neck with one hand, aware of the stiffness there.

The door of his office exploded inwards, propelled by a thunderous impact from the other side. It slammed back against the wall behind, hitting it so hard it almost came off the hinges.

Brennan froze, his gaze fixed on the door.

The figure that had burst through into his office was a man in his thirties. Tall, heavyset but hunched over slightly, his face contorted by a look of pain so intense that Brennan had never seen anything like it before. The man took a couple of faltering steps towards him, one hand outstretched towards the doctor.

It was only as he drew nearer that Brennan could see the man's eyes were tinged with red, blood shot. In fact, as he looked more closely, he could see nothing but red. It was as if the man opposite him was looking at him through two pools of blood. Only the black pupils were visible through the crimson where the whites should have been. There were several lacerations around the eyes too and, as Brennan looked more closely, he saw that the man also had similar cuts around his mouth. Part of the bottom lip was actually hanging off, dangling like a piece of raw meat from the gaping maw of his mouth.

The man croaked something, his face contorting once more into a mask of agony.

Brennan took a step nearer, one hand closing over his phone in his pocket. He knew he should call the police but how he was going to do that, with the man so close to him, he had no idea.

And now he noticed the smell that seemed to fill the room. A rancid stench of decay that almost made him gag. He put a hand to his face, trying to mask the fetid odour but it was impossible.

Brennan tried to help the man onto the chair opposite his desk, but the newcomer merely brushed him aside, swaying uncertainly, his face still twisted in a look of incredible pain.

"Let me examine you," Brennan offered, more than a little disconcerted by the man's appearance and his sudden, explosive entry into the office. "I need to know what happened to you."

The man grabbed him, strong hands gripping his throat, then he let out a low roar of agony, his entire body quivering madly. He pushed Brennan away, propelling him into the wall with an impact that knocked the breath from him.

Brennan glanced at the open door, trying to calculate his chances of reaching it. Of escaping from this madman who had barged into his office.

"Help me," the man roared at him, his red eyes blazing.

He snatched up the mug that stood on Brennan's desk and brought it down hard against the hard wood, shattering it. Pieces of china sprayed in all directions and the man grabbed the largest of these, pressing it to his forearm.

"No," the doctor shouted, realising what the newcomer was about to do.

Brennan watched helplessly as the man drew the sharp edge down his arm from the elbow to the wrist. The flesh and muscles opened like a mouth; the wound so deep it had almost exposed bone.

The fluid that burst from the gash was not red but almost

clear.

Brennan gasped as he saw the liquid spurting from the savage wound, a new smell now filling the room. A smell he thought he recognised.

The man roared something unintelligible at him, digging three fingers into the huge laceration.

He brandished the digits at Brennan, more clear fluid dripping from them. And now the doctor understood what the new smell was.

Despite the insanity of the situation and contrary to everything he believed, he realised that the liquid spurting from the gaping wound in the newcomer's arm was embalming fluid.

TWENTY-SEVEN

THE BRITISH MUSEUM; LONDON;

Jonathan Sellers looked at the crate and tried to swallow but his mouth and throat were as dry as chalk.

"You must be amazed that it's finally here," David Mackay offered, seeing the look of apprehension on his face. Mackay was a well-dressed man in his sixties. A man who could easily have been mistaken for a banker rather than the director of the British Museum. He'd held the post for more than nine years and, during his tenure, he had seen attendances rise every year. Even though the museum was a place of learning, he'd always been keenly aware that it was also something of a business and the steadily rising attendances had certainly been a comfort to the art historian who now looked at the crate before him with the same kind of fascination and veneration he'd always had for the ancient artefacts that filled the museum.

"Amazed and relieved," Sellers confessed. "When we first found it at Machecoul, I did wonder if we'd ever manage to display it here."

"It's six years since its discovery isn't it?" Mackay mused.

Sellers nodded.

"I'm still surprised the French allowed it to be displayed here first," he murmured. "Well quite," Mackay mused. "As Gilles de Rais helped defeat the English during the Hundred Years' War, you'd think they'd celebrate him just for that."

They both laughed.

"But we know it's his other interests that make him less desirable," Caroline Bradley chuckled.

"The murder, rape and mutilation of over two hundred children," Sellers said, quietly. "You can understand the French reluctance to celebrate him as a hero, I suppose.

Despite his military achievements."

"It's more ironic knowing that Joan of Arc felt she was being guided by God when one of her lieutenants was a devil-worshipper," Mackay mused.

Sellers nodded.

"And conjurer of demons," he added.

"One of whom supposedly gave him the secret of alchemy," Caroline went on.

Again, Sellers nodded.

"That's right," he said. "Baron. A creature he owed so much to he had an image of it placed in a stained-glass window in his chapel at Machecoul."

"What happened to the window?" Mackay wanted to know. "It's a pity we couldn't have got hold of that too."

"It disappeared," Sellers explained. "A man tried to buy it. A multi-millionaire called David Callahan. He had it flown to Ireland, to his estate. He was looking for the secret that Gilles de Rais thought he'd found. The secret of immortality. If you believe that story anyway."

"De Rais didn't write the book you found though?" said Mackay.

"No. It was written by a man called Gaston Lavelle. Also a satanist like De Rais. He was supposedly possessed by a creature he'd seen during a black mass. When the book was finished, he hid it beneath the De Rais chapel at Machecoul. That was where I found it during the excavations."

"So, we're going to be displaying a book used in black mass ceremonies along with weapons and artefacts from the Hundred Years' War," Mackay exclaimed. "That should ruffle a few feathers within the scientific community."

They all laughed happily.

"Most of the visitors will be a lot more interested in the armour, swords and arrow tips than they are in the ramblings of some fifteenth century French satanist," Sellers remarked.

"But it's a fascinating relic," Mackay went on.

"The pilot who flew it from France might not agree with

you," Caroline mused. "I wonder what happened up there?" She pointed skyward. "What made those marks on the plane for one thing."

"What do you think made them?" Mackay enquired.

She hesitated for a second then simply shook her head.

"Are you afraid to say it out loud?" Sellers challenged.

"It can't be true. We both know that," she intoned, her own hand shaking slightly as she touched the lid of the crate.

"If the book inside this box was removed from the place where it was written then the demons it was used to summon would try to destroy it." Sellers spoke the words slowly and almost reverentially. "Whoever had control of the book had control of the demons too. They called them 'Guardians.'"

Mackay raised his eyebrows.

"You make it sound like some kind of weapon," he murmured, glancing towards the box.

"It's a book," Caroline said. "Nothing more."

"You know that's not true," Sellers told her.

"Christ, I thought I was supposed to be the hopeless romantic. You're meant to be the hard-bitten realist."

Sellers managed a smile.

"You know this book was vital to Gilles de Rais," he said. "That was why he protected it so strenuously. All the secrets he wanted were in there. The secrets of alchemy. Of conjuring demons. Of eternal life."

"And of bringing life to inanimate objects," Caroline added.

"I didn't know that was one of de Rais' interests," Mackay added.

"The book maintains that all objects have a life force, even inanimate ones," Caroline explained. "And that with the correct knowledge, those objects can be imbued with a kind of organic life."

"It was a favourite of the Hellfire Club," Sellers said, smiling.

Mackay raised an eyebrow in surprise.

"They were obsessed with finding copies of it and distributing it to their different chapters."

"How many copies were there?" Mackay enquired.

"Six that we know of. All handwritten by Lavelle himself. Three were destroyed by the Inquisition. The others were lost. This is the only surviving copy."

"Satanists, devil-worshippers and the Hellfire Club, are we guilty of promoting the darker things in life?" Mackay mused.

"I'm not sure all the details of the book should be included in our brochures for upcoming exhibitions," Sellers offered, his smile fading slightly.

"If people knew those things about the book, we'd probably double our attendances," Caroline said.

They all managed a subdued laugh, the sound fading rapidly inside the room as they turned back towards the box.

"We'd better have a look," Sellers went on, taking a step closer.

The lid had already been loosened carefully. All that remained was to remove it and take out the item within.

"Let's get it out," Mackay urged, pulling on a pair of white cotton gloves.

Sellers did the same thing and finally lifted the lid, placing it on the floor beside the desk the crate was perched on.

As Sellers reached inside the wooden box, they both noticed that his hands were shaking.

TWENTY-EIGHT

CENTRAL IRAQ;

Doyle climbed down from the rear of the Scania, wincing as he felt an ache at the base of his spine.

It's your age.

The gates of the compound were closed behind the convoy of lorries and those that had been riding in them began to spill out, disappearing rapidly into their own quarters for the night as they usually did. There wasn't a great deal of social intermingling among the workers here, something Doyle had been grateful for when he'd first arrived. He valued his own company and always had, and he was constantly puzzled when others didn't feel the same way.

There was a small communal area in a flat roofed building towards the centre of the compound. The building contained a pool table, a few fruit machines and some games consoles for those who felt they had to mingle or couldn't stand the solitude of their own quarters every night. There was a bar of sorts, despite the fact that the country frowned on alcohol consumption, but it had a small choice of liquor and was there ostensibly for the social opportunities it offered rather than anything else.

Doyle was standing watching the lorries disgorge their cargos when he felt a strong hand on his shoulder.

"How about that drink?"

He turned to see the American security man standing beside him.

"Not now, Texas," Doyle said, managing a smile. "Another time, eh?"

"I'm buying," the big American insisted.

Doyle looked at the man and saw something close to desperation on his chiselled features.

One drink. It's not going to hurt is it?

"What else you doing that's so important?" the Texan went on.

Doyle nodded.

"You've got a point," he conceded. "But just one, right?"

The big Texan grinned broadly and set off across the compound with Doyle in tow. Once inside the building, the American walked to the makeshift bar and banged his hand down on it hard, laughing his whooping laugh. Doyle was relieved that they were the only ones in there.

"What are you drinking, man?" the Texan said, slapping Doyle on the shoulder.

"Vodka," Doyle told him, running a hand over his closely cropped hair and wiping the perspiration on his trousers.

When the drinks arrived, the Texan raised his own glass in salute.

"Here's to the good life," he said, chuckling.

"Whatever that is," Doyle replied and sipped at his drink.

He glanced briefly at his watch, wanting to ensure that he didn't stay too long. Not that he had anything else pressing to fill his time, but the thought of an extended drinking session with this big American didn't exactly fill him with joy.

"What do you think that rag head saw earlier on?" the Texan asked, turning his glass between his thumb and index finger.

"I don't know," Doyle answered. "But whatever it was, it shook him up."

"Maybe he just scares easy."

Doyle raised his eyebrows by way of an answer.

"If he'd seen some of the things I've seen he'd shit in his pants," the Texan went on, laughing.

"What made you come here, Texas?" Doyle enquired.

"I needed the work, man."

"Was there nothing where you're from?"

"Lots of people don't like hiring vets. They think we have problems." He tapped his temple with the tip of one index finger.

116

"They're probably right," Doyle said, smiling.

"Were you in the army?"

"No. Counter Terrorist Unit. It was a different kind of war"

"'War is all Hell.'"

"General William Tecumseh Sherman, right?"

The American nodded.

"How did you know that?" he laughed.

"I read. More than I used to. More time on my hands I suppose."

"So, what kind of action did you see when you were in the Counter Terrorist Unit? That must have been a few years back." He whooped that loud and piercing laugh.

"Thanks for reminding me," Doyle grunted.

"Were you like a spy or something?" the Texan went on, smiling broadly. "That sounds like it was undercover work."

"It was."

"So, you weren't regular army?"

"We worked with the SAS sometimes but usually we were on our own."

"Why'd you quit?"

"I didn't. I was invalided out."

"Like me."

"You had psychological problems. They threw you out because you were crazy."

Doyle smiled and raised his glass in salute. The big Texan laughed and nodded vigorously. The two men sat in silence for a moment.

"Have you got any family?" Doyle asked, at last.

"I was married," the American told him. "I had a daughter."

"What happened?"

"We split up. I was away all the time; I don't blame her. We just drifted apart. She said, by the end, I wasn't the man she married. Whatever the hell that means."

"Do you still see your daughter?"

"When I'm back home I see her sometimes. Usually just for an hour a week."

"It's better than nothing."

"No, it isn't, man." He finished what was left in his glass and motioned for the man behind the bar to refill his glass. "Every time I look at her, I realise how much I miss her."

"How old is she?"

"She's sixteen now but she's still my little girl. Does that make sense?"

Doyle nodded.

"Her mother's got another guy. They live together and I'm cool with that. But I miss my daughter so much. I should be with her. A father is supposed to be with his kids, isn't he? Teaching them? Guiding them? And what the hell am I doing?"

Doyle regarded the other man impassively for a moment.

"When me and my wife broke up, my daughter lived with me, but I lost my job. I couldn't support us. She had to go and live with my wife."

"That wasn't your fault."

"If I'd been any kind of man, I'd have got another job, a better job. I'd have got two jobs. I should have done anything to keep my daughter, but I didn't. I'll never forgive myself for that."

"Do you give your ex money for your daughter?"

"When I can. But it's not enough. It's never enough."

Doyle looked at the Texan and saw the pain on his face. The big man took another swig of his drink, his eyes lowered.

"You want to see a picture?" he asked, his tone lightening a little.

Doyle nodded.

The American fumbled for his phone and scrolled through the photos, finally holding one in front of Doyle. It showed a young, blonde girl dressed in a T-shirt and jeans, seated on a little bicycle. She was waving happily at the camera and smiling to reveal braces on her teeth.

"That was on her tenth birthday," the Texan said. "When they're that age they think that you're some kind of hero. Then they get older and they realise you're not."

His smiled faded and he presented another picture for Doyle to look at. It was the same girl, but she looked older. The smile on her face wasn't as broad. There were spots on her chin and forehead. Her hair was shorter, and Doyle could see a silver stud in one nostril.

"They grow up so quick," the Texan mused. "That was taken the last time I saw her. God knows when I'll see her again."

"When are you due to go back to the States?"

The Texan shrugged. "Who the hell knows?"

"She'll still be there when you get home, Texas," Doyle told him.

"Maybe," the big man murmured. "I just think I'm losing her. I get scared that one day I'm going to meet her and she's not even going to know who I am. Or that she won't even care any more."

"You'll always be her father, no matter what happens. She won't forget that."

"I hope you're right."

The Texan drained what was left in his glass.

"I send her a message every night," he went on. "I send a text at the same time, every night, no matter where I am. I always put 'Love you very much.'" He managed a thin smile. "She never replies though."

"I'm sure she gets them. You know what kids are like, she's probably too busy talking to her friends to reply."

"Maybe. She probably just thinks 'oh, here's another message from that asshole. That guy who thinks he's my father. That guy who I never see. That guy who's never here.'"

"I'm sure she doesn't think that," Doyle told the big man, seeing the pain in his expression.

"Some guys are weekend dads; some are Saturday dads. Me, I'm a one hour a fucking week dad. I'm nothing to her now."

Doyle took a last gulp of his drink and set the glass down.

"Listen, I'm going to leave you to it, Texas," he said, quietly, getting to his feet.

"Have another drink," the American insisted.

Doyle shook his head.

"No," he said. "I've got to go. You take it easy."

The Texan nodded.

"Thanks for listening, man," the American murmured. "I don't get the chance to talk very often."

Doyle slapped the American on the shoulder and turned towards the exit, making his way across the room without looking back. The cool night air washed over him as he stepped out into the compound again and Doyle headed towards his own quarters, glancing up at the star-spattered sky once or twice. There were clouds gathering too and the breeze he felt was getting stronger.

Doyle fumbled in his pocket for his keys, preparing to let himself into his quarters. However, as he pushed the key into the lock, the door swung open slightly.

He stepped back slightly, one hand sliding inside his jacket, his fingers touching the butt of the 9mm automatic.

Had he forgotten to lock the door before he left that morning?

No. He never forgot. This lock had been expertly picked.

Doyle slipped the Beretta from its holster and moved silently inside, alert for the slightest sound or movement.

He raised the pistol in front of him, ready to confront whoever was inside his quarters.

He saw the figure immediately.

Doyle let out a gasp of surprise, the Beretta still held before him.

"What the fuck are you doing here?" he murmured.

TWENTY-NINE

The figure stood up as Doyle entered, a slight smile on his face.

The man was in his sixties but there was a vibrancy to his expression and something behind his eyes that belied his years.

He extended his right hand towards Doyle as if it was the most natural thing in the world to do and Doyle, almost in spite of himself, first holstered the automatic and then shook the offered appendage firmly, a smile spreading across his face.

"How did you get in?" Doyle wanted to know.

"I broke in," the newcomer told him.

"Breaking and entering at your age. You should be ashamed of yourself."

Jonathan Parker smiled.

"You didn't answer my question," Doyle went on. "What the fuck are you doing here?"

"I could ask you the same question, Doyle." Parker looked around him. "It's not exactly your usual environment is it?"

"I haven't got an environment any more," Doyle told him, slipping off his jacket and the Kevlar he wore.

"Times change," Parker murmured.

"Times, but not me," Doyle grunted.

"How long have you been here?" Parker wanted to know.

"Fourteen months in Iraq."

"It's not the most picturesque country in the world is it?"

"It's a shithole but there's work here."

Parker nodded gently.

"How did you find me?" Doyle wanted to know.

"Just because I'm not head of the Counter Terrorist Unit any more doesn't mean I haven't still got contacts. I asked around. Eventually I found you. I've been watching you for the last day or two."

Doyle grinned.

"Why?" he enquired.

"I was waiting for the right moment," Parker said, smiling. "You're not the kind of man to sneak up on, Doyle."

"I'm surprised anyone at the CTU remembered me."

"It was difficult finding someone. Most of your former colleagues were dead."

"Yeah, I can imagine."

"And things have changed so much," Parker went on. "Even in the last few years. People retire or move on or die. It's hard to keep up."

"I know the feeling."

Doyle placed a glass in front of his former superior and held the bottle of vodka before him for a moment before pouring a small measure.

Parker nodded, waiting for Doyle to fill his own glass.

"I thought you retired from the CTU," Doyle mused.

"I did. Six years ago."

"What happened? Did you get bored?"

"There's only so much daytime TV, gardening and reading any man can take," Parker chuckled.

"I can't imagine you watching daytime TV."

"I started writing a book. About the Counter Terrorist Unit, my days in it, that kind of thing."

"I hope you mentioned me."

"You were in the chapter entitled 'Mad Bastards.'"

Both men laughed.

"I was only doing my job," Doyle reminded him.

"And you were very good at that job, despite your faults," Parker mused.

"What kind of faults?"

"Your attitude. Your arrogance. You were the most ruthless agent we had. We didn't assign you, we unleashed you."

"I'm going to take that as a compliment," said Doyle, raising his glass in salute.

The two men sat in silence for a moment then Parker smiled

more broadly.

"You got results," he murmured. "That was all we were concerned about. We just couldn't show we were happy with the way you worked. There were guidelines we all had to follow."

"I was only interested in getting the job done."

"Your lack of restraint served us well on a number of occasions."

Doyle smiled.

"Now tell me what you want?" he said. "You didn't come out here to tell me how good at my job I used to be."

"Straight to the point as usual." Parker took a sip of his drink, coughed and then fixed his gaze on Doyle. "I don't quite know how to say this, Doyle, but we need you back. Something's come up and, to be honest, there doesn't seem to be anyone capable of dealing with it other than you."

"After all this time? I'm not exactly a young man, in case you hadn't noticed."

"I know how you feel."

"I doubt it," Doyle grunted. "Your memories of what I did are probably more use than anything I could do now. You know what they say, 'the memories of a man in his old age are the deeds of a man in his prime.'"

"Tennyson?"

"Pink Floyd."

Both men laughed again.

"There must be someone who can take care of the problem," Doyle muttered. "Someone already in the CTU."

"Apparently not. The current head of the CTU contacted me with details of the case and your name was mentioned."

"I'm listening."

THIRTY

Parker took a deep breath, as if what he were about to say was somehow painful.

"Do you remember a mission you were sent on some years ago, in Ireland? The man was called Callahan. David Callahan," he began. "He was a billionaire arms dealer. He'd been selling weapons to the IRA among others."

"I remember," Doyle told him. "He didn't want the Good Friday Agreement to go ahead because it would cost him so much in lost weapon sales. He paid some renegade IRA men to kill politicians and public figures who were trying to secure the peace."

"That's right. We sent you and another agent to Ireland to stop them and Callahan. The other agent was killed."

Doyle nodded, lowering his gaze.

"I remember," he said, softly.

"I believe you and she were quite close," Parker continued. "Her name was Georgina Willis and..."

"I remember her fucking name," Doyle snapped, interrupting. "Get to the point."

Parker regarded Doyle warily for a moment.

"That's what I was trying to do," he protested. "You and Willis were sent to kill Callahan and the IRA men. It was an operation conceived and executed under the strictest secrecy."

"They all were."

"But this operation was never officially cleared. You didn't know it, but you were working without authorisation."

"That was nearly thirty years ago. What the fuck does it matter?"

"Do you remember what happened to Callahan?" Parker wanted to know.

"He was killed. There was a firefight at his house in Ireland."

"You should know, you were involved in it."

"I saw Callahan die. I saw too many people die that day."
Doyle swallowed hard.

"What else did you see?"

"What do you mean?"

"In addition to being an arms dealer, Callahan was also obsessed with..." Parker sighed. "I'm not even sure how to say this. With certain aspects of the black arts. He had been collecting items from around the world concerned with things like that. He was trying to acquire the secret of immortality. He thought he could do that by possessing a stained-glass window that had been in the chapel of a man called Gilles de Rais, hundreds of years earlier."

"He was fucking insane," Doyle muttered.

"You're probably right."

"Look, I still don't get this. What's this got to do with me? And why now? So long after all this shit happened?"

"Callahan's house and the land it stood on was recently acquired for a building project," Parker said, taking a long breath. "When excavations in the grounds were being carried out, the coffins of Callahan and his wife were accidentally dug up." Parker took a sip of his drink. "But two other bodies were found at the site of the grave. Two men who'd been working on the construction. The body of David Callahan was missing."

"I still don't know what that's got to do with me," Doyle said, quietly.

"How much of that night do you remember? The night Callahan was killed?"

"Not too much."

"You were badly injured during the firefight. We weren't even sure you'd make it but, when you did, when you started to recover, you underwent extensive debriefing about what happened at Callahan's house."

Doyle nodded.

"You said you saw something that night inside his house," Parker went on. "Something you described as a creature. A thing that Callahan summoned."

"I remember."

"What was it?"

"I don't know. I didn't know then and I don't know now."

Parker let out a low sigh.

"Well, whatever you saw, we think it's linked to the disappearance of Callahan's body."

"Are you fucking serious?"

"Doyle, I'm fully aware of how ridiculous this whole situation sounds. Believe me, no one was more sceptical about it than I was. But other evidence has come to light. Evidence it's becoming increasingly difficult to ignore."

"You came here to ask for my help recovering the body of a man I killed nearly thirty years ago?" Doyle grunted, a slight smile on his face.

"I came to tell you that Callahan never died. He's walking around now. As free and as dangerous and as animated as the night you thought you killed him."

THIRTY-ONE

D oyle smiled.
    Then Parker watched as he took a sip of his drink.
    He waited for the other man to speak. It was, he
    told himself, like waiting for a bomb to go off.

"Alive?" Doyle said, quietly, his words softer than Parker had anticipated. "Callahan is alive?"

Parker nodded.

"I know it's difficult to believe," he said. "God knows I had enough trouble accepting it myself."

"It's impossible."

"Everything logical would seem to back that up."

"It's impossible," Doyle repeated, a little more forcefully.

"Normally I'd agree with you. But, having reread your notes from the debrief when it first happened and with what we know now..."

"It's impossible," Doyle snapped, angrily, interrupting and getting to his feet.

Parker watched him as he walked back and forth inside the small room, his face now ashen.

"I put four or five .44 calibre bullets into him myself," Doyle hissed. "I blew his fucking head off. He can't still be alive."

"I'm telling you what I was told."

"Who identified him?"

"Local police from descriptions and from their records."

"And when did all this happen?"

"Over a week ago."

"So, where's Callahan now?"

"No one knows. That's why we need you to find him."

"And you think I'm the only one who can do that? You think I'm the only one who can find this fucking zombie who just got up and started walking again after thirty years?"

"I'm offering you a chance, Doyle."

"A chance for what? To prove I'm completely off my fucking head. I was an agent, not a zombie hunter."

"Callahan isn't a zombie."

"Well, whatever you want to call him."

"This is as ridiculous to me as it is to you."

Doyle sucked in a deep breath, held it and then slowly let it out.

"How much do you remember about Callahan's death?" Parker wanted to know.

Doyle shrugged.

"I killed him," he said. "What more do you need to know?"

Doyle was gazing at the far wall of the room, as if seeing something there that was only visible to him. As if he were somehow gazing back into a different time and place.

"You saw him die?" Parker persisted.

"I shot him five times, that normally does the trick," Doyle grunted.

"And the creature?"

"What fucking creature?"

"The creature you mentioned. The one you spoke about in your debrief. You described it and..."

"I was out of it for months after that night," Doyle snapped. "I don't know what the fuck I said and didn't say."

Doyle poured himself another drink and held the bottle close to Parker's glass, but the older man shook his head.

"You said that you saw something standing over Callahan," Parker continued. "Something you also shot."

"There you go then. I killed Callahan and his pet monster." Doyle downed his drink in one.

"Doyle, I'm as curious about what happened as you are. But you were there. You saw what happened."

"That doesn't mean I know what the fuck I saw. The mind plays tricks you know. Yours must do because you think I can still do a job I was doing thirty fucking years ago."

"Don't you?"

"I don't know until I try. I still don't understand why you

128

need me."

"I told you why. But there will be considerations."

"Like what?"

"You'll have to undergo some physical and psychological tests. Just so we know you're fit for service again."

Doyle laughed but the sound was hollow and mirthless.

"I couldn't run for a fucking bus now without collapsing a lung," he said, smiling.

"We'll see."

"Look, Parker, don't dangle this in front of me and then just snatch it away."

"I don't know what you're talking about."

"I've got work here. Hopefully it'll go on for a few more months. I don't want to chuck it in and then find out you're full of shit."

"Come back to England with me. The flight's already booked. Go through the tests you need to go through. You won't be reinstated at your original level, but you'll be part of the CTU again."

"And then?"

Parker shrugged.

"You do as you're told," he said, smiling.

"By you?"

"By whoever happens to give the orders. Can you do that?"

Doyle nodded slowly.

"It's a second chance, Doyle," Parker told him. "Not many people get those."

"I still don't know what the fuck you want me to do. Hunt down a guy who I thought I killed thirty years ago? I'm not sure who they're going to lock up first, you or me."

"Is that a yes?"

"Yes, I'll do it. What have I got to lose?"

"Your life possibly."

"What else is new?"

The two men regarded each other silently for a moment then Doyle refilled his glass again.

"When do we leave?" he wanted to know, his gaze fixed on the older man.

"Tomorrow morning."

Parker finally noticed Doyle's unwavering stare on him.

"Is there something on your mind?" he asked.

"I get the feeling you're not telling me everything," Doyle exclaimed.

"I'm telling you as much as you need to know at the moment."

Again, Doyle nodded.

"Just like old times," the older man murmured.

"Not quite," Doyle smiled. "But, like the man said 'it ain't like it used to be, but it'll do.'"

He raised his glass in salute.

THIRTY-TWO
MAGDALEN COLLEGE; OXFORD;

T he only light in the room came from the screen of the laptop.

A dull bluish-white light that illuminated very little other than the face and hands of the man who sat before the device.

He was in his early twenties but the light from the laptop made his skin look pale, as if all the life had been sucked from him. If he was honest, that was how he felt.

It was almost three in the morning; he knew that because he had just glanced at the time in the bottom left hand corner of the screen. He'd removed his own watch an hour ago when he first sat down before the computer.

It had taken him that long to summon up the courage to write the e-mail that was still open before him. All he'd managed was the opening salutation and it seemed horribly trite and inappropriate. But then again, nothing seemed adequate to open this message he was about to send.

He rested his fingers on the keyboard and stared fixedly at the screen, as if that simple act would somehow spark much needed inspiration. It didn't.

He took a deep breath and wondered if he should refill his glass with whiskey. He'd already drunk half the bottle of Glenfiddich but his mind was still surprisingly sharp and for that he was grateful. What he was about to do demanded clear thinking. He didn't want the liquor to cloud his reasoning.

Again, he looked at the blank screen and it stared back like a challenge.

He deleted what he'd written, waited a moment and then typed the same words again;

DEAR MUM AND DAD

And again, his fingers seemed incapable of moving over the

letters. He froze once more, closing his eyes for a second.

The silence was almost overwhelming. The rooms were quiet at the best of times but, at this early hour, nothing seemed to be stirring. Other students were sleeping, he guessed.

He got up from his chair and walked across to the window, peering out into the darkness.

What was he hoping to see? Some signs of hope? Some reason to go on?

He remained there for two or three minutes then returned to the desk and, once more, rested his fingers on the keyboard.

Again, he gazed at the words he managed to type so far and, as he did, he found his fingers moving slowly across the keys;

I LOVE YOU BUT I CAN'T STAND THE PRESSURE.

I CANNOT GO ON LIKE THIS.

He looked at the fresh words he'd typed. At the flickering cursor. At his fingers, now shaking on the keys.

I LOVE YOU.

I'M SORRY.

LOVE, YOUR SON, CHARLES.

He sat back on his chair, looking at the cursor blinking above the 'send' button.

Once it was gone that was it. They wouldn't see it until the morning and by then it would be over. Done.

He felt cold. As if someone had wrapped his shoulders in a towel they'd just pulled from a freezer. The feeling passed slowly. He hit the 'send' button. The e-mail was gone now. 'Your message has been sent' the laptop proclaimed. He nodded almost imperceptibly. For long moments he sat back on his chair, his head tilted backwards, his mouth open slightly, and his eyes closed.

It was time now.

When he got to his feet his legs were shaking slightly but he walked briskly and determinedly across the room. He didn't want to hesitate. He didn't want to think. Not now. He'd done enough thinking prior to this moment. He had done nothing but consider his position and his alternatives and it had become more and more clear to him that he had no other choice but the one he'd made.

Above him, the noose he'd placed there earlier hung from the beam.

He got onto the chair he'd placed below, slipping the noose around his neck, standing there stiffly for a moment then he began to rock gently backwards and forwards, trying to cause the chair to overbalance. The wood creaked loudly beneath his weight as he continued his movements, rocking until it finally fell away from under him.

He dropped into empty air, the noose tightening around his neck.

It was silent in the room once more.

THIRTY-THREE
LONDON;

Rain had been falling for the last hour or so. Drizzle that hung over the city like a damp blanket. As the man walked, he occasionally glanced up at the sky, seeing the great dense banks of grey cloud scudding across the heavens as they dumped more of their moisture on those beneath.

It had been a long time since he'd walked these streets and it was taking longer than he'd expected to readjust. Not just to the almost constant crush of people but also to the buildings that rose on either side of the streets. They made him feel claustrophobic and, combined with the never-ending cacophony of noise from the traffic, he began to experience feelings of unease that were quite alien to him. He didn't enjoy these feelings and he wanted to be away from the throngs of people and the noise and the buildings.

But he knew that it would be like this. He'd suspected as much. He'd been away from it for so long that it was only natural he should experience a certain amount of anxiety and unease. Perhaps as time passed and he became accustomed again to the hustle and bustle of everyday life, he would begin to relax within this environment. He certainly hoped so.

As he waited to cross the street a small child looked up at him and smiled.

The man nodded by way of acknowledgment and the child's grin broadened.

The child was holding a small pink cuddly hippo and she brandished it in the man's direction as if it were some kind of trophy.

Again, he nodded, even managing a smile himself.

"Her name's Mary," the child told him.

The woman holding the child's hand looked at her and

shook her head, as if to silence the youngster's outpourings, wondering why her child was talking to this stranger. The man merely continued to smile.

He could see the trepidation in the woman's eyes. She tried not to look at him too much.

Almost subconsciously, he touched his cheek, just along the bone beneath his slightly sunken eyes. He was only too aware of the scars there. Just like he was aware of those on his lips and chin. They were healing slowly, and he was conscious of them.

He didn't need this woman's thinly disguised revulsion to remind him of his appearance.

The man glanced at her, taking in details of her appearance. The shoulder-length brown hair. The narrow face. Full lips. She was in her late twenties. Slim. Very slim in fact. That detail accentuated by the tight jeans she wore. He wondered if the child was hers or if she was a nanny or au pair. Did people still have those? He smiled to himself, aware that walking around a busy city wasn't the only thing that he would have to get used to once again.

The lights were about to change to red, holding up the traffic and enabling the man, the woman and the child to cross the road. The little girl looked up at him again.

There was no distaste in her eyes. Nothing to say she found his appearance abhorrent.

Not like the woman with her.

The woman with the slim hips who he now took a step closer to.

She was aware that he had moved nearer, and she edged a little further from him, prevented from going too far by the other people standing at the pedestrian crossing.

The man wondered what she'd look like naked.

He tried to imagine how she would look spread-eagled before him with her slender legs wide open.

He wanted to know how she tasted. Perhaps he'd lick his way up from her toes to her ankles, then higher up to her knees and her thighs before sampling the flavour he knew lay between her legs.

It had been a long time since he did that to a woman.

Too long.

He reached out a hand and ruffled the little girl's hair, smiling down at her.

For a second he wondered how she would taste too.

He'd never been with a child before. Never sampled that particular forbidden fruit. He wondered if this five-year-old girl would taste the same as the woman in her late twenties. Probably not, he reasoned. The little girl would be sweeter, he told himself.

He looked at the woman once more, trying to decide what he would do with her after he'd tasted her.

The man wasn't sure whether he'd fuck her before or after he killed her.

Or possibly even during.

He could strangle her while he was thrusting deep inside her. The death throes would make her vagina grip him even more tightly than normal. And then he would concentrate on the child.

The man smiled more broadly.

The lights changed, the traffic stopped, and the woman hurried herself and the little girl across the street, anxious to be out of the rain and even keener to be away from this man and his piercing looks.

The man walked on slowly, never letting the woman or child out of his sight.

PART TWO

"No more nightmares, I've seen them all,
From the day I was born, they've haunted
my every move."

Queensrÿche.

THIRTY-FOUR

As the BMW pulled away, Doyle looked down at the two black holdalls that the driver of the vehicle had placed on the pavement next to him.

Two holdalls.

That was it.

Not much to show for a life is it?

Doyle picked up the bags and walked towards the main entrance of the building. The drive from Heathrow had taken less than two hours and now Doyle glanced up briefly at the facade of the red brick edifice before him. Like many buildings in this part of Notting Hill, it had been converted recently from a town house into six self-contained apartments.

Doyle was to occupy number 6.

It was, he had been told by Parker, a perk of the job. As he had nowhere of his own to live at present, the Counter Terrorist Unit had allowed him to make use of the apartment in Clanricarde Gardens that they had used in the past as a safe house. It had not been occupied for more than eight months; he'd been informed.

As Doyle climbed the stairs towards number six, he glanced at the other doors, wondering who lived behind them. Men like himself. He doubted it.

The thick carpet on the steps muffled his footfalls, absorbed them. It was silent within the building as he climbed higher, finally standing outside the door of his latest dwelling. Doyle selected the key and let himself in. Just before he closed the door behind him, he glanced in the direction both of the stairs and of the other door leading off from the landing.

Just checking.

It was force of habit. A habit that had helped keep him alive over the years.

He was pleasantly surprised by what he found inside the

apartment.

A sitting room. A small kitchen. A bathroom and a bedroom. Tastefully decorated. Well kept.

Doyle dropped his bags in the bedroom then wandered back into the sitting room and flopped down on the sofa, gazing in the direction of the TV. He could see himself reflected in the blank screen.

He rubbed his eyes, aware of how tired he felt. The flight from Iraq had been smooth and uneventful, the BMW waiting at the airport to bring him here to the heart of London. The driver hadn't been particularly talkative, but Doyle could understand that. He hadn't exactly felt like a prolonged conversation himself as the black vehicle had sped him back into the heart of the city. He'd been surprised at how much had changed since he'd been away. It would take time getting used to it again, but Doyle was looking forward to reacquainting himself with the capital.

He sat silently for a moment then got to his feet and crossed to the large picture window behind the sofa. He looked out into the street, watching as a woman pushed a pram along the pavement on the other side. He saw a mail van drive past, watched as two other people sauntered unhurriedly along the thoroughfare.

This time yesterday, he thought, he had been looking at sand and dust and now he was back. Back in the city where he had spent most of his life, both growing up and working. And from tomorrow, he would be working again. Doing the only kind of work, he had ever been any good at. The thought was a welcome one, but it also brought its own doubts. Would he really be able to function within the CTU like he had before? It was a psychological as well as a physical challenge, but one that Doyle relished. This was him. This was what he did.

It's what you used to do. When you were younger.

He took a deep breath and held it, releasing it slowly. He wanted a cigarette. He wanted a drink. Doyle smiled to himself and watched as an elderly woman made her way down the street, a small dog on a lead beside her. It waddled along even more slowly than the woman, stopping occasionally as if it simply couldn't suck in enough breath to continue walking. Doyle saw the woman disappear into another building, finally stooping to pick the dog up.

He continued gazing out of the window for a moment longer then he moved into the kitchen and checked the fridge and the cupboards.

There was milk, bread and some cans of food left in there for him.

Very thoughtful.

But he'd still need some more supplies. He decided to make a list and get his shopping later in the day.

For now, there was something else he had to do first.

THIRTY-FIVE

T he sword was at least three feet long.

Double-edged and wickedly sharp.

The pommel had been skilfully shaped to resemble the head of a dragon, the grip wrapped with strips of leather that were now cracked and peeling due to age, but it still looked a formidable weapon.

It was at the top of a display that also featured several smaller swords, some clubs, a mace and several daggers.

To the left of that, there was a selection of longbows and crossbows with arrows and bolts displayed beneath them to illustrate the kind of projectile that each weapon fired. Woodcuts of battles from that era were also displayed, showing the role that each weapon played in the bloodbaths that passed for battles during the Hundred Years' War.

Axes, war hammers, spears, clubs, daggers and swords of all sizes and design filled the gallery, a testament to the barbarity of man. Interspersed between these tools of death were the uniforms of the time. Gleaming suits of armour, some reconstructed in full and standing like sentinels, others disassembled and displayed to show each part of the suit, vied with position with the uniforms of the more lowly foot soldiers. Belts, footwear and helmets were also on view, many of the helmets bearing dents and scratches testifying to the fact they had been worn in the heat of battle.

In the centre of the gallery there was a huge diorama, peopled by small and beautifully painted model soldiers, showing the positions of the armies at the Battle of Agincourt in 1415. Another similar model showed the same armies at Crécy. Both displays were enclosed by glass to prevent any curious fingers from touching the tiny figures or the perfectly constructed bases.

On all four walls of the gallery there were huge flags and

banners of all colours and designs. Some had belonged to lords and knights who had fought in the battles of the Hundred Years' War, others had been carried by more simple men, used as rallying points for soldiers caught in the maelstrom of combat all those years ago.

As Caroline Bradley walked slowly through the gallery she smiled, looking around at the vast horde of historical paraphernalia, happy that everything was finally in place. It seemed as if this particular display had taken longer than most to realise. She was sure that the members of the public who turned up in their droves to view these artefacts had no interest in how they finally arrived in the museum, but she felt a sense of accomplishment when she looked around the gallery.

The first day of the exhibition had been very successful. She had no idea how many people had pored over the weapons, the uniforms and the other elements on display but every time she had visited the gallery it had been busy. There were statistics that she could look at to show exactly how many people had visited but Caroline had no interest in them. She still felt the same enthusiasm and excitement about her subject as she had when she'd first begun studying it and that had not diminished over the years. To see so many others sharing that enthusiasm was wonderful.

She walked towards the end of the gallery, noticing that it was not, as she'd originally thought, empty.

There was a man staring at the book. He was bent forward slightly as if his eyes were taking in every detail of the words written on the yellowed pages.

The book was displayed in the glass case, lit from above by a single spotlight.

As Caroline approached, the man didn't seem to notice her despite the clacking of her heels on the polished floor. Only when she was next to him did he finally acknowledge her presence.

"We are about to close, sir," she said, quietly, almost

apologetic to interrupt his reverie.

The man nodded.

"I'm sorry," he said, softly, his eyes still fixed on the book. "I was fascinated by this."

"It is a wonderful piece," Caroline agreed.

"And invaluable," he murmured.

"You're obviously interested in this period?"

"It's this book that interests me the most. The book and its writer. And its owner."

"Do you know much about Gilles de Rais?"

"I made a study of him at one time. A very complex man."

"He certainly was."

The man brushed at his left cheek with slender fingers, never looking away from the book.

"How much do you know about the writer?" Caroline persisted.

"Gaston Lavelle?" the man mused; his gaze still fixed on the ancient volume before him. "Only what I've read."

"He's not as well-known as Gilles de Rais."

"That's probably not surprising when you consider his beliefs."

The man continued to look raptly at the book and Caroline was beginning to wish that he would just leave. It had been a long day and she wanted to close the gallery and get home, but she felt a little guilty about having to eject this man from the museum. He hadn't taken his gaze from the book the entire time they'd been speaking.

"We're open again tomorrow at nine," Caroline reminded him. "Come back and have another look."

"I will," he said, smiling, but still he didn't move.

Caroline glanced theatrically at her watch and was about to comment that it was getting late when the man took a step closer to the book.

"How long will the exhibition run?" he wanted to know.

"It's scheduled for six weeks," Caroline told him. "If it proves to be very popular, we can extend that."

The man nodded.

Again, Caroline looked at her watch.

"We really must close up, I'm afraid," she offered, hoping her latest entreaty might goad the man into leaving. "As I said, you should come back and have another look tomorrow if..."

"I'm leaving," the man interrupted, still not looking at her. "Thank you."

Caroline was delighted and stepped aside as the man turned, took one last look in the direction of the book and then began walking back up the gallery towards the exit.

She watched him for a moment longer, seeing that he turned and looked back as he reached the exit, as if leaving was some kind of effort for him.

He stood motionless in the doorway for a second longer then turned and wandered out.

THIRTY-SIX

As he stood at the main gate of Norwood Cemetery, Doyle had one thought.

What if he couldn't remember where the grave was?

He walked slowly along the paved driveway, headstones and crosses on both sides of him, stretching away to the furthest reaches of the necropolis.

But even as he walked, he found that he was doing so with purpose. He knew where he was going despite not having been near this place for almost six years. Doyle glanced down at the small bunch of red carnations he held, the cellophane that they were wrapped in rattling in the breeze that had sprung up.

He walked slowly among the headstones, as if his slower pace was something of a show of respect to those who lay around him. He glanced at names and dates on the monuments as he passed. Old people. Young people. Even children. Death, as he knew only too well, was not choosy and a number of the graves still bore fresh flowers, a sign that the burials had only happened recently. Some of the other graves were more overgrown and uncared for, and Doyle assumed that many of those were of older people who no longer had anyone to look after their final resting places.

He walked on, eyes moving over the vast array of grave markers, finally spotting the one he sought.

Black marble with gold lettering.

Doyle slowed his pace as he drew nearer, a slight smile touching his lips.

He read the inscription.

GEORGINA WILLIS

AT PEACE

"Hey, you," he said, softly. He kissed the tip of his index finger and pressed it lightly to the headstone, feeling the cold marble beneath his touch.

For long moments he stood there motionless, his gaze fixed on the black stone, the cool breeze whipping past him then, Doyle knelt down, laying the carnations on the grass beside the grave. He took a cloth from his jacket pocket and began wiping the headstone and its plinth. Apart from the grime on the stone the grave was relatively respectable, and Doyle realised he had the gardeners at the cemetery to thank for that. There was one about two hundred yards away from him now, carefully lopping the low branches from an oak tree.

Doyle watched the man for a moment then continued with his task, cleaning the stone and the plinth, pulling some weeds from among the gravel that topped the grave. There was a metal vase on the plinth, parts of it rusted, and Doyle wiped that down too, then he carefully placed the carnations inside.

When it was done, he stood up, hands clasped before him, gazing down at the grave, his eyes resting once more on the dates it displayed. She'd only been twenty-eight when she died.

What a waste.

Doyle let out a long, low breath. A sigh of disappointment as much as sorrow. He had seen death in so many guises during his working life. It had become almost passé for him. He feared it but he knew it was never far away. When Georgie had died it had been different. He'd never felt that kind of pain before. God alone knew he'd experienced enough physical pain but the agony that her passing caused to him had been as bad as any of the wounds he'd suffered.

He lit a cigarette and stood there beside her grave, drawing deeply, allowing the smoke to fill his lungs.

What would they have been doing now if she had lived? Would they have married? Would they have had children? Doyle smiled to himself. He'd never thought about that before. Sean Doyle the Dad. The thought made him shake his head. It might have been good but what was the point of dwelling on what might have been? That wasn't for him. No point thinking about things that would never happen. They were joys he would never experience. Like so much more.

He reached out again and gently brushed his fingers across the top of the headstone.

"I miss you," he murmured, then he walked slowly away from the grave, back towards the driveway that snaked through the cemetery.

As he made his way back, he noticed other people attending some of the other graves. One was a woman in her early twenties and Doyle wondered who she had lost.

He thought the same about an elderly man who was sitting on a bench beside the driveway gently stroking a dog that looked even older than him.

The older man nodded amiably at Doyle as he drew level with him, and Doyle returned the gesture.

"Rain on the way," the older man said, pointing at the sky.

"There always is," Doyle murmured.

"That's true," said the man, smiling more broadly.

The dog waddled across to Doyle who dropped to his haunches and stroked it gently. The animal looked up at him, appreciating the attention.

"My wife spoiled that dog," the older man mused.

Doyle kept on stroking the animal.

"She's been gone ten years now," the other man informed him. "It seems like yesterday."

"They say it gets easier with the passing of time, don't they?" Doyle mused.

The older man sucked in a weary breath.

"They lied," he said, flatly, getting to his feet.

He carefully attached a lead to the little red collar the dog was wearing then both of them waddled off in the opposite direction.

"Take care," the older man called without looking around.

"And you," Doyle offered.

He watched them go, disappearing beneath some low hanging trees, swallowed by the deep shadows there.

As Doyle turned, he felt the first droplets of rain begin to fall.

THIRTY-SEVEN

Mark Granger brought the car to a halt and switched off the engine. He sat motionless for a moment then took a deep breath, cleared his throat and hauled himself out of the vehicle. He set off across the car park towards the main entrance, his face set in firm lines, his eyes fixed on the double doors ahead of him as if he feared that to look away would somehow divert him from his mission.

As he reached the doors he paused, dug a hand inside his jacket and pulled out his phone. He thought about calling his wife. Perhaps he should tell her that he'd arrived safely. Just in case she was worrying and...

What was the point? What was he going to say?

"I've just got to the hospital to identify our dead son. Hopefully it won't be too traumatic. Don't worry about dinner, I'll get something on the way back."

Granger slid the phone back into his pocket, realising how pointless the entire episode would be. She wouldn't be worrying about him anyway; she was probably just sleeping as she had been for most of the time since they learned of their son's suicide. It was either episodes of sleeping or hysterical crying. Granger knew it was to be expected but it didn't make it any easier to deal with. If he was honest, he was happy to be out of the house for a few hours, even if it was to complete so devastating a task as the one he was now about to undertake.

He moved inside the hospital, narrowly avoiding an elderly man in a wheelchair who grunted something irritably at him as he manoeuvred himself through the main doors. Granger moved on, finally approaching the reception desk and catching the eye of a thin woman who looked as if she'd have been better off occupying one of the beds in the hospital's

149

oncology unit.

He explained who he was and that his son's body had been brought to the hospital the previous night. The woman directed him to the relevant area of the hospital and Granger nodded curtly and headed off in that direction, lost in his own thoughts. He took the stairs rather than the lift down to the lower levels where the post-mortem examination rooms were. Granger slowed his pace as he reached another reception desk in this lower level, struck by how quiet it was.

"I'm here to see my son," he said, softly.

The man behind the desk nodded and got to his feet, beckoning Granger into a small anteroom.

There was a door in the far wall of that room, and, beyond it, Granger knew what awaited him. He swallowed hard, attempting to maintain his composed facade. He could feel his heart thudding harder against his ribs now and, as he waited for a doctor to join him, he paced slowly up and down the room.

When the doctor finally joined him, he expressed his condolences and motioned for Granger to join him as he passed through the door of the anteroom into the chamber beyond.

Granger clenched his fists as he saw the gurney standing in the room, a white sheet covering its occupant.

The doctor crossed to the gurney and gently pulled the sheet back as Granger looked down, his teeth gritted.

"Yes, that's my son," he said, stiffly, gazing blankly at the body of his only child.

He looked at the pale skin, the vivid red welts around the neck where the rope had cut into the flesh and, almost despite himself, he reached out and gently touched the face of his son.

"We had to order a post-mortem," the doctor told him almost apologetically. "It's standard practice in the case of a suicide."

Granger nodded.

"Would he have...suffered?" Granger enquired; his gaze still fixed on the boy's face. "Would he have felt any pain?"

"Mr Granger, that's very hard to say."

"Would he?"

"It's difficult. I wouldn't want to hazard a guess. I..."

"Would he have felt any pain?" Granger roared, the explosion of sound reverberating inside the room. He glared at the doctor, his eyes bulging wide.

The doctor hesitated a moment and then shook his head.

"In my opinion, no," he said, softly. "His neck would have been broken as he fell. Death would have been more-or-less instantaneous."

Granger nodded. He himself pulled the sheet back over his son then he turned away, heading for the door of the room. The doctor trailed behind him.

"You can request a full copy of the pathologist's report from the coroner's office if you want to," he offered.

"That won't be necessary," Granger said, still walking.

"I'm very sorry," the doctor said.

"So am I," Granger murmured. He kept walking.

THIRTY-EIGHT

As she rode the lift to the ninth floor of the Dorchester Hotel, Carla Watson brushed specks of imaginary fluff from the sleeve of her jacket.

It was a nervous reaction; she was sure of that. She always felt the same way before any new job. There was always that element of uncertainty and doubt. What would the guy look like? Would he be young or old? Would he be nervous or confident? Was he going to have some weird kink that would surprise even her? So many imponderables, Carla thought, affording herself a smile. She also tried to remind herself that the advantage was with her. She was the one in control.

Wasn't she?

She checked some of the details on her phone as the lift slowly rose. The agency didn't tell her much. Just names (which were usually false) and location. Sometimes they'd tell her the clients age but that was about it. And, if she was honest, in the grand scheme of things details didn't matter. It was another job, pure and simple. More money. Whatever the client wanted was up to them. They were paying for it after all. What did she care if some of them just wanted to watch her play with herself? It made no difference if others just wanted to piss on her or her to piss on them (that cost a little extra). Two had paid double to get her involved with their own partners (one male, one female). One had even filmed her and himself with his camera phone.

She didn't care. The money was all that mattered.

Some went too far. She had scars to prove that much. But, as long as they paid, she could grit her teeth and she had done on a number of occasions when the pain had become almost intolerable. But she was twenty-eight now, a five-year veteran of this game. She lived a good life. Some might say luxurious. Her customers were all rich men with more money than sense and she was happy to relieve them of that wealth.

It had helped pay for the best for her son and that, ultimately, was all that mattered.

She didn't see as much of him as she would have liked but that would change as he got older. He was only two now and she was happy to leave him with friends when she was working. The money she could earn compensated for the lack of contact with him.

The lift bumped to a halt and Carla stepped out into the corridor beyond, her high heels sinking into the thick carpet there.

She glanced at her reflection in one of the many mirrors on the walls as she passed, satisfied that she looked good enough for whoever was waiting for her. The Versace suit she was wearing had cost almost two thousand pounds and she brushed the sleeve again as she approached the door of the room she sought.

She knocked on the door, remembering to switch her phone to silent as she waited.

The man who opened the door was tall and powerfully built with close-cropped brown hair and pale eyes. The charcoal grey suit he was wearing looked expensive and she could smell his strong aftershave when she moved closer.

"Hi," she beamed, plastering on her best professional smile.

He ran appraising eyes over Carla and beckoned her inside, closing the door behind her.

"This way," he said, again beckoning to her, leading her towards another closed door beyond which he finally opened onto a huge bedroom.

"My name is Carla," she told him.

The man didn't answer.

"Did the agency tell you about prices?" she asked.

"Not for me," the man told her, shaking his head, and Carla caught the hint of an accent when he spoke. Eastern European she thought.

"You wait in here," he told her, jabbing a finger towards the centre of the room.

Carla was about to speak again when the man moved out of the room again, pulling the door closed behind him.

She glanced around at the sumptuous surroundings. The huge bed with the velvet curtains around it, the light spilling through the windows that looked out over Hyde Park. Furniture and fittings that probably cost more than her own flat. And that smell. Always that smell that only luxury hotels carried, as if it had been impregnated in the walls and floors. A combination of fresh laundry and newly cut flowers mingled with expensive soaps. It was intoxicating.

Carla perched on the edge of a nearby chair and waited, her vigil was finally broken when the door of the bathroom opened, and another man emerged.

He looked at her blankly then sat down opposite her.

"Hi, I'm Carla," she said, looking at him more closely.

He nodded.

"The other man showed me in," she announced. "If he's going to be involved too then it'll be more."

"He won't be involved. It's just me," the newcomer told her.

"It might be best if we sorted out the business first."

"I've left your money in the bathroom. You can change in there too if you need to."

"I had hoped you'd like what I'm wearing now," Carla said, smiling enthusiastically.

The man ran appraising eyes over her, his gaze finally settling on her face.

"You're very pretty," he said, quietly.

"Thank you."

"You remind me of my wife. We stayed in this hotel many times when she was alive."

"When did she die?"

"Probably before you were born," he told her.

"I'm sorry."

"I'm sure you are. But you didn't come here to offer me sympathy, did you? That's not what I'm paying you for."

"What are you paying me for?" Carla asked, rising to her feet and moving towards him. "What do you want me to do?"

The man smiled.

"Just stand there," he instructed. "I want to look at you."

Carla did as she was told and, once more, he looked carefully at her, his gaze travelling up from her feet as if he were memorising every single inch of her.

"Yes, you look a lot like my wife," the man told her again. "She was only about your age when she died. We used to come to this hotel a lot. She loved it here. She liked nice things. We used to travel the world and wherever we went we stayed in the best hotels, but this was always her favourite."

"What was her name?"

"Laura."

"That's a nice name."

He nodded, his gaze never leaving Carla.

"You can call me Laura if you want to," she said, cheerfully.

The man's expression darkened slightly.

"No," he breathed, shaking his head. "I don't want to do that. My wife wasn't a whore like you."

Carla caught the vehemence in his tone, and she felt the first ripple of fear brush her skin like cold fingers.

THIRTY-NINE

Sean Doyle sucked in a deep breath and held it.
    He was experiencing something he hadn't felt for years and he didn't like it.

He was nervous.

Seated in the large office in the building on the banks of the Thames, looking out over the greyish-brown waters of the river, he sipped at the vending machine tea he'd collected on his way in, his hand quivering slightly. He thought how ridiculous this situation was. He had faced death so often in his working life and barely thought about it but now, alone in this office, he was on tenterhooks. Probably, he told himself, because this was out of his control. There was little he could do to alter the outcome of what was approaching. If he'd been in a firefight somewhere then that was different. He knew how to handle that.

Doyle hated being out of control, he always had. He liked things on his terms. On his ground. This office wasn't his ground.

The building he had entered twenty minutes earlier was a recently built addition to the many already lining the banks of the Thames, one of several operations bases that the Counter Terrorist Unit had occupied upon leaving a more central home in Mayfair a few years earlier.

Doyle got to his feet and crossed to the window that ran the full length of the office wall. He stood there silently, trying to concentrate on the slowly moving river, trying to focus on anything other than the fact his heart was beating so fast. When he heard footsteps and muffled voices outside the door he hurried back to the chair where he'd been sitting.

Two men walked in. One was Jonathan Parker; the other Doyle didn't recognise.

He was a thickset man in his late thirties, dressed in a navy-blue suit that looked as if it had been carefully tailored for him. His hair was cropped short and the glasses he wore seemed to make his eyes look larger. When he looked at Doyle it was like being scrutinised by some kind of well-dressed owl.

Parker moved to a seat next to Doyle, the other man took up a position behind the large desk opposite.

"Sorry to have kept you waiting," the other man said, laying out some papers on his desk. He then glanced at his computer screen, tapping on his keyboard a couple of times and inspecting the information that appeared before him. "Things to take care of," he murmured.

"I know what you mean," Doyle offered.

"No, I don't think you do," the other man said, dismissively. He sat back in his seat and looked appraisingly at Doyle. "Things have changed so radically since you were a part of this department, Mr Doyle," he went on. "You have no idea how we function these days."

Doyle met his gaze, shifting slightly in his seat.

"I'm a quick learner," he said, flatly.

"Have you heard the saying 'you can't teach an old dog new tricks', I hope that doesn't apply in your case, Mr Doyle. I don't like wasting time and this venture smacks of that."

Doyle opened his mouth to say something, but he was interrupted before he could speak.

"Doyle, this is Mark Granger," Jonathan Parker interjected. "He'll be your superior."

"Wonderful," Doyle murmured.

"If you're accepted back into this unit," Granger added quickly. "Something that I must confess I was against."

"Why?" Doyle wanted to know.

"So many reasons," Granger said. "Your age. Your lack of experience..."

"Lack of experience?" Doyle snapped. "I was in the CTU for fourteen years."

"Things were different then," Granger told him.

"Terrorists don't change," Doyle offered.

"But their methods do, Mr Doyle," the bespectacled man went on. "We're more concerned with cyber terrorists now. With men that have been radicalised, like IS operatives. This is different to the world you knew. It isn't like running up against the IRA."

"At least you knew where you were with them," Doyle said almost wistfully.

"That's as maybe but this is a very different world," snapped Granger.

"Doyle is aware of that," Parker interjected. "He knows he wasn't brought back to participate in front-line operations."

"Most certainly not," Granger added.

"Then what the fuck am I here for?" Doyle wanted to know, his eyes never leaving the man opposite him.

"I thought that had been explained to you," Granger said. "There's been some activity in a case that you were involved with a long time ago."

"Well why not just get one of your clued up, younger men to deal with it?" Doyle snapped. "Men who know about cyber terrorism and radicalisation."

Granger sucked in a breath.

"That wasn't meant as a slight against you, Doyle," he said, wearily. "I was merely highlighting how much this department has changed since you were a part of it."

"When I went after the IRA, eventually someone had to pull a trigger," Doyle said. "I'm assuming that's still the case. Or do you kill them with kindness now?"

Granger wasn't slow to pick up the sarcasm in the older man's voice.

"We try to avoid slaughtering our opponents wherever possible, Doyle" he muttered. "We've found that it's best to use interrogation to find out what we need from them. It's a little difficult questioning a corpse." He afforded himself a smile.

"So, how many *IS* guys have you caught and interrogated?" Doyle asked. "That's irrelevant. Our methods have been very successful."

"If you say so."

There was a long silence and then Doyle spoke again.

"So, tell me, what is it you want from me?" he asked.

FORTY

"It concerns a man called David Callahan, the man you were sent to neutralise more than twenty years ago but failed to do so."

"I killed him," Doyle hissed.

"Apparently not," Granger chided. "He has been identified in several places since the initial sightings in Ireland." Granger pushed several black and white photos across the desk towards Doyle who glanced at them.

"That is Callahan isn't it?" Granger asked, looking first at Parker and then at Doyle.

"Where did these pictures come from?" Doyle asked, scanning the images, his gaze fixed on one particular man.

"From CCTV at Heathrow airport," Granger told him.

"Why didn't someone arrest him when he landed?" enquired Doyle.

"Because technically he hasn't broken any laws," Granger mused. "Not since his...reappearance anyway."

Doyle looked more closely at the images before him.

"That is Callahan isn't it?" Granger persisted.

Doyle eyed the photos more closely, focusing on the figure Granger indicated.

It's him. You can see it's him.

"Yes," Doyle murmured, finally.

"So, he's not dead after all?" Granger said.

"He was the last time I saw him," Doyle snapped.

"Well he's clearly not, is he? You were obviously mistaken all those years ago, Doyle."

"I killed him. I know I did."

"Then who is that man in the photo, passing through customs?"

Doyle looked at the pictures again. "I know what I saw," he said. "I know what I did. I'm not fucking senile you know."

"I wasn't implying that you were. Merely that you were involved in a firefight at Callahan's residence and that some men don't function as well under fire. You might not have remembered all the details."

"My memory is fine," Doyle assured him.

"I read the report you gave when you were debriefed," Granger went on.

"Good for you," Doyle muttered.

"Who else died that night?"

"What's that got to do with anything?"

"You were working with another operative that night. You and she had been working together for some time."

"So what?"

"You were close to her. Closer than you should have been probably."

"I assume there is a fucking point to this?"

"She was killed that night. That would have clouded your thoughts, affected your ability to think straight."

"So, you think because my partner was killed, I can't remember shooting Callahan?"

Granger regarded him silently for a moment then continued.

"Callahan was spotted two weeks ago," he said. "There've been no sightings since. He may have attempted to alter his appearance either with some kind of disguise or with plastic surgery."

"But he's in London? He can't have just disappeared."

Granger nodded and pushed several more photographs across the desk towards Doyle.

"Who's the other guy?" Doyle wanted to know, inspecting the images. They showed Callahan once again but this time he was accompanied by a thickset man with a bull neck wearing a pair of dark glasses.

"Vasili Gorchev. He was a member of the Berkut, the Golden Eagles, the Ukrainian secret police but he was thrown out for various reasons. He set himself up in business shortly afterwards."

161

"Russian Mafia?" Doyle mused.

"He's been involved with human trafficking, smuggling and drugs for the last six years," Granger went on. "He moved out of the Ukraine when a rival gang tried to kill him. He moved to France and then to this country."

"How did Callahan get hooked up with him?" Doyle wanted to know.

"We have no idea, but Callahan is using two of Gorchev's men as personal bodyguards. It's a safe bet they're involved in some kind of venture. We just don't know what as yet."

"Can't you use your hi-tech equipment to find out?" Doyle said, a slight smile on his face.

Granger glared at him and held his gaze, watching as Doyle sat back in his seat.

"Callahan's been...away for nearly thirty years," he began. "How the fuck does he just appear again and pick up the threads of his life as if nothing ever happened? Where's he getting his money from for a start?"

"Callahan had money stashed everywhere when he disappeared," Parker interjected. "Accounts in Jersey, Bermuda and the Cayman Islands. Property he owned around the world. Artwork he'd purchased over the years. It wouldn't have been hard for him to get his hands on that."

"Wasn't it seized after his death?" Doyle wanted to know.

"Those photographs would seem to indicate that he's not dead," Granger said, dismissively.

Doyle shot the other man an angry glance.

"It must be costing him a pretty penny if he's using Gorchev's men as hired hands," Granger added.

"I'll find him," Doyle said, flatly, getting to his feet.

"Not yet, you won't," Granger informed him. "There are certain protocols that must be followed. Matters that must be resolved before you can begin to act under the auspices of the Counter Terrorist Unit again."

"Like what?" Doyle hissed.

"Certain physical and psychological tests that you have to

undergo."

Doyle regarded the other man evenly.

"And if you fail to reach a specified level," Granger went on. "Then this is all over. You will also have to vacate the apartment we provided. I am not having men under my command performing at anything less than maximum level."

"I'll do your tests," Doyle told him, defiantly.

Granger nodded and sat forward slightly; his attention caught by something on his monitor.

"When you've completed them, we'll speak again and reappraise the situation," he said, quietly. "You can go."

Doyle hesitated a moment longer then turned and headed for the door, Parker in pursuit.

As the two men stepped out into the corridor beyond Granger's office, Doyle spun around and looked at the older man.

"He's a bigger cunt than you used to be," he snapped, pointing towards the office door.

"Praise from Caesar," murmured Parker, raising one eyebrow.

"Did you know about this when you came to get me?"

"I had an idea."

Doyle shook his head.

"When do I start these tests?" he wanted to know.

"Now would seem like a good enough time," Parker said, smiling.

FORTY-ONE

Carla Watson raised the fine crystal to her lips and took a sip of the mineral water.

When she lowered the glass, her hand was shaking slightly.

"How many men do you think you've slept with?"

The words seemed to come out of thin air and Carla jumped slightly as she heard them, looking once again at the man who sat opposite her.

"Does it matter?" she asked.

"I was just curious," the man went on. "I've been curious all my life about different things. About sex. About death."

Carla swallowed hard and reached again for her glass.

"The two are very closely linked you know," the man continued. "The French even call an orgasm 'la petite mort.' That means 'little death'."

"I'm more interested in sex than death," Carla said, trying to force a smile.

"Obviously. Or you wouldn't be in this line of work, would you? Do you enjoy it?"

"I like the money."

"At least you're honest."

She looked at him again, noticing that he'd barely moved since he'd entered the room. His gaze had remained fixed on her too, constantly appraising.

"But you must like what you do," he said at last, his voice low.

"It depends on the client," Carla confessed. "If they're young and attractive it makes things easier."

"I can imagine," he said, smiling.

"Have you done this before?" Carla asked, falteringly.

"Hired a whore? Of course I have. Life's all about experiences and sometimes you have to pay for those experiences. Sometimes only a whore will do the kind of things I want to do."

Carla took a breath, her heart beating a little faster.

"What do you want to do?" she asked.

"Don't get me wrong. I never did it when my wife was alive. If I wanted to sleep with another woman, my wife didn't mind. She'd help me get the woman and then she'd join in if she wanted to. Sometimes she'd just watch."

"I can get another girl if you like."

"For a price."

"Everything's got a price."

"Even life."

He smiled again.

"How much do you think your life is worth?" he asked, the smile slowly fading.

"I've never thought about it," Carla said, trying to smile.

"You know what price you put on your cunt or your mouth or your arse. Why not your life?"

"How can anyone ever know that?"

"What would you give someone not to kill you? How much are you worth as a person?"

"I haven't got much money so I couldn't pay much."

"So, you really are a cheap whore?"

Again, he smiled and there was something unsettling about it, Carla thought. There was a kind of disjointed distance in the gesture. No shred of warmth.

"Tell me more about your wife," she said, clearing her throat.

"We had the same interests," he told her. "The same beliefs. The same goals. We did everything together. She supported me. Encouraged me."

"She sounds lovely."

"She was. She didn't deserve to die."

"I felt like that when my brother died. He..."

"I don't care about your fucking brother," he snapped, cutting her off. "Get on the bed. I've talked enough."

Carla got to her feet, her body trembling slightly.

The man also began to undress, dragging his tie free, hurriedly undoing his shirt buttons as he watched Carla slowly pull off her own clothes. As he dragged his shirt open, she saw several blemishes on his torso. Scars that stood out darkly against the paleness of his skin. She turned away, continuing to remove her own garments.

When she was down to her bra and knickers, he stopped her, moving close to her, turning her around so he was standing behind her. She could feel his erection pressing against her buttocks.

She could also smell something she hadn't detected before. A thick, cloying stench that she didn't recognise. It clogged in her nostrils and the back of her throat as she desperately tried to identify it.

He reached around, both hands closing over her small breasts.

Carla sighed and pushed back against him, aware that he was now slipping out of his underwear. When he rubbed against her again, she could feel the warmth of his stiffness against her flesh. He pulled at her bra and tugged it free, dropping it on the floor before her, then he clamped his hands onto her breasts again, the thin fingers digging into the soft flesh.

The smell she had noticed was now almost intolerable.

He bent his head and she felt the hard edge of his teeth brushing against her neck and shoulders.

He bit her hard on the point of her shoulder and she yelped, surprised by the pain, wondering if he'd drawn blood with the action. She felt him press more urgently against her, moisture from the tip of his penis smearing her backside.

"Take these off," he demanded, still clutching her breast with one hand but pulling at the flimsy material of her knickers with the other.

Carla did as she was told, wincing again as he bit her other shoulder hard. This time he did draw blood and she tried to turn to face him, wanting him to stop this.

"Don't turn around," he breathed and, as he did, he slid his

166

free hand between her legs, fingers probing at her, searching for the warmth there, wanting to feel moisture between her thighs.

He bit her again on the right shoulder and the pain was intense, trickles of blood seeping down her chest, mingling with his saliva.

She heard him grunting close to her left ear, smelled his warm breath.

And again, that foul stench was so strong in her nostrils.

When he bit her left ear lobe, hard enough to make it bleed, she began to whimper softly, wanting him to stop. Again, she tried to turn to face him but, again, he held her firmly, the hand that had been touching her vagina now moving deeper, fingers probing at her anus.

He pushed two fingers into that tightest orifice, and she shuddered as he almost lifted her off the ground. As he did, he bit her back just below the nape of her neck. The pain was excruciating and as he forced a third finger roughly into her anus, it was all Carla could do not to weep.

Somehow, he forced a fourth digit into her anus and she thought for a second that the tender flesh there was going to split as he rammed his fingers in as far as the third knuckle. She wanted to tell him to stop, to do anything but this. This pain was as bad as the bites.

Then he spoke again.

"I'm going to hurt you. I'm going to hurt you more than you've ever been hurt before."

Carla Watson began to cry softly.

David Callahan smiled.

FORTY-TWO

Doyle had no idea how long he'd been on the treadmill but it felt like a long time.

Sweat was soaking through the T-shirt he wore and every now and then he used the back of his hand to wipe more of the clear liquid from his eyes.

He could feel it coursing down his face as he pounded the moving conveyor belt beneath his feet.

More than once he glanced at the figure standing nearby, as if seeking permission to stop, but the man didn't even acknowledge him. His only concern was with the small bank of machines that were connected to Doyle by a series of wires and tubes. He was a tall, lean man in his forties whose hair was impossibly dark for his age, his eyes fixed on an iPad he held when he wasn't checking readings being produced by Doyle's exertions.

Occasionally the man would mutter what were obviously meant to be words of encouragement, but they were wasted on Doyle. He was wondering how much dye the other man had to use on his hair to keep it looking so lustrous. Anything other than acknowledge the pain that was now lancing through his calves and thighs as cramp began to set in.

His legs were beginning to feel heavy, but he drove himself on, his gaze fixed on the wall before him.

The room he was in was in the basement of the building. White-walled and filled with various types of gym equipment ranging from wall bars to exercise bikes, climbing ropes to punch bags. Doyle wondered which of the pieces he was next to encounter. He felt like a heretic in a torture chamber, wondering what kind of punishment was in store for him when he finished on this one.

He continued to run, trying to control his breathing, fearing that his heart might just burst if he continued for much longer.

When the man close by finally told him to stop, Doyle almost overbalanced, stepping off the treadmill with a mixture of relief and gratitude. He grabbed for a nearby bottle of water and drank half of it in several large gulps.

"Got anything stronger?" he gasped.

The man with the dark hair merely smiled and checked something on his iPad.

"Do you drink?" he finally asked.

"Sometimes," Doyle confessed.

"How many units?"

"I don't usually count."

"Smoke?"

"Sometimes."

"How many a day?"

"Depends on the day."

The man nodded slowly. "It's bad for you," he observed.

"So is too much exercise," Doyle grunted. He drained what was left in the bottle and wiped his mouth with the back of his hand. "How am I doing? Is there much more of this shit?"

"By that I gather you mean are there other physical disciplines to be surmounted?"

"That's what I said," Doyle grinned.

"An hour on the bike," the man told him. "Some time on the bars and a little more of the treadmill. Then I'll start collating your results so far."

Doyle wandered across to the nearest of the bikes and clambered onto it, sitting patiently while the dark-haired man attached new electrodes to his body, pressing them into place on his already slippery skin.

"And when you're finished with me?" Doyle asked, sucking in a deep breath.

"There are a number of physical and psychological tests to come," the man told him.

"Like what?"

"They'll want to check your competence with weapons."

"No problem."

"And your familiarity with the software we use."

Doyle looked perplexed.

"Computers?" he murmured.

"Most of our business is conducted online now," the man told him. "You've got to know what you're doing. Then there's the psych evaluation of course."

"Great," Doyle sighed, wearily.

"All operatives go through a refresher course every six months. They like to keep us sharp."

Doyle nodded and started pedalling.

"I'll tell you when to stop," the dark-haired man told him. "Do you want some more water?"

Doyle nodded.

"There's something else," he said.

The dark-haired man looked quizzical.

"I could murder a cigarette," Doyle told him.

FORTY-THREE

The blood that dripped onto the white marble spread out like flower petals.

There were droplets of it on the gleaming floor too.

Leading from the shower and then to the bidet like some kind of crimson trail.

Carla Watson was shaking as she used tissues to mop up the worst of the blood flow from her anus and vagina.

She could barely stand, her legs shaking uncontrollably beneath her as she sponged and cleansed those two most sensitive areas. The towel that she'd used to staunch the initial flow of red fluid was balled up and useless on the side of the bath. Little more than a crimson rag now.

Carla whimpered softly to herself as she attended to the damage, sometimes glancing at herself in the mirror as she continued with her labours. When she did catch sight of her pale reflection, she could see the numerous red and angry marks on her shoulders, neck, ears and face that had been caused by the bites she'd sustained. The one on her bottom lip had torn that soft flesh so badly that a small portion of it was hanging free, tendril-like.

Waves of nausea kept sweeping over her and Carla sat down again, feeling as if her entire body was on fire with the pain.

When she turned, she could see more red wheals on her back and buttocks. One particularly savage bite had gouged deeply into the flesh of her backside causing fresh blood loss. She had wondered at the time if he'd actually ripped the flesh and muscle away but as she studied the injury more closely, she realised that was not the case. A flap of skin and muscle now opened and closed over the wound like a lid when she touched it.

There were more bruises and contusions on her thighs and calves.

Even on her feet.

He had made her sit on the edge of the bed while he had kissed and licked his way down her calves, finally licking her toes and biting hard on them as he masturbated in front of her.

Carla shuddered both at that recollection and also at the memory of the other things he'd done. She had passed out on two occasions when the pain had become too intense but, each time, he had revived her with powerful slaps to the face. When this didn't work the second time, he tugged her hair so violently that he ripped out several clumps of it.

She could see the bloodied portions of scalp when she looked, a single drop of blood oozing down her face from her hairline.

As she stood up, she felt her legs buckle once again and Carla shot out a hand, supporting herself on the marble of the nearest washbasin. The feeling passed and she moved as quickly as she could across the bathroom, scooping up the bloodied tissues and toilet paper she'd used, shoving them all into the small waste bin.

She dressed as quickly and carefully as she could, wanting now only to be away from this place and the man she had left sitting in the bedroom beyond. He had been drinking a large brandy when she finally staggered away from him to begin her ablutions. She had her money. There was no more reason for her to stay. All she wanted was to leave.

She stood motionless for a moment, steadying herself, one hand on the doorknob of the bathroom.

When she padded out into the bedroom, the man turned and glanced briefly at her. He was sitting at a writing desk close to one of the wide picture windows that overlooked Hyde Park, his attention on a laptop before him. He watched as she slipped her shoes back on, wincing because of a wound on the arch of her right foot.

The man in the charcoal grey suit who had originally let her into the suite was standing at the main door, hands clasped behind his back and head bowed as if he were observing a minute's silence. He heard Carla gasp in pain as she finally got her shoes on then that pain intensified as she walked across the room, her lower body feeling as if it had been dipped in fire.

The older man returned his attention to the laptop, his back to her as she headed gratefully for the exit.

The man in the charcoal suit walked as far as the elevator with her then he turned without speaking and strode back up the corridor towards the suite. Carla watched him go as she waited for the elevator to arrive. As she pressed the call button again her hand was shaking and the pain seemed to envelope her, coursing through her like some malignant drug in her bloodstream. The worst of the spasms passed, and Carla closed her eyes momentarily.

When the elevator bumped to a halt, a couple in their thirties stepped out, the woman casting her a cursory but disgusted glance as she passed. The two of them disappeared along the corridor, their voices gradually dying away and Carla walked into the elevator, riding it to the ground floor. As she walked across the reception area, she was aware of the curious and horrified looks she was drawing but she kept walking, her eyes straight ahead as if the main doors of the hotel signalled some kind of final escape.

She paused outside and the uniformed doorman took a step towards her but, before he could offer help of any kind, Carla hobbled off.

As she walked, she left a trail of crimson droplets behind her on the path. They soaked into the concrete like forgotten memories.

FORTY-FOUR

Doyle slammed the magazine into the butt of the Beretta 92FS, pulled back the slide and fired off the fifteen rounds in rapid succession. Each successive discharge echoed inside the room, the weapon bucking violently in his grip as the bullets erupted from the barrel. Doyle pumped the trigger until the slide flew backwards, signalling that the weapon was empty.

As he ejected the clip he glanced through the pall of greyish, white smoke towards the target he'd fired at.

As it came sliding back towards him, he removed his ear protectors and glanced at the man who was standing to his right in the shooting range.

When the backboard finally arrived, the man moved in front of Doyle, inspecting the holes in the target that the 9mm slugs had made.

"That's not bad is it?" Doyle said, also seeing the pattern of shots he'd inflicted on the silhouette of a man.

"He wouldn't be coming back for more," the other man mused, without looking at him, entering the results on the iPad he was carrying.

Doyle moved along to the next cubicle and saw a sub-machine gun laying on the counter. He picked it up, hefting it before him, testing the weight.

"Heckler & Koch G36," the other man told him. "Seven hundred and fifty rounds a minute. Dual sighting system. An optical scope and a red dot reflex sight. Ever used one?"

Doyle shook his head, lifted the weapon to his shoulder and sighted it.

As he squeezed the trigger a stream of spent cartridge cases spewed from the weapon, arcing into the air before hitting the ground like metallic confetti. Doyle adjusted his position slightly, slipped the weapon to single shot and pumped another ten shots into the target. Each impact slammed the stock of the weapon back against his shoulder, but the recoil was negligible, and Doyle nodded approvingly as he laid the sub-machine gun back down, smoke rising from the barrel.

"There is a version equipped with a rocket launcher, but we won't try that one out in here," the other man said, smiling thinly. "We also use the MP5K, but I think you're familiar with that."

Doyle nodded.

"It's highly unlikely that you'll need to use any of these weapons to be honest," the man went on. "I was told to monitor your capabilities with them. Just in case."

"So, what the hell will I be using?" Doyle grunted.

"One of the weapons you've just been using will be issued to you dependent on the circumstances."

"And who decides what's appropriate?"

"We have a number of tactical and situational analysts who decide on that."

"So, when you have to use guns you call a committee meeting?"

"There's a bit more to it than that, Doyle."

Doyle picked up the G36 again and pressed it to his shoulder, squinting down the sight. He watched as the red laser dot settled on the head of the target.

"Everyone keeps telling me how things have changed since I was last here," he murmured.

"Our operational procedures are probably completely different to those you were used to," the man confirmed. "It's called progress." He smiled.

Doyle rested his finger gently on the trigger.

He fired one shot that tore into the target in the very centre of the head of the silhouette.

"So, everybody keeps telling me," he said, quietly. "It worked all right then."

"That was a different kind of war, Doyle."

"Tell me about it."

He fired one more shot into the target, the blast echoing inside the range.

"You knew where you stood then," he murmured. "Your enemy had a face. You knew who to go after."

"Enemies now have faces too. We just go after them in a different way."

"Satellites. Drones. Dirty bombs. The Internet," Doyle muttered as if repeating a litany. He pulled the weapon into his shoulder and steadied himself before sending another round speeding down the range.

"What's your background?" he enquired, still peering down the sight. "How did you come to join the CTU?"

"I was approached when I was at university."

"Approached? Things really have changed. Who approached you? It wasn't Granger was it?"

Doyle fired off another round.

"No," the other man said, smiling. "Mr Granger's too high up the food chain to do that. How do you know him?"

"I don't know him. I only met him earlier today."

Doyle flicked the weapon to automatic and fired a short burst.

"Mr Granger's a very able man," said the other man. "Well respected."

"By who?" Doyle grunted, dismissively.

He put the G36 back on the counter.

"Have you got any other toys for me to play with?" he said, smiling.

"No," the man told him. "But there's someone who wants to talk to you. Come on."

FORTY-FIVE

The room was more like a cell.

Twelve feet square, completely empty apart from a wooden table and two chairs. Walls the colour of a dying man's flesh.

As Doyle sat down, he glanced around him and noticed that one wall sported a huge mirror, which he guessed was two-way in the manner of a police interview room.

What the fuck is this?

He made himself as comfortable as he could in one seat and glanced in the direction first of the two-way mirror and then of the only door into the room.

Who's watching? Hope you enjoy the show.

The door opened at last and a rotund man in his late thirties walked in. He was carrying a manila file and an iPad.

They all had fucking iPads.

The man seated himself opposite Doyle and extended his right-hand which Doyle shook firmly.

"My name is John Porter," the man announced, settling himself. "I've got to ask you some questions."

Doyle nodded.

"Do you know why?" Porter asked.

"So, you can find out if I'm crazy?" Doyle said, raising his eyebrows.

"Not exactly," Porter told him, smiling. "How have the other tests been going?"

"Not bad. I don't know when they'll give me the results."

"Did you do things like this when you first joined the Counter Terrorist Unit?"

"There were endurance tests, physical stuff. Like the sickeners the army do now."

Porter nodded.

"It was easier then," Doyle continued.

"You were a young man then," Porter reminded him.

"Don't rub it in."

"You must have killed men during the course of your work. How did you feel about that?"

"I didn't feel anything. It was part of the job. And it was usually them or me. People didn't sit around analysing their feelings like they do now, Doc. We just got on with it."

"Do you think it affected you?"

"I've never thought about it."

"You lost someone close to you during an operation. Do you ever think about that?"

Doyle eyed the other man suspiciously for a moment then merely shrugged.

"Sometimes," he admitted.

"Do you blame yourself for what happened to her?"

"No. She knew what she was doing. She knew the risks. We all did."

"Do you still think about her?"

Doyle fixed Porter in a withering gaze.

"Is this fucking relevant?" he wanted to know. "I thought you were testing my mental state not my emotional condition."

"I was just asking. Did you ever receive any kind of counselling?"

"For what?"

"It's common practice now for operatives to undergo grief counselling if they've been involved in violent incidents."

Doyle shook his head.

"It's possible you could have suffered some kind of PTSD when you were operational."

"How would I know?"

"From some of the symptoms you would have suffered. Anxiety and depression, emotional numbness, nightmares, hallucinations linked to a specific violent event."

Doyle shook his head almost imperceptibly.

"Hallucinations," he murmured. "Seeing things, you mean?"

"Have you experienced anything like that?"

Tell him about the nightmares involving Georgie. Tell him about seeing her.

Again, Doyle shook his head.

Porter looked at him for a moment then referred to his notes. He glanced at his watch and cleared his throat.

"There are certain questions I have to ask you, Doyle," he said. "In addition to those I feel are necessary."

"Like what?"

"Well, it seems a little archaic now, but we still like to do a spell of word association."

Doyle smiled.

"Go on then," he murmured.

Porter nodded.

"Death," he began.

"Life."

"Fear."

"Pain."

"Work."

"Ambition."

With each response that Doyle gave, Porter tapped something on his iPad and also made a mark on the piece of paper before him.

"You've done this before haven't you?" Doyle said, a slight smile on his face.

"Once or twice," Porter told him. He looked at Doyle for a moment then shrugged his shoulders.

"Sorry," Doyle murmured. "Carry on."

"Love," said Porter.

"Hate," Doyle replied.

"Sex."

"Blood."

Porter paused momentarily.

"Was that the first word that came into your mind?" he wanted to know. "You're not supposed to think about your responses. Just say what comes into your mind."

"I did," Doyle told him. "Maybe I'm sicker than you thought I was."

"Dreams," Porter went on.

"Nightmares," Doyle murmured.

"Gun."

"Kill."

"Authority."

"Pointless."

"Boss."

"Cunt."

Porter found it hard to suppress a smile. He glanced at his watch again.

"Do I win a goldfish if I get all these right?" Doyle enquired.

Porter returned to his list.

An hour later he was still throwing words at Doyle.

FORTY-SIX

David Callahan took a sip of his coffee and sat back in the chair, gazing out across Sloane Square.

He was the only one sitting at one of the pavement tables outside Cafe Colbert and that was fine by him. He didn't want any company just yet.

That would be arriving in due course.

For now, he was content to merely gaze at the traffic that drove by or to watch the pedestrians who moved past the restaurant. One of the dark-uniformed waiters hovered around him for a moment, checking if he needed anything, but Callahan merely shook his head and continued with his contemplations.

A pigeon landed nearby and moved slowly towards him. Only when it was almost beneath the table did Callahan notice that it had one foot missing. The bird was leaning slightly to one side and Callahan found himself gazing at it. It hobbled around close to the table and Callahan picked some crumbs from the tablecloth and dropped them onto the pavement. The bird gobbled them up gratefully.

Callahan was about to give it some more when it suddenly flew off, wings flapping as it soared into the sky.

The seat beside Callahan was suddenly occupied by a heavily built man in jeans and a black jacket. He sat down with a grunt.

"You're late," Callahan told him.

"I have other business to see to," the man told him. "Not just you."

"For what I'm paying you, I should be top of your list of priorities," Callahan snapped.

The other man looked around, glanced at Callahan's coffee cup and then jabbed a finger towards it.

"Do you want a drink?" Callahan wanted to know.

"Just coffee. I don't drink when I'm working," the man told

him. His accent was strong and although Callahan had known it was East European, he hadn't been able to pinpoint exactly where this man came from the first time they'd met. Only as time had gone on had he learned that he originated from a village close to Kiev in the Ukraine. He was about ten years younger than Callahan, but his face looked thin, his deep-set eyes rheumy.

Callahan ordered him a coffee when the waiter returned and the two men sat in silence for a moment, both looking out across Sloane Square.

Vasili Gorchev sipped at the dark fluid, slurping loudly as he drank.

Callahan shot him a disapproving glance.

"I don't want any mistakes," he said, flatly. "Your men better know what they're doing."

"They know," Gorchev assured him. "You should stop worrying."

"I'm not worried. I just don't want any of your gorillas messing this up. There's too much at stake."

"Gorillas?"

"Your men. The idiots who work for you."

"They work for you too when you pay me. When do I get the rest of the money?"

"When I have what I want."

"Why is it so important to you?"

"That's not your business. You're being paid to get me what I want. Why I want it is nothing to do with you."

"I know men like you," Gorchev said. "I know them all my life. Men who think they can buy anything with money."

Callahan sipped at his coffee.

"Money can buy anything," he said, quietly. "Why do you think everyone wants it? It bought you a way out of that shithole village you used to live in didn't it? If it wasn't for money, you'd still be working in a factory in Kiev for ten roubles a week or smashing in heads in the Berkut."

"I got out because I was a businessman."

182

Callahan grunted.

"You got out because they threw you out," he said, smiling. "You terrorised girls into prostituting themselves and then took ninety per cent of what they made."

"And you? You sold weapons. How does that make you better?"

"I'm not criticising your methods, merely pointing them out. That was why I chose to work with you. Your track record."

"What are you talking about?"

"Someone told me you were a nasty cunt," Callahan grinned. "That was what I needed. In fact, someone said that you weren't just a nasty cunt, you were the nasty cunt. The nasty cunt that other nasty cunts looked at and said 'fuck, he is a nasty cunt.'"

Gorchev grinned.

Callahan took another sip of his coffee.

"I didn't get you here today to talk about the relative merits of how we both made our money," he said, dismissively. "I got you here to make sure that everything was in place."

Gorchev's phone rang and he moved to answer it but Callahan merely shook his head.

"Leave that," he said. "Whatever it is can wait. I got you here to discuss our arrangements, not to watch you stumbling through your own pathetic business deals."

Gorchev let the phone ring.

"You will have what you want in two days' time," he said. "Just as we agreed. And then I want the rest of my money."

"You'll get it once I've inspected the merchandise and I'm satisfied with it."

"Don't try to fuck with me, Callahan," Gorchev said, leaning closer to him. "I want my money."

"When the job's done."

"What if I want it now?"

"Then you're out of luck," Callahan hissed, turning to look at the other man.

Gorchev leaned forward slightly and, as he did, his jacket

opened to reveal the butt of a Sig-Sauer P320. The 9mm pistol was pushed into a shoulder holster, clearly visible as the Russian moved.

Callahan smiled.

"Are you trying to frighten me?" he said, softly, picking up the fork that was lying on the table.

Gorchev glanced towards the utensil, his right hand moving to the inside of his jacket.

"Put your hand down," Callahan hissed, raising the fork. "Did you hear me, you low bred scum? Put that hand down or I'll cut it off."

Gorchev grinned but the expression faded rapidly as he saw Callahan pushing the tines of the fork against the palm of his own left hand.

"Don't think you can frighten me," Callahan told him, pushing harder on the fork until the tips of the prongs punctured flesh. The metal bored deeper, blood welling from the small wounds. Callahan kept pushing, driving it deeper into his palm, ignoring the blood that dripped onto the gleaming white tablecloth. He kept his eyes fixed on Gorchev's, never looking away, even when the tines had been pushed to their root. There were small marks on the back of Callahan's hand now where the tips of the tines were actually stretching the flesh there, ready to tear through if he pushed a little harder.

"If you try to cross me, I'll do the same to your eyes," he said, softly.

Gorchev said nothing but sat mesmerised, staring at Callahan's skewered hand.

"Do you understand?" Callahan insisted.

"You're fucking crazy," the Russian said under his breath.

Callahan ripped the fork free and hastily wrapped his hand in one of the napkins on the table.

Blood began to soak through the material immediately.

Gorchev swallowed hard, his heart beating faster now.

"We meet in two days' time as arranged," Callahan said,

getting to his feet. He dug in his pocket and pulled out a twenty-pound note that he tossed onto the table in front of Gorchev. "Pay the bill with that. And leave the change."

Gorchev nodded and watched him walk away, disappearing into the crowd.

FORTY-SEVEN

S ean Doyle could feel himself dozing off as the train rumbled out of West Norwood station.

He looked down at his hands and saw they were stained with dirt from where he'd pulled weeds from Georgie's grave. He'd washed them quickly beneath the cold cascade of water from a tap near the grave but there was still dirt beneath his fingernails and Doyle set about cleaning them as best he could.

The exertions of the day, both physical and mental, had taken more of a toll on him than he'd thought, and he could barely keep his eyes open as the train made its way slowly back towards Central London.

Doyle cupped his hand over his eyes, peering out at the darkening sky and the landscape that was now falling into heavy shadows as evening approached.

He sat back on his seat, relieved that there was no one else in the carriage. It would be another half hour or more before he got to his destination, he might well have a nap.

A nap? You're getting old.

"Fuck off," Doyle murmured, glancing at his reflection in the window, as if that had been responsible for the words inside his head.

The results of his tests with the Counter Terrorist Unit would be known in the next couple of days, he'd been told. He was reasonably pleased with his performance in most aspects of the tasks they'd presented him with but, as he knew too well, his opinion counted for nothing. It was what Granger and his cronies thought that ultimately counted and if they binned him off that was the end of it.

Doyle sucked in a deep breath and tried to force the thoughts from his mind. He closed his eyes again and tried to relax. He was asleep almost immediately, dozing off with his head against the window as the train rumbled on.

When he opened his eyes again the carriage was still empty.

And yet, Doyle was certain he could feel someone close to him. He glanced around and saw that his instincts were correct.

There was a young woman sitting close to the end of the carriage, her face turned away from him. He assumed she'd got on at one of the stations the train had passed through while he'd been dozing.

He couldn't see her face properly because she was sitting with her hand raised and her head lowered, as if she were deep in thought. Doyle could only see the blonde hair that hung as far as her shoulders.

And then she stood up.

"Oh Jesus," Doyle murmured.

He watched as she walked slowly down the aisle of the carriage towards him.

"Not now," Doyle said, his voice barely more than a whisper.

She sat down opposite him and smiled.

"Why?" he asked. "Why can't you just leave me alone?"

"You don't want me to leave you alone," she said, softly. "We belong together. We always did."

Doyle ran his gaze slowly over her.

"You're not real," Doyle whispered.

"I am to you," she told him.

"Why are you trying to hurt me?"

"I would never hurt you. I love you."

"Then leave me alone."

"You're going after him again, aren't you?"

"Who?"

"Callahan. The man who caused my death."

Doyle swallowed hard.

"How do you know that?" he murmured, the colour draining from his face.

She smiled at him.

"He'll kill you," she said, softly.

"Please, Georgie. Leave me alone," Doyle insisted. "I don't need some fucking ghost following me around."

She laughed and it was the musical sound he thought he'd forgotten. It sent a shiver through him.

"I'm not a ghost," she said.

"Then what the fuck are you? I just put flowers on your grave."

She reached out a hand to touch his face, but Doyle pulled back, as if fearing that to feel that touch would somehow infect him.

"Get the fuck away from me, Georgie," he hissed, gazing deeply into her eyes.

"Callahan will kill you," she breathed.

"You've already told me that."

"Then listen to me." Again, she moved nearer and once more he recoiled. "You know how dangerous he is."

"I killed him once. I'll do it again."

"You can't kill him. No one can."

"Bullshit."

She stood up, looking down at him, her face set in hard lines. She put out a hand and Doyle saw something dark drip from her fingertip. It landed on the left knee of his jeans, soaking into the material.

"Now why don't you fuck off back to wherever it is you came from?" Doyle hissed.

There was a tunnel approaching and the lights inside the carriage flickered slightly as the train swept through it. For fleeting seconds, the carriage was filled with impenetrable darkness. When the lights flashed back on, Doyle was alone once more.

He rubbed his face with both hands, looking anxiously around to ensure that he actually was alone again. He was relieved to see that there were only two or three stops left now until the train reached its destination. Outside, darkness had descended. Night was draped across the country like a cloak.

Doyle looked down, something catching his eye. Something

on his left knee.

There was a dark stain there. It took him a second to realise that it was one single, solitary drop of blood.

FORTY-EIGHT

As Mark Granger hauled himself out of his car he let out a long sigh. The tightness he'd been feeling across his shoulders and neck had intensified throughout the day and was now threatening to turn into a full-blown headache.

Granger locked the car and stood motionless in his short driveway for a moment, looking towards his house. Despite the fact that it was late, and the evening sky was growing darker by the second, there were no lights on inside the building and Granger shook his head slightly as he fumbled for his keys and let himself in.

He slapped on lights inside the hallway, hung up his jacket and headed through into the sitting room where he dumped his briefcase in a chair.

He put on lights in that room too, also switching on the television before walking through into the kitchen.

No lights in there either. Granger switched some on and let out another deep, almost painful sigh. He continued through the house, switching on lights as he went, anxious to banish the gloom within the house. By the time he reached the bottom of the stairs that led up to the first floor most of the ground floor was now bathed in light. Granger set off slowly up the steps.

He was halfway up when he heard the crying.

Slowing his pace slightly he sighed once more, the sound growing louder as he drew nearer the landing. He hesitated at the top of the steps, the sobbing intensifying. Almost reluctantly he walked towards the nearest bedroom, the place where he knew the sound was coming from.

He found his wife inside the room, seated on the bed, smoothing the duvet with one hand, as if that simple act would eventually remove every single crease from the material.

Like the other rooms in the house, this one too was in darkness and Granger reached for the switch, the lights bursting into life and flooding the room with brightness.

Theresa Granger didn't turn or look up when the lights came on, she merely continued with her robotic movements, her hand gliding across the duvet over and over again.

Granger looked around the room briefly, although he already knew its contents by heart. The posters, the books, the albums and the video games that decorated the walls. The TV, the games console, the brand-new electric guitar and its amp. All these things seemed so pointless now he thought.

"I'm going to make something to eat," he said, softly, still standing in the doorway.

Theresa merely shook her head.

"Have you already had something?" Granger persisted.

"I'm not hungry," she told him without looking around.

"You've got to eat. You know the doctor said it was important. Come down and I'll get us something."

"I don't want to."

"Well at least come downstairs."

"I want to stay here. In his room. I want to be close to him."

Granger let out a low breath and lowered his head slightly.

"How long have you been in here?" he wanted to know.

"Does it matter?" she countered. "You weren't here. I've got no one else to talk to. Not any more. Not now he's gone."

"I was at work, you know that. If I could have got away earlier, I would have."

"You always say that."

Again, Granger sighed wearily.

"Are you coming downstairs?" he wanted to know. "Let me cook you something. It'll make you feel better if you eat. The doctor said you were supposed to eat before you took your tablets."

"I don't want food," she snarled. "And I don't want those bloody tablets."

"They're to help you."

"I just want my son back." The words were shouted and when she turned to look at him there was something in her eyes that he'd come to recognise only too well during the last few days. A look that combined desperation with fury. And something more that looked like hatred. "He's dead because of you."

"Theresa, we've been over this before," Granger protested.

"He killed himself because of the pressure you put on him," Theresa went on, jabbing an accusatory finger at her husband. "You wanted him to go to that university. You pushed him into it. You knew he couldn't cope with the pressure."

Granger turned away from her, prepared to walk back onto the landing but she followed him, slapping him angrily between the shoulder blades with one shaking hand.

He didn't turn but simply kept walking, wishing there was something he could say to her. Wishing there was something he could do to ease the pain she was feeling.

"He hung himself because of you," she roared again, her words dissolving into another fit of sobs.

Granger turned slowly, watching as she dropped to her knees, finally curling into a foetal position on the landing, her sobs growing louder. He hesitated a second then moved towards her, trying to help her up but she lashed out, striking his hand and pushing it away. He looked down at her for a moment then simply walked away, heading back down the stairs.

As he reached the bottom, he too began to cry.

FORTY-NINE

The gallery seemed busier than usual this particular day, Caroline Bradley thought. She glanced around at the faces as she walked slowly from one end of the hall to the other, gratified that so many had come to view the exhibits. It was always pleasing, from an organisers point of view, when the public responded in such large numbers to any new exhibit. It was almost as if her own passions and interests were vindicated by the popularity of something she had helped to stage.

She paused beside one of the huge dioramas, watching the look of delight on the faces of two children who were gazing raptly at the many miniature soldiers on view there. She saw one take out his phone and take some pictures of the tiny Agincourt reconstruction. Further down the gallery, several people were gathered around one of the full-sized suits of armour, also posing for selfies or pictures with the battered metal outfit.

A security guard in his black trousers, dark blue sweater and black peaked hat nodded amiably at her as she passed him.

There was another of his colleagues further down on her left, the man gazing at passers-by, occasionally asking people not to put their hands on some of the glass cases that held particularly delicate or rare artefacts.

Another guard was standing talking to a couple of American tourists, posing a little awkwardly for a picture with them, and Caroline smiled to herself as she saw the pained expression on the guard's face. The Americans seemed happy enough with his contribution to their holiday and they moved on, towards the glass framed book written by Gaston Lavelle that sat beneath its single spotlight just ahead of some more suits of armour. It looked as if the empty figures were guarding the tome, Caroline thought, adding their own presence to the safeguarding of this most valuable volume. Several people' were standing around the exhibit, one of them reading the short description on a plaque attached to the display case. Another was peering at the open book, looking at the Latin and Romance words that had been scrawled there by Lavelle more than six hundred years earlier. Caroline wondered if the man looking so raptly at those words was able to read them. A part of her hoped he couldn't.

She walked on, towards another part of the gallery where members of the public were actually allowed to touch and handle some of the weapons on display. This part of the exhibit was one of the most popular and, she'd found over the years, that anything tactile and physically involving like this was always a huge hit with visitors. She stood and watched a man in his twenties trying to lift a double-handed sword, struggling to raise it as high as his chest, while several others looked on and laughed or smiled at his predicament.

Close to him, a woman was trying to hold a large shield that was almost as big as she was. She lifted the implement before her, raising it with the battered leather grips on the back, held it for a moment then lowered it again, contenting herself with inspecting the embossed gilt lions and fleur-de-lis on the front instead.

A man was inspecting some arrows that had been shot from a longbow, while another visitor was attempting to pull the bowstring back but finding it difficult due to the fact that the bow had been newly strung to the same pressure that the weapon would have exhibited during the period of its use. English longbowmen at that time were not unusually well developed in the upper body for no reason, Caroline thought, watching the man struggle and fail to pull back the string. The woman with him was laughing at his efforts and Caroline too afforded herself a smile.

She was still smiling when she saw two men striding purposefully down the middle of the gallery, one of them pushing other visitors aside angrily if they blocked his way.

This particular man, a tall, dark-haired individual in a black bomber jacket, was looking around as he walked as if he were seeking someone or something. His companion, also tall but wearing only a dark sweatshirt over his jeans, looked even more determined, his face set in hard lines as he stalked through the gallery.

Caroline watched them for a moment, feeling unaccountably concerned by the appearance of these two newcomers.

One terrifying thought popped into her mind and stayed there as if it was illuminated with neon.

Terrorists.

The word reverberated inside her head like an alarm bell.

Because of a series of recent terror attacks in London and other parts of the country, all the staff at the British Museum had been given instruction on how to try and spot terrorists and how to behave if an attack of any kind was mounted within the museum or close to it.

Two uniformed men from New Scotland Yard had visited them only three weeks earlier to deliver a talk on this very subject and, while assuring everyone that an attack was about as likely as getting struck by lightning (there had been a rumble of nervous laughter at that point), they had stressed the need for vigilance. Mentioning that all public places were likely targets. Someone had asked how it was possible to spot a potential terrorist and had been told that they would probably look anxious or nervous, possibly even frightened. They might be perspiring. They would be moving quickly, not wanting to lose the momentum that they had been imbued with.

And now, as Caroline watched the man in the bomber jacket and his companion in the sweatshirt, she felt the hair on the back of her neck rising. It was an irrational and unfounded fear that enveloped her, but she couldn't shake it.

Her heart was hammering against her ribs and she was breathing quickly and unevenly as she watched the two men.

She glanced in the direction of a security guard who was making his way down to the far end of the gallery but he didn't see her and merely continued to amble through the hordes of people, unaware of the two men blundering their way through the centre of the hall.

Caroline prepared to try and attract his attention, not wanting to alarm any of the visitors but now finding it increasingly difficult to control her growing anxiety.

The two men had now reached the area where the weapons were displayed and, as Caroline watched, the one in the bomber jacket suddenly snatched up an axe, hefting it in both hands before him.

When he ran at the nearest display case and brought the axe crashing down upon it, Caroline screamed.

FIFTY

The sound mingled with the explosion of shattering glass as the case disintegrated under the savage impact. Pieces of glass exploded outwards and 'Bomber Jacket' struck again, sending the display case crashing to the ground. Its contents spilled out, pieces of parchment falling across the floor.

His companion in the sweatshirt pushed one of the suits of armour which also toppled over and crashed to the ground, the helmet coming loose.

And now Bomber Jacket was moving towards the case at the end of the gallery, the case holding the book.

He used the axe to smash the glass there once again but this time he grabbed at the volume and pulled it free of the case, handing it to his companion who took it from him just as one of the security guards rushed at him.

Bomber Jacket didn't hesitate. He swung the axe with all his strength, catching the guard across the forearm. The impact was powerful enough to shatter the radius and the guard dropped to his knees, trying to support the broken limb, blood pouring through the rent in his sweater. A woman nearby screamed.

Another security man ran at the two intruders, but Bomber Jacket saw him coming and spun around, again swinging the axe furiously. The guard ducked beneath the first swing, slamming into the man, both of them crashing into more terrified onlookers. But the guard recovered first and he managed to pin Bomber Jacket beneath him, slamming his arms down against the hard floor, causing him to drop the axe.

The man in the sweatshirt snatched up the fearsome weapon and brought it down on the security guards back, driving the sharp blade into his lumbar region, severing the spine and pulverising vertebrae. The guard let out a scream of agony and Bomber Jacket shoved him to one side, scrambling to his feet in an effort to escape.

Bystanders were now running from the gallery, desperate to escape this carnage.

Caroline joined them as alarms began to sound loudly inside the room. As she reached the nearest exit she turned, wanting to know where the intruders were and she saw them rushing towards the other side of the gallery, the one in the sweatshirt still clutching the antique book.

The two men hurtled back through the museum, barging into anyone who didn't get out of their way.

More security men were now following them as they reached the main doors of the building, the dark-uniformed men desperate to catch up with the two thieves.

Alarms were ringing loudly, the sound mingling with the shouts of visitors. Screams occasionally punctuated the cacophony of sound.

The two men burst out into the open air, one of them stumbling, almost falling down the stone steps that opened out onto the paved area before the building.

The sound of sirens was now cutting through the air too, but the men seemed untroubled by the possibility of approaching emergency services.

As the two men ran out into Great Russell Street, a black Audi screeched across to them, rear doors springing open as if triggered by their very presence. They both scrambled in and the car sped away, the driver turning the wheel, narrowly avoiding two pedestrians.

And now the first of the police cars roared into view, speeding after the Audi.

From the back seat, one of the men in the Audi saw the pursuing vehicle and shouted something to the driver who eased down on the accelerator, coaxing more speed from the black car. He hit a waste bin as he turned a corner, rubbish flying in all directions, but he drove on, all too aware of the police car behind him closing the distance on him.

More shouting from inside the Audi and then one of the rear windows was lowered. One of the men eased himself out slightly and the driver of the police car realised what was happening.

He didn't recognise the weapon that was poking out in his direction from the back of the black car, but he felt his heart increase its pace.

There were two short bursts of fire from the HK33.

The first tore across the bonnet of the police car, blasting holes in the metal and causing the driver to swerve madly. The second burst took out most of the windscreen, glass exploding inwards, causing the driver to shield his face with one hand as he wrestled to keep the police car steady.

Next to him, in the passenger seat, the other policeman also ducked down as far as he could as more automatic fire struck the road and the police car.

Shots ricocheted off the tarmac, one blasted away a headlight and several others tore into the vehicle itself, one of them slamming into the arm of the police driver. The bullet tore through his shoulder, erupting from his back and punching through the seat itself.

Shocked by the impact and the pain, the driver lost control and the police car mounted the pavement, slamming into a wall.

Up ahead, the Audi roared off, swallowed by traffic.

The man in the passenger seat stumbled from the stricken police car, his face cut in several places by the flying glass that had been blasted back into the vehicle. He dropped to his knees, unconsciousness rushing in on him.

The last thing he saw was another police car hurtling up the street after the fleeing Audi, sirens blaring.

And then, darkness.

FIFTY-ONE

Sean Doyle sat back in his seat, turning the photographs over in his hand as if they were playing cards.

"The robbery happened four hours ago," Mark Granger told him.

"So, they walked in without any weapons?" Doyle muttered, his attention still on the photographs.

"They didn't need them," Granger said. "And security had no idea they were dangerous until the attack happened."

"All they took was that old book?" Doyle murmured. "What's that got to do with the CTU?"

"This was from the museum's CCTV," Granger said, turning the monitor on his desk around slightly so that Doyle could see the images on it. "The two men have been identified as Ivan Petriv and Oleg Shushkevich. Both known associates of Vasili Gorchev."

"The guy who's working for Callahan?"

"If they're involved with Gorchev it's a fair bet that Callahan is implicated somewhere. That's why this concerns us, Doyle."

Doyle looked again at the CCTV footage.

"So, all we have to do is find him?" he murmured.

"And figure out what the hell he might want with that book."

"What's so special about it? What makes you think Callahan might want it?"

"We have no idea at the moment. Someone needs to speak to the British Museum, if only to eliminate Callahan from the investigation."

Doyle got to his feet.

"Sit down, Doyle," Granger said. "I didn't call you in here today to assign you to this job."

"What did you call me for then?"

"The results of your tests."

Doyle sat down; his gaze fixed on Granger.

"It isn't good news, Doyle," the younger man went on. "I'm reluctant to put a man back into the field who is manifestly unfit for the tasks demanded by this department."

"So that's it? Goodbye?"

"Ordinarily I'd say yes."

"Were the results that bad?"

"Quite the contrary. Your aptitude with weapons remains. Your fitness levels for a man of your age are adequate. I'm more worried about the psychological aspects."

Doyle held the other man's gaze.

"You're a dinosaur, Doyle," Granger went on. "Your methods worked before but now I think you're likely to create more problems for this department than you solve. However, I will consider allowing you to become a field operative again as long as your efforts are confined to the Callahan case."

"That's fine by me."

"But there are conditions."

"Like what?"

"I want to be kept informed of every development, no matter how trivial. I want to know what is happening with this investigation."

Doyle nodded.

"Any deviation from the usual protocol and you're out," Granger persisted. "I won't tolerate the kind of loose cannon that you used to be." He took a deep breath. "In order to ensure this doesn't happen I'm only prepared to allow you back into the field on one condition."

"What's that?"

"You work with a partner. Someone who knows the way we work now. Someone I trust."

"I work alone."

"You used to work alone, Doyle. That was then, this is now. Times have changed."

"So, everyone keeps telling me."

"There is another reason you can be of help to the department on this matter."

Doyle raised his eyebrows.

"You're expendable," Granger told him, flatly.

"That hasn't changed then," Doyle muttered.

"You will work with your partner," Granger said. "Listen to him, Doyle. Learn from him. And do as you're told."

Doyle gritted his teeth, the knot of muscles at the side of his jaw pulsing angrily.

"Now, I think it's time you two met," Grange mused, leaning forward. He hit a button on the console on his desk and spoke. "Send in Vale."

A moment later the door opened.

Granger motioned to the newcomer.

"Sean Doyle," he said. "Meet your new partner. This is Gideon Vale."

FIFTY-TWO

Doyle took a step towards the newcomer and extended his hand.

The man who stood before him was over six feet tall, dressed in a dark blue suit. He had a thin, pale face and his light brown hair was thinly cropped at the sides, but the rest looked as if it had been piled up on top of his skull.

He shook Doyle's hand but there was no strength in the grip.

"Gideon?" Doyle said. "Your parents had a sense of humour."

"So did the guy who sold you that outfit," Vale countered, glancing at Doyle.

Doyle squeezed his hand a little harder, noticing something sparkling when Vale turned his head.

"Nice earrings," Doyle said. "Does your handbag match them?"

Vale pulled his hand away and ran an appraising gaze up and down the older man.

"Sit down, both of you," Granger said, jabbing a finger towards the two seats before his desk and both men did as instructed.

Doyle glanced at the newcomer and saw that he was heavily tattooed on his arms, edges of the designs visible when he moved, and his cuffs rode up. There were also traces of ink around his neck.

"Vale is a strategic analyst," Granger began. "He's one of our most experienced operatives. Your skills should complement each other."

"When do we start?" Doyle asked.

"Now," Granger said. "Go to the British Museum, find out as much as you can about what was stolen. Find out why Gorchev and Callahan are involved."

"If they are," Vale offered.

"It's a fair bet," Doyle countered.

"I'm not a betting man," Vale said.

"How much do you know about Callahan?" Doyle wanted to know.

"You can discuss that on your way to the British Museum," Granger interjected. "Vale, a car has been assigned to you. You drive."

"I can drive a car you know, or do you guys drive a different way as well, now?" Doyle mused, a slight smile on his face.

Granger shot him a disapproving glance.

"What about weapons?" Doyle wanted to know.

"We're going to the British Museum, not the O.K. Corral," Vale grunted.

Doyle glanced at his partner then back at Granger.

"You've been assigned weapons too," Granger said. "You can pick those up from the armoury when the time comes."

"Do you have to count the bullets first?" Doyle wanted to know.

"Just go," Granger said. "And remember, I want to be kept informed at every step of this investigation."

Doyle and Vale got to their feet and turned towards the door.

"Age before beauty," said Vale, stepping back so that Doyle could exit the room first.

"Shit before shovel, you go first," Doyle chided. "After you."

"Just get out," Granger said, wearily.

As Doyle and Vale walked towards the lift, Doyle glanced again at his new partner.

"That's a nice suit," he commented. "But I thought we were supposed to be undercover."

"We're only going to the British Museum," Vale reminded him.

"Do you change into your 'street clothes' when you're on the job then?" Doyle mused.

Vale chose to ignore the comment.

"Do we even know that David Callahan is involved in this robbery?" he said.

"Not yet. Granger's just assuming he is because some of Gorchev's men pulled it off," Doyle muttered.

"They're Russian Mafia, aren't they?"

Doyle nodded. "Hard bastards," he added.

When the lift arrived both men stepped inside and Vale hit the button marked G.

"Have you ever come up against them before?" Vale wanted to know.

"No. They were never terrorists, were they? Not in this country anyway."

"They're still criminals."

"They're police business. Not ours. Not until now."

"Any threat to the safety of this country is our business isn't it?"

"Callahan isn't a threat to this country."

"We don't know that yet."

"We don't even know that he's involved in this theft. What the fuck would he want an old book like that for?"

"I think that's what we're supposed to find out," Vale murmured.

The lift bumped to a halt and the doors slid open.

"I need to get some cigarettes before we get to the museum," Doyle offered. "Just pull over at the nearest garage or supermarket."

"You smoke?"

"Yes. You got a problem with that?"

"I don't smoke."

Doyle raised his eyebrows.

"Somehow I didn't think you would," he sighed.

FIFTY-THREE

When Doyle clambered back into the black BMW X5 M he found Vale glancing at his watch, checking the timepiece against the clock on the SUV's dashboard.

Doyle pushed the cigarette packet towards his younger companion but then smiled and withdrew it again.

"Sorry, you don't do you?" he murmured.

Vale shook his head.

"You're not going to smoke in here are you?" he sighed.

Doyle pushed a cigarette between his lips but didn't light it.

"Look, we've got to work together, right," he exclaimed. "You obviously don't want that any more than I do but let's try and ignore each other's little faults, shall we?"

"I'm not going to ignore something that could kill me. I don't want to inhale your secondary smoke. You want to kill yourself that's your business but you're not killing me too."

"Oh, fuck off," Doyle snapped. "Stick your head out of the window. The air in this city is worse for you than my fucking fag smoke."

Vale merely jammed the car in gear and drove on.

"So, how many field missions have you been on then, Vale?" Doyle wanted to know. "How many times have you done this shit before?"

"Are you going to lecture me on how much more experienced you are than me?"

Vale grunted.

"No. I was just asking."

"Like you asked why I joined the Counter Terrorist Unit? Or how long I'd been with them? Or any other of the questions you've been asking?"

"Just making conversation."

"You don't have to."

"That suits me, Vale. Personally, I couldn't give a flying fuck about you or what you've done. I was just trying to be polite."

"I read your file, Doyle. I don't think politeness is one of your strong points." He smiled to himself.

"Did you know we were going to be working together then?"

"Mister Granger told me two days ago we'd be partners."

"So you thought you'd check up on me?"

"Forewarned is forearmed or whatever they say."

"What was in the file then? What did you find out about me?"

"Enough."

"That puts me at a disadvantage. You know more about me than I do about you. I don't like being at a disadvantage."

"What do you want to know?"

"You married?"

"No."

"Girlfriend? Boyfriend?"

"Would that be a problem? If I had a boyfriend would it bother you?"

"I don't care about your sexual preferences, Vale. If you're a pillow biter that's your business. It doesn't affect how you do your job."

"See what I mean? A pillow biter. What the fuck is that supposed to mean? Are you implying I'm gay?"

"I'm not implying anything. If you object to pillow biter how about donut puncher? Turd burglar? Dirt-box mechanic?" Doyle smiled.

"Old guys like you, bigots I mean, always have hilarious names for things like that don't they? I bet you still call women birds, don't you?"

"I never have. I've got too much respect for them."

"Yeah, right."

"And don't call me a bigot. You don't know anything about me or about what I think."

"I know enough."

"You know what you read in a fucking file and that's it."

"You're like my Father."

"I'll take that as a compliment."

"Don't. He's always moaning as well. Old people are always moaning."

"Don't lump everyone over forty in together, Vale. I didn't even vote for Brexit you know." Doyle smiled. "You've got a bad impression of my generation."

"My father always said that too."

"What does your dad do for a living?"

"He's dead. He has been for five years."

"I'm sorry."

"He was a headmaster at a private school in Surrey."

"Is that where you're from?"

Vale nodded.

"Does your mum work?" Doyle continued. "Or doesn't she have to?"

"She does a lot of work for charity," Vale told him.

"That's how the middle classes get over their guilt at having so much money isn't it? By helping out the poor?"

"Are you going to hold my class against me as well as my age?"

"It wasn't your fault you were born with a silver spoon up your arse."

"So, what are you? Some kind of working-class hero?"

Doyle grinned.

"And don't call me mate, or son, or chief, or kid or anything like that, will you?" Vale continued. "Just because I'm younger than you doesn't mean you can treat me like a child."

"I wasn't going to."

"And I promise not to call you Grandad or Pop. How's that?"

"I wouldn't call you 'son'. It would imply we were close. I don't want anyone thinking that. What would you like me to call you?"

"My name would be good."

"I can think of a few names I might call you."

"Beginning with C no doubt."

"I know a few others as well."

"You haven't got any kids have you, Doyle?"

"Not that I know of."

"Thank God for that," Vale murmured. "The quicker your gene pool dries up the better."

"Cunt," Doyle muttered.

They drove in silence for a mile or two then Vale spoke again.

"I had a girlfriend. We split up about six months ago," he said, quietly.

"Whose fault?" Doyle wanted to know.

"It was sort of a mutual thing. We were drifting apart and the demands of the job meant we didn't see too much of each other."

"Your job?"

"Hers too. She was a nurse. She worked long hours. What about you? Is there a woman in your life?"

"Not at the moment."

"But there used to be?"

Doyle nodded almost imperceptibly. "Wasn't there anything in the file?" he asked.

"Not about your love life."

Doyle smiled.

"Why were you out in Iraq?" Vale wanted to know.

"Work. You have to go where the work is don't you?"

"Counter terrorism?"

"No. Just security."

"How the mighty are fallen," Vale mused, a slight smile on his face.

Doyle shot him a glance then finally lit his cigarette.

Vale let out a sigh but after a couple of minutes he slowed the SUV to a crawl, guiding it slowly along Great Russell Street. Doyle could see the huge edifice of the British Museum beyond the iron fence they were driving parallel to.

"What are you doing?" he asked.

"Looking for a parking meter," Vale told him.

"Are you fucking serious?" Doyle grunted. "We're on official business. Just stick it on the pavement."

Vale hesitated then turned the wheel, allowing the BMW to mount the pavement. As he did, Doyle clambered out, standing beside the open passenger side door for a moment.

"Then you'd better ring Granger," Doyle went on. "Just to let him know you haven't crashed the fucking car driving over here." He smiled and slammed the door.

Vale shut off the engine then followed Doyle through the main gates.

FIFTY-FOUR

There were policemen everywhere.

As Doyle and Vale walked through the main entrance of the British Museum it seemed that most of the Met had been called to the building. Half of the monolithic structure had been evacuated and the other half, it seemed, was populated by members of the emergency services.

They walked past a number of cordoned off areas, flashing their identification, moving deeper into the heart of the building towards the place they sought.

When they reached the gallery, they needed both of them stood gazing around at the exhibits inside, Doyle in particular, fascinated by what he saw. He moved towards one of the dioramas, inspecting the hundreds of model soldiers, bending down so he was level with the beautifully sculpted and painted terrain.

"This is brilliant," he said, smiling. "I used to collect these things when I was a kid." He gestured towards the models.

Vale glanced disinterestedly at the diorama and walked on.

"We've got work to do here," he said.

"I know that," Doyle snapped, following him.

Ahead of them he saw a woman with short hair talking to a policeman. She looked distraught and she kept shifting her feet, conscious that she was standing on broken glass. The shards had come from the smashed display case just ahead of her and Vale moved towards her, aware that Doyle was following but also aware that the older man seemed more interested in the weapons and armour on display than he did in speaking to anyone at the museum.

Vale beckoned to Doyle to join him and Doyle finally ambled over.

"Could we speak to you, please?" Vale said, trying to smile as he approached Caroline Bradley.

The policeman standing next to Caroline frowned but Vale showed his ID and the uniformed man merely nodded and stepped away.

Vale also showed his ID to Caroline, who glanced at it as if not sure what she was seeing.

"It wasn't a terrorist attack," she said, quietly.

"We're aware of that," Vale told her. "But the men who carried out the robbery may be linked to a terrorist organisation." He reached for his iPad and held it in front of Caroline, allowing her to see the footage and the photographs there.

"Do you recognise either of those men?" Doyle interjected.

"No," Caroline said, shaking her head.

"Have you got any idea why they would have taken the book?" Vale asked.

"No," she told him.

"Was it valuable?" Doyle wanted to know.

"Only to anyone who knew what it was. If they'd stolen gold or jewels, I could understand it but..." She allowed the sentence to trail off. She was still looking at the screen of Vale's iPad as he showed her more pictures of the two thieves, but she suddenly shot out a hand and pointed at the screen. "I've seen him before."

Vale glanced at the picture she'd indicated.

"I've seen that man before," Caroline went on.

"Where?" Doyle wanted to know.

"Here in the museum," she went on. "He was here nearly every day when the exhibition opened."

"This exhibition?" Vale echoed.

"He was here every day," Caroline said again. "I spoke to him a couple of times."

Doyle looked at the image more closely. It was David Callahan.

"And you're sure it was that man you saw here?" he offered.

Caroline nodded.

"Who is he?" she wanted to know.

"Just a man," Doyle murmured.

"What can you tell us about the book?" Vale asked. "If you could give us some information about it we might have more idea why it was taken."

Caroline shrugged.

"It's called Domus Vitae, the House of Life, it was written by a man called Gaston Lavelle in the fifteenth century," she began. "He was a satanist. A devil-worshipper."

"Why was the book here? Why was it part of the exhibition?" Doyle enquired. "I thought this was about the Hundred Years' War."

"Lavelle was a friend of Gilles de Rais and Gilles de Rais was one of Joan of Arc's lieutenants during the Hundred Years' War," Caroline told him. "It's a bit of a tenuous link I know but the book has never been displayed before. It's always been something of a pariah among historians and experts."

"Why?" Vale asked.

"Because of its subject matter and because of its links to De Rais," she said, warming to her subject. "It laid out details of the black mass, how to perform it. What was needed to conjure demons, that kind of thing. People would laugh at it now but in the fifteenth century they took it all very seriously. Some people even blamed Lavelle for the Black Death."

Doyle was gazing raptly at her, his expression fixed.

"Why?" Vale wanted to know.

"Because one of the demons he claimed to have summoned was believed to carry the Black Death," Caroline informed him. "Many peasants at the time held Lavelle personally responsible for the outbreak of the plague."

"But it was carried by rats," Vale protested.

"We know that now," Caroline conceded. "But if you'd been an ignorant peasant in the fourteenth or fifteenth century you might have blamed Lavelle too, Mr Vale." She smiled. "Lavelle was a misanthrope. He hated other people because he thought they were ignorant. He despised anyone who didn't believe the things he did. He felt that mankind was evolving too slowly, that it was resisting changes that he wanted."

"What kind of changes?" Vale wanted to know.

"Lavelle felt that God was no longer relevant, that the whole idea of religion was obsolete," Caroline went on. "He hated the Church and the way they controlled the population. That was why he wanted revenge against the rest of the human race. He thought they deserved to die for not being able to recognise how they were being used and manipulated."

Vale nodded slowly.

"What else was in the book?" Doyle murmured.

"It also contained details for raising the dead," Caroline told him, a smile touching her lips.

"Charming," Vale said, smiling.

"But Lavelle being the way he was, he even added a kind of 'fail safe' to that privilege," Caroline continued.

"What do you mean?" Doyle enquired.

"Well, because of his hatred of the human race, he wanted even that secret to carry some kind of punishment. If anyone used the book and actually managed to revive a dead body of their choice, a loved one for instance, then the price they had to pay was that other corpses would also rise."

Doyle frowned, watching her intently.

"The world would be overrun with walking corpses," Caroline went on. "Consumed by them. What might have started out as an altruistic act, returning someone who'd died to life, would end in disaster and death for the whole world."

"And people believed that?" Doyle said, flatly.

Caroline nodded.

"Where was the book found?" Vale enquired.

"It was discovered in a secret chamber beneath De Rais' estate of Machecoul in France, hidden under the chapel there."

"De Rais believed in immortality too, didn't he?" Doyle interjected.

"Yes, he did," Caroline confirmed. "Do you know anything

about him?"

"A little," Doyle said, quietly. "Wasn't there a stained-glass window taken from his chapel that supposedly contained information about that?"

"That's right," Caroline beamed, evidently happy that someone else apart from herself and her colleagues shared this kind of knowledge.

"How do you know that?" Vale enquired, looking at Doyle.

"Is there any way of us knowing what's in the book?" Doyle wanted to know. "Have you got a copy of the text?"

"It was transcribed a few years back, I did it myself," Caroline told him. "We've got it on file."

"Could I see it?" Doyle asked, urgently.

Caroline nodded, noticing that the colour had drained from Doyle's face.

FIFTY-FIVE

"**A**re you fucking mad? He will kill us all."
Andriy Demko's voice echoed inside the small
room as he turned and looked at one of the other
men gathered there.

"He's a business man like us," Ivan Petriv countered. "He will understand why we're raising the price."

"No, he won't," Demko protested. "All he will understand is that we are fucking him over. We stole the book because he paid us to do it and now we're going to ask for more money from him. No."

"It isn't his money anyway," Bohden Malinski interjected. "Someone else is paying him and he's paying us. What the fuck would he want with something like this."

He jabbed a finger towards the book lying on the table close to the men.

"It must be valuable to someone," Oleg Shushkevich murmured.

"Gorchev made his money from prostitution and porn, what the fuck does he want with a book like this?" Malinski insisted.

"I just fucking said, he doesn't want it but someone does," Shushkevich snapped.

The men regarded the ancient tome with a combination of bewilderment and disdain.

Demko rubbed a hand over his heavily stubbled chin.

"How much more do you think he'll pay?" he muttered.

"Another fifty thousand at least," Petriv told him.

"Is that what you value your life at? Fifty thousand?" Demko asked. "Because that isn't enough. Our lives will be worth nothing if we double-cross Gorchev."

"How much would you ask for?" Petriv enquired.

"I wouldn't ask for anything more because he will kill us if we do," Demko snapped.

"So, go now, walk away," Petriv said, dismissively.

Demko hesitated for a moment and then reached out and touched the cover of the book, running his fingers gently across the cracked leather binding.

"What if he won't pay?" Shushkevich asked.

"Then we keep the book," Petriv told him. "We find someone who wants it and we sell it ourselves."

"What kind of fence deals with books?" Malinski wanted to know. "I know they trade in diamonds and artwork but who do we go to with this?" He pointed at the book.

"We won't need a fucking fence," Petriv snapped. "Gorchev will pay what we want for the book."

"And then what?" Demko wanted to know.

"We get out. We take our money and we leave," Petriv told him.

"He'll come after us," Demko insisted.

"Once he's got the book, he won't give a fuck," Petriv countered.

Malinski took a sip of his drink and carefully opened the book, peering myopically at the Latin and Romance words that were visible on the pages. He ran his fingers over the ancient pages, feeling the texture of the parchment. He frowned, wondering if his mind was playing tricks on him.

The pages felt warm.

As if they'd been left in strong sunlight for an hour or two.

He withdrew his hand for a moment, gazing down at the tome, then he gently laid the digits on the page again, running them from the top to the bottom of the parchment.

This time he felt nothing but the harsh texture of the paper.

"I'm going to call him," Petriv said, reaching for his phone. "He needs to hear our proposal." He smiled thinly and found the number he sought.

Malinski leafed through more pages of the book, wondering what the words before him meant, curious as to who would pay such an amount to possess this tome.

Again, he felt that warmth from the pages and again he pulled his hand away.

"What's wrong?"

The voice close to him caused him to start and he turned to see Demko standing over him looking down at the book.

"Nothing," Malinski told him. "I think my mind is playing tricks on me."

"Why?" Demko wanted to know.

"Put your hand there," Malinski instructed, pointing at the open pages of the book.

Demko did as he was instructed, pressing his fingers gently to the parchment.

"Do you feel it?" Malinski enquired. "It feels...It's warm."

Demko nodded gently, his face pale. He lifted his fingers and glanced at the tips, as if fearing there was some kind of imprint or mark upon them, then he touched the book again.

The page felt cool now. Like dead flesh.

He turned in Petriv's direction, seeing that the older man was deeply engrossed in a conversation, the phone pressed hard to his ear as he listened to the voice on the other end of the line. When he finally put the phone down, he swallowed hard and then looked around at the other men in the room, all of who were now gazing in his direction.

"We meet him in two hours," Petriv said. "At the place where we agreed."

"Is he bringing the money?" Demko wanted to know.

"He said we'll get whatever we asked for," Petriv told him, smiling.

"And you believe that?" Demko challenged.

"He's a man of his word," said Petriv.

"I don't trust him," Malinski offered.

"We have no choice. We have to trust him this time," Petriv grunted.

"He'll take the book and kill us all," Malinski said.

"You think I am fucking stupid?" snapped Petriv. "You think we're going to take this fucking book there and just wait for him to turn up? We will be ready for him."

Malinski held the other man's gaze.

"I hope you're right," he said, quietly.

Petriv dug a hand inside his jacket and pulled the Glock 9mm from its holster. He pulled the slide back, chambering a round.

"I'm ready," he said, smiling. "Are you?"

FIFTY-SIX

"How do you know about this kind of thing?" Gideon Vale asked, watching as Doyle scrolled slowly through the translated pages of Domus Vitae, each page appearing on the monitor as he read.

"I don't," Doyle told him. "But I ran into some people who did."

"Have you any idea at all who would want to take the book?" Caroline Bradley asked. "I can't see how it could mean anything to anyone other than another historian or antiquities collector."

"Maybe the guys who took it were from another museum," Doyle mused.

"I don't think so," Caroline protested.

"I was joking," Doyle told her, raising his eyebrows.

"Who do you think took it?"

The newest voice in the room belonged to Jonathan Sellers.

Caroline performed introductions quickly and Sellers ran appraising eyes over the two counter-terrorists.

"What's this got to do with terrorism?" he wanted to know. "Why aren't the police taking care of it?"

"There is a police investigation," Vale informed him.

"We have more specific interests in the book and who might have wanted it," Doyle added.

"We have a right to know who took it," Sellers snapped. "If you know, you should tell us."

"You have a right to know precisely jack shit at the moment," Doyle told him, smiling thinly. "This is a classified operation."

Sellers looked angrily at him.

"I do apologise for my colleague's rudeness," Vale interjected.

"This is a priceless item," Sellers went on, angrily. "I want to know what's happening."

"As soon as we've got any information you'll be informed," Vale told him, apologetically.

"Who else knew about the book?" Doyle wanted to know. "About its origins? Where it came from? Where had it been before you acquired it?"

"It had been held at the Louvre in Paris," Sellers explained. "That was where it was meant to go back to after we'd finished with it."

"Why didn't they display it?" Doyle murmured.

Sellers merely shrugged.

"They didn't want it on show," Caroline Bradley added.

"Why not?" Doyle asked.

"They're afraid of it," Caroline told him, flatly.

"It's a book," Vale said, smiling.

"Until you understand its power and how to use it," Sellers intoned.

"Whoever took it could be in danger too," Caroline added.

Vale looked at Doyle, but the older man merely continued to gaze at the translation on the screen before him.

"That's what you believe?" Vale said.

"Belief is a powerful weapon," Caroline told him.

"What would anyone want with the book?" Sellers asked. "Unless they understood what it can do, it would be of no interest or use to them."

"I think whoever wanted it knows exactly what they're getting," Doyle explained.

"You found it didn't you?" He pointed at Sellers.

"Yes. There was an archaeological dig in France, and I discovered the book," Sellers told him.

"Was that the purpose of the dig?" Doyle enquired.

"No. It was a kind of happy accident that we found it," Sellers confessed. "We were looking for relics concerning Joan of Arc. That's why we were at Machecoul, because of Joan's links with Gilles de Rais. We never expected to find anything like the book."

Doyle got to his feet.

"We'll be in touch when we've heard anything," he said, quietly.

"You've got to get it back," Sellers told him.

Doyle held the man's gaze for a moment then he and Vale headed for the door that would lead them out of the room.

"If we find the book, we find Callahan," Vale said as they made their way through the museum.

Doyle nodded but didn't speak. His mind was elsewhere, and they were thoughts he didn't want to share.

FIFTY-SEVEN

"You know these men, you're supposed to be able to trust them," Callahan snapped, looking up at the facade of the building in Soho.

He turned and glanced briefly at Vasili Gorchev who was seated in the back of the Jaguar.

"Trust is hard to come by in this business," Gorchev replied, shifting uncomfortably.

"They've worked for you before," Callahan reminded him. "You should have known."

"You pay the extra and you get the book," Gorchev said.

"No. I'm paying you enough already. How do I know you're not involved?"

"Because I don't fuck people, I do business with."

"How do I know that?"

The driver glanced at Callahan and then at Gorchev.

"I will go and get the fucking book for you," Gorchev announced, irritably. "Take care of this bullshit once and for all."

"You stay where you are," Callahan snapped. "I'll get the book." He slipped a hand inside his jacket, fingers brushing against the butt of the Sig-Sauer P226.

"You might need some help," Gorchev offered.

Callahan threw him a disdainful look and hauled himself out of the car. He stood on the pavement and opened his jacket slightly, motioning to the Sig beneath his arm.

"I sold these for years," he said. "I know how to use them." He turned away from the car towards the door he sought. It was sandwiched between a fish and chip shop and a health food emporium.

Callahan pushed the door open and walked into the tiny hallway. Ahead of him, a narrow wooden staircase stretched upwards towards the three floors of the building. It smelled of fresh paint but there were also handwritten signs displayed on the newly decorated stone and plaster.

CHEC MODEL

One of them proudly proclaimed.

PHOTO MODELS 2ND FLOOR

Another told him in handwritten black marker pen.

GORJUS GIRLS

A third boasted.

Callahan moved slowly up the stairs, the wooden steps creaking beneath his weight.

As he reached the first landing he paused and looked around. There was a green door to his left.

LITHUANIAN MODEL – JUST KNOCK FOR ME.

The sign on the door announced.

On this first floor the paint on the walls was peeling off in places. Huge scabrous lumps of it were flaking away from the stone beneath. There were posters Blu-Tacked to the walls showing the most stunning blonde and brunette women. Callahan was fairly sure that the images bore little resemblance to what lay beyond those closed doors on either side of him.

He moved onto the landing, turning to his right to continue up the steps where there were more posters and signs. He heard footsteps above him and instinctively reached inside his jacket, touching the pistol again.

The girl who began to descend the stairs was in her early twenties. Dark hair, almost anorexically thin, she eyed Callahan warily as he beckoned her forward, stepping aside to allow her passage on the stairs. He could smell her freshly washed hair as she passed, and he looked her up and down approvingly for a moment before continuing up the steps.

He was halfway up when he heard sounds of laughter.

Two, possibly three voices, Callahan mused, and he continued climbing. As he reached the landing, he saw that there were two rooms ahead of him and the doors of both were open.

A large man with a couple of days of stubble emerged from

one of the rooms and glanced at him.

"No girls up here," the man said, in a thick Eastern European accent. "You stay downstairs for girls."

"I'm not looking for girls," Callahan told him.

"You can't come up here," the man insisted. "Is office up here. You go down."

"I've got business here," Callahan said, flatly, glancing around to see where the others might be.

"What business?" the man demanded.

"I'm here to collect something. A book."

The unshaven man smiled, revealing stained teeth.

"I know who you are," he said.

"And you've got something that belongs to me. I want it."

The man reached backwards, pulling a Glock 19 pistol from his belt. As he did, another man joined him on the landing.

Callahan looked at the newcomer and saw that he was stockier, heavier. He was wearing a T-shirt that could barely contain his bulging stomach. He too looked as if he needed a shave.

"He is here for the book," the first man told his companion.

"You are Callahan?" the fat man said. His accent was also East European.

The Englishman nodded. "Yes. I want what I paid for."

"You have the money?" the fat man enquired.

"I want the book," Callahan told him.

"No money, no book," grinned the fat man.

"Where is it?" Callahan wanted to know.

"You pay, you get to see," said the first man, also smiling.

Callahan didn't smile.

"If you give me the book now you've got a chance of walking out of here," he said, evenly. "If not, I'll kill you all."

FIFTY-EIGHT

The fat man laughed.

His companion also chuckled but he took a step backwards as he did, glancing towards the door of the office beyond.

"You are rich man but you're a stupid man if you think you can get the book now," said the fat man, cheerfully.

"I know it's here," Callahan went on. "This is where you planned to hand it over to Gorchev originally."

At the sound of Gorchev's name, the fat man's expression of amusement faded rapidly.

"He's outside now," Callahan went on. "He's waiting for me."

"He knows what we want," the man with the stubble offered. "Just pay us the money."

Now it was Callahan's turn to smile.

"I can almost understand you thinking you could double-cross him," he said, quietly. "All your type are the same. You all crawled out of the same sewer. But thinking you could double-cross me?" He shook his head. "You fucking scum." The venom in his tone was almost palpable.

The fat man stood before him impassively. His taller companion was now leaning against the frame of the door behind him, the Glock still gripped in his large hand.

"You come back with the money and we talk," the taller man began.

Callahan slid one hand inside his jacket, pulled the Sig free of its holster and swung it up in one fluid movement.

He pumped the trigger three times.

The sound, inside the small landing, was deafening. Callahan gripped the pistol tightly, bracing himself as the recoil slammed it back against the heel of his hand.

The first shot tore into the wall close to the fat man, blasting pieces of plaster away and sending dust billowing into the air. The second slammed into the man's left shoulder, ripping through and exploding from his back, spraying blood and tiny pieces of flesh and clothing all over the taller man behind him.

The third shot caught the fat man in his pendulous belly, ripping through to macerate intestines. As he dropped to his knees his companion swung the Glock around and fired three times at Callahan.

The heavy grain slugs slammed into wood and plaster, the thunderous retorts now echoing inside the landing too. Callahan moved to one side, firing again, pumping the trigger another couple of times.

The first shot hit the man in the face, smashing into his jaw where it splintered several front teeth.

The second screamed past him into the office beyond where it struck a window, shattering the glass.

The taller man dropped like a stone, tumbling over his fallen comrade who was still attempting to pull the gun from his belt. Callahan stepped forward, firing down at the fat man, pumping another shot into him.

He paused at the office door, ducked low now, wondering what lay beyond.

As he moved into the room he fired again, spent shell cases spewing from the Sig.

The stink of cordite was strong in the air now and Callahan ducked through the greyish-white smoke that had settled in the air, glancing around the room.

There was another body lying behind a desk. The man had fallen backwards, hit in the chest by a stray bullet. Callahan could hear ragged, uneven breathing as he moved towards the figure, and as he looked he could see that a bullet had ripped through the man's chest and punctured his lung. That was what was making the rasping noise. His eyes were still open and, as Callahan stood over him, he looked up helplessly, his lips quivering soundlessly.

Callahan held his gaze for a moment then moved behind the

desk, kneeling beside the man.

"Where's the book?" he said, through clenched teeth.

The man coughed, bright blood spilling over his lips.

Callahan slipped a hand beneath the man's shoulders, feeling blood on his hand as he raised him up slightly. He could see that the crimson fluid had soaked into the dark shirt the man was wearing. Callahan undid the shirt slightly, looking at the wound in the man's chest. It was choked with blood, pale around the extremities, and there were small pieces of flesh hanging from the hole.

"Where's the book?" Callahan said again, leaning closer to the man without looking at him now.

Again, the wounded figure tried to speak but all that he managed was a mucoid gurgle.

Callahan used his index and middle finger and pushed them hard into the bullet hole, working them around inside the wound.

The man tried to scream, his body shaking madly as fresh pain tore through him.

Callahan worked his fingers deeper.

"Where is it?" he snarled, forcing a third digit into the savage wound, ignoring the blood that poured out and covered his hand.

The man closed his eyes, barely able to take any more of the agony he was feeling but Callahan slammed his head down onto the floor of the office.

"Don't you pass out on me yet, you bastard," the Englishman rasped. "Where's the book?"

The man managed to raise one shaking hand, pointing towards an old safe that stood next to a large filing cabinet on the other side of the office. Only then did Callahan allow him to drop back to the floor, dragging his fingers clear of the wound, wiping the blood from his hand on the man's already sodden shirt front.

The safe was unlocked and for that Callahan was grateful. He pulled the door open and looked inside.

FIFTY-NINE

As the lift bumped to a halt on the third floor of St. Thomas's hospital, Doyle glanced across at his companion.

Gideon Vale was gazing straight ahead, seemingly lost in his own thoughts.

"You all right?" Doyle asked.

"I hate hospitals," Vale told him. "My father died of cancer about five years ago and every time I go inside one, I remember all the trips back and forth to see him."

Doyle nodded.

"Were you close to your father?" he asked.

"Very. I hated seeing him that way. He seemed to die a little more every time I saw him, does that make sense?"

Again, Doyle nodded.

"I felt so helpless," Vale went on. "There was nothing I could do but sit and watch him slip away and the night he finally died I wasn't there. I can't remember why. I never even got the chance to say goodbye to him."

"I know what you mean," Doyle said, quietly. He looked around. "The only times I ever saw the inside of these places, I was a fucking patient."

"Wounded in the line of duty?" Vale quipped.

Doyle nodded.

"They always seem more depressing at night, like now," Vale went on.

"They're depressing all the time," Doyle grunted.

The two men stepped out of the lift and headed along the wide corridor beyond, moving towards the reception desk just ahead of them. There was a large and formidable looking woman sitting there, intermittently tapping away at her keyboard and consulting a pile of papers to her left. She smiled broadly as Doyle approached and the smile didn't even fade when he showed her his identification.

"We're here to speak to Andriy Demko," Doyle told her.

"He's sedated," she said, the smile still in place.

"Well, can you wake him up then, please?" Doyle persisted. "This is important."

"I'll have to speak to a doctor," the nurse confided.

"You do that," Doyle said, gratefully. "We'll wait here."

The nurse reached for the phone on her desk and hit one of the buttons.

Doyle wandered over to a nearby notice board, glancing at leaflets that covered everything from Alzheimer's to strokes, gazing blankly at the words before him as the nurse chattered on the phone. Vale stood immobile near to the reception desk, only moving when a doctor appeared from a doorway to the right. He shot Vale an appraising glance.

"You want to see Andriy Demko?" the doctor asked.

Vale nodded.

"I thought the police had already questioned him," the doctor went on.

"We're not the police," Doyle explained, moving across to join his companion. Both he and Vale showed their identification. The doctor hesitated for a moment then led them further along the corridor to a private room. There was an armed, uniformed policeman outside who put down his copy of The Mirror and got to his feet as the little group approached. He inspected the ID Doyle and Vale showed him, nodded and sat down again, returning to his paper as the doctor opened the door slowly and moved inside.

As Doyle walked in, he could hear the constant blip of an oscilloscope cutting through the stillness of the dimly lit room.

Andriy Demko was lying in the bed in the middle of the room, tubes and leads connecting him to a number of drips and machines. Doyle glanced around, his eyes focussing on the bedside table.

"No get-well cards," he said, raising his eyebrows. "Not very popular, is he?"

"He's lucky to be alive," the doctor said, irritably, watching as Doyle moved closer to the bed, looking down at the Ukrainian.

"Wake him up," Doyle said, without taking his eyes off the prone man before him.

"He's supposed to rest," the doctor protested. "He's still on the critical list."

"If you don't wake him up, I will," Doyle said, glancing at the doctor.

Before either of them could move, Demko's eyes flickered open. He looked up, glancing first at Doyle and then at the doctor, then he tried to sit up slightly but was prevented from doing so by the heavy bandaging around his chest and neck.

"You can leave us now, doc," Doyle said, flatly.

The doctor hesitated for a moment then made his way to the door.

"Don't tire him," he called before disappearing.

Doyle ignored the remark, his attention now fixed on Demko.

"Can you hear me?" he said, leaning closer.

The man didn't answer.

"Where's Gorchev?" Doyle persisted. "Where's the book?"

Still Demko didn't speak.

"Perhaps he doesn't speak English," Vale offered.

"You speak English, don't you?" Doyle said, smiling down at Demko. "You know what I'm saying?"

Demko remained silent.

"You going to talk to me?" Doyle persisted.

Demko eyed him impassively.

Doyle reached for one of the clear plastic tubes that had been attached to Demko. He rolled it gently between his fingers.

"How about if I pull one of these fucking tubes out?" Doyle breathed. "Will you speak to me then?"

"Doyle, you can't do that." Vale snapped, taking a step

231

forward. "If he can't understand you, how can he answer you?"

"He can understand," Doyle hissed, turning his gaze back on Demko. "Can't you, you cunt?"

Demko shifted slightly in his bed.

"Where's Gorchev?" snapped Doyle.

"This isn't the way, Doyle," Vale protested.

"It might not be your way," Doyle told him. "But it always worked for me."

"Well things are different now," Vale rasped.

"Then you question him." Doyle took a step backwards.

He watched as Vale moved closer to the bed, looking down at Demko.

"If you can understand me, Mr Demko, just nod your head," Vale began.

The Ukrainian moved his head slowly, tentatively. He nodded gently.

"Did you get a good look at who shot you?" Vale wanted to know.

Again, Demko nodded.

"Was it Vasili Gorchev?" Vale wanted to know.

Demko lay silently, staring at the ceiling.

"You work for Gorchev don't you?" Doyle interjected.

The Ukrainian let out a breath.

Doyle glanced at Vale and shook his head almost imperceptibly.

"Fucking hard man," Doyle grinned.

Demko took a breath and looked at Doyle but he remained silent. Even when Doyle pulled the Beretta 92F from its shoulder holster, he didn't make a sound.

Only when the barrel was pressed against his cheek did he let out a frantic breath.

SIXTY

"What the hell are you doing?" Vale snarled, watching as Doyle pressed the metal against the Ukrainian's cheek.

"I'm not known for my patience" Doyle hissed, the remark aimed at either his companion or the man in the bed. "Now, where's Gorchev?"

The blip of the oscilloscope increased its pace as Doyle continued to hold the Beretta against the helpless man's face.

"Why did Gorchev shoot you?" Doyle persisted, glaring down at the Ukrainian.

Demko looked at him, his eyes bulging wide in their sockets.

Doyle thumbed the hammer back on the pistol.

"Doyle," Vale snarled, reaching out a hand to try and stop the older man.

"It wasn't Gorchev."

The words seemed to echo inside the small room.

Doyle looked at Demko and smiled thinly.

"Gorchev didn't do it," Demko went on, his breath coming in gasps now.

"Who did?" Doyle wanted to know, pulling the Beretta away from the Ukrainians face.

"I don't know," Demko told him.

Doyle frowned and pushed the pistol back against the wounded man's cheek.

"I never saw him before," Demko said, frantically. "I don't know who he was."

"Tall? Short? Black? White?" Doyle went on.

"English," Demko croaked. "He was English. About your height." He nodded towards Doyle.

Now it was Vale's turn to step closer to the bed. He pulled his phone from his pocket; found the photograph on it he sought and held the device before Demko.

"Was that the man who shot you?" he asked.

Demko nodded as he looked at the picture.

"Callahan," Doyle murmured under his breath.

"So, this man shot you and killed two of your companions?" Vale asked.

The Ukrainian nodded.

"Why?" Doyle demanded.

"He wanted the book," Demko said.

"The book you stole from the British Museum?" Vale interjected.

"He paid us to steal it," the Ukrainian went on, wheezing slightly now.

"Why did he want it?" Doyle enquired.

Demko merely shook his head slightly.

"Do you know where he is now?" Vale asked.

Again, the Ukrainian shook his head.

"What about Gorchev?" Doyle went on. "Where's he now?"

"I don't know," Demko sighed. "I'm not his fucking keeper."

Doyle held Demko's gaze for a moment longer.

"What do you know about the book?" Vale interjected. "The book you were hired to steal?"

"It's an old book. That's all I know," Demko said.

"You don't know why Callahan wanted it?" Vale pressed.

"I don't give a fuck. He paid for it. That's all I care about."

"And he killed two of your mates and came pretty fucking close to killing you too," Doyle reminded him. "How did he manage to do that? Did you just stand there and let him have some target practice? Were you too fucking dumb to shoot back?"

Demko sucked in a painful breath and glared at Doyle.

"You tried double-crossing him and you got what you deserved," Doyle went on. He smiled. "You were lucky he let you live."

Vale suddenly took a step forward.

"Maybe Callahan let him live for a reason," he murmured.

Doyle looked puzzled.

"He killed the others without a second thought," Vale continued. "Why let this one live?"

Doyle was considering his answer when the door of the room opened. The doctor who entered was the same man who had shown them to the room when they'd first arrived.

"I need you gentlemen to leave now," he said, briskly. "I told you I didn't want Mr Demko overtaxed."

"We're done now anyway, Doc," Doyle told him, as he and Vale moved towards the door.

"Mr Demko was very helpful," Vale added.

As the two counter-terrorists reached the door, Demko coughed then pointed accusingly at them.

"He will kill you," the Ukrainian called.

"He'll try," Doyle murmured.

SIXTY-ONE

Maitland Hall stood in twelve acres of its own grounds about five miles north of the town of Gerrards Cross.

Built in the late eighteenth century it had been presented as a gift from a grateful nation to one of the main participants in the Battle of Waterloo and that was when it had acquired the name it now sported and had proudly borne since 1815.

General Sir Peregrine Maitland had commanded the 52nd Regiment of Foot at the titanic battle and his men had been instrumental in driving off the final French attack and securing victory. For this contribution, Maitland himself had received a number of awards and titles and also the hall that would go on to bear his name.

He had been the one who had supervised many aspects of the landscaping in the grounds, most of which survived into the twenty-first century, including a huge pond to the rear of the property that also featured a small island in its centre, connected to the rest of the grounds by a purpose-built stone bridge.

From the windows at the front of the imposing edifice there was a view of the rolling countryside that surrounded it and also of the river that cut through the land. Ornate and beautifully kept gardens surrounded the buildings on three sides, approachable only by a wide driveway that snaked through the grounds after leaving the network of narrow country thoroughfares. There was a small wood masking the front of the main house, separated from it by a huge expanse of lawn.

To the rear of the house there were tennis courts, an outdoor swimming pool and also a guest house. Years ago it had been the servants quarters but, successive affluent owners had seen fit to convert the building into what it was now. A small staff consisting of a butler, chauffeur and two house keepers had actually lived at the hall as recently as five years before but they had left with the previous owners.

The house had stood empty since that particular departure.

Exactly why it had not been snapped up by another buyer, no one knew.

The estate agents handling the sale had been surprised by how long the property had remained unoccupied. It was, after all, not only a luxurious residence, it was also within thirty miles of London, easily reachable by train or car.

When it had finally been acquired, they had been relieved and not only because of the size of their commission fee, it wasn't good for business to have a property on the market for so long without a buyer.

People living in the area had also wondered why Maitland Hall had remained empty for so long. There were no neighbours in the immediate vicinity, the closest dwelling was two miles to the west, but those who lived in the town itself had seen quite a lot of one of the previous residents. A singer with a rock band, he had made it his business to become as much a part of the local community as possible, but he too had moved out after living for less than two years in the hall.

His departure had been sudden and unexpected, as had those of the previous owners, and some local residents had seen fit to look into the history of the house and discovered that in fact, three out of the last four owners had all left within two years of purchasing the property and that those departures had been swift and unexpected. Someone on social media had suggested the place might be haunted but the theories and the interest in the hall had died away as quickly as they'd begun.

As David Callahan stood on the terrace at the rear of the property, he smiled to himself.

What would people say if they knew of his background? He sipped the whiskey he had poured himself and gazed out over the huge lawn towards the wood beyond.

Behind him, the house was quiet and in relative darkness apart from one room where the light inside was prevented from spilling out into the night by the thick curtains placed at the windows.

It was into that room that Callahan would go when he had finished his drink.

Above him, thick banks of cloud rolled away momentarily to reveal a watery moon and Callahan looked up towards it, peering at the silvery circlet for a second. Then the clouds returned, blotting out the moon once more, plunging the landscape into blackness again. And yet, even in the gloom he could see the dark outlines of bats whirling and swooping through the air, trying to catch the insects that seemed so plentiful in the humid stillness.

From the wood, an owl hooted, and Callahan listened to it and to the other sounds he could hear for a moment longer. There was a dog barking somewhere, the noise carried on through the stillness.

He turned towards the house again, his eyes drawn to the well-lit room hidden by the thick curtains. He drained what was left in his glass and decided he needed a top-up before he entered that room again.

SIXTY-TWO

Gideon Vale waved a hand in front of him as he drove, trying to waft away the smoke drifting from Sean Doyle's cigarette.

Doyle glanced at his companion then took another drag on the Rothmans.

"All right, don't panic," Doyle grunted. "I've nearly finished."

"It's a filthy habit," Vale snapped, dismissively.

"So, you're perfect are you, Vale? No bad habits?"

"Not antisocial ones like smoking."

"Oh, fuck off. You're like an old woman, moaning all the time." He took another drag. "It relaxes me."

Vale raised his eyebrows.

"What do you do to relax?" the older man wanted to know.

"I have the odd joint now and again," Vale confessed.

"Fuck me. You're bellyaching about me smoking this and you're into drugs?"

"Cannabis isn't a drug."

"It's illegal."

"It used to be used as a pain killer. It still is in many places. It's legal in lots of States in America."

"But we're not in the States, are we? So, don't criticise my smoking when you're a fucking pothead."

"Doyle, you really are so far out of touch, you're practically on a different planet."

"What do you do when you really want to relax? Shoot up? Snort some cocaine?"

"Now you're being ridiculous."

"They're all drugs."

"Marijuana grows naturally on the planet."

"So, does fucking cactus but you don't smoke it do you?"

"Actually, peyote is made from cactus and that's an hallucinogenic."

"So, we finally found a subject you're interested in."

"So, what do you do to relax, Doyle? Get drunk? Smoke extra cigarettes?" Vale grinned.

"I watch TV. Not that it's any of your fucking business."

"Listen to music?"

"Sometimes."

"What kind?"

"Rock music. What do you like?"

"I like Coldplay."

Doyle snorted.

"Fucking lift music," he said, smiling.

"And I like RnB. Some Grime. Depends on my mood."

"Remind me never to borrow your record collection."

"I've got everything on my phone. It's all digital. If you weren't so old, you'd know that. It's all about convenience now, Doyle."

"Downloads. Streaming. All that bollocks?"

Vale drove on, finally glancing at Doyle again.

"So why do you think Callahan left Demko alive?" he said, finally.

"Who knows how his mind works?" Doyle murmured.

"You got as close to him as anyone. I thought you might have an idea."

"I don't think trying to kill him counts as getting close, does it? What about you? How much do you know about him?"

"Only what I read in the files. Multi-millionaire. Made his fortune running guns. Obsessed with the occult."

"And immortality."

"Who wouldn't want to live forever?"

"That depends."

"On what?"

"On what kind of world you're living in."

"I also read the reports on your debriefing. You know, what happened the first time you were sent after him. What you did and saw that night at Callahan's place in Ireland. Some of it makes for pretty interesting reading."

"I'm not even sure what I saw."

"A demon?"

Vale couldn't resist a smile.

Doyle saw the expression and shot him an angry glance.

"Callahan's wife was killed that night, wasn't she?"

Doyle nodded.

"Her and a few others," he sighed.

"Like your partner?" Vale enquired.

"You read the reports. You know what happened," Doyle snapped.

"You shouldn't blame yourself, Doyle. She knew the risks. She was a professional like you."

"Thanks for the expert guidance, now stop the car."

"I'll drop you outside your flat," Vale protested. "It's only another few hundred yards."

"I need some fresh air first. Drop me here." Doyle jabbed a finger towards the pavement.

"There are people at the CTU who you can talk to about the way you feel," Vale offered. "Therapists. Experts on grief and..."

"Vale," Doyle snapped. "You are a cunt. Do you know that?"

The younger man shrugged and brought the SUV to a halt, watching as Doyle clambered out. He set off briskly, heading away from the stationary vehicle, not looking back.

Vale watched him for a moment longer then pulled his phone from his pocket.

He found the number he sought immediately and was relieved when the recipient of the call picked up straight away.

"I just dropped Doyle off," Vale said into the phone. "I thought you'd want to know."

The person at the other end of the line thanked him and terminated the call.

Vale glanced at the phone for a moment then slid it back into his pocket. He waited until Doyle had disappeared around a corner then he drove off.

SIXTY-THREE

He didn't have any photographs of her.

Why should he? Those hadn't been the days of selfies and smart phones and taking snaps every few seconds to document every single moment of a life. If they'd been young now there would have been endless pictures of them together. Draped over each other, joined together like Siamese twins or posing in front of famous monuments and sites.

But Doyle had none of that. All he had were his memories of Georgie.

Of the woman she had been and that he had known so briefly. And now, as he sat on the sofa in the flat, a cigarette in one hand and a drink in the other, he thought again of just how short their time together had been. Weeks? Months? Certainly, no longer than that and yet, in that time, she had made such an indelible mark upon him and upon his life that he sometimes felt as if they'd been together for years. For ever.

Doyle let out a long sigh and took another drag on his cigarette. He felt tired. More tired than he had for a long time.

You're getting old. You can't keep up any more.

But along with that tiredness he also felt a kind of exhilaration he had not experienced for many years. On a number of occasions during the day he had felt that unmistakable surge of adrenaline he had known and loved. It was the kind of feeling someone experienced upon seeing a long-lost friend and he welcomed it, however fleeting it might be. It made him feel alive again. It made him feel worthwhile.

He got to his feet and refilled his glass, gazing out of the window, looking out into the night.

And as he looked, the recollections flooded back into his mind as if someone had opened a sluice gate in his memory.

That night, nearly thirty years ago, in Ireland. That night that was burned into his soul like a brand. The images were still fresh. Still vivid.

Flames from a wrecked car leaping through shattered windows. Curtains ablaze, thick smoke filling the air.

Georgie lying on her stomach in the centre of the room, her body twisted into a foetal position, one arm crushed beneath her. Blood spreading in a dark puddle all around her.

Bullet wounds in her body and gashes on her face where she'd been thrown through the windscreen. Her blonde hair matted with blood, plastered across her face. Her eyes closed.

He remembered kneeling beside her, closing her half-open eyes gently and reverentially, his fingers smeared with blood when he touched her.

And then moving through that house, Callahan's house, through the smoke and the flame, driven by a need for revenge that he had never felt before. Consumed by the desire to kill the man who had been responsible for Georgie's death. And he remembered finding that man. Finding him in a room with...

With what? What the fuck had that thing been?

Doyle swallowed more of his drink. As he lowered the glass, he found that his hand was shaking slightly.

Whatever had been in that room with Callahan had towered over him, red eyes burning insanely as it looked around.

Doyle had shot it twice in its broad chest, but it had remained upright. Not until he'd shot it between the eyes did it finally fall.

And it had disappeared.

Doyle wondered if he'd blacked out for a second and the monstrosity had somehow escaped the room in that brief moment of time and yet he knew that couldn't be. Despite everything, contrary to all the things he believed, the abomination had gone. And when he'd looked into its eyes and seen them glowing red and then looked into Callahan's eyes, also illuminated hellish crimson as if lit from within, he had understood.

The creature that Callahan had summoned now possessed him.

Doyle shook his head. Even now it seemed ridiculous.

You saw a monster.

"I killed him," Doyle said, softly. "I fucking killed him."

And yet now, nearly thirty years later, he was again hunting the man he had thought he'd destroyed.

Doyle spun around and hurled the glass at the far wall of the room. Overcome with a feeling of rage he could barely understand.

He crossed to the laptop he'd left on the sofa and he flipped the lid up. There was a picture of David Callahan there, an enlarged image taken from some CCTV cameras that had captured his face when he passed through Heathrow. Doyle sat looking at it for what felt like an eternity.

When he finally slammed the lid shut again, he did it with such force he practically broke it.

SIXTY-FOUR

The thing that struck him first was the silence.

As he walked slowly along the narrow country lane he stopped occasionally, sometimes even wandering on to the grass verge on one side of the tarmac, enjoying the stillness all around him.

Trees grew thickly on the other side of the lane, beyond the verge there was a low stone wall that overlooked fields and more trees.

There were birds singing in the trees, but they made their sounds almost reverentially, as if they too did not want to disturb the cloying stillness. The atmosphere was heavy, the silence closing in around him like an invisible glove. It was warm and the humidity grew more intense as he walked on, cutting through a copse of trees. The ground sloped away sharply down to a hollow that was filled with water, probably from the recent heavy showers they'd suffered, he reasoned.

He walked down to the edge of the hollow, careful not to slip in the mud there. In the thick ferns nearby something moved and he spun around, trying to see what had disturbed the silence.

A frog made its way unhurriedly from the ferns towards the sanctuary of the water. It paused on the edge of the hollow for a moment then launched itself into the dark depths, only a couple of air bubbles now signalling its presence. He watched it for a moment longer then made his way back up the slope towards the lane. Breathing a little more heavily than he would have liked, he continued down the lane. He could feel sweat trickling down his back, some beading on his face too.

As he rounded a slight bend in the lane, he heard the sounds. High-pitched voices. Joyful, playful voices.

There was another narrow thoroughfare leading off from

the lane up towards the wrought-iron gates of the school.

As he reached the end of this other walkway, he could see children beyond the gates. They were running backwards and forwards, enjoying the afternoon break. There were girls skipping or playing hopscotch. Boys kicking a ball about or chasing each other. They seemed oblivious to the cares of the world around them but that was how it should be for children between five and eight, he thought wistfully. They should have no concerns. Nothing to worry them. He stood at the end of the short walkway for a moment longer, gazing at the children, his eyes focused particularly on a little girl with long blonde hair who had rolled both her socks down to the ankles. She was skipping back and forth just inside the gate, apparently alone but untroubled by the fact she had no one to play with.

He watched her more intently then walked slowly up the pathway towards the gates.

There was another path that led around the walled playground and he followed it, wondering where it would bring him out. As he walked, he could still hear the children beyond the walls and then, as he turned the corner, he found that the wall had been replaced by a low privet hedge. He could see straight into the playground from his new vantage point and he could still see the little blonde girl in the rolled-down socks. She was still skipping happily back and forth, untroubled by the other children playing around her in couples or in groups.

He guessed she was about six. He wondered what her name was.

A whistle sounded loudly, and the children all turned in its direction, hurrying across the playground towards the entrance to the red brick block they had emerged from earlier.

He watched them go, particularly the little blonde girl with the rolled-down socks. She was such a pretty little thing. He couldn't help but smile as he watched her running across the playground.

And he couldn't help but wonder what she would look like

cut open from groin to throat with her intestines pulled from her stomach cavity and her heart ripped out.

David Callahan smiled to himself and started walking again.

SIXTY-FIVE

Doyle turned and looked out of the side window of the SUV, glancing at the shop fronts and pedestrians as the vehicle moved slowly through traffic.

Occasionally he glanced towards the dashboard of the SUV, his gaze accusatory.

"Do we have to have that shit on?" he said, finally, jabbing a finger towards the radio.

Vale glanced at him briefly and frowned.

"It's just the radio," he murmured.

"Exactly," Doyle grunted. "You might be interested in hearing about what so-called celebrities are up to or listening to pop music but I'm not."

"I was waiting for the news," Vale told him.

"Then put it on a news channel."

"They have news on here."

"Well, unless they've got a new segment about finding Ukrainian gangsters and devil-worshipping gunrunners, who should have died twenty odd years ago, then there's not going to be anything to help us, is there?"

Vale shook his head wearily and turned off the radio.

"I can understand why you used to work alone," he said.

"What do you mean?"

"You never stop moaning. I doubt if anyone else wanted to work with you, did they?"

"I'd rather work alone."

"Like a cowboy?"

"What the fuck are you going on about?"

"My dad used to love western films and the leading characters in old westerns were always loners. Always drifting around the West on their own. Shooting people or rescuing people." Vale grinned.

"I'd have made a good cowboy," Doyle said, smiling. "I'd

have been a bounty hunter."

They rode in silence for a little longer, then Doyle glanced at his younger companion.

"Were you and your dad close?" he asked. "You said he died of cancer, didn't you?"

Vale nodded.

"I still miss him," he said, quietly. "We had the same kind of sense of humour."

"Did he know what you did? What work?"

"I tried to explain it as best I could but there's a lot you can't talk about. You know that."

It was Doyle's turn to nod.

"Was that why you were close to another agent?" Vale enquired.

"What do you mean?"

"You were in a relationship with another member of the CTU."

"Relationship might be pushing it a bit," Doyle said, smiling thinly.

"But you were close?"

"Oh, yeah. We were close."

Vale glanced up the road ahead, looking for a space to park the SUV, noting the police cars that were already parked around the entrance of the building in Hatton Garden.

"Are they expecting us?" Doyle asked, as Vale manoeuvred the vehicle into a gap between an ambulance and a police car.

Vale nodded.

Doyle clambered out of the vehicle and stood on the pavement looking up at the main entrance of Boleyn Mathis. Next to the thick, black painted doors there was a brass sign on the wall that proclaimed; SAFE DEPOSIT LTD.

As Doyle was running appraising eyes over the front of the edifice a uniformed policeman approached him and he pulled out his ID, showing the constable who nodded sagely and retreated back inside the building. Vale joined him on the pavement, also glancing around.

"This only happened an hour ago," Vale said, watching as two paramedics made their way from the building carrying a stretcher.

"How many killed?" Doyle wanted to know.

"Initial reports say two. Three more were injured. All employees here."

Doyle nodded and led the way inside the building.

The interior of the place seemed disproportionately large compared to its exterior that Doyle thought looked more like a town house. It seemed to stretch back a long way once its reception area was passed. A small desk on the left-hand side of the marble trimmed entryway was spattered with blood, Doyle noted. A tarpaulin had been laid across it but the red fluid beneath had soaked through in several places. Large glass double doors stood open, leading into the next area of the building.

Vale looked up at the CCTV cameras positioned in each corner of the room.

"We need to look at the footage," he murmured to Doyle.

"Why?" the older man said. "We already know what happened."

"I want to see it," Vale insisted.

They walked on, past more uniformed policemen. The vault was just ahead.

SIXTY-SIX

The floor of the vault looked like polished marble, reflecting the cold white lights set into the low ceiling. The luminescence also reflected from the gleaming metal fronts of hundreds of safety deposit boxes. Footsteps echoed inside the cavernous room when any of the men moved.

"So, this is how the other half live?" Doyle murmured, glancing at the array of metal boxes before them. "I couldn't afford to rent one of these fucking boxes let alone ever have anything worth storing in it," he grunted, smiling.

The small, tubby, middle-aged man who was with them glanced at each of the men in turn then wiped a pudgy hand across his bald head. He was shaking slightly.

"How many boxes did they empty?" Doyle wanted to know.

"Only one," the tubby man announced.

"The one belonging to David Callahan," Vale murmured.

The tubby man nodded and pulled at the neck of his shirt as if it had suddenly become too tight and was throttling him.

"What was in it?" Doyle asked, looking at the array of boxes, one of which was hanging from its place, open to show that the contents were now missing.

"I can't tell you that," the tubby man informed him.

"The men who did this, could you identify them if you saw them again?" Vale enquired.

The tubby man nodded and again tugged at his shirt collar. He finally loosened his broad cornflower blue tie slightly.

"It's important that we know what was in the box," Doyle went on, glancing at the rows of boxes and then at the tubby man.

"It's confidential," the man told him. "Only Mr Callahan is allowed access to the contents."

"Mr Callahan has been dead for nearly thirty years," Doyle

intoned. "No one has been near that box in that time. Whatever was in there obviously wasn't that important was it?"

"Whatever it was, it was the property of Mr Callahan and I am not at liberty to divulge the nature of the contents," the tubby man exclaimed, moving towards one of the wooden chairs in the room. He sat down wearily and used a handkerchief to dab at the sweat beading on his top lip and cheeks.

"Did you know him?" Vale asked.

"My predecessor met him two or three times," the tubby man announced. "I never did."

"So why are you protecting him?" Doyle demanded.

"I'm not protecting him."

"Then tell us what was in his safety deposit box."

"It's a matter of ethics and..."

"Fuck ethics," Doyle snapped.

The tubby man swallowed hard and glanced at Vale as if for support. He didn't like the harsh tone Doyle was using.

"Did you open the box for them?" Doyle continued, sharply.

"I showed them the box they wanted. They cut it open themselves with a drill and circular saw."

"We're going to need access to your CCTV footage," Vale told the tubby man who nodded.

"The employees who were hurt or killed," Doyle said, softly. "Did they try and do anything to stop the robbery? Were they trying to be heroes? Is that why they were harmed?"

"The men who robbed us..." the tubby man began, falteringly. "They opened fire as soon as they walked in. Firing into the ceiling and the walls. They shot one of our security men in the head." The tubby man blenched. He put a hand to his mouth as if to stifle the feelings of nausea that had filled him as he recalled the shootings earlier. "He never even moved but one of them just put the gun to his head and fired." The tubby man shook his head.

"When they spoke, what kind of accents did they have?"

Doyle asked. "Russian? East European?"

"Yes. How did you know that?" the tubby man enquired.

"We know them," Doyle told him.

Vale pulled his phone from his pocket, found some photographs and held the device before the tubby man.

"Do any of these men look familiar?" he asked, watching as the tubby man ran appraising eyes over the images. He nodded and pointed to two of them.

"That was the man who shot the guard," he mumbled.

"Ivan Petriv," Vale said, glancing in Doyle's direction. "One of Gorchev's men."

Doyle turned and stood over the tubby man.

"What was in the box?" he said, quietly.

"I can't tell you, I..."

"Money? Documents? Bonds? Jewellery?" Doyle went on.

The tubby man shook his head.

"Then what was it?" Doyle snapped.

"It...it was a knife," the tubby man said, exhaling as if all the air had left his body.

Doyle frowned.

"Some kind of antique," the man continued. "About eight or nine inches long. A plain handle. No jewels on it."

"And that was it?" Doyle said. "That was all they took. That was the only thing in the box?"

The tubby man nodded.

"Have you got any photographs of it?" Vale asked.

The tubby man nodded.

"You'd better show us," Doyle urged.

SIXTY-SEVEN

"It's a misericorde," Caroline Bradley announced. She nodded to herself as she looked more closely at the photograph Doyle had presented her with.

"A knife?" Vale offered, moving closer to the desk where Caroline was sitting.

The office inside the British Museum was large and yet still looked cluttered and overburdened by the sheer volume of files, books and artefacts it contained. Doyle had a cigarette between his lips, but he hadn't lit it. He seemed content to chew on it as if it were some kind of nicotine flavoured lollipop.

"An edge-less knife," Caroline went on. "More like a spike to be honest. It was a common enough weapon during medieval times. It was used to deliver the coup de grâce to wounded knights rather than let them die in agony on the battlefield. It was thin enough to fit through the gaps in plate armour."

Doyle himself looked at the photograph again.

"If a knight was mortally wounded it was thought decent to finish him off with the misericorde. Its name is derived from the Latin word misericordia, meaning mercy. Ambrose Bierce, the American writer, once said that the misericorde was used by the foot soldier to remind the unhorsed knight that he was mortal." Caroline raised her eyebrows and smiled, as if imparting this knowledge was somehow pleasurable for her.

Doyle nodded.

"And Callahan had that in his safety deposit box," he murmured. "That was all he had."

"And, as far as we know, it had been in there for more than twenty-five years," Vale added. "Why would he keep a weapon like that locked away in a vault?"

Caroline looked more closely at the photograph, studying

the outlines and silhouettes of the dagger as closely as she could.

"So, this was stolen?" she murmured, her gaze travelling slowly over the outlines of the weapon.

"By guys working for Callahan as far as we know," Doyle informed her.

"I thought this was classified," Vale interrupted.

"Who the fuck is she going to tell?" Doyle snapped at his younger companion. "And we need all the help we can get."

"Does that knife look valuable to you?" Vale enquired; his gaze fixed on Caroline as she continued to inspect the photograph.

"It's difficult to say without an actual physical examination," she murmured. "The sheer age of it would give it some value to a collector or to a museum but it doesn't seem to have any jewels and it's made from normal steel as far as I can tell, so I don't think it's unduly valuable in itself."

"So why steal it?" Doyle muttered.

"It must have some value to the man who wanted it," Caroline offered. "He obviously considers it worth enough to have it stolen."

"Where would Callahan have got something like that in the first place?" Vale enquired.

"Again, it's hard to say without an actual physical examination..." Caroline mused.

"In your considered opinion," Vale told her.

"It doesn't look familiar," she said. "It isn't some well-known artefact that's recognisable to every historian and medievalist on the planet."

"Not like the book," Doyle interjected.

Caroline and Vale both turned and looked at him.

"First Callahan has the book, the grimoire, stolen," Doyle went on. "Then this dagger. Both historical artefacts."

"And both from the same period," Caroline added.

"Are they linked in some way?" Doyle persisted.

"Not as far as I know," Caroline said, almost apologetically.

"But as I told you, I'm not an expert in this field."

"You're more of an expert than anyone else we know," Doyle told her, smiling. "Whatever you can tell us is helpful."

Caroline smiled.

"Callahan had a stained-glass window brought from Machecoul to his home in Ireland," Doyle said, quietly. "He paid big money for that. He also paid someone to steal a book that we know was, at one time, hidden underneath the same chapel where the stained-glass window came from."

"So how does that tie in with the stolen dagger?" Vale wanted to know.

"Machecoul belonged to Gilles de Rais," Caroline said. "He knew the man who wrote the grimoire found beneath his chapel, he believed the things he read in that book. As a knight of France, he would have owned a dagger like the one stolen."

"So that knife that was taken, the one that Callahan had been hiding for nearly thirty years in that safety deposit box, could have belonged to Gilles de Rais?" Doyle said, flatly.

The silence inside the room was deafening.

SIXTY-EIGHT

The blonde was young.
The youngest of the two girls.
She was barely nineteen.
The brown-haired girl was older by at least five years. More experienced probably but, even so, the blonde was more confident. More uninhibited. Much more comfortable with her nakedness. As he watched them both on the bed his attention was drawn repeatedly to the young blonde. Although, he mused, in a month or so the term blonde wouldn't be so apt. The dye had almost grown out of her long hair, only the ends were the platinum blonde she must have once sported everywhere. Just seven or eight inches of her sleek locks still held that colour with any lustre.

She rolled over, glancing at him briefly before returning her attention to the darker-haired girl.

She looked up, brushing some strands of her own long mane from her mouth, lifting her head slightly as the blonde kissed her gently, tenderly.

He watched them more intently, pulling at his penis as if it was dough, massaging it with his fingers, sometimes giving the same attention to his swollen testicles.

The brunette looked over at him now, kneeling up on the bed, shaking slightly. There were still red marks on her shoulders where he'd held her tightly as he'd driven deep inside her, letting the blonde watch then summoning her to join them. Instructing her what she should do as if he was a director on a film set.

Now he was content to observe.

He told the blonde to get on all fours.

"Spread your legs," he added, and she did as he instructed because, as she reasoned, he was paying well for the privilege. He reached around to the small table beside him and grabbed

257

a thick, black dildo that was at least ten inches long. Attached to a harness, the strap-on was a formidable looking accessory and he threw it onto the bed, smiling.

"Who do you want to put it on?" the blonde asked, looking down at the strap-on warily.

"You," he said, flatly.

As he spoke the word, the dark-haired girl shuddered slightly.

Both she and the man watched as the little blonde slipped her legs through the harness and pulled it into position, checking that the dildo was firmly attached to the leather that chafed against her inner thighs. When it was in place she kneeled up, displaying the fake penis as if it had been her own erection, she was so proud of.

He settled himself more comfortably in the chair at the bottom of the bed and eyed each girl in turn, pulling more intensely at his penis now, feeling it swell and grow in his hand.

"Suck it, you fucking whore," he said to the dark-haired girl who nodded and crawled closer to the blonde, finally taking the tip of the dildo in her mouth, allowing her tongue to play over the end of it. The blonde pushed her hips forward slightly and the long thick phallus touched the back of the dark-haired girl's throat. She pulled back slightly, gagging as the rubber scraped her tonsils.

"I said suck it," he snapped, watching as the dark-haired girl wiped her mouth with the back of one hand. She hesitated then returned her attention to the fake penis, placing her lips around the tip once more.

"You need this," he rasped, hurling a bottle of lubricant onto the bed with such force that it struck the blonde on the shoulder.

She looked warily at him but said nothing. Instead, she squeezed the bottle, coaxing some of the thick white lubricant from the bottle into the palm of her hand. She then applied it to the dildo, smearing the fluid from top to bottom of the implement.

As he watched, his penis grew stiffer.

"Turn around," he said, pointing at the dark-haired girl. "She's going to fuck you while I watch."

He smiled thinly at the blonde, getting to his feet and taking a couple of steps closer to the bed. When he was alongside the blonde, he picked up the bottle of lubricant and upended it over the dark-haired girl's bottom, allowing the liquid to flow between her buttocks.

"Get her ready," he hissed, his face inches from the blonde.

He watched as she spread the lubricant over the brunette's anus, massaging the cold liquid into that tightest orifice and then dripping more of it onto the dildo that was jutting from between her legs.

As he rubbed his own penis, feeling it stiffen fully in his hand, he slapped the blonde around the back of the head.

"Now," David Callahan gasped to the youngest girl. "Fuck her until she screams."

SIXTY-NINE

Gideon Vale pulled at the knot on his tie as he entered the office.

As he walked in, he nodded in the direction of Mark Granger then towards Jonathan Parker who was seated in one of the large chairs facing Granger's desk.

"Take a seat, Vale," Granger told him, his gaze still fixed on his computer screen, eyes seemingly glued to the images on his monitor.

Vale did as he was asked, nodding again at Parker.

"Where's Doyle?" the older man asked.

"I don't pick him up for another hour," Vale announced.

"Does he know you're here?" Parker enquired.

"Is that important?" Granger murmured.

"I think it is," Parker said. "He might not be too happy if he knew we were discussing him without his knowledge."

"Doyle's feelings are not our concern," Granger muttered, an edge to his voice. "I'm only interested in his suitability for this assignment and how he performs during it."

"I didn't think his abilities were in question," Parker said, flatly.

"What do you think, Vale?" Granger asked. "What's it been like working with him?"

"He's very direct," Vale said. "I can't say I approve of all his methods."

"He gets the job done, that's all that matters," Parker said, a slight smile on his lips.

"That might have been the case in your day, Parker, but there are other factors to be taken into consideration now," Granger exclaimed. "This department has no place for maverick behaviour. If Doyle's such a loose cannon, then he might endanger others as well as himself."

"He's certainly unpredictable," Vale offered.

"Is he unstable?" Granger wanted to know.

"That's hard to say," Vale said.

"You know his state of mind," snapped Parker. "You saw the results of his psych evaluation."

"Being in a combat situation is different," Granger went on. "He might not be able to cope now. He could crack."

"Oh, come on," Parker protested. "At least he has combat experience. Vale doesn't."

Vale raised his eyebrows.

"You watch him closely," Granger said to Vale. "Any signs of a problem, I want to know."

"Vale's his partner, not his carer," Parker said, irritably.

An uneasy silence descended, broken finally by Granger. He pushed a file across the desk towards Vale who opened it, glancing at the contents. There were several photographs inside and also a number of bank statements and other pieces of paper. Vale considered each one carefully.

"David Callahan had just over two million pounds in that bank in Piccadilly when he disappeared," Granger said, watching Vale poring over the documents.

"It could be a target," Parker added.

"Like the safety deposit box that the dagger was stolen from," Granger went on.

"If Callahan needs money, surely he wouldn't be stupid enough to steal it from a bank where he had an account," Vale said, smiling. "He'd know we'd be expecting that."

Granger didn't appear to share the younger man's amusement.

"Who knows how his mind works? Besides, he had more in there than just cash. His wife owned over eight million pounds worth of antique jewellery, acquired from all around the world. That's in there too," he said, flatly. "I'm telling you to be prepared. Doyle too."

"Why can't you just seize it?" Vale asked.

"Because as long as it's there, it's bait and it might just draw Callahan out."

There was a long silence.

"What's the significance of the dagger?" Parker wanted to know, breaking the silence.

"We have no idea," Vale admitted. He repeated the conversation they'd had at the British Museum but, apart from that, he could only shrug. "Doyle thinks it's related to Callahan's obsession with Gilles de Rais."

It was Granger's turn to raise his eyebrows. It was a gesture of scepticism and disdain.

"I don't really care what Doyle thinks," he said, dismissively. "All I care about is that he follows orders."

Vale looked expressionlessly at his superior. Granger was looking at his monitor again, his brow slightly furrowed. "You can go now," he murmured, glancing briefly at Vale who got to his feet.

"Do I continue to report to both of you?" the younger man wanted to know.

"Until further notice," Granger said, while Parker merely nodded. He too got to his feet, following Vale out of the office. As the two men emerged into the corridor beyond, Parker reached out and gently grabbed Vale's forearm, trying to slow him down.

"Listen to what Doyle has to say," he said. "He knows what he's doing. He can help you."

Vale nodded.

"Do you think he's unstable?" the younger man asked.

Parker smiled.

"I always did," he muttered.

SEVENTY

As the thick dildo slammed deeply into her stretched anus, the brunette girl gripped the sheet more tightly, trying to brace herself as the fake phallus drove hard into her.

She felt as if most of the lower part of her body had been dipped in fire, the pain and the sensations spreading up from her battered anus as the thrusting of the strap-on became more urgent.

Standing beside the bed watching the performance, David Callahan was rubbing his stiff penis, gazing intently at the brunette and her quivering body. Occasionally he would stroke the neck and back of the little blonde who was still furiously driving her hips forward, ensuring that the strap-on penetrated as deeply as possible into the tight, puckered hole of the brunette. Occasionally she would slow down or stop for a second, perhaps wondering if she was to suffer the ordeal next. But Callahan's hand on her back or bottom would then force her to continue.

The brunette was whimpering softly as each deep thrust sent fresh waves of pain coursing through her. Callahan reached across and pulled her hair, jerking her sagging head upright so that he could look more closely at the tortured expression on her face.

He could see one single tear trickling down her left cheek and he smiled thinly, rubbing himself more intently, forcing his swollen tip closer to her open mouth.

The blonde slowed down again for a moment, sweat beading on her back such was her exertion.

Callahan shot her a furious glance and she resumed the steady thrusts.

When the brunette let out a long wail of pain Callahan straightened up, glancing down to see that several droplets of bright blood had dripped onto the previously pristine cotton sheets. He glanced at her anus and saw that the dildo had indeed torn the tender flesh around that tightest of openings.

Again, the blonde hesitated, also seeing the slowly widening fissure in the puckered flesh, watching the blood well from it as the strap-on slammed deeper.

"Keep going," Callahan hissed at her.

The brunette was crying softly now and, again, Callahan grabbed her hair and pulled her head up so he could look into her eyes. He was smiling crookedly.

"Are you enjoying that you fucking whore?" he rasped, the grin stuck on his features like some kind of rictus. "There's a fine line between pain and pleasure you know. Have you come to that line yet?" His grin broadened.

The brunette shuddered as the dildo was driven deeply into her anus again and, at last, the blonde finished her movements and edged back slightly, the jutting strap-on glistening with lubricant, blood and tiny traces of faeces.

"I didn't tell you to stop," Callahan hissed at the blonde, his eyes blazing.

"No, please," the brunette gasped, reaching back with one hand to gently touch her battered anus. When she pulled the fingers away, she too saw the blood that stained them, and she sucked in a quivering breath.

"Both of you kneel in front of me," Callahan snapped, rubbing his penis more furiously now.

The blonde moved more quickly, perching on the edge of the bed, her head tilted backwards. The brunette joined her, moving a little more slowly, trying to cope with the pain that had enveloped her lower body as surely as if she'd been dipped in fire. Callahan gripped the blonde's hair and yanked her head back more sharply, forcing her mouth to drop open slightly. It was towards that glistening orifice that he pushed his throbbing penis.

Grunting loudly, he spurted his fluid into her open mouth, watching as most of the pearly liquid found its target. The other spurts hit the blonde on her chin or cheek. She gagged slightly, surprised at the sheer volume of ejaculate.

"Keep it in your mouth," Callahan hissed.

As the last spasms rocked his body, he pushed the two girls heads together.

"Kiss her," he snapped, glaring at the blonde.

Their lips brushed gently and then he saw some of the white fluid dribbling thickly from the mouth of the blonde into that of the brunette. Callahan took a step backwards, enjoying the spectacle. He stood there for a moment longer then turned his back on the two girls.

The blonde was already undoing the strap-on, anxious to take it off. She looked at her companion and saw that the brunette was rocking gently back and forth, her eyes screwed tight shut. Blood was spreading, soaking slowly into the sheet beneath where she sat. The blonde wiped her mouth with the back of her hand and dropped the dildo and its harness on the bed.

Callahan gazed at them for a moment longer then turned his back.

"Now get your clothes and get out of here," he said, evenly.

SEVENTY-ONE

oyle took a final drag on the cigarette and flicked the butt out of the half-open window.

Vale looked at him disapprovingly and returned his attention to his phone.

Doyle noticed that his younger companion was gazing at the device and sighed.

"Checking your Facebook?" he said, smiling, cryptically. "Seeing how popular you are?"

Vale shook his head dismissively.

"Or are you tweeting?" Doyle persisted. Again, he smiled, his gaze fixed on the building across the street.

The facade of the bank in St. James's Square wasn't exactly imposing but that was the idea. Understatement and anonymity were two of the watchwords for Grayson and Bellsher private banking facilities. They'd been operating on those principals since 1864 and it had served them well. The building looked as if it was hiding in one corner of the square and Doyle watched as a motorbike dispatch rider dismounted and walked towards the main entrance of the building, a small package gripped in his gloved hand.

"Social media is important," Vale said, still gazing at his phone.

"If you've got no life or if you're a so-called fucking celebrity," Doyle grunted. "They're the only fuckers who use it."

"It can be a powerful tool."

"It's used by tools."

"Just because you don't understand something you don't have to ridicule it, you know. And anyway, I'm not on Facebook, not that it's any of your business."

"Instagram?" Doyle grinned.

Vale exhaled deeply and stretched his arms in front of him.

266

His shoulders were stiff and so was his neck.

"How long do we have to sit here like this?" he groaned.

"This is part of the job," Doyle told him. "A big part."

"The police should be doing it, not us. We could even do the surveillance using drones. It wouldn't be the first time."

"Fucking technology."

"It's designed to make your life easier. Welcome to the twenty-first century, Doyle. Just because you can't handle technology doesn't make it a bad thing. Everyone else seems to manage."

The two men eyed each other for a moment then Doyle broke the silence.

"You can get out and have a walk around if you want to," he said. "Stretch your legs. I'll keep my eyes open."

"That's thoughtful of you."

"I just thought it would get you out of the fucking car for a few minutes, so I didn't have to hear you whining about surveillance."

Vale shook his head.

"I might go and get us a coffee or something," he mused.

"Good idea. Get me a doughnut, will you?"

"They're bad for you. How the fuck have you stayed alive so long? You smoke, you drink, and you eat rubbish food."

"I'll take that over an alfalfa wrap," Doyle grinned.

Vale glanced over at the entrance to the private bank.

"It doesn't look very impressive does it?" he murmured.

"Appearances are deceptive," Doyle told him. "These fuckers make Coutts look like an Oxfam shop."

"Coutts?"

"The rich people's bank. Google it."

"Callahan certainly moved in privileged circles, didn't he?"

"He made a fortune running guns and other ordnance. He could afford to. He even sold tanks to some dictator in Liberia at one point."

"Why was he so interested in medieval history?"

"When we find him, we'll have to ask him," Doyle said,

quietly.

"Do you think we will find him?"

"I know we will."

Vale hesitated a moment longer then dug in his pocket for his wallet.

"I'm going to get that coffee," he announced. "I saw a place around the corner."

"Take your time."

"I'm sure you'll tell me all the excitement I've missed when I get back," he sighed, pushing open the door of the SUV.

"Wait a minute," Doyle said, glancing at his watch and then towards the bank again.

Vale hesitated.

"How long does it take to deliver a package?" Doyle mused. "Two minutes? Walk in. Get a signature. Walk out? That dispatch rider went into the bank more than five minutes ago."

"Perhaps he can't find who he's looking for," Vale offered.

Doyle didn't look convinced. When a silver-grey BMW pulled up in front of the bank and remained there, the engine idling, he sat up more stiffly in his seat, his gaze flickering over the front of the building once more. Almost unconsciously he reached inside his jacket, touching the butt of the Beretta 92F in the shoulder holster there.

Vale saw his growing agitation and pulled the door of the SUV shut gently, sliding behind the steering wheel once again.

A moment later the dispatch rider came striding out of the bank, swung himself onto his bike and roared away.

Doyle slid down in his seat slightly.

When the silver-grey BMW pulled away from the kerb he reached for his cigarettes and lit another one, glancing at Vale.

"Two sugars in the coffee, please," he said, smiling.

SEVENTY-TWO

David Callahan poured himself another drink and stood close to the window, peering out at the perfectly landscaped gardens of Maitland Hall.

One of the team of gardeners who kept the grounds immaculate was trundling up and down on a large mower, manicuring the lawns.

Another of the men was busily pruning the rose bushes that had been planted so densely in beds leading up to the terrace at the rear of the building.

Callahan watched them for a moment then turned back into the room, taking another sip of his drink. The sun filled the room with bright shafts of light, motes of dust turning lazily in them as Callahan glanced around him, his mind somewhere else.

He had never been a patient man. It had never been his way. But now he knew that he must find that quality somewhere deep inside himself. He had to find a way to maintain his composure while he waited.

And waited.

The time was coming, he knew that only too well but he didn't want to wait. He wanted that time to be soon. Even better, to be now.

He finished what was left in the glass and wandered out of the room, heading down the short corridor he emerged into, his footfalls muffled by the thick, expensive carpet that covered the floor. He passed through another door and this time found himself on bare stone floor. It stretched away before him towards the rear of the house and Callahan walked on, finally coming to another wooden partition.

This one was locked.

Callahan stood before it for a second then reached into his pocket and retrieved a small key. He pushed it into the lock, turned it and stepped through into the area beyond.

The stairway that led down from the door was bare stone and Callahan's footsteps echoed inside the narrow confines. He made his way slowly down the steps towards another heavier door which he also unlocked using a key on the same ring. As the door swung open, he was aware of an odour of dampness and neglect that had struck him the first time he descended into the subterranean chamber.

He slapped the light switch and a bulb fizzed into life, spilling some dull yellow illumination into the otherwise stifling blackness.

Whether the large underground room had once been used as a wine cellar he had no idea, but it had not been maintained as well as the upper floors of the house and in several places bare brick wall was visible through rents in the plaster. There was mould in a couple of the corners, an indication of the dampness of the room and somewhere, water was dripping. Callahan knew that there had once been a stream that ran through the grounds of the house and he wondered if that had contributed to the moisture here below the main structure.

He walked slowly across the room. It was bare but for a large wooden table to his right. Callahan made his way towards the far wall, grateful for the dull light given off by the bulb above.

He stopped a few feet from the wall, arms folded before him contemplatively, his gaze moving slowly over the objects that lay against the wall.

There were four children, ranging in age from five to fourteen.

All were heavily bound and gagged, but the thick cloths that had been pushed into their mouths to mask their cries were hidden from view by the hoods they all wore over their heads.

It had been easier than he'd thought to take them.

All had been snatched within the space of three days.

He'd been careful to ensure that each of them had been taken from a location no closer than twenty miles from his house. The police would come eventually, he knew that, and he was prepared for it. But by then it wouldn't matter.

One of them heard Callahan approaching and they began to move about frantically, bumping into the other figures around them. Callahan could hear the muffled sounds rising from inside the hood and one of the others briefly joined in the frenzied shuffling. Callahan merely stood watching them, knowing that they could never escape. The bonds had been tied too tightly and too securely. They would remain here until he was ready.

They were fed twice a day, taken individually to different parts of the subterranean vault and forced to ingest the sustenance that was brought to them. Callahan knew he had to keep them alive until the time came. Until they could serve their purpose.

He needed one more and then he was ready.

It could begin.

SEVENTY-THREE

The sun was high in the sky as Gideon Vale walked slowly back towards St. James's Square.

The heat had been growing steadily throughout the morning and now, the blazing orb suspended in the cloudless blue heavens had reached its zenith and the temperature had risen to barely tolerable heights. Vale paused, setting down the cardboard tray he was carrying on the windowsill of a nearby shop. He could already feel sweat beading on his forehead and at the back of his neck. He wiped it away and then picked up the coffees again.

He glanced into the window, looking at the clothes on display there. A nice navy-blue jacket he mused. Some shoes that might go with a pair of trousers he'd bought the week before. Vale smiled to himself and continued walking, not wanting to take too long on his little excursion. Doyle would only complain if he had to wait.

He always found something to complain about.

Vale rounded the corner into the square, glancing across towards one of the entrances to see a couple of young women entering. One was leading a pug on a pink leather leash, the unfortunate animal finding the heat of the day more difficult to cope with than any of the humans around it. Vale eyed the two women, aware that the one in denim cut-offs had seen him looking.

She waved as she and her companion disappeared into the green expanse beyond the wrought-iron fence and bushes. The girl with the pug picking the animal up as if she was aware that it had suffered enough physical exertion for the day.

Vale walked on, back towards the parked SUV, paying little attention to the white Peugeot 308 GTi that had pulled up about twenty yards further away.

As he drew closer to the SUV, he could see Doyle slumped

in the passenger seat, one foot propped against the dashboard, his gaze fixed on the bank nestled in one corner of the square.

Vale pulled open the driver's side door and climbed in.

Doyle shot him a brief glance then returned his attention to the front of the bank.

"One latte and a doughnut," Vale announced, pushing the items towards the older man.

Doyle sipped at his drink then took a bite of the doughnut as Vale settled himself behind the steering wheel and lowered his window, the heat inside the vehicle intolerable.

"There's no breeze," Vale exclaimed, fanning himself with one hand.

"I hate the heat," Doyle murmured.

"You hate everything," Vale reminded him.

Doyle smiled thinly, watching a tall man with a bald head enter the bank. He stepped aside to allow an older couple to leave. The older man was having trouble walking even with the aid of a stick, his wife supporting him as they made their way along the pavement away from the bank.

"Is that what it comes to?" Doyle murmured, watching the old couple. "Getting old. Waiting to die?"

"Cheerful as usual," Vale muttered.

"I hate getting old," Doyle said.

"It beats the alternative."

"Maybe Callahan is right about wanting to live forever."

"Do you believe that?"

"Why not? I wouldn't mind living forever."

"But all your loved ones would die. You'd see people you loved dying while you lived on. Wouldn't you hate that?"

"No."

"Wouldn't you have your dad back again if you could?"

Vale considered the question for a moment then nodded.

"I still miss him," he said, quietly. "I only used to go home two or three times a year after I moved to London but even now I miss our little chats. I could talk to him about anything. He was more like a mate than my dad."

"That's nice. Not everyone has that kind of relationship with their parents."

Doyle took another sip of his coffee, washing down the chunk of doughnut he was chewing.

Two bank staff walked out of the main door; Doyle assumed they were on their lunch break. He watched them as they wandered across the street and out of sight.

"Why didn't you just retire?" Vale asked. "Why come back to this?"

"Retire?" Doyle grunted. "I'm not that fucking old. Besides, you need money to retire. I'd go crazy if I just had to sit around all day doing nothing. I'm never retiring."

He swallowed more of his coffee.

And then the alarm went off.

SEVENTY-FOUR

As the strident sound cut through the heavy air, Doyle turned and looked in its direction.

It was definitely coming from the bank.

He sat bolt upright; his gaze now fixed on the building jammed in the corner of St. James's Square.

"Is it their alarm?" Vale murmured, also peering towards the main entrance.

Doyle nodded; his heart thudding harder against his ribs now.

When he heard the gunshots, it hammered even harder.

The sound was unmistakable. At least it was to a man like Doyle who had heard the retort of a weapon so often. The fire-cracker explosion of a gun sounded three times, the noise reverberating across the stillness of the square. Barely had the retorts died away than two men walked slowly from the main entrance.

"What do we do?" Vale asked, an edge to his voice.

"Start the engine," Doyle told him, his gaze never leaving the bank and the two men who had just emerged.

Both were dressed in dark clothes, even down to the leather gloves they wore. Both were heavyset, powerfully built men and the two of them were wearing masks. One was carrying a large black holdall and it was he who broke into a run, hurrying towards the edge of the pavement, looking around anxiously.

The sound of the alarm was suddenly eclipsed by the roar of a car engine as a vehicle came hurtling down King Street and screamed across towards the front of the bank. The two dark-clad men both moved towards it, but Doyle was already out of the SUV, dragging the automatic from its shoulder holster, swinging it up into position.

One of the dark-clad men saw him and turned in his

direction.

Doyle saw him pull the MP5K from inside his jacket and fire.

Bullets drilled into the car next to Doyle and he hurled himself to one side as the 9mm slugs tore into the bodywork, blasting a wing mirror away.

Doyle used the car as cover, knelt up and squeezed off five shots in the direction of the armed man and the waiting car.

Two of them screamed up off the tarmac, one struck the driver's side of the car and another two, more by luck than judgement, blew the front tyres out.

Doyle fired again, aware now that the driver of the car was scrambling out, knowing that his vehicle was incapacitated. He and the two dark-clad men froze for a moment and then the driver ran towards a green Skoda Octavia vRS that was moving slowly through the square, the driver looking for a parking space. Doyle saw the man drag open the driver's door of the Skoda. He could see the woman who was behind the wheel, could see her screaming and lashing out at the man who was trying to drag her from where she sat.

And now the other two men were running towards the Skoda and one of them was pulling at one of the rear doors, trying to clamber inside as his companion fought with the screaming woman.

As the back door was torn open, the woman struggled even more manfully and now Doyle realised why.

He saw the baby on the back seat, strapped into the black booster chair. He watched as one of the men dragged the chair free of its straps and hurled it into the road, the baby still inside it. The woman's screams intensified and now, as the first man finally succeeded in dragging her from behind the wheel, she scrambled towards her child, desperate to reach the stricken baby. The three men piled into the Skoda, the back wheels spinning as the driver stepped hard on the accelerator, wanting only to be away from this place now. He missed the woman and her baby by inches as he drove past.

Doyle swung the Beretta up again, preparing to fire, but was suddenly aware of the black SUV screeching to a halt beside him. Vale leaned over and pushed the passenger door open and Doyle didn't hesitate. He clambered in and, as he slammed the door shut, Vale stepped on the gas and sent the SUV streaking after the fleeing Skoda.

They roared past the screaming woman who was trying to pull her baby from the remains of the car seat that had been thrown into the road.

Ahead, the Skoda turned into Duke of York street, catching a parked car and scraping the paint from its wing. Vale followed, his eyes fixed on the fleeing vehicle, his shoulders slightly hunched as he gripped the wheel tightly.

The Skoda shot left, roaring along Jermyn Street, narrowly avoiding two pedestrians who were crossing.

One of them gestured angrily towards the green car and many heads turned in the direction of the speeding vehicle as it screamed down the narrow thoroughfare. Vale followed, manoeuvring the SUV expertly as it powered along. Next to him, Doyle checked his pockets for spare magazines and found two. He lowered the passenger side window slightly, wondering when his chance to get a shot at the Skoda might come.

The SUV was no more than ten yards behind the fleeing car and Vale was careful to maintain the distance.

From his vantage point he could clearly see the man in the back of the car who was now kneeling up on the back seat, something metallic gripped in his hands.

He blew out most of the back window with the first blast of the shotgun, glass spraying out onto the road.

The discharge missed the SUV, punching a hole instead in the windscreen of a parked car.

Vale gripped the steering wheel more tightly, gritting his teeth as the thunderous retort reverberated in his ears. The man in the back of the car worked the slide of the automatic shotgun and fired again, the recoil slamming the weapon back against his shoulder. That too missed the SUV but blasted in several glass panels of a nearby phone box.

Doyle ducked involuntarily as the second blast came, shoving his right arm out of the open passenger window. He squeezed off three shots.

Two hit the back of the Skoda, thudding into the boot.

Before he could fire again, the green vehicle lurched violently to the right and Doyle watched in bewilderment, not quite believing what the driver was attempting.

Still moving at about thirty, he guided the Skoda into the entrance of the Piccadilly Arcade.

SEVENTY-FIVE

"**W**hat's he doing?" Vale snarled.

"Escaping," Doyle snapped. "Follow him."

Vale glanced briefly at his companion and then twisted the steering wheel, the SUV hurtling towards the entrance of the arcade, bright sparks flying from its sides as it roared into the narrow thoroughfare.

Ahead, the Skoda was speeding through the arcade, the driver oblivious to pedestrians who were diving desperately for cover in the shop doorways, terrified by the sudden appearance of the vehicle.

People inside the shops looked out in horror as the cars tore up the narrow thoroughfare.

The sound of the engines, amplified by the acoustics inside the low-ceilinged arcade, was deafening. Doyle steadied himself, knowing that, for precious seconds at least, the Skoda would be forced to travel in a dead straight line. He leaned sideways, gripping the 92F firmly, one hand supporting the butt as he aimed. He pumped the trigger frantically, empty shell cases flying into the air as the SUV sped on. Doyle kept firing, the slide on the Beretta finally flying back to signal that the gun was empty.

Doyle grabbed a fresh clip, ejected the old one and slammed the new one into the butt, firing almost immediately, the sound mingling with the cacophony of noise already filling the arcade.

And then the Skoda was bursting free of the arcade, slamming into two pedestrians as it exploded into Piccadilly.

One of them was knocked into the street, the other catapulted into the air by the massive impact.

Vale managed to avoid them both as he guided the SUV free of the entrance, keeping control as he turned hard left, not allowing the Skoda to escape. It was already roaring along the wide expanse of Piccadilly, colliding with a taxi as it shot away. Vale swerved into oncoming traffic briefly, desperate not to allow the Skoda out of his sight.

There were traffic lights just up ahead, but the fleeing green car showed no sign of abiding by the sequence of colours showing.

Red had just begun to flame when the Skoda rampaged through. Vale followed, sweat beading now on his forehead.

Doyle watched as the other vehicle sped onwards. On the pavements on either side of the road pedestrians were standing to watch the pursuit, shocked and frightened by the sight of the two cars barrelling along Piccadilly. Some drivers, unaware of what was happening around them, merely looked on in bewilderment as first the Skoda and then the SUV tore past them.

And now another sound began to fill the air to join that of roaring engines. It was the sound of sirens.

Police cars suddenly joined the chase from both sides as if they'd been magically summoned by some huge invisible force. Doyle saw the first one clip the side of the Skoda, causing both vehicles to skid but the Skoda driver recovered first, forcing his car along the road.

The police car lost control, spinning across the street and slamming into the window of a cafe. Doyle glanced briefly behind to see the huge plate glass partition shatter and fall under the impact.

He saw the other marked car ease in only a foot or so behind the speeding Skoda, chasing it down towards The Ritz hotel, through another set of lights and a chorus of blaring hooters and squealing brakes.

Doyle saw someone in the back seat of the Skoda rise into view, saw them swing a weapon into sight.

He realised that it was a Kalashnikov.

The barrel flamed, bullets tearing across the bonnet and windscreen of the pursuing police car.

The driver was hit three times, slammed back against his seat by the impact of the high-calibre slugs. The third shot blasted off most of his bottom jaw, a confetti of blood, bone and teeth filling the car briefly as he pitched sideways, the police car going out of control. It swerved violently across the road, slamming into an oncoming bus.

The noise was deafening, and Vale winced as he saw the carnage.

He drove on, desperate not to allow the Skoda to escape, seeing that the driver was now turning right again. Vale followed, pressing down harder on the accelerator as the Skoda turned.

It took him a second to realise it was turning into a one-way street.

SEVENTY-SIX

That was Vale's first thought as he saw the traffic flooding from Berkeley Street.

He dragged hard on the wheel, narrowly avoiding a car that was crossing the junction, the driver banging on his hooter as Vale swept by.

Other vehicles joined in the cacophony of blaring as both the Skoda and the SUV

hurtled up the narrow thoroughfare

Again, pedestrians leapt for cover as the two vehicles roared along the pavement, two or three people dashing into the road to escape the oncoming cars.

If the Skoda driver saw the scaffolding up ahead then he certainly made no attempt to avoid it. The green car struck the supporting aluminium poles, scattering them like giant toothpicks. Part of the wooden platform they supported came crashing down, a portion of it slamming down onto the rear of the Skoda. Vale drove over the planks, keeping the SUV only a few yards behind the fleeing car, sticking as close to it as he dared as it continued along the pavement.

Doyle braced himself in his seat, his gaze also fixed on the speeding Skoda. He could clearly see the man on the back seat, and he could also see the AK-47 that he was wielding. Doyle knew that if the man opened up on them from such close range they were fucked. He gripped the Beretta more tightly in his fist, ready to get off more shots first should it come to that.

The Skoda swerved violently, skidding into the road for a moment, but Vale held the SUV on the pavement, accelerating slightly to get alongside the green car. Doyle saw his chance and, as the two vehicles drew level, he fired off three more shots.

One of them blasted in a side window of the Skoda.

Another punched a hole in the passenger side door and the third screamed off the roof.

The driver of the green car also accelerated, guiding the Skoda towards the end of the street and the open expanse of Berkeley Square.

Even over the roaring of the engines and the screeching of the tyres, Doyle could hear more sirens now and he glanced ahead to see that there were several flashing blue lights approaching from the far end of Berkeley Square. Vale also heard them, pressing down harder on the accelerator as he swung the SUV back onto the road, ready to follow the Skoda as it turned into the square.

But, ahead of them, the Skoda driver suddenly floored the accelerator. The car shot forward at incredible speed, hurtling across the traffic lights and missing a van by inches. The green vehicle slammed into the metal railings around Berkeley Square, flattened them and shot across the grass, sending occupants of the park scattering. The rear wheels skidded on the slippery surface, but the driver retained control of the vehicle and drove on.

Vale didn't hesitate. He pressed down on the gas and sent the SUV speeding after the Skoda, roaring over the well-manicured grass, knocking a wooden bench flying as he accelerated in pursuit of the Skoda.

Doyle gripped the Beretta more tightly, aware that Vale was gaining on the Skoda, moving closer and closer.

He rammed the speeding car, the jolt shaking them, the impact causing part of the Skoda's back bumper to come away. Portions of shattered back light also skittered onto the gravel pathway they were driving over and now Vale coaxed greater speed from the black vehicle, guiding it up alongside the fleeing Skoda.

Doyle fired again.

Two of the bullets hit the man in the back seat and he was hurled backwards, blood spraying from two wounds in his throat and shoulder. But Doyle saw the man in the passenger seat grab the dropped AK-47 and, seconds later, the barrel of that assault rifle was shoved out of the window and Doyle saw the black maw yawning menacingly in his direction.

He slammed in a fresh magazine and pumped the trigger again, the retorts thunderous inside the car.

Vale hit the Skoda broadside, sending it skewing across the grass, obliterating a bench that it struck.

The driver of the Skoda managed to keep control for a moment longer as the two vehicles hurtled, side by side, for the far end of the park, roaring towards the railings.

They slammed into them, obliterating two motorbikes parked close to the metal partition. Vale hit the brakes to prevent the SUV colliding with an oncoming car and, as he did, Doyle fired again, shot after shot smashing into the green car.

But the AK-47 also flamed, bullets ripping across the front of the SUV, two of them puncturing a front tyre.

Both Vale and Doyle knew what was coming next.

The Skoda swerved violently, cutting across the SUV and roaring towards Mount Street but the SUV careened on at breakneck speed, Vale struggling to control it but failing. It slammed into the kerb, catching the tail end of a white Porsche parked outside the front of Morton's Club.

Doyle covered his face as best he could as the impact came.

The SUV jack-knifed, the rear end swinging up so that it somersaulted, crashing through the front window of the club.

Glass sprayed inwards, showering diners and drinkers and the SUV was left on its roof, smoke and steam rising from it.

Of the Skoda, there was no sign.

SEVENTY-SEVEN

Sirens.
More fucking sirens.
Always sirens.

Doyle opened his eyes slowly, partly due to the fact that blood had covered most of his face and the congealed red liquid was almost sealing his lids.

He reached up with one hand and wiped some of the blood away, aware that he was feeling pain from his lower back and also from his right shoulder. He managed to undo his seat belt and push open the door of the SUV, not quite realising what had happened. Only as the door swung open did it strike Doyle that the vehicle was upside down. He tumbled from the SUV onto the pavement, vaguely aware that several uniformed figures were running towards him. There were police cars and ambulances parked nearby.

Always an ambulance.

Doyle stood up, felt the nausea and giddiness hit him like a wave and he dropped to his knees again, the pain from his shoulder growing more intense. He could smell petrol and glanced back to see that the fuel tank of the SUV had ruptured, and the fluid was spilling across the road.

As the first of the paramedics reached him, he looked back towards the wrecked SUV and saw that Vale was still motionless behind the wheel. Even as another paramedic was trying to get him to lay down on the cold concrete, Doyle could see policemen and more emergency personnel trying to release Vale from the black vehicle.

Another wave of nausea hit Doyle, accompanied by an overwhelming feeling of faintness that he could not stave off.

As Vale was pulled from the SUV, Doyle passed out.

When he woke again the sirens were still cutting through the air, but the wail was much less intense than before and it took Doyle a moment or two to realise the reason for that was that he was now lying in a hospital bed.

The sirens were coming from outside the building, dying away into the distance as the ambulance sped away on another mission of mercy.

Doyle tried to sit up, wincing as he felt the stiffness in his lower body and shoulder. One of his hands was heavily strapped and when he tried to flex his fingers, he found it was impossible. He let out a weary breath and muttered something to himself, blinking myopically as he looked around the room, trying to make out his surroundings.

The room he was in was small but looked more like an apartment in a boutique hotel than a place designed to treat the sick and injured. Lit only by a couple of low wattage bulbs on either side of the bed, the room was like an oasis of calm within the busy hospital.

But which hospital?

Where the fuck am I?

Doyle remembered the chase. The gunfire. The crash and Vale...

Where was Vale?

He'd looked in pretty bad shape when they were pulling him from the wreck of the SUV. Was he dead? Critically injured? Again, Doyle tried to sit up, and again he gave it up as a bad job due to the pain it caused him trying to accomplish such a previously simple action. He was settling back against the pillows behind him when the door of the room opened.

Doyle raised his eyebrows in surprise when he saw the identity of the visitor.

Mark Granger nodded affably in his direction as he walked into the room. He looked as unruffled as usual and Doyle watched him as he stood beside the bed, his hands clasped behind him.

"How are you feeling?" Granger said, curtly.

"I've felt better," Doyle told him.

"I can imagine. Your injuries were relatively minor considering the amount of damage you caused."

"Just send me the bill," Doyle murmured.

"You might find it amusing, Doyle, but your actions endangered hundreds of innocent civilians today."

"I was doing my job," Doyle reminded him. "What the fuck was I supposed to do? Just let the guys who robbed the bank get away? You told us to watch that bank and that's what we were doing. When they hit it, we tried to stop them."

"And failed."

"What about the police? Did they manage to find them?"

"No. They got away."

"I tagged one of them. I know I did."

"You're quite correct. His body was found about an hour ago. It seems as if they just pushed him out of the car when he died."

"Who was he?"

"One of Gorchev's men. Russian Mafia."

"Tied in with Callahan?"

"It looks like it."

"What did they get from the bank?"

"The antique jewellery that had belonged to Callahan's wife. That was all they took."

Doyle nodded almost imperceptibly, wincing slightly when he felt pain from his right leg.

"I didn't come here for a social call as you may have gathered," Granger went on. "I wanted to see how you and Vale were, obviously, but that wasn't the only reason for my visit."

"Where is Vale?"

"He's in another room nearby. He's recovering. He's got a couple of cracked ribs and lots of cuts and bruises but he's on the mend. Just like you."

Again, Doyle nodded.

"So, if you didn't come to bring grapes and flowers," he said. "Why are you here?"

Granger smiled thinly and then spoke softly.

"I came to tell you that we've located David Callahan."

SEVENTY-EIGHT

Doyle looked directly at his superior, shifting his position in bed slightly.

"Where?" he wanted to know.

"He bought a place in Buckinghamshire about a month ago," Granger explained.

"Quite a spread. It set him back over twelve million."

"A month ago? And no one knew until now?"

"The sale was done through solicitors and agents, paid for by offshore funds, it's a wonder we found out as quickly as we did. Callahan's a master at operating under the radar, you know that."

"How was he identified?"

"We'd been tracking any activity from his accounts, the ones we knew of. And we finally got positive identification of him from some CCTV footage."

"Buckinghamshire?"

"It's a huge place. Isolated. Well away from prying eyes. Similar to the house he had in Ireland." Granger pulled his phone from his pocket, scrolled through some folders and held the device before Doyle. The picture he was presented with showed Maitland Hall. A shot taken from the air that showed the building and a large portion of its considerable grounds. "That's what he now calls home."

"I can see why he went for it," Doyle murmured.

"No one bothers him. No one even knows he's there."

"Apart from us."

Granger nodded.

"So now what?" Doyle wanted to know.

"We wait. Let him think he still has his anonymity. Allow him to believe he's escaped us. He's not going anywhere. We have time on our side." He smiled. "Don't worry Doyle, you're not going to miss out on the chance to finish what you should have finished nearly thirty years ago."

Doyle looked impassively at the younger man.

"It will be difficult though." Granger went on. "He shouldn't be underestimated. And he's being guarded by more of Gorchev's men."

"How many?"

"We think there could be twelve or more in and around the house. He's well prepared."

"I wouldn't have it any other way," Doyle said, flatly.

"This isn't the Gunfight at the O.K Corral, Doyle."

"We'll get him," Doyle said, flatly.

"I want him alive when the time comes."

"That might not be possible."

"Make sure it is."

There was a long silence then Granger spoke again.

"You and Vale will be fully briefed when you get out of here," he said. "I want this done right."

"How long will that be?"

"The doctors say you'll both be fit enough to leave in a couple of days."

"I might want to stay longer," Doyle said, smiling. "It's a nice room."

"This hospital has a wing purely for our use. We look after our people."

"It was a Band-Aid and some aspirin when I started in the CTU."

"It's called progress, Doyle."

Granger brushed some specks of dust from the sleeve of his jacket.

"Why did Callahan want his wife's jewellery stolen from that bank?" Doyle enquired. "It's not like he's going to fence it."

"There was an item among the things that were stolen that he needs."

"Needs?"

"We showed the collection that was taken to some experts and they confirmed that one of the pieces was from the same period as the book Callahan had stolen from the British Museum and also the dagger that was taken. We feel they're linked."

"So that was why that bank was hit? To get that one piece of jewellery?"

"It's a gold medallion of some description. The inscription around the edges of it is in the same language as the grimoire. Medieval Romance. Our experts think they're linked."

Doyle considered the information carefully

"And Callahan had kept that hidden in the bank too?" he asked.

Granger nodded.

"Don't you think it's a bit...I don't know...easy?" Doyle murmured.

"What do you mean?"

"He gets guys to rob two places where he's got stuff hidden, where he's had it hidden for nearly thirty years," Doyle began. "And he buys a big place here in England. All this within the last month or two. He's not trying to hide."

"I told you, the purchase of the house was done through third parties and the robberies were committed by men working for him. He hasn't drawn attention to himself directly. What are you driving at?"

"I just think it's too easy. Why buy a place here? He knows we're on his tail. Why here in England? Why not in the States or somewhere else in Europe? Somewhere that puts distance between himself and us? He could afford to live anywhere in the world, but he chooses to live thirty minutes from London. It makes no sense."

"I think you're over-analysing it, Doyle. He's just been careless."

"But that's the point, Callahan isn't a careless man. He sold guns for years without anyone being able to nail him. No one knew what he was up to. He moved about in the fucking shadows."

"He's still in the shadows."

Doyle shook his head.

Granger sucked in a weary breath.

"We'll discuss this again when you're out of here," he said, turning towards the door. "You need to rest."

"If you say so," he murmured.

"Is there anything you need?" Granger wanted to know.

"A cigarette?" Doyle said, hopefully.

Granger merely shook his head and sighed.

"I've had some files and photographs downloaded concerning Callahan's new place and also the items that were stolen," he said. "You can see them on your laptop tomorrow. Get some rest now."

"I'll try," Doyle said, managing a smile.

Granger hesitated at the door then raised a hand in a perfunctory gesture and disappeared.

"Twat," Doyle murmured under his breath.

PART THREE

"Revenge, the sweetest morsel to the mouth that ever was cooked in hell."

Sir Walter Scott.

SEVENTY-NINE

There were three items lying side by side on the large wooden table.

David Callahan looked at each one in turn, his gaze moving slowly over them. He reached out and trailed his fingertips over the book, touching the stiff parchment pages, sometimes tracing the outline of the letters. The smell that reached his nostrils was of damp and mould, as if the book were decaying in front of him. He closed the ancient volume and stood silently before it, considering the hardened leather cover.

There was no design on it. No illustrations. It was just plain black leather, cracked and faded with the passage of time. As smooth as dead flesh.

Callahan turned his attention to the dagger that lay beside the book.

The long blade glinted in the dull light and he picked it up by its hilt, hefting it before him, running one thumb up the long slim spike.

Despite its age, the blade was still gleaming, and Callahan could see his own features reflected briefly in the metal as he looked at it. He replaced it finally and picked up the last item on the table.

The medallion was gold. A circlet about two inches in diameter, suspended on an equally heavy gold chain from which several of the links were missing. The precious metal was dark and stained in places but still retained enough of its lustre to be impressive. Callahan lifted it closer to his face, turning it in his fingers as he scanned the ancient engravings and inscriptions on the edges and rear of the artefact.

The words there meant nothing to him. He didn't understand their meaning, but he appreciated their worth.

"I hope they're worth what you paid for them."

The words echoed through the stillness.

Callahan didn't turn or acknowledge them or their speaker, he merely continued to gaze at the medallion.

"Very few people understand their value," he said, finally, his attention still fixed on the items before him.

"How much are they worth?" the voice enquired.

"They're priceless," Callahan said, without taking his eyes from the objects. "You'll see."

Vasili Gorchev stepped forward from the shadows, standing beside Callahan, casting his own curious gaze over the articles on the table. The Ukrainian reached out towards the book, but Callahan slapped his hand away.

"Don't touch it," he said, flatly.

"You were happy enough for my men to touch it when they stole it for you," Gorchev reminded him.

Callahan didn't answer. He laid the medallion down again and moved back slightly.

"Why are you still here?" he said, at last, glancing dismissively at the other man. "You brought me the medallion. You've been paid. Our business is complete."

"Twelve of my men are still guarding this fucking house," Gorchev reminded him. "I lost another one getting that...necklace for you. Our business isn't over."

"Do you want money for the man you lost?" Callahan wanted to know.

Gorchev held his gaze for a moment longer.

"How highly do you value his life?" Callahan went on. "How highly do you value your own?"

"You think you can buy everything with your money."

"I can."

"They will come for you," Gorchev said, quietly. "They will find you and they will come."

"Let them come," Callahan breathed, anger in his voice. "I'll bury them all."

EIGHTY

D oyle sat back from the laptop and rubbed his eyes. The sunlight that was pouring through the window of the hospital room felt pleasantly warm against his skin.

Beside him, Gideon Vale got to his feet, using a crutch to help support his weight.

"You need a parrot to go with that," Doyle said, nodding towards the younger man.

Vale didn't smile.

"The doctors said I should keep any pressure off it for a few days," he answered. "There was some damage to the ankle ligaments."

"I'm not surprised the way you drove that SUV."

"What does that mean?"

Doyle shook his head and smiled, his attention returning to the photographs on the screen of the laptop. There were several views of Maitland Hall. Some of Callahan himself, more of Vasili Gorchev and the men believed to be guarding Callahan in the huge house and its grounds.

"What you said earlier about Callahan, what did you mean?" Vale murmured, glancing at the pictures. "About him not hiding?"

"If you were on the run would you have paid twelve million for a pile like that, thirty minutes away from an organisation trying to nail you?" Doyle said.

"What are you talking about?"

"It doesn't make any sense. Callahan should be miles from here by now. Not setting up home that close to London."

"Perhaps he doesn't think we're capable of finding him."

"He knows. He'll be expecting us."

"That's what I'm afraid of."

"Granger said Callahan bought this place more than a

month ago and yet we've only been told in the last day or two. I don't understand why he's waited. If the CTU want Callahan that badly why not move in on him straight away?"

"I'm sure there's a reason."

Doyle raised his eyebrows.

"How much do you know about Granger?" he wanted to know.

"He's my boss. How much do I have to know about him?"

"You knew enough about me from reading my files. What about him?"

Vale shrugged.

"He's been head of the CTU for the last six years," he said. "He was high-up at MI5 before that. Public school and Cambridge educated. Married. His son, Charles, committed suicide not long ago."

"Why?"

"How the hell do I know? They don't put that kind of information in departmental files. It must have hit him pretty hard."

"He never showed it."

"He's too professional for that."

Doyle smiled thinly and glanced again at the photographs before him. He studied the house and its grounds, consigning the details to memory. Then he moved on to the pictures of the Ukrainians thought to be guarding Callahan and his home. By the time he got to the pictures of the grimoire, the dagger and the medallion, Vale had joined him. He sat down next to Doyle, gazing at the artefacts displayed on the screen.

"I wonder why he wants them," Vale said, quietly.

Doyle had no answer.

EIGHTY-ONE

The silence was overpowering. Almost oppressive in its totality. David Callahan could hear his own breathing echoing in his ears as if it had been amplified.

He sat naked on the floor of the subterranean room, illuminated only by the dull yellow glow of several candles that had been lit and placed in holders nearby.

Callahan was breathing slowly but heavily, his exertions of the past hour or so having taken something of a toll on him.

He got slowly to his feet, almost slipping in one of the puddles of dark liquid that now stained the floor all over the room.

The smell filled his nostrils too. A thick, coppery stench that clogged in his nose and seemed to block those orifices as surely as if someone had pushed coins inside. The smell of blood was distinctive and impossible to mistake. Callahan knew it well after all these years and now he was smelling it again, fresher and stronger than he had for a while.

The source of the blood lay a few feet from him.

The four dead children were also naked.

They had been stripped before the ceremony had begun. Prepared in a way that was specified and that had to be followed to the letter. A way set out in the grimoire.

The book itself was lying on the large wooden table at one side of the underground room. Callahan had consulted it a number of times during his ritual, but its very presence was enough for him and for his purposes.

As was the medallion which he now wore around his neck.

Blood had spattered onto the golden circlet a few times and now it was congealing thickly on the precious metal as Callahan walked slowly, almost drunkenly, across the stone floor.

The blade he still held.

It had been a much more important part of the ritual. Necessary to what he sought. He had pushed that spike of metal slowly into the base of each child's skull as demanded in the grimoire. He had watched as the child's eyes had seemed to swell in their sockets, looking intently as the life, like their blood, left them. And when they had finally shuddered and shaken in their death throes, he had hacked their heads off using a larger, single-bladed knife.

The misericorde was necessary for taking their lives. It had been designed for that and he had used it carefully and skilfully. The stiletto blade wasn't robust enough to sever their heads, not even with prolonged cutting but it was beautifully adapted for snuffing out the initial spark of life.

Callahan held it lightly in one bloodstained hand as he continued across the room, the shadows that hovered thickly beyond the range of the candlelight hiding his target. But Callahan could see the pale outline of the figure cowering in the gloom, the gag that had been tied around his lower jaw and jammed into his mouth preventing him from crying out.

The last of the children was a boy of six.

Naked like the others, his wrists and ankles had been bound roughly with thick rope, the knots tied so tightly that the skin had been rasped away by the hemp. He pressed himself back against the stone wall as Callahan advanced, his body shaking both from the cold but mainly from fear.

He had seen the fate of those before him. He had watched helplessly as they'd died and now, he could still see their severed heads lined up on the table near the grimoire, displayed like hunting trophies in the den of some maniacal trapper.

When Callahan reached the boy he knelt down, looking at the boy impassively but then smiling thinly.

He reached out with one hand and gripped the boy by one shoulder.

Tears were rolling down the boy's cheeks and Callahan reached forward with one bloodied index finger and wiped them away, shaking his head almost reproachfully.

"Don't cry," he whispered. "You're helping me. You should be happy about that. The others helped me too." His smiled broadened and he gestured behind him towards the other bodies all lying like broken, red stained, mannequins on the stone floor, covered with blood and excrement. "But you are the last. The most important. And I want to thank you."

Callahan leaned forward and gently kissed the boy on the forehead.

"You have no idea how grateful I am to you," he whispered.

He smiled at the child who looked up at him, tears still rolling down his face. Callahan held the boy's chin gently and tilted his head back slightly.

"Thank you," he said, softly.

As he spoke, he pressed the misericorde gently against the back of the child's neck, pressing it harder into the hollow at the base of the skull.

The boy struggled a little more violently now, perhaps realising what was happening to him, but Callahan held him firmly, gazing into his eyes with all the attentiveness and care that would normally be reserved for a lover.

As he pushed the blade into the boy's trapezius muscle, he felt him stiffen, then try to pull away, but Callahan merely shook his head gently in a gesture of admonishment.

When the boy tried to scream, he clamped his spare hand over the gag that he'd pushed into his mouth earlier, keeping the bellow of pain and fear trapped inside the child.

Callahan pushed harder on the blade, driving it upwards through the boy's cervical vertebrae, feeling it grate against the bone as it had with two of the others. And now the boy's eyes bulged madly as Callahan gazed deeply into them, pushing with even greater force on the spike until he had forced it into the child as deep as the hilt. It punctured the occipital lobe of the brain effortlessly.

At that point the boy's body began to spasm, his legs and arms jerking uncontrollably. Callahan held him tightly, his eyes never leaving those of the boy until they rolled upwards in their sockets.

Only then did Callahan slowly lower the body to the blood-drenched floor.

As he kneeled over the corpse he looked down and realised that he had an erection.

Callahan smiled.

EIGHTY-TWO

D oyle closed the door of the flat behind him then walked into the sitting room, not bothering to turn on the lights.

Only in the kitchen did he finally flick a couple of switches and allow cold white light to flood the room. He reached into his jacket pocket and took out the painkillers the hospital had given him, setting the small plastic container down on a worktop. He'd already decided that he wouldn't take any unless he really needed them. Doyle was fairly sure that over the years he'd built up some kind of immunity to painkillers.

God alone knew he'd taken enough of them in his time. He smiled thinly to himself and got a glass from the cupboard above the sink. From the small fridge-freezer he took a bottle of vodka, poured himself a large measure and downed half of it in one swallow.

Only when he'd finished the measure and refilled the glass did he move back into the sitting room.

Doyle seated himself on the sofa, pulled his laptop towards him and found what he wanted.

The information on Mark Granger wasn't exactly classified. A Google search revealed photographs and articles about him as far back as his university days. There were items about his appointment to the higher echelons of the CTU. The usual generic stuff. Not exactly what Doyle was looking for. He wanted details about the man's background, private life and family.

He sighed, knowing that someone like Vale would have been able to access countless websites and files that would have revealed the information he sought. Doyle stared at the laptop as if it was his worst enemy in the world. He downed more vodka and then tried a search for Granger's son.

There were articles about the suicide. Photographs of the university where he ended his own life. More pictures of Granger himself. Not as much information as Doyle would have expected and definitely not as much as he wanted.

He finally closed the laptop, massaging the bridge of his nose between his thumb and forefinger. When he got off the sofa, he felt the stiffness in his back and the pain that was beginning to become more prevalent. For a moment he wondered about taking a painkiller but decided against it. Probably not a good idea to mix them with alcohol either but, right now, he needed the booze more.

He switched on the TV, lowered the volume until it was barely audible and wandered through to the kitchen again to refill his glass. He was happy to be out of hospital. The three days in there had passed with infinite slowness and he was hoping it would be a long time before he had to see the inside of one again.

For some reason, thoughts of hospital made him think of Callahan.

Tempting fate?

The last time he'd run up against Callahan he'd ended up in hospital for five months.

He lowered his head, as if the memories themselves were as painful as the bullets that had torn more scars into him that night nearly thirty years ago.

And now it was all going to happen again.

Wasn't it?

Doyle moved back into the sitting room, crossing to a window to gaze out into the street. A taxi had just pulled up across the road and he could see a man and a woman clambering out of it, the woman laughing loudly as the man slapped her backside. Doyle smiled as he watched them, sipping his drink, peering down on the little tableau.

He stood there a moment longer, silhouetted in the window. Something he might not have done had he realised he was being watched.

EIGHTY-THREE

David Callahan awoke with a start.

He sat up, glancing around, blinking myopically and rubbing his eyes.

It took him a moment or two to realise that he was still naked. It was cold inside the room and Callahan shivered as he looked down at his own unclothed body. From the pains in his shoulders and back he realised he must have spent the whole night passed out on the stone floor.

Had the exertions of the previous night really taken such a heavy toll on him? He took a deep breath, tasting something rank. The air itself seemed to be tainted. Filled with a smell that he couldn't recognise at first. He knew the metallic odour of blood but there was another, stronger smell filling his nostrils and mouth now. It reminded him of rotting meat.

Lying on the far side of the room he could see the bodies of the dead children.

They had served their purpose.

Hadn't they?

Callahan got slowly to his feet, swaying drunkenly as he stood in the centre of the room. He looked down again and saw that much of the bottom half of his body was covered with dark stains that he knew to be congealed blood.

Why couldn't he remember much from the night before?

The grimoire, the misericorde and the medallion were lying on the large table nearby. They too were spattered with blood. Callahan closed his eyes for a moment, as if that simple action may well cause the memories of the previous night to come flooding back but it didn't.

He walked slowly towards the door of the room wanting to shower as much as anything. He wanted to wash away the rusty coloured mess that had spattered him.

As he stepped out of the room into the vestibule beyond,

he was struck by the silence.

The house was usually quiet but this particular morning it seemed preternaturally still. Callahan could usually hear some of the staff moving around but now, as he stood motionless, he heard nothing but the blood rushing in his own ears. Only as he reached the hallway did he hear sounds of movement from the first floor of the house.

He continued up the wide flight of steps, not caring that one of the staff might be up there and might see him in his state of undress.

As he reached the top of the stairs, he realised that the sounds were coming from the bedroom directly ahead of him. His own.

Someone was moving about inside the room. He could clearly hear footsteps moving back and forth across the floor despite the thickness of the carpet in there. Callahan slowed his pace as he drew closer to the door, stopping to listen for a moment longer before reaching for the door handle.

He heard only silence now.

Whoever was in there had either stopped walking or had moved into the large en suite bathroom attached to the main room.

Callahan opened the door and stepped inside, thinking that whoever was in there was going to get more of a shock than he was. He even smiled thinly to himself as the thought entered his mind. Indeed, as he closed the bedroom door behind him, he realised that there was someone in the en suite. It was, Callahan decided, one of the maids. He walked towards the half-open door and pushed it, standing silhouetted in the doorway.

The figure inside turned to face him.

EIGHTY-FOUR

As the slide on the Beretta 92F snapped back into position, the loud metallic click filled the SUV.

Gideon Vale turned his head sharply in the direction of the sound, seeing that Doyle was inspecting the weapon closely.

He did the same with the two MP5K sub-machine guns he'd taken from the large metal bound case, previously stored in the boot of the vehicle. Doyle also checked each of the spare fifteen-round magazines, ensuring that each was filled to capacity.

The six G60 flash-bang stun grenades that were housed in the case he also scrutinised carefully, removing each one in turn and checking it.

"Do you want to check mine too," Vale said, sliding the Sig-Sauer P226 from his shoulder holster. "Or do you trust me?"

"You know what you're doing," Doyle murmured without looking at him. "You're a big boy now."

"You know Granger wants Callahan alive?"

"He told me. But he's not here is he?"

"Doyle..."

"I'll tell you what I told him," the older man snapped. "It might not be possible."

"This isn't a revenge mission you know."

Doyle didn't answer. He merely continued to gaze out of the windscreen of the SUV, looking at the thick woodland around the stationary vehicle. The evening sky was darkening, and Doyle welcomed the growing gloom. It would make it easier to approach their target.

"Initial intelligence says there are twelve people inside Maitland Hall now," Vale offered.

"How do they know?"

"A drone sweep about ten minutes ago. Thermal imaging

showed twelve individuals in and around the buildings."

Doyle nodded.

"Our support is in position," Vale told him.

"Fuck the support," Doyle snapped. "We don't need it."

"Doyle, this is a carefully planned operation."

"Have any of the men in the support groups had combat experience?"

"How the hell do I know?"

"I'm betting they haven't. They're all CTU, right?"

"What's that got to do with it?"

"We needed military support for this operation."

"Callahan is a civilian and technically so are the men guarding him."

"So, it's all by the fucking rule book?"

"It's always by the rule book."

Doyle shook his head.

"We've got six guys backing us up," he murmured. "Just six."

Vale looked intently at him.

"You're a strategic analyst, what's your fucking strategic analysis of this situation?"

"Six isn't enough."

"You're fucking right it isn't. And who assigned the men?"

"Granger."

"He knows the risks. He knows that Callahan is being guarded by Russian Mafia. He knows their capabilities and yet he sends us six guys as fucking backup?"

"What are you trying to say?"

"I don't trust him."

"You don't trust anyone."

"You're fucking right," Doyle snapped. "How do you think I've stayed alive so long." He pushed open the door of the SUV and clambered out.

Vale also swung himself out of the vehicle.

"Where are you going?" he wanted to know.

"I'm going to have a look around," Doyle informed him. "You stay here."

"You don't need to do that. We've got details of the terrain and the buildings."

"I'm going to have a look."

Doyle raised a hand and waved it dismissively in Vale's direction before disappearing into a small copse.

"Doyle," Vale called.

"Don't wait up, dear," Doyle replied, his voice fading as he moved further away.

Vale shook his head.

"Prick," he muttered and retreated back inside the SUV.

Doyle was already out of sight.

EIGHTY-FIVE

As Doyle advanced deeper into the overgrown trees he realised that the ground was sloping away gently before him. Fallen branches and small bushes covered the ground and, more than once, he almost stumbled, moving on as assuredly as he could in the ever-growing darkness. As the slope grew even steeper, Doyle used the trees as support, easing himself down the incline until he reached a stone wall that he presumed marked the perimeter of Callahan's land.

Beyond the stone wall there were more trees, but these grew less densely, and Doyle could also see that the ground was levelling out somewhat. He could hear running water and realised that there was a narrow stream just ahead. About fifty yards to his right there was a battered old stone bridge spanning the small waterway, but Doyle was convinced he could cross it by simply stepping on the large rocks that protruded from the water in several places.

He steadied himself and put one foot on the first of the rocks, moving nimbly from one to the other until he reached the other bank. Doyle clambered up it and found himself in another copse of trees. Beyond those, he could see some open ground leading towards the better kept and maintained gardens of Maitland Hall. The building itself had several lights burning.

If Callahan was in there, Doyle thought, he certainly wasn't hiding.

Doyle moved on, taking a breath, aware of how thick and cloying the air seemed. It was a humid night, and, within the confines of the trees, it seemed even more difficult to get a breath. A cloud of midges, no doubt attracted by the closeness of the stream, flew past him and Doyle waved a hand before him to dispel the seething insects.

He could feel perspiration trickling down the back of his neck as he advanced, his eyes never leaving the outline of the huge edifice before him.

Nervous?

About fifty yards to his left there was a gap in the trees and what looked like a narrow path, the ground worn smooth by the passage of many feet over the years. The path led up to what looked like a stone culvert that sank into the earth. Doyle moved towards it.

He had a small torch stuffed in the back pocket of his jeans, but he didn't reach for it, prepared instead to squint through the gloom at the partially bricked-up hole. It was about four feet in height, half that in width and shaped like an arch. Doyle thought that it must at one time have been linked to the sewage system of Maitland Hall. As that thought struck him so did another. If it had been part of that system, then it must lead deeper into the grounds and possibly even under the house itself. It might be a way in without risking approaching the place via the open gardens and grounds.

Doyle finally reached for his torch, clicking it on. He stuck it through the hole in the brickwork and shone it around.

Sure enough, the culvert stretched away into thick darkness, but he could see the damp walls clearly in the beam of the torch. The tunnel was moist at ground level, stagnant water having puddled in several places. There were also numerous lumps of masonry lying on the floor of the tunnel beyond and Doyle realised that the brickwork was crumbling due to age and lack of maintenance. He pushed gently on some of the bricks, unsurprised when one of them gave way. Doyle smiled to himself. How come Vale hadn't known about this with all his hi-tech shit?

A way in.

He was still considering that possibility when he heard movement close by.

Doyle spun around, scanning the gloom, trying to pick out what had made the sound.

He could see nothing in the darkness, but he stood still, ears alert for any more sounds.

When they came, they were closer.

Whatever was making the sounds was coming in his direction.

EIGHTY-SIX

Doyle squeezed himself into the culvert entrance as far as he could, hoping the archway and the darkness would shield him.

He heard the sounds nearby once more and tried again to pinpoint their source.

High up in a tree an owl hooted.

Doyle tried to control his breathing, crouching lower as he scanned the heavily wooded ground around him.

The sounds were coming closer and he slipped his hand inside his jacket, fingers touching the butt of the Beretta briefly but then withdrawing. Instead, he reached for one of the bricks that had crumbled away from the culvert opening. The sound of a gun would carry for miles in this stillness and Doyle didn't want to give any more clues to his presence than he had to. He gripped the lump of brick more tightly as the sounds grew louder.

One of Callahan's bodyguards doing a sweep of the grounds?

Be careful.

Doyle took a breath and held it.

A rustling of leaves. A twig snapped loudly, the sound echoing with almost supernatural volume. Doyle gritted his teeth.

And there it was, on the narrow path leading to the culvert entrance. The source of the sound.

The badger was large, and Doyle gazed at it for a moment as if mesmerised.

He'd never seen one in the flesh before. Big bastard. Bigger than he'd thought. They looked smaller on TV. Doyle smiled to himself, watching as the animal snuffled around, trying to pick up the trail of a rabbit or mouse or whatever it was tracking.

"Watership Down is that way," Doyle whispered, smiling and nodding at the badger when it finally saw him.

It stood motionless for a second then headed off into some thick bushes. He could hear it moving away from him. It didn't seem unduly perturbed by his presence. It seemed more concerned with finding a meal. He gave it a moment or two to get clear then dropped the brick he'd been holding and turned back towards the culvert once more, shining his torch through the gap with one hand while pulling at the crumbling stone with the other. The bricks came free with very little force and, in less than five minutes, Doyle had opened up a gap large enough to squeeze through. As he pushed his way through his own hastily created entrance, two more bricks came loose and dropped noisily to the ground, the sound echoing through the tunnel and inside Doyle's ears.

He shone the torch again, up and over the curved walls and ceiling of the tunnel. It was high and wide enough for him to walk through, even though he had to crouch to avoid scraping his head on the crumbling ceiling.

He put up a hand to touch the brickwork, surprised at how easily it crumbled under his touch. Small clouds of dust came free at each contact, particles filling the air. Doyle waved a hand before him in an effort to dispel the miasma, attempting not to cough or sneeze when it filled his throat and nose.

He had one brief but telling thought. What if the whole lot collapsed? But he pushed that thought to the back of his mind and advanced slowly.

A very large spider scuttled away from the bright beam of torchlight and Doyle shuddered involuntarily as he saw the huge arachnid retreat towards a hole in one of many webs that seemed to decorate the narrow space.

He didn't like spiders. He hadn't since he was a kid. And that fucker was big by anyone's standards. There must be thousands of them down here he thought, swallowing hard.

Doyle moved a few feet further into the culvert, the torch beam illuminating every detail of the tunnel. About twenty feet further ahead, at the very limit of the torch beam's cold white gleam, he could see that the tunnel curved slightly to the right, towards Maitland Hall. Doyle smiled again.

Satisfied that his theory about the tunnel running underneath or certainly close to the house was correct, he switched off the torch and retreated back up the tunnel, careful not to disturb the spiderwebs above him. He had to fetch Vale. Had to show him this.

As Doyle emerged into the night again he jammed the torch back into his jeans pocket, moving assuredly in the gloom, picking his way through the trees and bushes as he moved away from the culvert and towards the ground that sloped upwards back to where Vale was waiting.

He was just crossing the narrow pathway when he heard a twig snap close by.

Another badger? A fox? Something else looking for a meal in the blackness? Again, the owl hooted, as if that sound was some kind of death knell for one of the smaller creatures that inhabited the woods.

Doyle moved on, only slowing his pace when he heard leaves rustling more loudly, this time much closer to him.

He ducked down behind some bushes and a fallen tree, again trying to work out where the sound was coming from and what was making it.

Perhaps the same badger had come back, he reasoned as he heard more movement.

He was still considering that possibility when he saw the figure emerge into view.

EIGHTY-SEVEN

The man loomed out of the darkness like a tangible shadow.

Even from where he hid, Doyle could see that the newcomer was carrying a weapon and it was unmistakably an AK-47 gripped in two large hands before him.

The barrel yawned as Doyle looked at it, realising that the man carrying it was pointing it in his direction.

He's seen you.

Doyle crouched lower, reaching for the Beretta but then he realised that he was still hidden from view by the trees and the gloom. The man merely stood motionless for a moment, looking back and forth but seeing nothing but night. Doyle kept his gaze fixed on him, taking in as much detail as he could. The man was in his thirties. Over six feet tall and heavily built. He swiped irritably at a mosquito as it flew around his head then he reached into his pocket for a packet of cigarettes and lit one up.

Fuck off. Not now.

Doyle remained where he was, trying to keep low, attempting to maintain his shallow breathing. The slightest movement in this kind of solitude would give him away. When the tall man lit his cigarette the click of the lighter seemed to reverberate throughout the woods. He drew on it, finally blowing out a stream of smoke into the humid air.

Move, you cunt.

Doyle heard more sounds and it took him only a second to realise that it was the hiss of static. The tall man muttered something under his breath and, after hanging the Kalashnikov from his shoulder by its strap, reached for the two-way radio he was carrying, silencing the static. He spoke into the two-way, his words barked in a language Doyle couldn't understand but assumed was Ukrainian. For all he knew the man could be giving his colleagues Doyle's position right now. Any moment, half a dozen more heavily armed men could descend on him.

Goodnight.

Doyle tried to shift position slightly. His right leg was beginning to ache beneath him, his knee stiffening.

Old wounds.

The tall man was still snarling words into the two-way, occasionally pausing to listen to the answer. He took a drag on his cigarette as he received instructions, using the stream of smoke he expelled to drive off more of the insects that were flying around him. As Doyle watched, the Ukrainian moved along the narrow path towards the culvert, pulling out a torch of his own that he aimed at the opening. He sent the beam over the brickwork, finally bringing it to bear on some of the masonry Doyle had pulled away to allow himself entry into the tunnel.

Could he tell it had been newly disturbed?

Doyle saw him drop to one knee and pick up one of the crumbling bricks.

Surely, he didn't know, did he?

Doyle touched the butt of the 92F again but then hesitated. If he knew for sure that he'd been discovered, then he'd pull the automatic and shoot this fucker without a second thought. But what if he was wrong? What if he was still undetected? If he was, then a sure way would be to open fire. The sound would draw everyone in the house and for miles around.

Doyle eased himself up onto his haunches, actually managing to move along through the bushes and among the trees with relative ease in this position. He moved closer to the big man, keeping twenty or thirty feet between them but never allowing his gaze to drop from the Ukrainian who was now peering into the culvert itself. The big man reached for his radio again and Doyle heard him speak, again wondering what the hell he was saying.

Was this a set up? Had he been meant to find the culvert?

Doyle moved a little closer, careful not to step on any fallen branches or twigs.

Had Callahan been expecting this?

There was another crackle of static on the two-way and the big man pushed it back into his jacket, seemingly finished with his communication. He stood before the culvert for a moment, now seemingly more interested in finishing his cigarette than anything else.

Doyle ducked down as the Ukrainian shone his torch around, the beam illuminating everything nearby. It cast its white glow over trees, bushes and flowers, even catching a fluttering bat in its wide sweep.

The Ukrainian looked up as the bat swooped and dove close to him, no doubt attracted by the insects that were flying around the culvert entrance. Then he finished his cigarette, threw the butt away and walked off slowly along the narrow pathway.

Doyle eased the Beretta back into its shoulder holster, relieved that the big man was finally leaving.

He took a step backwards and trod on a piece of fallen branch.

It snapped loudly under his weight.

The Ukrainian spun around, swinging the AK-47 up to his shoulder, squinting down the sight into the gloom.

Doyle froze, his heart hammering against his ribs. For interminable seconds he remained in that position, his gaze fixed on the big man who was similarly statuesque, the Kalashnikov still held tightly against his shoulder, his finger poised on the trigger.

Then, with infinite slowness, he lowered the weapon slightly and Doyle afforded himself a muted sigh of relief.

At least he did until he saw the big man walking back in his direction.

EIGHTY-EIGHT

Doyle waited a second, wanting to be sure that the Ukrainian was indeed heading towards him.

In the blackness of the night and with the trees as cover, Doyle knew that he was hidden until the other man was within a few yards so he had a split second to move if he could. Ducked low to the ground and with his eye on the advancing man, Doyle moved towards the culvert, wanting the extra protection should the man open fire. Trees and bushes would be precious little protection against the bullet from an AK-47. Doyle knew that if he could reach the culvert he would be in a stronger position. But, if either of them opened up then the sound would alert others and bring them running.

The Ukrainian stopped in the middle of the pathway and looked around, eyes squinting through the night, desperate to see what had made the sounds close by. When he could not pick out the source of the noise, he pulled out his torch again, sweeping the broad beam back and forth over the trees and bushes.

Doyle froze again.

From where he waited, he could hear the crackling and burbling coming from the Ukrainian's two-way radio. Words barked out. The big man hesitated a moment then jammed his torch back into his belt and grabbed the radio. As he spoke, he walked slowly forward, closer and closer to Doyle who was now less than ten feet from him.

The big man muttered a few more syllables into the radio then switched it off again. Silence momentarily descended, every sound inside the wood amplified by the stillness.

Doyle heard what sounded like a muted thud.

It took him a second to realise that it was the sound of a pistol shot, muffled effectively by a silencer.

The bullet hit the Ukrainian in the back of the head, stove

in a portion of the occipital bone, ripped through the brain and erupted from his left eye. He stood stiffly for a second then pitched forward, landing flat on his face close to Doyle who scrambled out from the bushes, looking around to try and find the source of the bullet.

He saw Gideon Vale striding through some trees, his gaze fixed on the fallen Ukrainian.

Doyle smiled thinly.

"Is he dead?" Vale asked, softly.

"Dead enough," Doyle told him, digging the toe of his boot into the body of the big man. "Thanks."

"I thought you'd been gone for too long. I thought I'd check."

"Good timing."

Doyle dragged the AK-47 from the dead Ukrainian, rolling the body over to check for anything else that might be useful.

"Let's get this bastard out of sight," he grunted, grabbing the big man by the wrists. Vale did the same with the ankles and they hurried towards the culvert, finally dumping the corpse near the entrance.

"What's this?" Vale wanted to know, looking at the mouth of the tunnel.

"A way in," Doyle breathed. "Our private route straight to Callahan."

Vale pulled the torch from his jacket and shone it around the culvert, taking in details.

"How do you know?" he murmured.

"I don't. It's a hunch."

"What if you're wrong?"

"Then I'm wrong. We just come back out and approach the house the way we said we would to begin with but let's at least try this way."

Vale nodded.

The dead Ukrainian's two-way crackled again and Doyle looked down at the body, wondering why Vale was reaching for the device.

He watched as the younger man grabbed the radio and raised it to his mouth. When he spoke, the words were in perfect Russian. He nodded as he spoke, even managing to laugh mutedly as he finally signed off. He stuffed the radio into his pocket.

"I didn't know you spoke Russian," Doyle said.

"There's a lot about me you don't know," Vale muttered.

"What were you saying to them?"

"Someone wanted to know if everything was quiet. I told them it was. I said there was no one around. Do I get a gold star?"

Doyle smiled.

"We need the other weapons," he said. "I'll go back to the car and fetch them. You stay here."

Vale nodded, ducking back further into the culvert.

The darkness swallowed him.

EIGHTY-NINE

The darkness inside the tunnel was almost palpable. The gloom so impenetrable that even the torch beams could only penetrate it five or ten feet at a time.

Doyle moved forward through the shaft, ducked low, careful to avoid the sometimes-crumbling roof. Behind him, Vale also walked slowly, one hand touching the wall as if to reassure himself. In the confined setting, the breathing of the two men sounded like ruptured bellows.

"I hate confined spaces," Vale whispered.

Doyle merely nodded by way of an answer. He had no idea how long they'd been inside the culvert, but it felt as if it had been a long time. The old pipes must run for miles beneath Maitland Hall. As they moved further, the ground became soggier, soaked through in places by underground leakage from God knows where. The brickwork too was damp, even wet in places. Pieces of walls or ceiling had come away and now lay on the floor of the tunnel. Vale stumbled over one particularly large lump of stone, muttering angrily under his breath.

He swept his torch around, his heart thudding faster. He felt as if the walls were closing slowly around him.

Doyle slowed down slightly.

"What is it?" Vale wanted to know.

"Just ahead," Doyle told him, motioning forward. "The tunnel splits."

Vale peered through the gloom to see that the culvert did indeed branch off in two directions.

"Which way?" he breathed.

Doyle pointed to the right.

"That's going in the direction of the house," he said. "Or we could split up?"

"No. We might never find each other again down here."

Doyle hesitated a moment and Vale pushed past him, taking the lead now, moving into the right-hand branch of the tunnel. It curved around slightly and Doyle also thought that he felt the ground beneath their feet sloping downwards slightly. He aimed his torch at the wall of the tunnel and saw several holes there in the stonework. Low down, close to the damp floor. There was matted fur around the entrance to one.

Rats?

Doyle shuddered. Rats. Spiders. The sooner they found their way out of here the better. He would rather face bullets than those he told himself, almost managing a smile.

Ahead of him Vale grunted irritably, almost falling over some more fallen bricks that were hidden by the increasingly deep water at the bottom of the tunnel. The stagnant fluid was now up to their calves as they walked and the stench inside the tunnel was becoming stronger with every yard they advanced.

"Is this still part of the sewer system?" Vale asked. "It fucking stinks."

"Just keep moving," Doyle told him, ducking his head a little more as it became increasingly obvious that the tunnel was narrowing.

Both men were now bent almost double as they walked and Vale finally stopped and shone his torch around him, keeping it aimed at the roof of the shaft.

"What are you doing?" Doyle wanted to know.

"We should turn back," Vale said.

Doyle shook his head.

"The tunnel is getting narrower," Vale protested. "We won't be able to go much further."

"We've got to try."

Vale hesitated for a moment then turned away, ducking down further and moving on as best he could, cursing under his breath. Doyle followed, feet splashing through the water that he was sure was rising. He shone his torch down, playing the beam over the surface of the reeking fluid and then at the sides of the tunnel. The green mould that had formed in places on the brickwork there was never more than a foot or so above the floor of the shaft. The stonework higher up was dry. Doyle assumed this was because the water level never rose higher than that. He smiled, congratulating himself on his powers of detection, slightly more relieved as they pushed on.

Something moved close behind him.

Doyle spun around, again aiming the torch at the surface of the water and the area where the sound had come from.

He saw the rat as it entered the water.

"Fuck," he snarled under his breath.

The furry horror had disappeared under the surface, he hoped in the opposite direction, but he kept his torch trained on the hole it had emerged from, wanting to see if any other vermin emerged.

For a full fifteen seconds, Doyle kept the light focused on that gap in the brickwork, his breathing low but laboured.

Nothing else appeared. No more rats. Nothing.

He moved on, increasing his pace to catch up with Vale who was now several yards ahead of him. When Doyle caught up, he found the younger man standing motionless in the middle of the narrowing tunnel.

"We've got to go back," Vale said, quietly.

"Why?" Doyle wanted to know.

Vale turned his torch on the area ahead of them.

The tunnel was bricked up.

NINETY

Doyle stood looking at the wall across the shaft, his face set in hard lines.

"So much for your great idea," Vale breathed, also glaring at the obstacle.

Doyle pushed past him and put one hand on the wall ahead, pushing gently. It was built of the same bricks and stone that the rest of the culvert was, eroded and worn by the passage of time. They weren't new bricks. They were stained in places by the same black mould that grew in the lower reaches of the remainder of the shaft and the mortar holding the bricks together was crumbling here and there.

Doyle drove one foot against the wall, smiling when several bricks fell away.

"We can get through here," he insisted, slamming his foot again into the barrier.

More bricks fell away, most toppling away from the point of impact. Energised by his success, Doyle continued with his assault, only pausing when he had opened a gap large enough to peer through. He moved forward, aiming his torch through the new hole into the darkness beyond.

The tunnel stretched away before him. Wider once more. Doyle nodded gratefully.

He pushed and pulled at the bricks around the hole he'd made, tearing more away until the hole was large enough for the two men to scramble through. Doyle led the way, hauling himself through into the next part of the tunnel, relieved that the water level was also much lower in this latest section of shaft. He stood on the other side of the brick partition, waiting for Vale to join him, shining his own torch all around in an effort to pick out details of this newest subterranean walkway. By pushing several other lumps of brickwork away, Vale was also able to clamber through and he joined Doyle, wiping brick dust from his jacket.

"Why was it bricked up?" he murmured.

"Fuck knows," Doyle said, looking around. He noticed that there was lots more fallen stone on the floor of the tunnel now and, as he trained the torch beam on the ceiling of the culvert, small stones fell close by. "Come on," he urged, walking ahead, again forced to duck his head.

Vale walked along behind him, also aware of the dust and stones falling from the ceiling of the tunnel with increased regularity now. He could feel his heart beating faster and, for a fleeting second, he had a terrible vision of the entire structure collapsing on their heads. As if to emphasise his growing anxiety, a lump of brick the size of his fist dropped into the tunnel with a thud.

"I wonder how close we are to the house?" Doyle said, quietly.

Vale didn't answer. He was too concerned with the state of the tunnel roof. As he shone his torch upwards, he could see the motes of brick dust turning in the cold white beam. It seemed even the vibrations caused by their footfalls was causing a minor reaction such was the decaying state of this antique brickwork. He stretched out a hand and touched the wall, as if that simple gesture would somehow reassure him. As his fingers scraped over the stones more dust filled the air and Vale coughed, shielding his mouth and nose from the particles.

Despite the welcome lack of rancid water standing in this part of the culvert, there was still a foul stench permeating the air. One that was even more rank and fetid than they had encountered earlier. Vale waved a hand before him as if to dispel the smell, but it clogged in his nostrils and made him cough. Ahead of him, Doyle was also finding it hard to breathe in the increasingly noxious atmosphere. He coughed and spat, trying to clear the taste as well as the smell from his system. If this had been a sewer many years earlier, he reasoned, it couldn't have smelled much worse than it did now had it been filled with excrement. He shone his torch ahead, wondering how much further they would have to travel in this subterranean gallery. The house must be close by now surely.

Doyle walked on, his shoulders and back beginning to ache from having to walk constantly hunched over.

The torch picked out two dark shapes just ahead and Doyle slowed his pace slightly.

Rats.

Both dead. Both seething with maggots. Doyle looked down in disgust, watching the vile white forms writhing madly inside the dead rodents' eye sockets, mouths and ears and, as he drew closer, he groaned softly as he saw one of the rat's bellies split open to reveal more of the maggots inside. Like grains of animated rice, they spilled from the swollen maw of the stomach, floating in the puddle of fluid they had created while feeding on the soft internal organs of the dead rodent.

Doyle stepped past the two dead creatures, revolted by what he'd seen. Vale too shook his head as he eyed the furry bodies and the parasitic mass within them. And, further on, there were more dead rats.

Dozens of them.

Each one swollen and bloated. Every one a banquet for the carrion eating maggots that were swelling from every orifice. And now, Doyle heard squeaking ahead of him. The high-pitched shriek of the vermin he hated so much. As the culvert turned gently to the right, once again, he saw them emerge from the blackness ahead.

Hundreds of them.

Thousands.

Filling the tunnel from roof to ceiling, pressing against its walls, such was their numbers. They squealed and screamed and hissed as they advanced. A new wall comprised of filthy matted fur and scaly bald tails. Of yellowed protruding teeth and sharp claws. But there was something worse. Something impossibly wrong with these rats and Doyle shook his head gently as he backed away from the oncoming swarm, wondering if his mind had finally imploded and was now refusing to accept what he saw. Where a narrow-pointed head should have ended in a twitching snout and whiskers, there was nothing like that. Instead there was only something that not even the most fevered of nightmares could have produced.

Every single one of these monstrosities had the twisted, bloodied, screaming head of a child.

NINETY-ONE

D oyle took a step backwards, colliding with Vale and both of them stood motionless for a second, gazing dumbly at the oncoming horde of creatures.

"What the fuck are they?" Vale said, his breath coming in gasps.

Doyle had no answer.

He was just grateful that Vale could see the things. For a moment he'd thought that they might be the product of his own fevered imagination.

He pulled the Beretta from its shoulder holster and held it at arm's-length, watching as the monstrosities spilled over each other in their eagerness to reach the two men. If he fired, it would be impossible to miss. There were so many of the vile creatures, but Doyle was only too aware that he had just fifteen rounds in the magazine. Even if he hit something with every shot there would still be hundreds left. If he and Vale both fired constantly and hit their chosen targets with every single discharge it seemed unlikely that they could halt this onslaught.

Doyle and his companion backed up further, realising now that the stench they had been aware of for so long was coming from the swarm of creatures advancing upon them. The horde that seemed to have slowed its approach towards them. The initial frenzied rush forward had given way to a more sedate and more menacing approach. But, Doyle reasoned, why did they need to hurry? He and Vale had nowhere to go. They couldn't outrun these things, not in this small environment. And the creatures were obviously more than aware that their prey was all but helpless. There was no rush to overwhelm them now, just that slow, inexorable advance.

Doyle looked at the contorted faces. The skin on them was yellowish-white, as if the flesh was jaundiced. Large cuts and

329

lacerations, most infected and oozing thick pus, scarred their features. Eyes gaped, throbbing in the sockets and threatening to burst free from those pits as if pushed from behind. As their mouths yawned open, they showed discoloured teeth that were as sharp as knives. And all the time they advanced, those behind crawling through the excrement left by the leading ranks.

"Use a stun grenade," Vale suggested, his breath coming in gasps now.

"In here?" Doyle hissed. "It'll kill us as well as them."

The two men continued to back away, only too aware that there was another thirty or forty yards before they retreated to the brick wall and, even then, they would be forced to scramble through the gap they'd made. The rats or whatever the hell they were, would have them at their mercy then.

Doyle regarded the hordes of creatures, wondering why they didn't just attack. If they had swarmed forward now, they would have overwhelmed both men, but instead, they just kept up that same slow, deliberate and almost tortuous advance. Were they enjoying the terror they inflicted? Could they sense it somehow, the way a dog detected fear?

Something struck Doyle on the shoulder and he glanced around, realising that a portion of the culvert roof had fallen, striking him before it fell to the ground and was swallowed by the reeking water.

Another portion followed. Then another.

Great choice. Eaten alive by these fucking things or buried alive when the tunnel caves in.

He glanced up apprehensively, seeing dust and small particles of brick billowing from the roof like gas.

And still the rats came on.

He still held the Beretta before him, the barrel pointed at the monstrosities as they advanced.

But it was Vale who fired first.

The sound inside the confines of the culvert was thunderous despite the silencer jammed into the barrel of the

Sig-Sauer automatic. The muzzle flashes lit up the entire tunnel for brief seconds and Doyle was blinded by it as he fell backwards, the noise of the retorts throbbing in his ears as Vale pumped the trigger four times. Vale too stumbled away, his head bowed, his ears ringing from the muted detonations.

The smell of cordite drifted through the air, but it was a welcome change from the nauseating stench emanating from the rat creatures and the reeking water in the base of the culvert.

Both Doyle and Vale looked along the tunnel, towards the creatures, and saw nothing.

They were gone.

Every single one of the monstrosities had vanished as if swept away.

NINETY-TWO

Both men gazed blankly into the darkness, breathing heavily. Doyle was the first one to sweep his torch beam back and forth over the confines of the tunnel.

They were alone inside it once again.

There wasn't a trace of the rat creatures.

The only sound now was the low breathing of the two men as they stared at the place previously filled with writhing rodent bodies. Doyle took a couple of steps forward, moving cautiously as if he expected the furry horde to swarm into view again at any second.

He looked at the walls for burrows or holes where they might have disappeared but there was nothing to be seen. It was as if, when Vale fired, the whole mass had simply disappeared into thin air. As ridiculous as that thought was, Doyle couldn't explain where else the monstrosities had gone. Unless they were waiting somewhere further along the culvert. Hiding. Preparing an ambush?

He moved further along the tunnel, Vale close by, both men shining their torches around them to keep themselves behind a barrier of light.

"Where are they?" Vale murmured.

"I don't know," Doyle snapped, as if to discuss it further would require answers that he could not provide. Answers that might question his sanity. He continued on, eyes fixed ahead, scanning the gloom for any signs of movement.

Some more small pieces of masonry fell from the roof of the tunnel and both men looked up nervously.

On the walls up ahead, Doyle could see something thin and tendril-like clinging to the brickwork. He shone his torch over the spindly matter and saw that it was roots. They must have penetrated the brickwork over a period of years and now they protruded from the crumbling stones like hardened veins.

"Maybe this wasn't a sewer," Vale offered. "It could be connected to a priest's hole or something like that. During the Reformation lots of houses and monasteries had them. Places for the clergy to hide if someone came looking for them. This tunnel might be linked to one of those."

"So what?"

"If it is then you're right about it leading near the house, maybe right into it."

Another piece of brickwork fell away from the roof of the culvert.

"If we don't find a way out soon, we won't have to worry about that," Doyle said, anxiously. "We'll be buried in here."

Vale also cast a wary glance upwards, reaching up to touch the roof of the culvert, dragging his fingers across the brickwork. When he pulled them away they were coated with reddish-brown dust. The entire tunnel seemed to be decaying around them. The two men moved on, ever vigilant for sounds and movement inside the culvert.

"Those things..." Vale said, falteringly.

"Forget it," Doyle told him.

"That's not easy, Doyle. You saw them. What the hell were they?"

"There's a description in the grimoire of creatures like that. Guardians of the book. If anyone threatens it or its owner, they defend them."

"They had children's faces."

"I saw them," Doyle rasped. "I saw them. As clearly as you did."

"But their heads..."

"Supposedly the guardians represented the victims of Gilles de Rais. The children he murdered. Their souls were trapped inside those things."

"It's impossible. It's just a story. Superstition."

"Maybe it is, but how else do you explain those...things?"

Vale had no answer.

"When it comes to Callahan, nothing is impossible," Doyle

said. "Trust me."

Doyle played the torch beam over the roof of the culvert, noticing that the brickwork further along was of a different colour. The red of the bricks was brighter. They didn't look so old or fragile. He wondered if they were newer. Possibly added recently as some kind of renovation?

There was a small metal grille set in the tunnel roof within these newer bricks.

When Doyle walked beneath it, he shone the torch onto the rusted iron and held it there for a moment before switching it off.

In the darkness, he saw a sliver of natural light from above. He could see the starry night sky through the grille and the shaft that led up from it.

"Can we get out through there?" Vale asked, joining him beneath the grille.

Doyle didn't speak but a slight smile spread across his face.

NINETY-THREE

The shaft that led up from the grille to ground level was narrow in the extreme. Doyle was sure it wasn't more than three feet across. As he climbed, he could feel the bricks on either side scraping against his shoulders and arms and he wondered if, at any time, he might become stuck in the narrow crawl space.

The grille had come away with relative ease from the bricks and Doyle had been delighted to see that a narrow metal ladder led from it up to ground level. Exactly whereabouts in the grounds of Maitland Hall he was going to emerge he had no idea but, for the time being, he was just grateful to be out of the culvert.

He finally hauled himself up from the hole, rolling over, glancing around quickly to take in his new surroundings.

There were thickly planted flower beds all around him and, beyond that, an open expanse of lawn. Beyond it, Doyle could see the impressive edifice of Maitland Hall itself. There were lights burning brightly in several of the windows. He guessed the main house was less than two hundred yards away. However, there was precious little cover leading up to the objective. All he could see was what looked like another walled garden about sixty or seventy yards off to the right. If Callahan had men patrolling the grounds here, then it would be difficult to reach the building without being seen.

As Doyle crouched there peering at the house, Vale pulled himself free of the shaft. He also looked around, more relieved to be free of the subterranean tunnel than concerned about his new situation.

Doyle glanced at him then pointed towards the high brick wall to their right.

It would provide them with at least some cover from any prying eyes and CCTV cameras that might be trained on the gardens.

The two men set off towards the wall, bent low, gazing around constantly for any signs of danger.

There was a gravel path leading up to the wrought-iron gate that marked the entrance to the walled ornamental garden, and it crunched loudly beneath their feet as they reached it. Doyle pulled the gate open and ducked through into the garden, following the path, letting Vale trail in his wake as he hurried across towards the gate on the other side.

From where they stood, they could clearly see the main house of Maitland Hall. Both of them saw two figures walk slowly past the well-lit French windows on the lower floor. Each of the men was armed with an AK-47.

"How do you want to play this?" Vale asked, his voice low. There was a hint of nervousness in his tone.

"You're the strategic analyst," Doyle murmured, his gaze never leaving the two armed men. "What's your strategic analysis of this lot?"

"Take out his guards and get inside the house," Vale offered.

Doyle nodded.

Vale suddenly reached into the pocket of his jacket. He pulled the two-way clear and turned a couple of dials on it, trying to mute the sound of crackling static.

Doyle watched him as he raised the device and spoke into it rapidly, his Russian impeccable. After a moment or two, Vale switched the two-way off again and shoved it back into his pocket.

"I said that there was a car parked to the north of the property," he murmured. "I said it needed investigating."

"That's where our backup is," Doyle exclaimed.

"It'll keep some of them busy."

Doyle smiled, noticing that the two armed men outside the French windows were already moving away from their positions.

"I suppose all Russians must sound the same on a two-way," he murmured, still smiling.

"Brains are sometimes better than brawn, Doyle."

"You might be right. Now come on. Let's get inside before they realise someone's been fucking with them."

The two men sprinted from the walled garden, across the wide expanse of lawn and towards the stone steps that led up to the French windows. Doyle glanced around, spotting a CCTV camera perched high up a wall nearby. He wondered who was watching them, wondered if, at this precise second, more armed men were heading towards them, but he pushed the thought to the back of his mind, more intent on finding a way into the house.

The sash window close to them opened easily and Doyle slid it up, scrambling over the windowsill into the room beyond. Vale followed him, closing the window behind him.

The room in which they found themselves might once have been a drawing room of some description but now it was sparsely furnished. Empty but for a couple of chesterfields and some coffee tables, displayed before towering bookcases that bore hundreds of volumes, mostly antique tomes that gave off a fusty smell that filled the air like invisible dust. Doyle looked quickly around the room then moved towards the wooden doors on the far side of the large space, his eyes drawn to the strip of light he could see beneath them.

As he put his hand on the door, he pulled the Beretta from its shoulder holster, gripping it tightly in one fist. He glanced at Vale who was gripping the MP5K in both hands.

"Set?" Doyle murmured.

Vale nodded.

Doyle eased the door open slightly, peering out cautiously into the carpeted corridor beyond. Directly opposite him, hanging from the wall, was a huge painting of a man in military uniform. Doyle wondered if it was the man who the place was named after. He was wearing the familiar red jacket of the British Foot Guards from the Napoleonic period. Doyle was sure he was gazing at Colonel Maitland himself. He smiled and nodded in salute.

To his right was another door. To his left the corridor turned sharply to the left.

Which way?

He was still wondering when the first burst of automatic fire tore across the door.

NINETY-FOUR

D oyle ducked back inside the room, bullets punching holes in the wood of the door. Dust, smoke and splinters of wood filled the air and Doyle muttered something under his breath, turning away from the riddled door.

Vale stepped forward and Doyle could see that the younger man's face was a little pale. He glanced at Doyle as if for guidance.

"When I open the door," Doyle murmured. "You go left, I'll go right."

Vale swung the MP5K up into the firing position and nodded.

"Just open up on whoever's out there," Doyle added, one hand gripping the handle of the door. "Set?"

Again, Vale nodded.

Doyle wrenched the door open and Vale stepped forward, his finger tightening on the trigger of the sub-machine gun.

The barrel flamed and nine-millimetre rounds erupted from the weapon as he raked it back and forth, making sure he fired only short bursts. The thirty-round magazine could be emptied in seconds with prolonged pressure on the trigger. Empty shell cases rained down and Vale stepped into the corridor, Doyle joining him, pumping the trigger of the Beretta.

Bullets tore into the walls of the building as both men fired and the two figures away to their left both ducked back behind the wall seeking cover, desperate to avoid the fusillade of fire.

Doyle pulled a stun grenade from his pocket and hurled it towards their foes, ducking and covering his ears as the G60 hit the ground.

The explosion was thunderous.

A shrieking eruption of white light, three hundred thousand

candle power, filled the corridor, while a blast registering one hundred and sixty decibels shattered ear drums.

The two men who had been sheltering around the corner were helpless before the detonation.

One of them staggered drunkenly from cover, blood seeping from both his ears, his eyes wide open and staring madly.

Doyle shot him twice.

The first bullet smashed two ribs before ripping through his lung and erupting from his back, carrying portions of macerated tissue and bone with it. The second bullet punched in most of his left temple and he dropped like a stone, gouts of blood fountaining from what remained of his skull.

Vale also fired in the direction of the man, some of the short blast catching him in the leg and hip, causing further damage to the corpse. Doyle flattened himself against the wall and advanced towards where he knew the second assailant was sheltering. He stuck his hand out around the corner, using the wall as protection, and fired four times.

He heard the groan as the man was hit and, as Doyle ejected the empty clip of the automatic, Vale stepped past him and fired two short blasts at the stricken Ukrainian. The bullets caught him in the stomach and chest and sent him stumbling backwards against a wall. He remained upright for a second then slid down leaving a huge smear of blood on the paintwork.

Vale advanced and kicked the legs of the fallen man, satisfied that he was dead. Doyle slammed in a fresh magazine and advanced with him, moving towards the foot of a wide staircase that led up to the first floor. The stink of cordite and gunpowder was heavy in the air but both men moved swiftly through the greyish-white mist, making their way swiftly up the stairs towards the landing.

They were halfway up when another man appeared at the head of the stairs.

He swung his Kalashnikov up to his shoulder and fired.

Bullets tore into the balustrade, blasting some of the polished wood to splinters, and Doyle dropped to one knee, squeezing off three shots in the direction of the newcomer.

One of them hit him in the left shoulder, more by luck than judgement, and he staggered back, holding the AK-47 in one hand now, unable to control it as it spewed out more rounds, the sound filling the stairwell.

A stray bullet tore off the top of Vale's right ear and he hissed in pain, blood spattering onto his face.

He swung the sub-machine gun up and fired too, happy to see that some of the fusillade had hit the Ukrainian in the thigh and stomach. The man dropped to his knees then slumped forward, blood spreading out rapidly around him.

Doyle hurried to the top of the stairs, reaching the nearest door. He dragged it open and stepped into the room beyond, aware that Vale was close behind.

Below them he heard angry shouts and then pounding feet on the stairs.

More men were coming up after them.

NINETY-FIVE

Vale slammed a fresh magazine into the MP5K, trying to control his breathing as he heard more footsteps pounding up the stairs.

Doyle could see that his younger companion looked nervous and the paleness of Vale's skin seemed to make the blood that had splashed across his face appear even more vivid in colour. Every now and then he would gently touch what was left of the top of his ear, wincing in pain as he felt the torn flesh there.

"Don't worry, it's not serious," Doyle murmured. "It missed your earring."

"Fuck you, Doyle," Vale snapped.

The older man hid a smile and glanced around the room, looking for another way out. A connecting door or anything that would allow them to escape this room.

On the other side of the main door, voices were now clearly audible. Words were barked in Ukrainian. Doyle wondered how many men were out there. But, irrespective of numbers, he was sure of one thing, that they were all armed to the teeth and they weren't going to stand outside that door forever.

Towards the back of the room Doyle saw a connecting door, almost hidden by a table and a high bookshelf but he moved towards it and turned the handle slowly, relieved to discover that it was unlocked. He motioned to Vale to join him and the younger man retreated across the room, keeping his eyes and his gun trained on the main door all the time, ready for the onslaught that they both knew would come.

And now, silence had descended. It was more disturbing than the sounds before it.

The calm before the storm.

Doyle eased the connecting door open and glanced quickly into the next room.

It was another bedroom. Sparsely furnished apart from the large bed at its centre and the floors were bare wood. Doyle stepped over the threshold carefully, making sure he didn't put too much weight into each step. The sound would carry in the stillness. He didn't want their opponents to know they had moved into another room.

The first board creaked beneath his weight and he muttered under his breath. He moved on, gripping the Beretta more tightly, a single bead of sweat popping onto his forehead.

Vale stood in the doorway, his gaze still fixed on the main door, his ears still straining for any sounds coming from beyond it.

Doyle moved towards the door of the bedroom, also aware of the presence of the men beyond. When he reached the door, he pressed himself against the wall next to it, one hand reaching slowly for the handle, the other gripping the automatic more tightly. His heart thudded evenly against his ribs. As if he was moving in slow motion, he turned the handle.

The metal mechanism squeaked loudly, and Doyle dragged his hand away as if the lever had suddenly become red hot.

Anyone standing on the landing would have heard the sound. Wouldn't they? Doyle waited a second then reached for the handle again, turning it quickly and pulling open the door, jamming the Beretta forward, his finger tightening on the trigger.

The landing was empty.

If there had been men there before, then they were now gone.

Doyle edged slowly out from the doorway, glancing in all directions, desperate to locate those who had been gathering outside the room he and Vale had been in. He saw no one. If they'd been there, they weren't there now. Again, Doyle spun around, peering into the alcoves and hiding places on the landing as he tried to work out where the men had disappeared to. He looked over the balustrade, down into the stairway and beyond but there was still no sign of anyone.

Vale joined him, also looking around. Similarly puzzled by the sudden disappearance of the men who had been after them.

Doyle made his way carefully along the landing, one hand sliding across the polished wood of the balustrade as he walked, the Beretta held at the ready should it be needed. There were more closed doors up ahead and the landing turned sharply to the left, making it impossible to see what lay around that corner. Doyle slowed his pace and stepped across to the far wall, so he had some cover.

Vale waited a moment then joined him, watching as Doyle peered cautiously around the corner.

Nothing.

The landing widened and Doyle could see a set of double doors ahead of them. Above those doors there was a CCTV camera and the red motion sensor light on it was blinking. If either of them should advance towards the doors then someone, somewhere inside the house would see them. Doyle moved back, still pressed against the wall.

"Now what?" Vale wanted to know; his voice low. "They know we're here. It's only a matter of time before they come back."

"We've got to find Callahan," Doyle told him.

"How?" Vale snapped. "It's like a fucking maze in here. He could be anywhere."

He glared at the older man. "You're the expert. What do we do?"

Doyle was about to speak when a bullet slammed into the wall just above his head.

NINETY-SIX

Dust and plaster drifted from the bullet hole and both men dropped to their haunches, unsure of where the shot had come from.

Vale sent a quick burst of fire across the landing, bullets smashing into walls and blasting portions of the balustrade to matchwood.

As the sound of automatic fire filled the air once more, Doyle ducked around the corner and sprinted towards the double doors beyond, raising his pistol as he ran. He fired three times, the second shot obliterating the CCTV camera above the door.

"Come on," he called to Vale, who tightened his finger on the trigger of the MP5K once more, the barrel flaming as more 9mm slugs cut across the landing and the head of the stairs.

Just before he ducked around the corner, Vale saw two men pounding up the stairs in pursuit. It was the leading man who fired a burst from his Kalashnikov. The 7.62mm rounds hammered into the wall and floor around Vale and he dashed off after Doyle, knowing that the men were now at the top of the stairs.

Doyle crashed into the double doors ahead of him, making no attempt to hide his presence.

The doors flew back to reveal a much larger, unfurnished room beyond and yet another staircase leading off to the right.

Doyle didn't hesitate but headed straight for the steps, taking them two at a time as he tried to put some distance between himself and the men pursuing.

He heard the deafening retort of a gun from nearby but couldn't pinpoint the source. The bullet hit him in the left forearm, tore through the flexor muscle and sent blood spraying into the air. Doyle hissed in pain, aware of the burning sensation that spread rapidly from his elbow to his fingertips, but he was relieved that the bullet had passed right through without causing worse damage. As another shot hit the ground near his feet, he swung the Beretta up and fired off two shots, not really sure what he was firing at.

Behind him, Vale saw the muzzle flash from above them and he too fired in its direction.

As the two men reached the top of the stairs, Doyle dashed towards the nearest door but found it locked. He drove his foot against the wooden partition, ducking down as more bullets tore into the wall close by.

He felt sudden searing pain in his left side as another round caught him just above the hip. Again, he was lucky that it passed straight through, blood and fragments of flesh and clothing spattering the wall behind him. Doyle snarled angrily and gritted his teeth, turning to see the source of the gunfire. The man was directly across the landing from him, about to fire again.

Doyle and Vale opened up simultaneously and the man was hit four or five times, each bullet powering into him and dropping him like a stone. As Doyle turned back towards the recalcitrant door, Vale saw blood trickling from the wound in his side and looked questioningly at him, but Doyle said nothing and merely redoubled his efforts to break through the barrier. Vale swung the sub-machine gun up again, waiting for more attackers to emerge but, as he stood there, none appeared.

The door finally gave under Doyle's assault, flying back on its hinges and the older man dashed inside. Vale followed.

The room was in darkness. Complete impenetrable darkness. Only the light flooding from the landing area illuminated anything close to the doorway but, as he squinted through the gloom, Doyle could see very little inside the room. It appeared to be unfurnished, the floor nothing but bare wood and, on that bare wood, on the far side of the huge room, he could hear footsteps on that bare floor.

Before he could fire into the gloom, he heard two loud thuds from inside the darkness.

Sharp pain spread from his chest and shoulder and Doyle stumbled backwards, gasping for breath.

He knew he'd been shot but he guessed that the calibre of the weapon was fairly small. Anything more than a .22 and he'd have been cut in half.

That realisation wasn't much of a comfort as he dropped to his knees, his head swimming. He felt nauseous, saw shapes swimming before him, one of which was Vale, who was now lying prone on the floor behind him.

What the fuck is going on?

Doyle fell forward onto his face, the Beretta slipping from his hand as oblivion swept in upon him. He gritted his teeth, trying to stave it off, knowing what was happening to him now and fearing it. As he tried desperately to cling to consciousness, he was aware of lights flashing on around him and of a figure walking towards him.

Doyle rolled onto his back, gazing towards the figure.

The man was looking down at him, eyeing him appraisingly, almost dismissively.

Doyle opened his mouth to say something, but no sounds would come forth. He fought to keep his eyes open, but it was impossible. The man was standing above him now and Doyle could see that there was something else in his expression. Something that looked like distaste. Hatred even. And Doyle finally understood.

The man looking down at him was David Callahan.

Doyle blacked out.

NINETY-SEVEN

Pain.

Darkness.

Familiar things. Unwelcome things.

Doyle opened his eyes slowly and with difficulty. It felt as if someone had sewed his eyelids shut and, when he finally got them open his vision was still clouded. It was as if he was looking through running water.

As he tried to sit up, he realised that he was tied firmly to the wooden chair upon which he sat. He tugged against his bonds for a moment then slumped back, defeated, realising that his struggles were futile and also because the pain from his shoulder and side intensified when he moved too violently. Glancing down at his torso he could see the wound in his side and also a smaller one in his chest just above his heart. He looked around slowly, his vision clearing a little more. Doyle blinked hard, hoping that would help and it did. He felt sick and, as his stomach somersaulted gently once more, he wondered if he was going to vomit. Thankfully, the feeling passed, and he sucked in a deep breath and held it for a moment before exhaling.

The room he was in was small, no more than ten or twelve feet square with a small window. The walls were bare, the floor covered by a thin grey carpet. There was a wooden table directly in front of Doyle, three more chairs set around it as if for some impromptu meeting.

"I thought you were dead."

The voice came from behind him.

"Isn't that what you wanted?" Doyle grunted.

"If I'd have wanted you dead, you'd be in the ground now," the voice said, coldly.

Doyle sensed movement to one side of him and then, as he watched, David Callahan walked into view and seated himself at one end of the table, his gaze fixed on Doyle.

"Long time no see," Callahan said, flatly.

Doyle regarded the other man evenly for a moment, trying to take in details of his face.

"You know who I am?" Callahan murmured.

Doyle nodded.

A slight smile touched Callahan's lips.

"It is hard to believe, isn't it?" he began, quietly.

Doyle stared intently at the other man.

"I killed you," he said, finally. "Nearly thirty years ago I shot you."

"All evidence to the contrary," Callahan breathed.

"What happened?"

"I don't understand all the details myself. But the fact is, I'm here, now. You're not imagining it. You're not dreaming." Callahan drummed his fingers gently on the table top. "There are, as they say, more things in heaven and earth than are dreamed of in our philosophy." He smiled.

"Fuck you, Callahan."

"Still as charming, I see."

Doyle shot him a glance.

"Where's Vale?" he wanted to know.

"Your companion? He's in another room. And before you tell me that your backup will be coming for me, it won't." Again, Callahan smiled. "Three men in a silver Land Rover parked about a mile from here. They were your backup, weren't they?"

Doyle nodded.

"They're dead," Callahan told him. "Some of my men found them and took care of them. No one's coming to get you, Doyle."

"If you're going to kill me why don't you just get it over with?"

"There's plenty of time for that. I thought you might like a little chat first. For old times' sake." Again, that smile flickered on Callahan's lips.

"How did you get away that night?"

"I didn't. You were right. You shot me. But there were other...forces at work. Stronger than anything anyone had ever encountered before. Things beyond anyone's understanding."

Callahan disappeared behind Doyle again for a moment and, when he returned, he was carrying a jug of water. Doyle watched as he set it down on the table and then retrieved a couple of glasses, both of which he filled with the clear liquid.

"I would offer you something stronger but that probably wouldn't be wise until the effects of the tranquilliser have worn off," Callahan told him. He raised the glass to Doyle's lips, allowing him to drink. He did so thirstily. "It was a mixture of ketamine, nitrazepam and chloral hydrate. I don't know the dosages exactly, but it did the job. Fired from a PAX-22 rifle. I thought you might like to know. You've been out for about two hours."

"Why Callahan?"

"Why what?"

"Why are you here? Why steal the book? And the dagger and the medallion? Why...all this? Why now?"

"You'd never understand."

"Try me."

"Because the time was right."

"You were dead."

"As I said, there are certain forces at work that are beyond the understanding of most."

"Fuck you. Stop talking in riddles. Tell me the truth."

"I told you, I don't even understand it all myself."

"What was that...thing that night...in Ireland. That creature or whatever the fuck you want to call it. It came from a stained-glass window. You summoned it."

"Just like I summoned the guardians."

"What the fuck are you talking about? What guardians? The Guardians of the fucking Galaxy? What?"

"The creatures you saw earlier."

"Those...rats? The ones in the tunnel?"

Callahan nodded.

"They can take the form of rats, bats, even dogs sometimes," he said, flatly.

"And you expect me to believe this voodoo bullshit?"

"I don't care what you believe, Doyle, but even you can't doubt the evidence of your own eyes. You shot me. Killed me. And yet, here I am. Explain that."

"I can't. But all I know is when I get the chance again, I won't fuck it up. And I'll bury you myself if I have to."

Callahan leaned nearer to Doyle, his eyes blazing furiously.

"You killed my wife that night," he snarled. "You and that...cunt you had with you."

Doyle eyed him angrily.

"She was the only person I ever loved," Callahan went on. "You took her from me. Do you know how that feels?"

"Yes, I do."

"You're going to pay for what you did, Doyle. You and the organisation you work for. Everyone connected to it."

He slipped a hand inside his jacket and pulled out a pistol that Doyle recognised as a Glock 22. Callahan pressed the barrel against the other man's forehead, pushing the gun hard against the flesh.

"Do it," Doyle said, closing his eyes. "Get it over with. Do me a fucking favour."

Callahan thumbed back the hammer.

"What do you want me to do?" Doyle rasped. "Beg you not to kill me?" He glared at Callahan who slowly withdrew the pistol.

"No," he breathed. "There'll be time for that." He slid the gun back inside his jacket. "Before that happens, there's someone I want you to meet."

NINETY-EIGHT

Gideon Vale felt as if someone had been using his skull as a football.

He opened his eyes slowly, raising his head with difficulty. The pain from his head seemed to have spread down his neck and shoulders as he gradually regained consciousness. He tried to stretch but quickly realised that his arms and his legs were both tightly tied. Vale clenched his fists, trying to ease some of the pressure around his wrists but the cable ties had been pulled so tight that his fingers felt numb. He wondered how long he'd been trussed up like this and also wondered if it was possible for gangrene to set in due to such a situation. The cable ties certainly felt tight enough to cut off circulation to his hands. He flexed his fingers, wincing at the effort.

At least, he reasoned, the headache and neck ache had momentarily taken his attention away from the fact that the top of his right ear had been shot off. He was, he told himself, disfigured by that injury. He swallowed hard at the thought then looked around the room in which he found himself.

It was a room that looked as if it belonged in a different age. The walls were oak panelled. The furniture looked antique. The paintings on the wall were in frames decorated heavily with gold leaf. Most of them showed military scenes and Vale even recognised a couple as showing the Battle of Waterloo. Others were portraits and he had no idea who their subjects were. A man in a military uniform. The same man standing next to a magnificent white horse. Vale regarded the paintings with indifferent eyes, his attention now caught by something that seemed curiously innocuous in such a room.

In one corner there was a CCTV camera and Vale could see that it was aimed at him. He moved slightly on his seat and the camera whirred into life, pinning him in its cyclopean gaze.

He was also aware of a low rumble coming from nearby. A muted sound he thought was conversation.

It was coming from the room next door and he wondered who was speaking.

The voices were sometimes raised but, even then, it was impossible to make out who was responsible for the words or to decipher their meaning or nature.

As Vale struggled to his feet the camera above him once more whirred loudly as it focused on him and he wondered who was watching him.

Was it Callahan? One of his men? Vale tried to ignore the device, more concerned with the low mumblings he could detect from the adjacent room. He sat back on the seat, allowing his head to tilt backwards until it was actually resting against the wall. He looked slowly around the room, his attention now fixed on the single door that led in and out.

What lay beyond it? The chance of freedom? If only he could get free of the cable ties, he might have a chance of getting out. He was still considering that fact when the door opened.

The man who walked in was in his late thirties. Tall, heavily built, almost brutish in appearance. As he moved closer, Vale could see the tattoos on his neck and face. There was even one on the top of his head. A huge spiderweb that extended over the dome of his skull. He was wearing two shoulder holsters, pistols jammed into each one. He walked over to Vale, slipped a box-cutter from his pocket and sliced easily through the cable ties.

"Are you letting me go?" Vale asked, flexing his fingers, relieved when the tips of his fingers lost some of their numbness.

The man merely grunted by way of reply. He eyed Vale appraisingly.

"Others will come after me you know," Vale insisted. "There are other men on their way here even now. Other agents. They were under orders to move in on this house if myself and my partner hadn't reported in by a certain time."

"Fuck you," the man sneered.

"It's true. They're coming."

"Let them come," the man intoned.

"They'll kill you. They'll kill everyone here."

The man looked unimpressed.

"Why did you come here?" he said.

"To see your boss," Vale told him.

"You will die. All of you."

Vale regarded him evenly but didn't speak. He was trying to judge his chances of overpowering the man. Even if he did there were at least seven or eight heavily armed guards still on the property. Men he would have to bypass or remove if he was to escape.

"Why didn't you kill us when you had the chance?" Vale wanted to know.

"You will wish we had," the man said, a grin flickering on his lips.

"What do you mean?" Vale demanded.

The man merely smiled more broadly then turned towards the door. As he reached it, he turned once more, looking back at Vale.

"You should never have come here," he said, his face impassive. "There is evil in this house."

He closed the door, locking it securely behind him.

NINETY-NINE

Doyle sat back in his seat and glanced at Callahan again.

"You still haven't told me why?" he murmured.

Callahan raised his eyebrows quizzically.

"The book?" Doyle went on. "Why is it so important to you?"

"What's the point in me explaining? You wouldn't believe me anyway. You saw what happened in Ireland all those years ago with your own eyes and you don't believe that. Why would you believe what I tell you about the book?"

"The book. The dagger. The medallion."

"What do you believe in, Doyle?"

"What do you mean?"

"Do you believe in God?"

"When you've seen some of the things I've seen over the years it's a bit difficult to believe."

Callahan chuckled.

"I'm with you on that," he said. "Someone once said, 'would a God that was good invent something like death?' I tend to agree with that. That's why I looked elsewhere. Other beliefs. Over the years men have tried to conquer death. To live forever."

"And you think you've done that?"

"Only time will tell."

"If I stuck a gun in your fucking mouth it'd put that theory to the test wouldn't it?"

"You still don't understand, do you?"

"Then make me understand," Doyle snapped. "Tell me your big secrets. I'm not going to be around for much longer to share them with anyone am I?"

Callahan lowered his gaze slightly.

"Why did you come after me?" he said.

"Because I was told to. It's my job."

"That's all?"

"No. It was personal too."

"Are you doing it for her?"

"What the fuck are you talking about?"

"Her name was Georgina Willis wasn't it?"

Doyle eyed Callahan furiously.

"Your partner that night in Ireland," Callahan went on. "She died. Just like my wife died. We both lost the only people we ever loved. We're similar in lots of ways, Doyle."

"I'm nothing like you."

Callahan chuckled.

"That's what you'd like to think," he said. "So, tell me about her. Tell me about...Georgie." Again, he smiled but there was a sneering, dismissive edge to his expression.

"Fuck you."

"What would you give to see her again?"

Doyle lowered his gaze, not wanting to look at the other man.

"Do you think you'll be together again when you're dead?" Callahan persisted. "Joined together in some heavenly reunion where you'll live out the rest of eternity in bliss?"

Doyle didn't answer.

"Or have you accepted that she's dead. Gone forever? Worm food?" Callahan laughed. "Twenty-eight years ago she died. There won't be much of her left by now. All you'll have will be your memories and in time they'll start to fade too. You'll forget how she smelled, how smooth her skin was, what her laugh sounded like."

Doyle looked at him unblinkingly.

"I was the same with my wife," Callahan confessed. "I knew that time would come. Every single day I wanted her back. The way she was. The way she'd been when she was killed." He stood up, looking down at Doyle, his expression darkening and anger filling his voice. "The way she was when you killed her."

"She was in the wrong place at the wrong time," Doyle hissed. "That was your fault. She died because of you."

Callahan pulled the Glock from inside his jacket once more, gripping it tightly, the barrel aimed at Doyle's head.

"Do it," Doyle snarled. "If you've got the balls. Pull the fucking trigger."

Callahan pushed the barrel harder against Doyle's forehead.

"This is what you wanted isn't it?" Doyle sneered. "Your revenge? This is what you've been waiting for. Do it."

Callahan pulled the gun away and turned in one movement towards the door of the room. He opened it, stepping back from the threshold, signalling to someone outside who Doyle couldn't yet see.

When the figure entered, Doyle froze. He felt as if the air had been sucked from his lungs. He shook his head slowly, his gaze never leaving the newcomer who walked slowly across the room and stood opposite him.

Doyle ran appraising eyes over the form before him, scanning from head to toe, trying to grasp what he was seeing.

The figure before him was Georgina Willis.

ONE HUNDRED

Callahan was smiling thinly now, watching Doyle's reaction as he continued to look blankly at her.

Doyle tried to take a deep breath but seemed incapable of filling his lungs. When he attempted to swallow, his throat was chalk dry.

"Hello, Doyle," she said, softly.

Tears began to fill Doyle's eyes. It was like hearing a previously forgotten tune of such beauty and resonance now played again through a crystal-clear sound system. He gazed raptly at the woman sitting opposite him, his mind reeling.

"I know what you're thinking," she told him. "It is me. You're not dreaming. You're not imagining it."

Callahan was looking on like some doting father watching his children playing together.

"I should leave you alone," he said, softly.

Georgie looked around at him and nodded, watching as he slipped out of the room, pulling the door shut behind him.

"Alone at last," she breathed, reaching across the table to brush the back of Doyle's hand.

He pulled his hand away as if it had been touched with a hot iron.

Georgie looked hurt and stood up, walking around the table towards him.

"Stay the fuck away from me," Doyle hissed under his breath.

"You don't mean that."

She perched on the edge of the table close to him and Doyle again ran appraising eyes over her. Over her? Over whatever this apparition in front of him was. He lowered his gaze then, not wanting to look at her any more. Not wanting to prolong this torment. This was a nightmare, some twisted fantasy sucked from a part of his mind he couldn't control. It couldn't be anything else.

"Please listen to me, Doyle," she said, softly. "I know this is insane but..."

"Insane?" He glared at her. "I'm the one who's insane. I'm sitting here talking to a fucking corpse."

"Do I look like a corpse?"

"You're dead. You've been dead for nearly thirty years. I saw you die." The words were forced out with disbelief and pain that was almost physical.

She reached forward and gently touched his forearm, tracing the outline of the bullet wound there.

"Another scar," she murmured. "You had so many."

Doyle shook his head and pulled his arm away as best he could and, once more, looked away from her.

"Don't touch me," he hissed. "You're not real."

The door opened and Callahan walked in, a smile still on his face.

"Is this your idea of a fucking joke?" Doyle snarled at him. "What else was in that fucking shit you shot me up with? A hallucinogenic? Something to make me see things?"

"You don't understand do you, Doyle?"

"I understand that I'm seeing things. I understand that she's not real." He nodded his head in Georgie's direction.

"What would it take to convince you?" Callahan said, quietly.

"First you try and convince me that you didn't die all those years ago and now...this?" Doyle rasped.

"You can see me. You can see her. Why do you doubt the evidence of your own eyes?"

"Because it's impossible," Doyle bellowed.

"You know about the grimoire," Callahan said, quietly. "You know about the man who wrote it, what he believed in?"

"He was as crazy as you," Doyle snapped.

"Because he was different?" Callahan snarled. "Because he could see beyond the narrow parameters of the beliefs we all grow up with? The beliefs that tell us that life ends when our hearts stop beating, that there is nothing beyond that final moment?"

Doyle shook his head dismissively.

"Why do you believe that?" Callahan went on.

"Because I've seen it so many times during my life," Doyle rasped. "When you're dead, you're dead. End of story."

"Don't be as blinkered as the rest, Doyle," said Callahan. "How can you be when you look around this room? What do you see?"

"I see two people who've been dead for nearly thirty years," Doyle told him. "I see something that I know can't be real."

"So, you'd prefer her dead, would you?" Callahan breathed, pointing to Georgie. As he spoke, he pulled the Glock from inside his jacket. He lifted it slowly and aimed it at Georgie's head. She recoiled slightly, a look of concern in her eyes.

"She's not real," Doyle grunted.

"Do you want to put that to the test?" Callahan insisted, pushing the gun closer to Georgie's head. "What is she, Doyle, if she isn't real? A mirage? A projection of thought? A ghost?"

Doyle swallowed hard, his gaze moving between Georgie and the barrel of the Glock.

"Put it down," he breathed.

"Why?" sneered Callahan. "If she isn't real then I can't hurt her, can I?" He thumbed back the hammer, the metallic click reverberating inside the room. "You saw her die once, why not again?"

Georgie tried to move away but Callahan kept the Glock aimed at her, his finger resting gently on the trigger.

"It's up to you, Doyle," Callahan said, softly.

"What do I care?" Doyle muttered. "Pull the fucking trigger,"

ONE HUNDRED AND ONE

"I was as sceptical as you, Doyle," Callahan confessed. "At first. And then I realised the extent of the power that the grimoire gave access too. That power is limitless."

Doyle regarded the other man expressionlessly, watching as he lowered the Glock again. Georgie looked grateful for that and sat down on the chair next to Doyle, concern still etched on her face.

"I was the same to begin with," Callahan went on. "When my wife returned, I wasn't sure what to do."

"Your wife?" Doyle sneered.

"The woman you killed thirty years ago," Callahan snapped.

"You really are crazy."

"It's true," Georgie interjected. "I've seen her. She's alive."

"She's here, in the house," Callahan added. "You can meet her if you like." He smiled.

"You should believe him," Georgie said, softly.

Doyle glared at her, allowing his gaze to move over her. She looked just as she had the last time he'd seen her. Her shoulder-length blonde hair looked almost luminescent, lit as it was by the harsh overhead lighting inside the room. She wore very little make-up, she didn't need it, she never had. Her skin looked flawless, her lips slightly parted as she met his gaze and held it. She was dressed in a pair of black jeans, a white cowl neck jumper and a pair of black boots.

She's dead you fucking idiot. Dead for nearly thirty years.

And yet, no matter how hard Doyle tried to convince himself of that fact, and of the insanity of this entire situation, he could not take his eyes from her. When she smiled thinly at him, he again felt tears welling up in his eyes. A part of him wanted to believe she was alive. Wanted to believe it with all his heart. Wanted to but dare not. Because if he did believe it then along that road lay madness.

She looked just as she was. Still twenty-eight years old. Still as young and full of life as she had been when she had died in his arms all those years before. Again, he shook his head.

If she took off those clothes would her body be disfigured by the bullet wounds that had killed her? Would those same wounds be filled with maggots feasting on her dead flesh? If he got close enough would he smell the stink of corruption and death on her? The scent of the graveyard and the odour of decay? Doyle felt as if his head was spinning.

"The power of the grimoire is beyond measure," Callahan went on. "What else could have done this? What else could have restored life to those we love?"

"No," Doyle sighed. "It can't be right. It can't."

"Just because we don't understand its power doesn't mean it isn't real," Callahan said. "Hasn't that been the basis of every religion in every country and every culture since time began? Religion promises things that none of us can ever hope to understand. Every religion promises eternal life, doesn't it? The conquest of death? The destruction of the power of death? The grimoire promises the same things, but it delivers on those promises." Callahan's tone darkened. "I didn't need a God for the things I've done," he snarled. "With the grimoire's power I am God." He tapped his chest triumphantly.

Doyle let out a long, almost painful breath and shifted his position on the chair as best he could. His shoulders were aching he'd been held in that same position for so long.

Georgie moved closer to him, slipped a small knife from her belt and cut effortlessly through his bonds, freeing him. Doyle looked at her then at Callahan as he rubbed his wrists, noticing that the flesh there had been rubbed almost raw.

"Am I supposed to say thanks?" he grunted.

"Say what you like," Callahan told him. "What you say and what you think doesn't alter the situation. Your doubts and lack of belief can't change the way things are. You're just like all the others, Doyle, blinded by your narrow-minded view of things. Unable to accept anything beyond the blinkered parameters of what you were taught to believe. I wonder if your colleague feels the same way."

Doyle looked puzzled.

"Who do you mean?" he asked.

"The young man you came here with," Callahan went on. "Vale. I wonder if he has the same problems accepting the evidence of his own eyes."

"What the hell are you talking about?" Doyle wanted to know.

"He was close to his father, wasn't he?" Callahan said. "The same way your boss, your superior, was so distraught when his son took his own life."

"What do you know about that?" Doyle snapped.

Callahan merely smiled. "You'd be surprised what I know, Doyle," he said. "Everyone has someone close to them who they've lost," he said, finally. "Someone who they'd give anything to be reunited with. Your superior, Mark Granger, would have given anything to have his son returned to him. Just like your partner, Vale. What do you think he'd have sacrificed to see his father alive again? Even if it was for just an hour or two?"

"So, you know how to reanimate corpses?" Doyle sneered. "So what?"

"Not corpses," Callahan told him. "Are you familiar with a story called 'The Monkey's Paw'?"

"An old woman gets three wishes," Doyle said. "She wishes for money and gets it. Her son is killed in an accident, so she wishes for him to be returned to life, but the problem is he comes back the way he looked when he fell into a machine. So, her husband uses the last wish to wish the son dead again. That old bollocks? Is that what you mean?"

"The history of mankind is littered with stories like that," Callahan said. "The dead return to life but they only have a limited time here, or they look monstrous or have homicidal tendencies. This is different. When the grimoire restores life it restores it exactly the way it was when it was first extinguished. No time limits. No catches." He smiled. "No... hidden extras." He pointed at Georgie. "She's alive. Just as you always knew her. Like my wife. No catch. No illusion."

"None of this will matter soon," Doyle breathed. "None of this bullshit."

"Why not?" Callahan wanted to know. "What do you mean?"

Doyle smiled at him.

"Since we arrived here, our progress has been tracked," he said, evenly. "The three guys in the silver Land Rover your men took out weren't our only backup. If we didn't report in after an hour there were orders that phase two of this operation should be put into motion." Doyle's smile broadened. "Right now there are two helicopters heading here carrying other CTU agents and they've got orders to wipe this place, and everyone in it, off the face of the fucking earth."

ONE HUNDRED AND TWO

If Callahan was feeling any emotion it certainly didn't show on his face. He looked blankly at Doyle and then moved slowly to the window, glancing out at the night sky.

"They're coming, I'm telling you," Doyle grunted.

"Let them come," Callahan hissed. "Do you expect me to be frightened? What can they do to me?"

"They'll kill you."

"I thought you were going to do that."

"Just give me the fucking chance," Doyle snarled.

Callahan shook his head slowly.

"You really are stupid, aren't you?" he breathed. "You can't kill me, Doyle. No one can."

"Let me fucking try, you cunt," rasped Doyle, getting to his feet.

As he did, Callahan dragged the Glock into view once more. He aimed it at Doyle's chest, smiled and turned towards the door.

"You two should have some time together before your colleagues arrive," he said, pointing at Georgie. "You must have lots to talk about after all these years." He walked towards the door, pausing there for a moment, casting a dismissive glance at Doyle then he stepped outside, closed the door and locked it.

Doyle got to his feet immediately and crossed to the door, pulling hard on the handle.

"I know where he's going," Georgie said.

Doyle shot her a glance.

"You're not real," he hissed, his attention still fixed on the door.

Georgie took a step towards him.

"Callahan's right," she snapped. "You are fucking stupid."

"And you're dead. Now get away from me."

She glared at him for a moment.

"You always were pig-headed," she told him, grabbing his arm. As Doyle swung around to face her, she moved nearer to him, pushing her face towards his, grabbing the back of his head and forcing him against her. Their lips brushed together, and she kissed him passionately. Doyle felt the warmth of her lips against his. A familiar moist warmth that he knew so well. The smell of her skin filled his nostrils. When he felt her tongue probing against his he pulled her closer, his fingers sliding beneath her sweater, trailing over the smooth flesh there. When they finally broke the kiss, he reached out and touched her cheek with his fingertips. The skin was warm, almost incandescent.

"Now do you believe I'm real?" Georgie said, softly.

Doyle swallowed hard, his fingertips still trailing gently over her flesh.

"I...I... how?" he mumbled. "I... can't..."

She kissed him again.

"Have you forgotten how I feel?" she said. "How I taste?"

Doyle held her tightly, inhaling her scent. The smell of her hair. Feeling her warmth against him.

"I saw you die," he murmured, his voice cracking.

"I know," she whispered.

"How can this be happening?"

"I don't know but it is happening. We shouldn't question it."

"Georgie..." Doyle began to speak but could barely force the words out.

"Thank you," she said, smiling.

"For what?"

"For saying my name."

She kissed him again.

"You remember what that feels like then?" Georgie breathed.

Doyle nodded.

"I remember everything about you," he said. "Every touch, every word. Everything."

"Then you should know I'm real. This is real. This is happening. You're not imagining it."

"What can you remember?"

She sighed.

"I remember that night in Ireland," she told him, wearily. "I remember...pain. Lots of pain. And fire. Something was burning." She touched her chest with one hand. "Then nothing after that."

"You died," Doyle said, incredulously. "I held you in my arms while you died."

"And Callahan brought me back. Don't ask me how but I'm here. Isn't that all that matters now? What does it matter that we don't understand it?"

"You're just as you were when I last saw you."

"You're not." She smiled. "You're old." The smile widened as she touched his face. "You've got wrinkles."

"Wrinkles and scars," Doyle murmured.

She traced the outline of one scar from his temple across his cheek and down to his jawline. When Doyle looked into her eyes, he could see they were moist with tears.

"I missed you so much," he said, quietly, his own eyes full of tears. "I blamed myself for your death. I..."

She pressed one index finger to his lips to silence him.

Doyle held her hand and kissed that digit, then another and another. He held her so tightly to him she feared he might snap her in two.

"I don't want to lose you again," he said, his voice again cracking.

"You won't."

For long seconds they held each other, eyes fixed on the other. Lost in a moment that neither had dreamed they would ever experience.

"We've got to find Callahan," Georgie said.

"You said you knew where he was going."

She nodded. "Under the house, there's a chamber of some kind. It's huge. It's where he keeps the grimoire. It's that book

367

that gives him his power. There are tunnels under the grounds that connect to it."

"How do you know?"

"I've seen it. I've heard him talking about the book. That's why he bought this house. He knew that chamber was there. It's been there for hundreds of years. The man who used to own this house, Maitland, he was a member of the Hellfire Club back in the 1820's, that's where he held his rituals. That's why this place is so important to Callahan. He wanted to harness all the evil that had gathered there over the years."

Doyle nodded.

"I knew there had to be a reason," he murmured. "The book, the knife, the medallion and now this house. He had to have those things in this setting, didn't he?"

"If we can destroy the book, we can destroy Callahan," Georgie said.

ONE HUNDRED AND THREE

D oyle didn't time it but he guessed that it took just under a minute to smash the door open.

The prolonged effect of him driving his foot against the wooden partition finally caused it to give, panels of the door flying loose as he kicked it. Once the panel close to the lock was shattered it was a simple matter of reaching up to the key that was still jammed in the mechanism there.

"Why did he leave the key?" Doyle grunted.

"Does it matter?" Georgie told him. "Just open it."

Doyle did as he was instructed, turning the key and pushing what remained of the door open.

As he emerged into the vestibule the sound of gunfire erupted and Doyle ducked back inside the room, almost knocking Georgie over. Like him, she dropped to her haunches, trying to see beyond the doorway to the source of the fire.

To their right there was a staircase, to the left the rest of what Doyle guessed had once been a drawing room. Pieces of modern furniture vied for space with antique items and a large coffee table and several footstools had also been arranged before a huge open fireplace that didn't look as if it had been used for ages. There were two long curved swords, crossed at their centres, hanging above the grate. They looked like cavalry sabres. To either side of the fireplace there were more weapons arranged in makeshift displays. Flintlock pistols and muskets, more swords, a couple of lances that still carried the red and white pennants they had flown during battles.

But it was the staircase and the doorway at its base that was Doyle's focus of attention because it was from that direction that the gunfire had come. He leaned close to the door frame, using it as cover as he glanced towards the bottom of the wide staircase.

If there was anyone there, he couldn't see them now.

That doesn't mean they're not there.

"I wish I had a fucking gun," Doyle murmured.

"How do you want to do this?" Georgie asked, her gaze also fixed on the area beyond the doorway.

"You go left, I'll go right," Doyle said, quietly.

Georgie nodded and prepared to sprint from the room.

As they both ran from the doorway another burst of gunfire sent bullets drilling into the wall to the right of the frame. Plaster and pieces of wood were blasted free by the high-calibre shells and both Georgie and Doyle ducked down as the fusillade of fire cut through the air. Georgie made for one of the large antique sofas close to the fireplace, throwing herself down behind it. Doyle scrambled towards the staircase, using the rise beneath the steps as cover. Once there he raised a hand briefly to signal to Georgie who returned the gesture, pulling her hand down sharply when another burst of fire tore into a chair not two feet from where she was crouching.

She got onto her stomach and crawled towards the fireplace, using the heavy furniture to guard her approach.

Inside the large room the retort of the gunfire was still echoing, the smell of cordite now becoming more noticeable as it drifted in the thin clouds of smoke from the weapon. From his position crouched beneath the stairs, Doyle could see Georgie edging closer to the fireplace and the weapons displayed there. He saw her hand close around the butt of one of the muskets there and he wondered what she was doing. It wasn't as if the weapon was going to be loaded and even if it was, the chances of hitting anything with a flintlock weapon were pretty slim even from such close range.

Doyle moved forward a foot or so, peering between the struts of the balustrade. He could see that the gunman was hidden behind the slightly open door at the bottom of the stairs.

There was a chance.

Doyle signalled to Georgie who, still clutching the musket, got to her feet and ran towards the bottom of the stairs, weaving her way through the other pieces of furniture, ready to drop down behind cover should the need arise.

She was less than ten feet from the door near the foot of the steps when the door opened again.

Doyle gasped, realising that Georgie was directly in front of the gunman. If he opened up now, she was dead.

Georgie swung the musket up but not to her shoulder, she hefted it above her like a spear and Doyle understood. As she hurled the weapon like a spear, he saw the light glint on the fifteen-inch bayonet that was attached to the barrel of the musket. The whole thing hurtled through the air, propelled by Georgie's throw. It caught the gunman in the chest just below the sternum, the steel tearing through him, puncturing a lung and burying itself at least six or seven inches into his torso. He toppled backwards, the musket protruding from him like a new limb. Doyle scurried towards the fallen man, kicking the AK-47 that he'd dropped away from his clutching fingers. He looked down at the stricken man then grabbed the musket, throwing all his weight on it, twisting and driving the bayonet deeper, forcing it through muscle, bone and sinew until the point finally burst from the man's shoulder. Blood began to spread around the fallen figure.

Georgie grabbed the fallen Kalashnikov and checked the magazine. The clip was more than half-full. She slammed it back into place, gripping the weapon with both hands.

Doyle dropped to one knee, pulling open the jacket of the dying man, delighted to find a Glock automatic in a shoulder holster there. He dragged the weapon free, gripping it tightly in his fist, casting one last look back at the twitching body of the man impaled on the bayonet. Blood was coursing from his mouth now and his body shook gently as he made one final attempt to drag the weapon free. His hands fell away weakly.

Doyle glanced at Georgie who hefted the AK-47 before her.

"Are you sure you can handle that?" he asked, a slight smile on his lips.

"Fuck you, Doyle," she muttered, also smiling.

"Come on," he murmured. "Let's go."

ONE HUNDRED AND FOUR

Gideon Vale heard movement outside the door of the room.

He could hear words being spoken hurriedly in Ukrainian. More than once those words were spoken by raised voices and there was panic in at least one of those voices. He stood close to the wooden partition, one hand moving to the door handle, turning it slowly despite the fact that he knew it was locked. The words beyond sounded muffled due to the thickness of the door but also because one of the speakers was obviously moving away, his final words shouted from some distance as he retreated.

Vale dropped to his knees, squinting through the keyhole of the door, trying to catch sight of what lay beyond, but he could see nothing. The voices he'd been able to hear had both disappeared and Vale looked intently at the door for a moment before driving one foot hard against it.

The door was thick, sturdy wood and didn't budge under the impact even when Vale struck it a second and third time. He paused momentarily, looking around at the contents of the room he was being held captive in, trying to pick out something that might be used as an implement to help him escape his temporary prison. Perhaps, he reasoned, the door wasn't his best escape route. There was a single sash window in the room and Vale now moved towards it, trying to slip his fingers beneath the frame. It was as futile as his assault on the door had been. Up in one corner of the room the CCTV camera turned and focused on him, the red light blinking.

Again, Vale looked around the room, his gaze coming to rest on a nearby chair. If he could break the window, he could easily clamber out and...

Don't you think they'd have thought of that?

He walked towards the chair.

It's too easy.

Again, he looked up at the CCTV camera, watching as it moved slightly to follow his passage across the room, the lens adjusting itself automatically to keep him in focus. Whoever was watching him could clearly see every movement he was making. If he did manage to smash the window, then they would be upon him in minutes.

Wouldn't they?

He wondered why the tattooed man had untied him in the first place. With his wrists bound by cable ties he had been helpless. Why had they released him? Vale sat down on the chair, his mind reeling. None of this made sense. His head was still throbbing from the after-effects of the tranquilliser that had been pumped into him and, as he sat there, he put one hand to his forehead as a wave of dizziness hit him.

Just sit tight. Wait for Doyle.

The thought stuck in his mind and refused to be shifted. But what if Doyle was incapacitated somewhere and waiting for his help? He might, Vale reasoned, already be dead. Thoughts tumbled around inside his mind as he massaged his temples, fearing that his aching skull might just implode at any moment.

Do something.

He got to his feet again, swaying uncertainly for a second before turning.

The window. It had to be the window. That was the most sensible escape route.

He heard more movement outside the door and then something else. Something he couldn't immediately identify. A louder noise that built and built like a gathering storm until it was almost deafening. But this sound was coming from outside the house. From above it.

And finally Vale realised what was happening.

He crossed to the window and peered out into the night and he saw lights up in the sky. Cold white lights that shone down on Maitland Hall and illuminated it. Lights that cut through the gloom as surely as a scalpel through flesh and, all the time, that low rumbling grew in intensity.

Vale could see the first of the Eurocopter AS565 Panther helicopters hovering in the night sky not more than a hundred feet above Maitland Hall. It was the twin turboshaft engines he could hear. Engines that could move the chopper at speeds of more than one hundred and ninety miles an hour but could also allow it to hover effortlessly above a target as it was doing now. He saw more lights. Another Panther swinging into position. This one swept over the house, turned effortlessly in the air then headed back again, gliding over the complex of buildings like a hawk searching for prey.

The other chopper merely hung in the air as if supported by invisible wires.

There could be ten men in each of the flying vehicles, all of them armed too. Vale wasn't surprised that the voices beyond the door of his temporary prison were tinged with panic. The attack was coming, it was just a matter of when.

And you're right in the firing line.

The sound of the spinning rotor blades grew louder until it seemed as if they were inside Vale's head, roaring inside his ears as surely as the sound of his blood rushing there. Time seemed to have frozen. Vale knew that the Panthers were equipped with 20mm cannons. If those opened up, there would be carnage.

The helicopters continued to hover.

ONE HUNDRED AND FIVE

A s Doyle approached the end of the narrow corridor he could see that it opened out onto a small landing and then that more steps led down from it to a wide hallway.

Behind him, Georgie pushed doors open as she passed them, glancing into each room in turn, squinting into the darkness there in an attempt to make out what lay inside.

Each one, so far, had been empty.

Doyle steadied the Glock and edged slowly out onto the landing, gazing over the balustrade down into the hallway.

Deserted.

Where the hell were Callahan and his men? Had they all run?

As Doyle moved slowly along the balustrade, one hand resting on the polished wood, the other gripping the automatic, Georgie moved to the left, checking the other doors there, pushing the first two open.

The third was locked.

She stepped back, pressing the flat of her hand to the wooden partition, pushing again but finding that it wouldn't budge. Gripping the Kalashnikov tightly, she raised it a few inches then struck the door handle with the stock of the weapon. The lever buckled under the impact and Georgie pushed the door again, watching as it swung back on its hinges.

She stepped inside, the weapon levelled and ready.

The figure inside the room raised his hands in surrender and she saw the look of concern on his face.

"Keep your hands up," Georgie commanded, keeping her gaze fixed on the individual. She took a step into the room, aware that Doyle was now close by, alerted by the sound of her voice. She wondered why he had suddenly started laughing.

"Georgie," he said, trying to regain his composure. "This is my partner, Gideon Vale." He nodded in the direction of the room's occupant.

Vale lowered his hands, glaring at Doyle.

"Vale, this is Georgina Willis," Doyle went on, nodding at the blonde.

Vale looked puzzled for a moment and eyed Georgie warily then he stepped forward.

"Nice to meet you," he murmured, glancing again at Doyle who merely shook his head. There were questions Vale needed to ask but he knew that now wasn't the time. Questions about the woman standing before him but, for the time being, he decided to ask just one.

"Where's Callahan?" he wanted to know.

"I'm not sure," Doyle confessed. "Making a run for it I'd say. Georgie thinks she knows where he's going."

Vale looked at the woman as if for confirmation.

"There's a room under the house," she explained. "A chamber. I think he's there."

"Where is it? How do we get to it?" Vale wanted to know.

"Through the cellar," Georgie told him.

"Do you know your way around this house?" the younger man demanded, holding her gaze.

Georgie nodded.

"Then we'd better follow you," Vale conceded, watching as Georgie hurried off towards the head of the stairs. As Doyle made to follow her, Vale grabbed him by the arm. "Is she the one who...?" he began.

"Yes," Doyle snapped. "It's her. Trust me."

"Can we trust her?" Vale went on.

"What choice have we got?" hissed Doyle.

They both advanced to where Georgie was waiting, a few steps down from the landing. The little procession made its way cautiously down the wide steps, watching for any sign of movement, alert for any sounds. In the open, like this, they were sitting ducks. If someone opened up on them now there would be no escape.

At the bottom of the steps there were double doors to the right and then, across the wide hallway, more doors.

Georgie paused for a moment.

"Which way?" Vale demanded.

"Through there," Georgie said, falteringly, pointing at one of the doors. "I think."

"You think," Vale snapped. "You said you knew this house."

"The cellar is that way, there's access to the tunnels through there," Georgie said.

"You'd better be sure," Vale told her, sharply.

"Do you want to find the fucking cellar on your own?" Georgie hissed.

"I'm not used to taking advice from a corpse," Vale rasped.

"Now, now, kids," Doyle grinned. "Save it for the playground."

Both Georgie and Vale glared at him.

Led by Doyle, they advanced across the open hallway, all too aware of how exposed they were to a possible attack. A portrait of Peregrine Maitland looked down impassively upon them as they moved closer to the doors Georgie had indicated. Vale moved towards the door first, turning the handle with ease when he found it wasn't locked.

"Do you think he knows we're coming?" Doyle muttered as they passed through into the narrow corridor beyond.

"It looks like he's banking on it," Vale added.

There was another door at the far end of the walkway and that too was shut tight. Doyle took one last look out into the hallway then followed Georgie and Vale into the narrow vestibule. As he did, he shivered involuntarily. It felt much cooler inside. The air itself seemed to be refrigerated. When he put out a hand to touch the wall, the stonework too seemed as if it had been coated with ice water. Doyle gripped the 9mm more tightly and walked on.

"Are you sure this is the right way?" Vale asked, nudging Georgie.

She nodded.

"How do we know you're not on his side?" insisted Vale.

"Because if I was, I'd have emptied this into you by now wouldn't I, hotshot?" she intoned, raising the AK-47 slightly.

"I'm saying nothing," Doyle whispered, looking past them both towards the door ahead.

As he reached for the handle, he was aware of the smell that seemed to be seeping from beyond the door. He recoiled slightly, wincing because of the noxious stench. There was something horribly familiar about it. A smell of death and decay that Doyle had come to recognise only too well over the years. He glanced around and saw that Georgie too had raised one hand to her face in an effort to block out the stench.

"Set?" he murmured, preparing to open the door.

The other two nodded and Doyle turned the handle.

ONE HUNDRED AND SIX

As the door swung open, the foul stench rolled over them like an invisible blanket, causing all three to falter slightly.

Doyle led the way down the flight of stone steps into the cellar itself, glancing around into the dark corners, trying to pick out anything moving in the gloom. Their footsteps echoed inside the subterranean room.

It was Vale who noticed the pale shapes away to their left.

Doyle and Georgie swung their weapons up, readying themselves. In the chill of the cellar, their breath clouded slightly in the air as they advanced towards the barely visible figures shrouded by the darkness.

"Oh, God," Vale gasped as they all drew closer.

The bodies of the children were naked, spattered with blood and, in at least two cases, already showing signs of decomposition. Doyle clenched his teeth as he stooped to examine the corpses more closely, noticing that each one had severe wounds to the face, neck and shoulders. One of the girls, lying on her stomach with her legs splayed, also displayed the wound that had killed her. The deep penetrating puncture in the base of the skull that was now blackened and clogged with congealed blood.

"Did Callahan do this?" Vale murmured; his gaze fixed on the dead children.

Georgie nodded.

"It's part of the ritual," she said, flatly.

"What fucking ritual?" Vale snapped, disgust in his tone.

"To raise the dead," Georgie went on.

"It's set out in the grimoire," Doyle added, shaking his head slightly as he regarded the bodies more closely. "Five children have to be sacrificed for each body raised."

Vale looked at the assembled corpses before him.

"There are more than five bodies here," he breathed.

Doyle realised that too. The small corpses lay on top of each other, some hiding others. He used the toe of his boot to shift one of them, the body flopping lifelessly to one side, the mouth open and filled with dried blood and clear fluid.

"Why so many?" Vale murmured, his gaze moving slowly over the bodies.

Doyle could only shake his head gently. He raised a hand to his face once more to block out the vile odour rising from the putrefying figures.

So young.

Lost in his own thoughts he didn't realise that Georgie had wandered away to the far side of the cellar. She was standing close to another thick wooden door, this one braced with heavy iron struts.

"This way," she called, gesturing to the two men who both hurried over to join her. "This leads down into the tunnels," she announced.

"Are you sure?" Vale wanted to know.

"I told you, I know this house," Georgie informed him.

"Then you go first," Vale demanded.

"Fine," Georgie snapped. "Do you want to help me get this door open then?" She tugged at the rusted handle, surprised at how easily the heavy door opened. The hinges creaked loudly but the door moved relatively easily.

"Callahan didn't lock this one either," Doyle mused.

"Perhaps he wants us to follow him," Vale offered.

"It's too easy," Doyle sighed.

Georgie was already peering into the darkness beyond. She dropped slowly to her haunches, reaching out with one hand towards something that Doyle couldn't yet see.

"Be careful here," she said, motioning towards a metal ladder that was attached to the wall directly in front of them. It led down into even more impenetrable blackness and, somewhere far below, Doyle could hear the sound of dripping water. He looked at the ladder, watching as Georgie slipped the Kalashnikov around her shoulder by its leather strap. She needed both hands to grip the metal ladder properly. "It leads down into the tunnels," she said, beginning the descent slowly, her back occasionally brushing against the moist wall of the shaft.

"After you," Doyle said to Vale, motioning towards the ladder but the younger man hesitated.

"Do you trust her?" Vale whispered. "Because I don't. Just because you fucked her thirty odd years ago doesn't mean she's okay now."

Doyle glared at the younger man for a moment.

"We've got to find Callahan," he snarled. "And if she's the only way to do that then that's fine with me."

"Maybe you should be as suspicious as I am, Doyle."

The older man watched as Vale pushed past him, clambering down the ladder behind Georgie. He himself hesitated a moment longer and then followed.

ONE HUNDRED AND SEVEN

The shaft that led down from the cellar was twenty feet deep. That was Doyle's guess as he eased himself down on the metal rungs, the sound of dripping water from below growing louder all the time.

As Georgie stepped off the bottom rung, she felt her feet sink into the thick mud there. She looked down, noting that she had sunk almost up to her ankles in the ooze but, as she took a couple of steps away from the base of the ladder, she was relieved to discover that the ground was firmer in places. Other parts of the tunnel floor were little more than puddles of filthy water and mud but, by keeping close to the left-hand wall of the underground walkway, she kept her feet on more-or-less firm ground.

Vale was the next one to leave the ladder and he too glanced around at the inside of the tunnel, taking in the damp stonework, the mould that covered the bricks in many places and the steady dripping of water from somewhere above. The smell of damp was strong, and Vale waved a hand before him, trying to dispel the odour.

Doyle dropped down from the last two rungs of the ladder, landing in a puddle, water splashing up around him. He muttered under his breath then followed his two companions as they moved slowly along the tunnel. If he stretched out both arms, he could touch the two sides of the narrow culvert. It was smaller than the one he and Vale had used to first reach the house.

"Are you sure this is the right way?" he murmured, keeping his voice low.

"It leads to the main chamber," Georgie told him, her own voice barely louder than a whisper.

"Callahan will be long gone by now," Vale offered.

"Maybe," Doyle said. "But we have to see."

They continued their advance, moving further into the passageway, eyes narrowed as they tried to see through the almost palpable gloom. More than once Doyle stumbled on the uneven ground, both times shooting out a hand to steady himself, feeling the damp stonework beneath his fingers.

He winced as he felt something brush against his face, realising with disgust that it was the diaphanous web of a spider. Doyle swept it away quickly, wiping his hand on his jeans, wondering where the spider that made the web was. In the almost total darkness of the tunnel it was impossible to see how many more of the webs were ahead of them. What he wouldn't give even for a pinprick of light. It was like being blind in the tunnel, blundering along helplessly in the darkness with only the sound of his companions for company.

Ahead, Georgie was finding the same problems. With the Kalashnikov still slung around her by its strap she walked on cautiously, bracing herself against the tunnel walls as she walked. As she took deeper breaths, she realised how cold the air in the tunnel was and it seemed to be getting cooler with each passing minute. It was like inhaling the air from a freezer. Georgie shuddered and walked on, sometimes ducking lower almost involuntarily as if she feared the ceiling of the culvert was getting lower. She reached up and felt her way along the stones above, realising that the cramped confines of the subterranean shaft were helping to create that illusion in her mind.

Beneath her fingers, something moved.

For a second Georgie thought that part of the crumbling stonework had come away but then she realised that the brickwork wasn't crumbling but undulating.

She pulled her hand away quickly, sucking in a breath that was audible inside the tunnel.

"What is it?" Doyle wanted to know, aware of the sharp inhalation.

"I don't know," Georgie said, breathlessly. "Something's moving."

"What are you talking about?" Vale snapped.

"The ceiling," Georgie breathed.

It was Vale's turn to raise his hands, his fingers trailing over the damp bricks above him.

"It was moving," Georgie went on, still trying to advance in the blackness.

"You're imagining it," Vale told her, dismissively.

"No, she's not," Doyle grunted, his own hands also raised to the bricks above.

He grunted as he felt something slither beneath his fingertips, something that was cold and slimy and oozed across the stonework he was touching. There was a low sucking sound coming from above too. A sound that grew in volume until it became a low hiss. Again, Doyle raised his fingertips to the ceiling of the tunnel and this time when he withdrew them, he realised that they were covered with something viscous. Something that clung to his skin like mucus.

"It's slime," he said, fearfully.

"From where?" Vale snapped, wiping more of the sticky fluid from his own fingers.

Something dropped onto Doyle's face. Something moist. Something that slid and contracted on his skin for a second before he brushed it disgustedly away. It took him only a fraction of a second to realise that it was a slug. A bloated, slime covered slug.

The ceiling of the culvert was covered in them. Thousands of them that slithered and crawled like animated faeces only a foot or so above. They clung to the roof of the tunnel, slipping and sliding over each other as they covered the stonework with the slime they exuded, more of them now beginning to drop from their precarious perch onto the trio of figures below them.

Vale stumbled backwards, trying to brush more of the creatures from his shoulders and head. Georgie stumbled on, trying to get clear of the mass above her but with no way of knowing how many of them were there. Even when she looked up towards the tunnel roof, she could see nothing but blackness. But still they fell from their perch, dropping into the reeking water below or falling onto the figures inside the tunnel. Doyle could feel thick droplets of their slime dripping onto him like putrid rain and he tried to brush it away.

All three of them blundered on in the darkness, desperate to be away from this place, away from the slugs. As each one fell from the ceiling it landed with a dull slap and tried to cling on. Doyle spluttered angrily as he spat slime from his mouth, desperate to dislodge a particularly large and corpulent slug that was on his cheek. He knocked it away, ducking low as more of them fell from above.

Ahead, Georgie realised that the tunnel was turning slightly to the left and she hurried on as best she could, hands sliding over the stonework as she tried to use the walls to guide herself through the blackness.

Then she saw it.

Up ahead, two hundred yards or more, a flickering pinprick of light that drew her attention.

She tried to run but stumbled on the uneven ground, falling to her knees as more of the slugs fell onto her, two of them tangling in her hair. She pulled at the bloated black forms with her fingers, squashing one and feeling more of the thick slime pumping from it but she persevered, finally dragging the slug free, hurling it away.

Doyle caught up with her and hauled her upright, forcing her on deeper into the tunnel, away from the creatures above them, trying to get clear of that seething mass that could, at any second, drop from where they clung.

They scrambled forward, joined by Vale who was using one arm to protect his head from the falling monstrosities. He too had seen the dot of light further up the tunnel and it seemed to be spurring him on, forcing more speed from him in the cramped confines of the tunnel as he sought desperately to escape the narrow walkway and its slimy denizens.

Despite his revulsion he shot a hand heavenward, feeling not slippery oozing forms beneath his fingers now but damp stone once again.

"I think we're clear," he panted, his breath coming in gasps.

Doyle too raised a hand and was delighted to feel just crumbling bricks. He nodded in the gloom, trying to control his breathing now.

Georgie moved on, still drawn by the almost hypnotic gleam of the light ahead of them.

"Come on," Doyle grunted, pulling Vale with him as they too headed towards the light.

"There might be more of those..." Vale allowed the sentence to trail away. "Those..."

"They were slugs," Doyle told him. "'Every crawling thing that doth feed on corruption and death'."

"What?" Vale gaped.

"It's from the grimoire," Georgie told him. "Callahan can control some creatures, some animals. The book gives him that power."

"Does it give him power over you?" Vale wanted to know; his question directed to Georgie. "Are you taking us to him now?"

She didn't answer.

"Just keep moving," Doyle instructed, pushing gently into Vale's back. The light ahead was closer now. Another fifty yards and they would be free of this tunnel. The thought seemed to spur all three of them on and they quickened their pace.

They were fifteen yards short when the first of the explosions came.

ONE HUNDRED AND EIGHT

The tunnel shook from the impact of the blast and Doyle glanced around, despite the fact that he couldn't see anything in the darkness.

"They took their time," Vale grunted, pressing himself against the nearest wall as the vibrations rolled through the tunnel.

"Granger must have given the order to attack," Doyle added. "He didn't care if we were in there or not, the bastard."

Georgie kept moving, drawing closer to the light, leaving the two men trailing in her wake. As the sickly yellowish glow grew brighter, she noticed that the tunnel dropped away, eventually opening out into a much larger room beyond. She swallowed hard, a tingle of familiarity running through her. The culvert finished abruptly, the end of it protruding out over a wide expanse of filthy water. Beyond that there was an island of what looked like mud rising in the centre of the room. The openings of several other tunnels also gaped wide into this cavernous chamber, each one leading from a different cardinal direction. She and her two companions were approaching from the eastern branch.

The central area of the chamber was dimly lit by the light from some candles that had been arranged in a rough circle and also a couple of hurricane lamps. It was that dull luminescence that had drawn Georgie and the other two.

"Where's Callahan?" Doyle murmured.

Georgie could only shake her head.

Doyle glanced around the chamber, noticing that there were three small archways towards the northern wall of the chamber, each one blocked by a metal door constructed of thick bars and sturdy cross panels. Candles burned in small compartments close to each of these doors.

"What the fuck is this?" Doyle breathed; his gaze still fixed on the scene before him.

"You know where Callahan is don't you?" Vale snapped, pushing Georgie.

"Get your hands off me," she hissed at him.

"Both of you, shut up," Doyle snapped, peering down from the end of the culvert at the filthy water beneath. They could lower themselves down with relative ease, but they had no idea how deep the water was. It might be a couple of inches or it might be deep enough to drown them all.

He was still considering that when two explosions came in rapid succession, both of them shaking the chamber, the second one causing a confetti of small stones and brick dust to fall from the high ceiling. The stones landed with loud splashes in the expanse of dirty water below.

Both Doyle and Georgie looked up towards the high ceiling of the chamber, seeing more pieces of stone falling from the curved roof. Doyle waited a moment longer then eased himself from the end of the culvert, dangling in mid-air for a moment before dropping the few feet into the water below.

He was thankful that the stinking fluid only reached his knees. He moved slowly through the water, his gaze fixed on the small raised area at the centre of the chamber and the doorways beyond them. Vale and Georgie followed him, also splashing slowly towards the firmer ground beyond.

There was another explosion and all three of them almost overbalanced. More debris rained down from above, larger pieces of stone that could have caused real damage if they'd hit. Doyle ducked down, raising one hand involuntarily to protect his head from the stones. A piece of brick about the size of a fist struck Vale on the left shoulder, momentarily numbing it, such was the force of the impact. He staggered and almost fell but Georgie shot out a hand to steady him, supporting him while they walked up onto the central area of the chamber.

Doyle grabbed one of the hurricane lamps, lifting it high above his head, trying to use the light, desperate to see any signs of movement. Something scurried away quickly off to his right, something that looked at him with red eyes and hungry interest. Something that disappeared into the central of the three archways. A rat? Or something larger? Something that had no name?

Above them, another explosion.

Doyle and the others ducked again, aware of smoke spilling into the chamber now from high above. Another shower of stones and pulverised brickwork rained down.

"The whole lot will collapse soon," Vale snapped. "We've got to get out of here."

Doyle looked around again, realising how useless the light of the hurricane lamp was. It barely cut through the gloom.

"Callahan's not here," Vale snapped. "He's long gone. Why did you bring us here?" he demanded, looking at Georgie. "Were you trying to lead us into a trap?"

Georgie was about to say something when Doyle jabbed a finger towards the middle archway, about twenty or thirty feet ahead of them.

As they watched, the barred door swung open and a figure, still shrouded by the gloom, took a couple of steps towards them. Georgie raised the AK-47 into a firing position while Doyle gripped the Glock more tightly, trying to draw a bead on the dark shape.

In the dull light of the lamps and the candles it was now possible to make out some of the features of the figure that was walking slowly towards them.

It was a man in his late fifties. Grey-haired. Thin faced but with the most piercing blue eyes Doyle had ever seen. They were almost luminescent. He was dressed in a worn grey suit and shoes so highly polished they glinted even in such inadequate light.

Doyle raised the automatic slightly, aiming at the man's head, his finger resting gently on the trigger.

Vale gently pushed the weapon down and advanced a couple of paces.

"What are you doing?" Doyle hissed.

As he turned to look at the younger man, he could see that tears were coursing down Vale's cheeks, his gaze fixed on the older man who had emerged from behind the gate. The older man smiled.

When Vale spoke, his voice was little more than a whisper, tears still pouring down his face as he looked at the newcomer.

"It's my father," he croaked.

ONE HUNDRED AND NINE

Without hesitation, Vale walked towards the grey-haired man, who now had his arms outstretched.

Doyle tried to hold him back, putting an arm across the younger man's chest in an effort to restrain him but Vale pushed past, only slowing his pace when he was a yard or so from the grey-haired man.

"Dad?" he murmured, fresh tears spilling down his cheeks.

The smile the grey-haired man wore widened and he nodded enthusiastically. There were tears in his eyes too.

Doyle looked on helplessly, watching as Vale drew nearer to the older man, slowing his pace slightly as they prepared to embrace.

"Vale..." Doyle murmured, but he couldn't force any more words out. He didn't know what to say anyway. All he could do was watch as Vale and the grey-haired man hugged each other, holding so tightly it seemed likely each would cause the other damage. The grey-haired man was sobbing uncontrollably now as he held Vale to him, his face contorted. Vale himself seemed incapable of speech, his own muted sobs echoing inside the chamber.

Another explosion rocked the subterranean room, causing another cascade of crumbling stone and brick to fall like lethal rain.

The grey-haired man looked up anxiously towards the roof.

"We have to go," Vale said to the older man, touching his cheek with one hand as if he were testing the malleability of the skin there.

"I don't understand," the grey-haired man said, falteringly. "Where are we? What's happening?"

"I'll tell you when we're out of here," Vale said. "When we're safe."

"Now, do you believe?" Georgie snapped at Vale.

"Who are these people?" the grey-haired man asked, his voice cracking. "Tell me where we are."

"Don't you know?" Vale asked.

The grey-haired man merely shook his head, his face pale and a questioning look in his eyes.

"What can you remember?" Vale wanted to know.

"I... I remember waking up in here...and..." the grey-haired man stammered, looking around helplessly. "I can't remember anything else."

Another explosion. This one much closer and more powerful. Several large lumps of debris slammed down onto the table behind them.

"Sorry to interrupt the family reunion," Georgie said to Vale. "But we really need to get out of here."

Another blast, this time so powerful the reverberations almost knocked Doyle off his feet. Smoke billowed from one of the culverts, spilling into the chamber like thick, noxious fog. Huge lumps of stone rained down, slamming into the top of another culvert, obliterating the tube of easterly facing stone wherever it was struck.

"That way," Doyle snapped, pointing at the culvert that opened from the north.

"How do you know?" Vale demanded.

"I don't," Doyle told him, hurrying through the knee-deep water towards the gaping mouth of the tunnel.

Vale and the grey-haired man followed, bent low as more debris hurtled from the roof of the chamber. The older man stumbled, pitching forward into the filthy water. Vale dragged him upright again, following Doyle and Georgie as they clambered into the mouth of the nearest culvert.

They didn't see Callahan emerge from one of the archways behind them.

He was carrying an MP5K in one hand and he squeezed the trigger once, sending a stream of bullets cutting across the wall close to Doyle and the others. As the rounds tore into the brickwork, Callahan moved closer, firing again. Each impact sent a spiral of smoke and dust flying from the wall, pieces of it chipped and blasted away by the heavy grain shells.

"Drop the guns," he roared, his voice echoing inside the huge underground chamber.

Doyle and Georgie turned slowly to face him, their ears still ringing with the sound of the gunfire.

"Drop them," Callahan insisted. "Now." He fired again. More bullets exploded from the weapon, tearing across the wall above the heads of his opponents. Doyle hesitated for a moment, wondering if he could swing the pistol up and squeeze off a couple of shots before Callahan opened up again but he decided against it and tossed the Glock away, watching as it landed on the central area of the chamber. Georgie waited a second longer then dropped the AK-47 too.

"You know this is all over, Callahan," Doyle said, his face fixed in hard lines. "The CTU are blowing the shit out of your house and your men. You're finished."

"Really?" Callahan said, flatly.

He fired another burst over the heads of Doyle and the others, watching as they ducked beneath the fusillade.

"I expected a little more gratitude from you Doyle," Callahan said.

"What the hell are you talking about?" Doyle wanted to know.

"Your...young lady," Callahan said, nodding towards Georgie. "I gave her back to you."

"Fuck you," Doyle rasped. "You gave me nothing."

Callahan pointed at the grey-haired man. "And your father, Mister Vale. How does it feel to see him again?"

Vale didn't answer but he moved closer to the grey-haired man.

"Where's the grimoire?" Georgie called.

Callahan's smile faded rapidly.

"It's safe," he told her. "And as long as it is then you're safe too. You understand that don't you?"

Georgie nodded.

"What the hell does he mean?" Doyle wanted to know.

"Tell him," Callahan snapped. "Put him out of his misery." The smile returned. Mocking and dismissive. "Perhaps you should tell Vale as well. I'm sure he and his father would be interested."

Doyle grabbed Georgie's arm and pulled her close to him.

"What is he talking about?" he snapped.

"It isn't her fault, Doyle," Callahan called. "She didn't ask for this. Neither of them did."

Again, Doyle glared at Georgie.

"Tell me what he means," he rasped.

Georgie pulled away from him, angered by his reaction even if she understood it.

"She's alive because of the grimoire," Callahan called. "The same as Vale's father. The same as my wife. The same as the others. It brought them back. It helped to give them life again..."

"Others?" Doyle interrupted. "What others?"

"That doesn't matter now," Callahan told him. "All that matters is that you know the truth about the power of the grimoire and about those it brings back to life."

"You said there were no catches," Doyle shouted.

"There aren't," Callahan assured him. "They're alive now as they were before. Just as you knew her. Just as Vale knew his father. Just as my wife was before you killed her." He pointed an accusing finger at Doyle, his expression darkening. "And as long as the grimoire is intact, they will remain alive. For ever."

Doyle looked puzzled.

"They can't die," Callahan shouted. "They're immortal. Like me."

ONE HUNDRED AND TEN

For a moment, Doyle was silent, struggling to digest what he'd just heard. The words seemed to reverberate in the air, hovering around him like bothersome flies. He glanced at Georgie, then at Vale and finally seemed to find his voice.

"I don't believe you," he roared.

Callahan was smiling thinly.

"You thought you killed me nearly thirty years ago," he said. "You shot me. Why didn't I die? Because I can't. You can't kill me. Not you, not anyone. And that is the gift that I have given to the others."

"Did you know?" Doyle said, glaring at Georgie.

"He's lying," she told him, her face pale.

"What if he's not?" the grey-haired man blurted. "I don't want to live forever. I don't want to see the people I love dying while I live on." He looked at Vale almost imploringly. "I can't do that."

Callahan took a step backwards, glancing towards the archways behind him. Doyle recognised the woman who emerged from one of them. Long dark hair, slender and dressed in expensive clothes. He had seen her before, years earlier. Watched her die.

Laura Callahan walked up alongside her husband and kissed him gently on the cheek. She was carrying the grimoire.

"Five children for each life, Callahan," Doyle called. "You killed fifteen kids to bring these three back?"

"There were more than fifteen," Callahan told him. "But it was a small price. Don't you agree?"

Doyle took a couple of steps forward, chancing a brief glance towards the Glock that was lying off to his left. If only he could reach it.

"So, she's immortal too?" he said, nodding towards Laura

who was still standing beside her husband.

Callahan smiled. "No one can separate us now. No man, no god."

Doyle continued to advance slowly, moving closer to the fallen Glock but always keeping his eyes on Callahan.

"I want to know if what he's saying is true," the grey-haired man said, his voice cracking.

"It's impossible," Vale countered. "It can't be true."

"I don't know whether your lack of faith is down to ignorance or stupidity," Callahan offered. "You can see with your own eyes that what I'm saying is true. The people you loved are with you again."

"For the rest of eternity?" Doyle grunted.

"They can't die," Callahan said, smiling broadly.

"Unless the grimoire is destroyed," Georgie called.

Callahan's smile faded rapidly.

It was Doyle's turn to look quizzical.

"'Whatever is restored by the book will cease to be when it is no more,'" Georgie breathed, her eyes fixed ahead.

"What the hell is she talking about?" Vale snarled.

"Words from the grimoire," Doyle told him.

"I do understand your doubts," Callahan said. "I really do. Perhaps some proof of what I say would make you more accepting."

His finger tightened on the trigger of the MP5K, bullets exploding from the barrel. The blast swept across the figures before him, drilling into the ground, ripping through the water and cutting through the air like a scythe.

Doyle dived for the ground. Vale and Georgie both dropped to their knees, ducking instinctively as the sound of the fusillade filled the chamber, roaring in their ears.

The grey-haired man stood motionless, frozen by the sudden blast, unable to react fast enough as a bullet ripped through his left shoulder, tearing through flesh and muscles, shattering his scapula as it burst from his back. Another powered into his stomach, a third into his right thigh. Blood burst from the wounds, spraying into the air.

The grey-haired man staggered uncertainly for a moment then dropped to his knees, hands clutching at the wounds, one finger slipping inside the bleeding maw of his stomach injury. He could feel something warm and slippery inside that hole and he realised that it was his intestine. He looked helplessly at Vale and fell forward.

Vale jumped to his aid, pulling him out of the water.

Doyle had managed to reach the Glock and he swung it up, finger pumping the trigger, the automatic slamming back against the heel of his hand with each discharge, the sound deafening inside the chamber.

And from above, another explosion rocked the chamber.

There was a deafening grinding sound and smoke came pouring into the subterranean room through a huge rent in the roof. Smoke, dust, pulverised bricks and stone all filled the air, lumps of masonry raining down like shrapnel. Doyle looked up in horror, realising that what they had feared was about to happen.

The roof was caving in.

ONE HUNDRED AND ELEVEN

Doyle grabbed Georgie by the arm and hauled her to her feet, almost dragging her towards the archways at the rear of the chamber.

However, she was more concerned with Vale, watching him trying to pull the grey-haired man from the water, seeing the look of horror on the younger man's face as he saw the bullet wounds still spurting blood. She pulled away from Doyle and hurried across to help Vale, both of them tugging and dragging the grey-haired man from the water into the central part of the chamber.

Doyle rushed on, seeing Callahan and his wife disappear into the central archway, desperate to escape the lumps of masonry that were raining down in such profusion. He peered into the mouth of the archway, ducking back hurriedly when a burst of automatic fire came from inside.

A splinter of stone nicked Doyle's cheek, opening a cut and causing blood to dribble down his face. He muttered something under his breath then stuck his hand into the archway and fired three times, the slide flying back as the hammer slammed down on an empty chamber. Doyle grunted angrily and backed off, looking across to where Vale was leaning over the grey-haired man.

"Get him in here," Doyle shouted, motioning to one of the other archways, aware that they needed to escape the chamber before the entire structure collapsed in upon itself.

Vale had his hand inside the grey-haired man's jacket, pulling his shirt open, trying to get a better look at the wounds. The older man lay motionless, his eyes open wide, gazing helplessly at Vale who was trying to support him with his spare hand.

"We've got to get him help," Vale gasped. "He's going to bleed to death."

The grey-haired man's skin was already the colour of milk and Vale realised it was a combination of shock and blood loss.

"Dad, hang on," he said, desperately. "I'll get you out of here."

As Georgie looked out into the chamber, she saw that the entire area was now filled with smoke and dust. Bricks and stones were still raining down, some pieces so large they caused the ground to shake as they hit.

"Get him up," Doyle snapped, gesturing towards the grey-haired man.

Vale and Georgie lifted the man, supporting him, forced to ignore his protestations of pain. They followed Doyle down the tunnel.

"If Callahan went down here, there must be a way out," Doyle announced, keeping close to the wall of the tunnel. "But we've got to hurry."

"Leave me," the grey-haired man croaked.

"No," Vale snapped. "I'm not leaving you. Not again."

They struggled on, deeper and deeper into the tunnel, swallowed by its enveloping darkness, stumbling over the uneven floor, only too aware of the chamber collapsing behind them.

Vale could feel the warm blood seeping onto him as he held the grey-haired man, trying to support him, trying to carry him away from this scene of carnage and destruction. Georgie too could feel the older man's life fluid soaking into her own clothes as she held him. He was moaning softly under his breath, his lips fluttering.

The tunnel curved around gently to the left and then the right and as they struggled on, Doyle felt cold air against his skin. He realised that it was coming from up ahead. The end of the tunnel must be within reach.

From behind them, there was a huge crash and smoke and dust filled the tunnel, causing them to momentarily slow their pace. Enveloped by the noxious fog, they could only stand helplessly as the clouds of smog turned the air around them opaque. Vale coughed loudly, trying to get his breath within the choking miasma. Beside him, still supported by him, the grey-haired man also coughed and, as he did, bright blood sprayed from his mouth, some of it spattering Georgie who looked with concern at the older man.

Doyle hesitated a moment longer then moved on, waiting for the others to catch him up, wanting to check that the way ahead was clear but only too aware that Callahan was somewhere in front of them and still armed. Moving through the darkness and the smoke it was almost impossible to see more than a yard or two, Doyle squinted in an effort to see more clearly in the tunnel.

But now the breeze was blowing more strongly, and he could see a dull light ahead. He realised that it was moonlight and that realisation cheered him somewhat. They were almost out of the tunnel, almost free of the subterranean complex. Still carrying the grey-haired man, Vale and Georgie were close behind him, also welcoming the gusts of cool air that greeted them the nearer they came to the tunnel exit.

The mouth of the tunnel finally opened into a wooded area that Doyle realised was still on the grounds of Maitland Hall. As he glanced around, he could see the hall itself about half a mile away to the west, smoke and flame rising from it in several places.

As Vale and Georgie emerged from the tunnel, they laid the grey-haired man down, Vale inspecting the wounds again. With his free hand he gently stroked the older man's forehead, brushing his hair back. The older man smiled up at him.

A second later they all ducked down as a burst of automatic fire cut through the woods, blasting branches from trees and causing Doyle to scramble for cover. He saw movement off to his right, a figure blundering through the bushes there as the echo of the gunfire died away on the still night. Then the roar of a car engine and he saw a Land Rover pulling away, back wheels spinning as it struggled for traction on the slight rise.

Behind the wheel he saw Callahan, his wife seated next to

him.

And as he watched, above Doyle, a helicopter hurtled across the sky, swooping low like a bird of prey in pursuit of a meal. The sound of the rotors was deafening in the stillness and Doyle watched as the chopper sped after the fleeing Land Rover. He saw brilliantly bright flames from muzzle flashes as the men in the helicopter fired down at the speeding car.

Bursts of fire also came from the Land Rover, cutting through the air and causing the chopper to swing away violently as the pilot tried to avoid it being hit. As Doyle watched, the AS565 swung around almost full circle and he realised that it was descending.

As it landed a hundred yards from him, he saw one of the doors open and witnessed a familiar figure beckoning to him.

"Come on," Mark Granger shouted.

Doyle hesitated a moment, aware of movement behind him. He saw Georgie emerging from the trees there. He waited for her to join him then both of them ran towards the waiting helicopter. Granger looked quizzically at Georgie as they both clambered into the Panther but then he too swung himself back into the chopper, the machine rising rapidly into the air.

There were two other men inside apart from the pilot, a heavily built individual dressed in black jeans and a black leather jacket and another man in his twenties with shoulder-length hair who was hunched over several monitors in the belly of the craft. Doyle could see various lights and images on the screens, but they meant nothing to him.

"We're tracking Callahan," Granger said, flatly, motioning to the screens. "Thermal imaging. He can't get away."

"Vale needs help," Doyle told his superior.

"I know," Granger said, nodding. "I'll send backup. Our priority now is Callahan." He reached inside his jacket and pulled a Beretta 92F from a holster there. He handed it to Doyle butt first. "I think you need that," he said, a slight smile on his face.

As Doyle took it from him, he too was smiling.

ONE HUNDRED AND TWELVE

"What happened in there?" Granger wanted to know.

"It's a long story," Doyle grunted.

"Tell me anyway," Granger murmured.

"Whatever Callahan was threatening to do with the grimoire, he's done it. Don't ask me how."

Granger glanced at Georgie who met his gaze for a moment and then peered out into the night, gripping the arms of her seat as the Panther banked sharply.

"This is..." Doyle began, nodding in Georgie's direction.

"I know who she is," Granger interrupted, cutting across him. "I read the files." Again, he looked Georgie up and down.

There was a moment of silence and then Granger continued. "We were tracking you the whole time you were in there," he said, flatly, now looking out into the gloom.

"Then why the fuck did you order the attack before we got out?" Doyle snapped.

"We couldn't wait all night," Granger told him. "As I said to you, the priority was Callahan."

"And you still missed him," Doyle said.

"We'll get him," Granger breathed. "Now we've got a fix on him he won't be able to outrun us. Visual and electronic surveillance, we're monitoring every move he makes. He can't sneeze without us knowing about it now."

"I don't think he cares about outrunning us," Doyle observed. "He's been ready for us at every turn."

"He's been lucky," Granger grunted.

"What if it's more than luck? What if he's got someone feeding him information? Someone on our side?"

"Why would anyone want to do that?"

"He's a billionaire for fuck's sake. He could buy anyone if he wanted to."

"Not everyone's for sale, Doyle."

"Bullshit. Everyone's got a price."

"What's yours?" Granger looked unblinkingly at him for a moment. "The return of your...former partner?" He smiled.

Doyle held his gaze.

Georgie reached across and gently squeezed his hand.

"How touching," Granger said, noticing the gesture.

Doyle wasn't slow to catch the scorn in his voice.

"Mister Granger."

The voice came from the pilot who was motioning to one of the many display units and monitors in the front portion of the chopper's cockpit.

"Callahan's turned off the main road," he said.

"Stay on him," Granger instructed. "I'll order in more units when the time comes."

"Any idea where he's going?" Georgie offered.

"None at all," Granger told her. "But wherever he's going we'll get him."

"You seem very sure of that," she said.

"You and Doyle might have let him slip away, twice, but I won't." He smiled thinly. "By the way, who's the man with Vale?"

"He thinks it's his father," Doyle said, softly.

"And what do you think?" Granger wanted to know.

"I'd say there's a pretty fair chance that it is," Doyle confessed.

Granger didn't answer.

The next voice that filled the cockpit was the pilot once again.

"Callahan's stopped," he said, flatly. "About half a mile to the east."

Doyle reached inside his jacket and touched the 92F, undoing the clip that held it in position in its shoulder holster.

The chopper banked violently, speeding towards its destination.

ONE HUNDRED AND THIRTEEN

The church stood on a low hill overlooking the countryside around it. Surrounded on three sides by trees and ringed by a high privet hedge that had long ago become overgrown just like the graveyard it protected.

A short pathway cut through the ancient headstones, tombs and crosses that marked the graves of those so long ago deceased, winding past these monuments until it came to the thick, iron-braced door of the church itself. Here there was a small porch, surrounded by scaffolding like most of the main building. The renovation work had been going on for several months already, the church closed to the public while essential maintenance was carried out on the roof and upper level. Particularly the bell tower which rose high above the rest of the building. Workmen were busy on the site for eight hours of every weekday, in fact some had even left their tools inside the building. Drills, saws and a selection of other implements had been momentarily abandoned on the wooden walkways of the scaffolding inside the church. Those who had left their tools seemed to trust that hiding them inside a house of God would ensure their safety. Who was going to steal from a place of such sanctity, seemed to be the thinking?

The church was a classic example of medieval architecture and similar to many other buildings of its type so numerous in the English countryside. It had stood like a beacon for the local community for more than seven hundred years now, a testament to those who had built it and also those who had worshipped within its walls over the centuries. In the local towns and villages for so many years people had lived who had in this one building, been christened, married, seen their offspring marry and then taken their turn in the earth just beyond its walls like so many before them. It had always been an integral part of local life. Fetes and fairs had been held in the large fields attached to the building, at one time church land too. Now those fields were slightly overgrown too and the whole church and the grounds around it seemed to signal a feeling of neglect more than anything else.

When the renovations were over that would be rectified, everyone was sure of that. With the church back to its pristine best then everything else would follow. Inside there was more scaffolding, in fact the entire building seemed to be supported by the network of steel pipes and wooden walkways.

Pews had been stacked neatly to prevent them being damaged and the nave, transept and aisles had all been covered with tarpaulin to prevent them sustaining any more damage than was necessary.

By taking a set of wooden stairs from the north or south transept it was possible to reach a balcony that ran around the church just below the roof and overlooked the inside of the structure. From this balcony it was also possible to see through one of the six leaded windows out into the darkness of the night and watchful eyes now peered through these apertures, looking into the gloom and towards the lights that flickered brightly in the sky.

Lights that glowed on the landing gear of a Panther helicopter as it swept closer, descending all the time, aiming for the field nearest the church.

Those watching eyes saw the AS565 gliding down, rotors spinning madly, engine roaring.

They saw figures spilling from inside the transport, heading towards the church across the expanse of open ground that led up to the hedge which marked its perimeter.

There was a wooden gate that opened into the graveyard and the same eyes now saw that gate being opened. Saw the leading figures hesitate as they reached the Land Rover that was parked close to that gate. A cursory inspection inside the vehicle and the figures moved on, into the graveyard, walking carefully along the path towards the church, others taking other routes between the grave markers, anxious to remain hidden by the obstacles and by the enveloping night.

The rotors of the helicopter had stopped turning now, only the lights inside the cockpit showed that the transport was operational. The silence had swallowed the Panther as surely as it had everything else around about. The footsteps of those approaching the main door of the church could be heard crunching on the gravel of the pathway.

The figures that had chosen to advance through the maze of grave markers and over the grassy uneven ground were close to the east wall of the church now, one of them darting ahead towards another narrow walkway that encircled the building. This path led to the area outside the ambulatory but there were no other doors into or out of the structure. Whoever was coming in would have to do so via the main door and it was towards that door that the watching eyes now turned.

The time had almost come.

ONE HUNDRED AND FOURTEEN

Gideon Vale let out a long sigh, got to his feet and walked out of the small room in the hospital, heading towards the vending machine at the end of the corridor outside.

The building was quiet, due to the late hour, and as he walked, his footsteps echoed on the gleaming floor. He reached the machine, fed in some coins and made his selection, finally lifting a coffee free. He took a sip, wincing as he did, both from the heat of the brown fluid and also at its bitterness. Vale pushed more coins in, got himself a cup of warm milk and decanted some of it into his coffee, sipping again and finding that it was now a little less bitter. He sighed and turned to walk back to the waiting room he'd left, glancing into some of the rooms he passed on his way.

None of them contained his father. He had been taken to Intensive Care upon arriving at the hospital an hour before. Vale had been sitting in the waiting room ever since or at least since his own wounds had been treated. He raised one hand to his injured ear, touching the bandages there, thankful that he hadn't been hurt more seriously during the time at Maitland Hall.

He sipped at his coffee again, considering everything he'd seen during the evening prior to the arrival at the hospital. It seemed like something from some fevered nightmare. Something that belonged in a horror film. Something...

Vale glanced at his watch. How much longer before there was some news of his father? Or did they already know all they could and they were just sparing him the agony for a few moments longer?

His father.

Even thinking the words seemed ridiculous. And yet he knew that man he had seen at Maitland Hall, the man who now lay in a bed in Intensive Care, was his father. There could be no mistake. The man lying up there was the man he'd seen die of cancer only five years earlier. As insane and impossible as that seemed, it was true. And now Vale feared he would lose him for a second time, on this occasion to bullets rather than some monstrous disease. He pushed open the waiting room door and walked in.

The man inside the waiting room was a little older than Vale himself. Clad in the long white coat of a doctor and carrying a stethoscope as if to reinforce that fact, he smiled warmly at Vale as he entered the room.

"Mr Vale," he said, extending his right hand. "I'm Doctor Elliot."

Vale shook the offered hand and nodded.

"Is it about my father?" he asked, his voice low.

Elliot nodded.

"I've just come from ICU," he said. "Your father is out of danger."

"Thank God," Vale breathed. He sat down heavily, almost spilling his coffee.

"In fact," the doctor went on. "He's not just out of danger, he's practically fit enough to leave here."

Vale looked in bewilderment at the doctor.

"That's impossible," he said, quietly.

"I agree. The wounds he sustained caused serious damage to a number of internal organs and the amount of blood he lost alone should have been enough to finish him off. And yet he was sitting up in bed when I left him."

Vale looked even more puzzled.

"How is that possible?" he asked.

"I was hoping you could tell me?" Elliot offered. "When he was brought in, he was critical. Less than two hours later he's as healthy as you or I. His vital signs are stable. His heart rate and respiration, his blood pressure, they're all perfect. Not what you'd expect from a man who'd sustained bullet wounds severe enough to kill him."

Vale could only shake his head.

"We took X-rays when he was brought in," Elliot continued. "They showed irreparable damage to the pancreas and part of the lower intestine. The left lung had collapsed, and the femoral artery had been severed. I checked fresh X-rays twenty minutes ago and those same areas looked...untouched."

Vale swallowed hard.

"It was as if the damaged tissue had somehow regenerated," Elliot went on. "Which I know is impossible. And yet...your father is...I don't know how, but he's not only alive, he's recovering at a speed I would have thought impossible for wounds of that severity. It's incredible. If I hadn't seen it with my own eyes, I wouldn't have believed it. In fact, I have seen it and I'm still not sure I believe it."

"Can I see him?"

"By all means. I'd prefer it if you didn't tire him to much but, from what I've seen, there's not too much chance of that."

Vale got to his feet.

"He's very confused and unsettled, Mr Vale," Elliot said. "But I can understand that."

"Is he in pain?"

"No. He says he has no pain at all. I don't understand that either."

"Let me speak to him," Vale said. "I'll see what I can find out."

He was out of the door before the doctor could speak again.

ONE HUNDRED AND FIFTEEN

D oyle slowed his pace slightly as he approached the large stone sarcophagus ahead of him. The tall grass that grew all over the churchyard was wet and he could feel that the lower parts of his jeans were already soaking. He glanced towards the church, trying to see any signs of movement from inside but he could detect nothing.

If Callahan was waiting inside, he was certainly keeping quiet. Doyle wondered what he was walking into.

He glanced to his left and saw another of the CTU men, the tall man in the leather jacket, hurrying towards some bushes near the pathway. They didn't offer much cover, but something was better than nothing. To his right, Georgie was also picking her way carefully among the grave markers, clutching the weapon that Granger had given her as they'd all exited the helicopter. She was holding a Ruger LCR .357 Magnum revolver, gripped in one hand as if it was an extension of her flesh and muscle. Doyle had seen her take two spare cylinders of ammunition from Granger too. He had a feeling she might need it.

Granger himself was bringing up the rear with the long-haired member of the CTU Doyle had seen in the chopper earlier. Only the pilot was left in the transport itself.

Doyle glanced around once or twice in Granger's direction, seeing that his superior was also moving through the churchyard, picking his way carefully through the long grass, steadying himself on the uneven ground when necessary. The long-haired man remained at the church gate, peering into the gloom.

Doyle reached the sarcophagus and ducked down beside it, one hand stroking the stonework unconsciously. He watched Georgie scurry towards one corner of the church, pressing herself against the wall there. She looked towards the porch and then behind her along the easterly wall. As Doyle watched, she bent low and moved off along that wall, ducking so that anyone inside wouldn't be able to see her through the leaded windows that looked out onto the churchyard.

She kept close to the cold stonework, glancing at each window in turn, ensuring that none had been opened and used as escape routes by those hiding inside the building. She continued right around the structure, trying to control her breathing as she reached each window, slipping fingers gently under the frame to test if it opened or not. If it didn't, she simply moved on. When she came to the wall of the north transept she paused then turned back and headed once more for the main entrance of the church.

Doyle saw her appear once more at the corner of the building then press herself against the wall as she moved slowly towards the porch.

He himself rose up behind the stone sarcophagus, watching as 'Leather Jacket' took up another position on the other facing corner of the building.

Doyle was about to move forward himself when a burst of fire ripped across the churchyard.

He ducked back behind the tomb, pieces of it blasted away by the bullets tearing from inside the church.

Doyle tried to pinpoint the muzzle flashes, attempting to work out where the gunfire was coming from. As more bullets tore into the ground close to him, he saw that barrels were flaming in two separate places inside the church. One of the windows near the front of the structure and high up in the bell tower itself.

Georgie stepped away from the wall, swung the Ruger up and fired three times, the weapon bouncing in her grip as the heavy grain slugs exploded from the barrel.

Leather Jacket too fired upwards towards the tower, the high-pitched scream of ricochets also filling the air along with the rattle of fire.

Small clouds of gun smoke drifted through the air and, as Doyle added his own fire to the fusillade from his companions, he smelled the stink of cordite in the night.

More gunfire from above and he hissed as a bullet nicked his boot, slicing through the sole.

He ducked down behind the sarcophagus again as the blasts slammed into the stonework. As Doyle kept himself pressed to the wall of the monolithic tomb, he could clearly see the inscription on the side of it;

FRANCIS DUGGAN

DIED MARCH 12TH 1856.

Doyle hoped he wouldn't be joining him any time soon.

He saw Georgie duck down behind a stone cross, firing off more rounds at the bell tower.

Leather Jacket too was sheltering behind another one of the grave markers, also firing back. For fleeting seconds, the night air was alive with the sound of gunfire and the scream of bullets as they cut through the blackness. Muzzle flashes looked like sheet lightning, illuminating the churchyard.

It was in one of those moments that Doyle saw something move close to him.

At first, he thought it might be a mouse or rat hiding in the overgrown grass but, as he looked more closely, he saw that it wasn't an animal causing the long blades to part and undulate. The ground beneath them was moving slightly. Rising and falling gently, small clods pushed upwards and sideways.

Doyle frowned, rubbing his eyes, annoyed that they were playing tricks on him.

But the ground continued to move.

He moved back slightly and reached for a small branch that had been blown off a bush near to the sarcophagus, using it to probe and dig into the mound of earth that was growing larger by the second.

A mole?

They were common in this part of the country, weren't they?

That had to be the answer. A mole was digging its way up

from the dark earth. They were nocturnal hunters weren't they, Doyle pondered, wondering where he had ever picked up that kind of useless information, but his gaze was now fixed on the steadily moving earth before him. Only suddenly it wasn't just before him. It was to his left and to his right.

There were new mounds of earth being pushed up on the graves on either side of him. A metal vase that had been standing on one of them toppled to one side, dislodged by the movements from beneath it.

What the fuck is going on?

Leather Jacket was also gazing raptly at the ground next to the gravestone where he sheltered. The earth there was undulating and rising too.

As it was close to Georgie.

As it seemed to be all over the churchyard now.

And then he heard a loud grinding of stone on stone and it was a moment before he realised that the lid of the sarcophagus was sliding slowly open. Pushed from within by a force that possessed incredible strength. That same force was coaxing movement from those lying deep in the earth of the churchyard.

As Doyle looked, his eyes bulging wide in the sockets, his mouth open wide, unable to accept or understand what was happening around him, a hand burst from the nearest grave and clutched at the night air.

It was followed by another.

And another.

All over the churchyard those buried so long ago in the dirt of this sacred place, tore through the mud and earth and fought to breathe the air once again.

Doyle shook his head disbelievingly, wishing that it was just his fevered imagination that was making him see the images before him but, despite his doubts, only one thing seemed certain. As ridiculous and insane as it was, his eyes told him the truth of it.

The dead were rising.

ONE HUNDRED AND SIXTEEN

Doyle saw another hand thrust upwards from the grave closest to him, driving higher until the rest of the arm appeared to. Pieces of rotting clothing clung to the limb, dropping away as the appendage was pushed further out into the night air.

And then, the entire upper torso of the grave occupant came into view as it hauled itself free of the enveloping dirt and mud.

Doyle moved back slightly, transfixed by the sight before him but also aware of the danger he was facing.

More and more of the graves disgorged their occupants. One of them, a man who had died in his thirties, dragged himself free of the earth and swayed drunkenly for a moment, using his own headstone to steady himself. He took a deep breath, filling lungs that had previously only contained the air of the coffin. Then he turned in Doyle's direction and lurched towards him but when he moved it wasn't with the stuttering, unsteady steps of some cinematic nightmare. He didn't stumble or stagger with arms outstretched the way Doyle had seen so many times in horror films over the years, instead he moved with disconcerting assurance and purpose towards the CTU agent.

Another body, a woman barely twenty, was dragging her legs from a grave near to Leather Jacket who was backing away in horror and revulsion, his eyes fixed on her as she finally pulled herself clear of the grave.

Just as they were when they died.

Two children, no more than five or six when they died, dragged themselves from the ground and stood beside the overturned earth that had marked their resting places, smelling the night for the first time in years. One of them pulled a maggot from its nostril and dropped it to the ground.

Close to them, something smaller emerged and, as it pulled itself into the freedom of the night air, it became obvious that it was a baby. Crawling across the grass as the mud of the grave fell away from its mouth and eyes. A worm dangled from its shoulder like an epaulette partially torn from an old uniform.

Georgie was gazing blankly at a body that had hauled itself free of a grave nearby. This one, a man in his twenties, was naked, the clothes long since having rotted away from his large form. He saw her and hurried towards her, his lips drawn back from his crooked teeth, his face twisted into an expression of pure rage.

Georgie didn't hesitate. She raised the .357 Ruger and fired.

The bullet caught the man in the cheek, blasted away most of his lower jaw and exploded from the back of his head, a flux of brain, pulverised bone and blood spraying out into the air behind him. He dropped like a stone, his eyes rolling upwards in the sockets. Georgie stood over him for a second, watching his body shudder involuntarily then she turned to see two more figures dragging themselves from the earth, both of them men, both of them with their attention now fixed on her.

Doyle followed her example and shot down the man running at him. Stepping over the body to confront whatever was emerging from the sarcophagus. The figure that rose into view was a man in his forties, hunched over as he had been in life but still powerfully built and possessing that same expression of fury on his face. He opened his mouth to roar his rage, but Doyle didn't hesitate, he shot the man twice, one of the bullets powering into that open mouth, smashing the spine as it exited, almost severing the head. The body toppled backwards onto the grass as more corpses dragged themselves into view, all it seemed, infected with the same look of fury.

Leather Jacket backed away until his back was against the wall of the church, shaking his head slowly as if he was still unable to accept what he was witnessing. Even when the young woman before him launched herself at him he could only look on dumbly.

The impact knocked him off his feet, slamming him harder against the wall and, as he fell, she shot out a hand, grabbing a large stone from the earth near the building. She gripped it in one fist and brought it down onto Leather Jacket's face with a strength that belied her fragile frame.

The stone smashed his sphenoid bone, driving it back into his face. Blood erupted from the wound as she struck again, knocking out two of his front teeth. Despite the agonising pain, and the rapidly rising feeling of unconsciousness sweeping over him, he managed to lash out with one hand and knock her backwards. She stumbled but then came straight back at him, using the stone as a missile this time, hurling it at him as he raised his gun and fired three shots into her. The third one caught her in the hollow of the throat and dropped her like a stone. As she lay on her face, he fired two more shots into her head, watching as the cranium exploded, slicks of brain spilling out onto the grass as the skull opened like an overripe peach.

He barely had time to enjoy his small victory when hands grabbed him from behind. Powerful hands that pulled him off his feet. Thumbs digging into his windpipe, causing him to gasp for breath. The man pinning him down was small but incredibly strong and, as he throttled Leather Jacket, he glared down at him with a look of complete hatred etched on his features. With a grunt he raised Leather Jacket's head then slammed it back down repeatedly.

On the edge of consciousness now, Leather Jacket tried to strike out at his assailant, but it seemed that all the strength had gone from his body now. Even though he was fighting for his life he found it hard to discover the last vestiges of power he needed.

His attacker suddenly drove both thumbs into his eyes, gouging and pushing, driving the sensitive orbs back into his skull, bursting them. Blood and vitreous liquid exploded into the air, drenching Leather Jacket's face and spurting onto the hands of the attacker who seemed to push harder. Leather Jacket screamed and tried to pull the hands away from his face.

Blinded by the attack he heard only the deafening retort of a pistol above him as Doyle put two bullets into the head of the assailant. Blood and other matter spattered across Leather Jacket's face and upper body and he felt the weight of his attacker suddenly slump across him.

Doyle dragged the other agent to his feet, trying to support him, trying to get him away from the churchyard. He snaked an arm around Doyle's shoulders to keep himself upright, his head swimming, the pain filling him. Blood was pouring down his face. He could taste it as it coursed over his open lips. Doyle muttered something to him, some garbled words of encouragement and they continued on through the necropolis. The roar of pistol retorts echoed in the night as Doyle fired.

Georgie joined him and they fired randomly into the mass of figures that were advancing from all four corners of the cemetery towards them.

From the gateway, Granger was firing short bursts of automatic fire into the corpses closest to him, watching them drop to the ground as the bullets tore into them.

Doyle guessed that there must be forty or more figures closing in around them now. Every grave and tomb had sent forth its former occupant and they advanced with unshakable intent.

Georgie reloaded, her breath coming in gasps. She fired off two more rounds, dropping more of the horde. But it wasn't enough.

Doyle too fired, pumping the trigger repeatedly, some of the shots hitting home, others screaming off the grave markers they hit, adding the high-pitched shriek of ricochets to the boom of pistol retorts. He looked at Leather Jacket who had now gone limp and was barely able to stand, even with Doyle's support, then at Georgie. He saw the concern on her face, and he felt it too. Neither of them spoke. Neither of them gave voice to the thoughts tumbling through their minds.

What the hell was there to say? For the first time in years, Doyle was gripped by the icy conviction that he was going to die.

ONE HUNDRED AND SEVENTEEN

Gideon Vale slowed his pace as he reached the end of the corridor leading into the Intensive Care Unit of the hospital.

As he watched, a woman in her forties, supported by a nurse, stepped sobbing into the corridor having just emerged from a room to the left.

He couldn't hear what she was saying through the muffled sobs she couldn't control. He did hear words of comfort from the nurse and he suddenly felt very conspicuous and unwelcome here. As if he were somehow intruding upon this poor woman's grief.

As she brushed past him, she looked first at him and then back into the room behind.

"My husband," she said, softly. "He died."

Vale could see the figure of a swarthy, dark-haired man in the room beyond, that individual sitting up stiffly against a stack of pillows, his mouth slightly open and his eyes closed. The jacket of his light blue pyjamas was open, revealing his chest.

"I'm very sorry," Vale replied.

"Just now. Heart attack," the woman told him before being led away by the nurse.

Vale nodded and moved on, anxious to be away from this scene. He had problems of his own to deal with now. As he drew nearer the room he sought, he caught sight of his own reflection in the large window ahead of him. He took a deep breath and pushed open the door of the room, peering around it, hesitating a moment before he walked in.

The grey-haired man was sitting up in bed, sipping slowly from a beaker of water. As Vale entered, the older man looked expressionlessly at him. Vale smiled and sat down on one of the plastic seats beside the bed. He reached out and squeezed the older man's free hand.

"How do you feel?" he murmured, his voice little more than a whisper.

The grey-haired man merely nodded gently but he didn't look at Vale. He kept his gaze fixed on the blanket that covered his bed, looking at it as if it bore some design or pattern that only he could see.

"The doctor said that you were getting better," Vale went on. "Can you remember what happened?"

"I remember being shot if that's what you mean," the grey-haired man said, his eyes still lowered. "I should have died. Why didn't I?" Only now did he look at Vale and the younger man could see that his eyes were filled with tears. "He was right, wasn't he? That man. The one who shot me. He said that I couldn't die and he's right. Those bullets should have killed me just like the cancer killed me five years ago." The tears that were welling up finally coursed down his cheeks.

Vale squeezed the older man's hand more tightly.

"Why am I still alive?" the grey-haired man wanted to know, his body shuddering gently as he cried.

"Because we managed to get you here quickly," Vale said. "A helicopter brought you here."

"I don't mean that," the older man rasped. "I mean why didn't those bullets kill me?"

"I don't know, Dad," Vale told him, his own eyes now filling. "But you are alive, that's all that matters. You're here. You're here with me. You're back. Imagine how happy Mum will be when she finds out." He tried to smile.

"No," the older man snapped. "This isn't right. I should be dead. How can I go on knowing that I'll never die? Seeing you and your mum pass but knowing that I'll never have that release to look forward to? I don't want to live forever. I couldn't stand that." He pulled Vale closer. "Please help me."

"What do you want me to do?" the younger man protested. "Put a gun to your head now?"

"What good would it do?" the grey-haired man hissed. "You

wouldn't be able to kill me anyway."

Vale sucked in a deep, almost painful breath.

"But without the fear of death, life would be so much better," he said, his own voice cracking.

"Would it?"

"Everyone is afraid of dying. No one wants to die but you don't have to worry about that ever again."

"There comes a time in a man's life when he knows that enough is enough. There's nothing else to strive for. Nothing else to look forward to. Nothing else to care about. When I had cancer I understood that. I'd accepted what was going to happen to me. But this is...unbearable. Knowing I'll never die but helpless to stop those I love from dying. I can't stand the thought of that. I don't want that."

Vale looked helplessly at the other man, almost feeling his pain.

He was about to speak again when he heard a scream from the corridor outside.

Vale got to his feet and crossed to the door, peering out into the walkway. He saw the nurse he'd passed moments earlier. She was backed up against one wall, her gaze fixed on something that Vale couldn't yet see. It was she who had screamed. As he watched she put one hand to her mouth, as if to stifle any other sounds she might let slip.

Vale was about to ask her what was wrong when he saw a figure emerge slowly from the room opposite her.

A swarthy, dark-haired individual in light blue pyjamas. A man who looked around in bewilderment, as if puzzled by his surroundings. Vale swallowed hard. Was that the same man he'd just seen lying in another room, propped up by pillows, dead of a heart attack?

When the nurse screamed again, he knew that it was.

The man in the light blue pyjamas looked at the nurse and then at Vale but it was the nurse that he dashed towards, grabbing her by the throat, slamming her up against the wall so hard he almost knocked her unconscious with that one crashing impact. She sagged uselessly in his grip, but he jerked her upright, driving her head back against the wall with such force that it cracked bones at the rear of her skull. As her eyes rolled upwards in the sockets, he let her slip to the ground.

His face contorted in a look of sheer fury, he turned towards Vale.

ONE HUNDRED AND EIGHTEEN

Doyle fired two more shots into the advancing horde, watching as one of them fell heavily and the other staggered backwards holding a wound in the shoulder.

"We've got to get inside the church," Georgie said, swinging the Ruger up, shooting down a man dressed in just a shirt.

Doyle nodded, trying to hold up Leather Jacket who was now unconscious.

"Leave him," Georgie said.

"I can't," Doyle hissed. "They'll kill him."

"He's half-dead now," Georgie said through clenched teeth. "We can't save him."

Doyle hesitated for a moment then gently let the other man slip to the ground.

Georgie put one bullet into Leather Jacket's head, meeting Doyle's questioning stare as he looked at her. Then the two of them turned and raced towards the main doors of the church, crashing through two more of the corpses, knocking them aside as they tried to grab them with dirt-stained hands.

"Where the fuck is Granger?" Doyle hissed as they both slammed into the heavy doors, trying to force them open.

Georgie had no clue and no answer. She drove her foot repeatedly against the thick partition, wincing once when Doyle fired close to her ear, taking down another of the advancing horde.

The figures were close but seemed reluctant to approach any further. It was as if they knew they had time. Their quarry was going nowhere. Why rush?

Georgie kicked furiously at the door once again and this time it swung open enough for her to slip through.

She dashed into the vestibule, Doyle seconds behind her. He slammed the door shut and threw his weight against it, forcing it closed. Georgie dropped the locking bar into position, sealing it. They both stepped away from the doors knowing that they were safe at least for the moment. Even if the figures outside managed to smash their way in, they could only get through the doors one or two at a time. As long as Doyle and Georgie had enough ammunition, any attack could be countered. As if in answer to that unspoken question, Georgie held up her pistol.

"I've got twelve left," she announced. "What about you?"

"Two mags," Doyle answered, his breathing gradually coming under control.

They could hear movement outside the church doors now. Shuffling feet but nothing else. The silence closed in around them.

"So, Callahan's controlling those things out there," Doyle breathed, his voice low.

"I don't think so," Georgie mused, thumbing fresh bullets into the empty chambers of the .357.

"Then who the hell is?"

"No one. It's because Callahan used the grimoire."

Doyle looked puzzled.

"It's like the price to be paid for bringing someone back," Georgie said, quietly. "Others will rise too. Because Callahan used the book to restore life..."

"Everyone else who died will come back too," Doyle murmured. "'A plague of hell brought forth by greed and longing.' That's what it says in the book isn't it?"

Georgie nodded.

"Callahan's longing to have his wife alive again," she said. "The book is a curse if it isn't used correctly," she went on. "It means life to those chosen but it's a death sentence for everyone else. That's what Gaston Lavelle wanted when he wrote it. It's his revenge on a world he hated."

"And Callahan's too," Doyle mused.

There was a loud thump against the church doors.

"The ones we shot, they'll come back too, won't they?"

Doyle grunted.

"They can't die. We could nuke them but an hour later they'll be alive again."

"That's a cheery thought," Doyle sighed, raising his eyebrows as the impacts on the church door increased in both volume and ferocity.

"The only way to stop them is to destroy the grimoire," Georgie announced.

"'Whatever is restored by the book will cease to be when it is no more,'" Doyle said, quietly. He looked at Georgie. "But that means you too. If we destroy the book, then you die as well."

"There's no other way," she told him.

"There has to be," he snarled. "I won't do that. I won't let you die. Not again."

"If I live, the rest of the world dies. Everyone in it."

"Fuck the rest of the world."

She held his gaze for a moment longer, her reverie interrupted by another impact against the church door.

"We've got to find Callahan," Doyle snapped.

He put one hand against the church doors, satisfied that they were sufficiently sturdy to keep out the would-be invaders for a good while yet. Then he moved a few paces across the vestibule, peering into the gloom of the church beyond. Even in the darkness the view down the nave was unobstructed. There were a few pews left in position on either side of the aisle and those that had been stacked were pushed up against the walls to the north and south. Scaffolding covered a large part of the inside of the structure, as high as the ceiling in places, but the walkway around the upper level of the building was clear. As were the stone steps that led up to the bell tower.

Callahan was up there. The direction of the gunfire they'd encountered earlier told Doyle that much.

There were narrow steps leading up from both sides of the vestibule towards the first level of the church and then, beyond that, to the tower itself. Doyle looked at Georgie who had finished refilling the .357. He himself slammed a fresh magazine into the Beretta, working the slide to chamber a round.

Something heavy struck the church door.

Doyle looked towards it and then at Georgie.

She nodded and they both moved towards the steps that led from the vestibule towards the bell tower above.

Doyle could feel his heart hammering harder against his ribs.

ONE HUNDRED AND NINETEEN

Vale could see the look of anger on the dark-haired man's face and he steadied himself for the attack he knew would come.

Fleetingly, the thought flashed through his mind that he'd last glimpsed this man dead in his bed but, as the pyjama-clad figure prepared to run at him, Vale found he had other matters to consider.

Alarms were sounding in other parts of the hospital for reasons that he didn't understand, and the strident wail seemed to spur the dark-haired man on. He rushed at Vale, slamming into him with great force, knocking him backwards.

Vale managed to roll free, driving one foot into the man's face as he lunged at him again.

The impact staggered him momentarily and Vale took advantage of the respite. He punched the man hard in the face, splitting his upper lip. Blood spurted from the cut and this only seemed to enrage the man further. He ran at Vale again but, this time, the younger man ducked to one side of the assault, grabbed the man's arm and swung him around, sending him hurtling towards the wall at the end of the corridor.

He hit the window and the entire structure shattered. The man toppled through, clutching at empty air for a second before hurtling from sight, racing towards the ground thirty feet below.

Vale ran to the remains of the window, looking down in time to see that the dark-haired man had hit the ground and was now laying still in a widening pool of blood. There were screams coming from below, from people who had seen him fall but also from others who were running frantically from the building, desperate to get away from something Vale could not yet see.

"What's happening?"

The voice beside him startled Vale and he spun around to see two orderlies had joined him in the corridor. One of them was hunched over the fallen form of the nurse, trying to help her sit up as she slowly regained consciousness.

The orderly next to him was a balding man with ruddy cheeks and a thick moustache. He looked as if he was sweating, beads of moisture on his forehead and cheeks.

"Who attacked her?" the orderly demanded.

"Him," Vale snapped, pointing out of the shattered window towards the prone body below.

"You've got to get out of here," the orderly said. "Everyone who can has to get out."

"Why?"

"I don't know what's happening," the man confessed, his eyes wide with fear. "I don't know..." The words trailed off as the man took a step back, shaking his head, his gaze lowered as if he were considering the images racing through his mind.

"Tell me what you've seen," Vale demanded. "Why are the people down there running?"

The orderly swallowed hard and let out a long sigh.

"I was taking a body to the pathology lab," he said, his voice cracking. "A woman in her sixties. She'd had a stroke or heart attack or something. Complications. They couldn't save her. She died. I took the body from the ward." He wiped his face with one shaking hand. "I got it down to Pathology."

Vale watched him, his face contorting as the memories flooded back.

"What happened?" Vale insisted.

The orderly was crying now, tears rolling down his cheeks.

"She got up," he gasped. "Got off the trolley. She'd been dead but I swear to God she got up."

It was Vale's turn to take a deep breath.

"There were more of them," the orderly went on, his eyes gazing into space. "I saw them coming out of the morgue. Four of them. They'd been dead. They were walking." More tears ran down his face. "I know you think I'm crazy."

Vale merely shook his head gently.

"When was this?" he wanted to know.

"Ten, fifteen minutes ago," the orderly told him. "I ran. What else was I going to do?"

Behind them, the other orderly was helping the nurse to her feet, wiping blood from her mouth with a tissue. Vale watched them moving away up the corridor.

"You've got to get out," the first orderly repeated. "I don't know what's happening, but you've got to get out." With that, he too turned and hurried away along the corridor.

From nearby, Vale heard more screams.

ONE HUNDRED AND TWENTY

The walls on both sides of the narrow stairway that led up to the bell tower were bare stone.

As Doyle moved slowly up the steps, he was aware of how cold they felt whenever he brushed against them and, the higher he climbed, the cooler the air itself seemed to get. He shivered involuntarily, gripping the Beretta more tightly.

Behind him, Georgie also climbed the steps cautiously, aware, like Doyle, of the insistent banging on the church doors as those outside continued their quest to get in. The darkness inside the tower was broken only by the natural light spilling in through the small windows in the walls but, for that they were grateful and, as they drew nearer the first level of the building, that light seemed to grow brighter.

Doyle paused at the head of the steps, peering into the gloom, trying to pick out shapes in the darkness. Seeing nothing he moved onto the wider landing area, the bare boards creaking under his weight. Georgie followed, also glancing around anxiously in the blackness. She looked up towards the higher levels of the tower.

Above them there was movement. Both of them stepped back, away from the central area of the tower.

The floorboards above creaked slightly and Doyle swung the Beretta up, considered for a moment squeezing off a couple of shots but then thought better of it.

Get closer. Make sure.

He moved towards the next flight of steps that would take them even higher, keeping his breathing low.

From outside there was more hammering on the church door. More powerful and insistent now. Georgie crossed to one of the leaded windows that looked out over the churchyard and peered down onto the necropolis. She could

431

see about ten of the figures gathered around the doors. The same number were wandering aimlessly around the churchyard. Where the rest had gone, she could only guess.

Doyle put his foot on the first step of the next flight of stairs. Slowly he began to climb. As he got halfway, he could see that there was scaffolding across the walkway. He ducked beneath it, careful not to bump into it. The wooden planks between the metal poles had several tools lying on them and if he knocked the frame then the sound would be heard throughout the church.

He moved higher, wondering how many more landings and levels there were before the very top of the tower was reached.

Callahan had to be up here somewhere. There was nowhere else to hide.

Georgie too ducked beneath the scaffolding, the .357 gripped more tightly in her fist. She was breathing more quickly now, her respiration almost matching the increased speed of her beating heart.

There was another landing a few steps ahead and she saw Doyle reach it and pause, holding up a hand to slow her down too. She moved closer to him, watching as he leaned forward slightly, trying to see around the balustrade. Attempting to get a clear view of the next level.

As he took a step onto the new landing, the roar of sub-machine gunfire erupted inside the tower.

Doyle ducked back but too late. A bullet hit him in the left shoulder, snapping the clavicle, tearing through muscle and exploding from his back. More shots hit the scaffolding, singing loudly off the metal poles. Georgie tried to duck back into the stairwell, but a bullet tore across her right cheek, ploughing a furrow in the flesh there. Blood burst from the nick, spilling down her face and she grunted in pain as she stepped back, gasping as another heavy grain shell caught her in the side. It sliced effortlessly through the flesh there, missing her pelvic bone by a fraction before exiting. She felt pain envelope her lower body and a numbness began to spread around the wound and her lumbar region.

Doyle saw that she was hit, and, despite his own wound, he stepped in front of her, trying to protect her. Shielding her as another round caught him in the chest and tore the breath from him. He yelled in pain and dropped to his knees, pumping the trigger of the Beretta, blasting off rounds in the direction of the gunfire that had wounded both of them. He kept firing until he saw a figure stumble forward from the deeper shadows. A figure that took a couple of faltering steps and then fell forward onto the wooden floor, blood spreading rapidly around it.

It was Laura Callahan.

She lay flat on her face, arms by her sides, her eyes open and turned skyward.

Doyle moved closer to her, prodding her body with the toe of his boot, inspecting the large exit wounds in her back where the 9mm slugs had exploded from her when she'd been hit. He knew without touching her that she was dead. If the wounds to her torso hadn't finished her then the one that had punched through her skull, just below one of her eyes and torn away most of the back of her head, had.

Doyle tried to suck in a deep breath but the wound in his chest prevented anything other than a shallow inhalation. He coughed, bright blood spilling over his lips and down his chin. He could barely lift his left arm and the pain from the wound there was excruciating. When he did manage to move the limb more than three or four inches, he could feel the two ends of shattered bone rubbing together.

"Fuck it," he grunted through clenched teeth.

Georgie joined him, one hand clapped to the wound in her side, blood spilling between her slender fingers.

"How bad is it?" she wanted to know.

Doyle swallowed and tasted blood in his mouth. By way of reply he shook his head, his gaze still fixed on the body of Laura Callahan.

"She's not dead, is she?" he gasped.

433

"She is for now," Georgie told him. "It gives me time to get to Callahan." As she spoke, she gestured upwards. It was the way they must go. Up, to where Callahan waited. "You wait here. Rest for a minute."

"No way," Doyle hissed. "I want that bastard. I'm going to kill him myself."

"You can't kill him," Georgie protested. "You know that."

"You fucking watch me," Doyle snapped, pushing past her. Ahead of him was the final staircase that would lead to the very top of the bell tower. As he put his foot on the first step of that last stairway there was a loud crash from below them.

The church doors had finally been forced open.

ONE HUNDRED AND TWENTY-ONE

Figures were spilling into the church.

Some rushed down the nave. Others contented themselves with walking around the vestibule, anxious to find their quarry. There were more than twenty of them. Some dashed towards the far end of the building, towards the altar and the steps that led up to the higher level of the church through the transepts. Georgie thought they were like hunting dogs with the scent of a prey they would not relinquish until they had it cornered. The thought made her shudder and she gripped the Ruger more tightly, glancing around when she heard Doyle cough again. He winced with each contraction of his chest and she saw more blood spilling from his mouth. He sagged against one wall, waving her away when she tried to support him.

"I'll be okay," he said, but there was nothing particularly reassuring in his voice.

"You wait here," she said. "Keep those...things back. Give me some time."

"I told you, I'm going to kill that cunt myself." He glanced upwards towards the uppermost level of the bell tower.

"Doyle..." she began, but he raised a hand to silence her.

He began to climb once again, wincing as the pain from his wounds swept through him but he forced himself on, moving closer and closer to the top of the bell tower.

As he reached the head of the steps he paused, peering into the uppermost chamber of the tower. Eight bells hung from the mechanism high up in the pinnacle of the tower, the smaller ones swaying gently when the breeze cut through the room from the ancient windows. Doyle moved up the last few steps into the belfry, his eyes scanning the area for the one he sought.

"Your wife's dead, Callahan." he called, wincing.

Silence greeted the words.

"You left her down there to die, didn't you?" Doyle went on. "To slow us down. Well, she didn't manage it. I blew her fucking head off. That's getting to be a bit of a habit with me." He smiled.

"She's not dead."

Doyle heard Callahan's words and immediately fired twice in their direction. The sound of the pistol retorts was deafening in the small space and, for several seconds afterwards, Doyle was deafened.

"You know she's not dead," Callahan called from another part of the belfry.

Again, Doyle fired in the direction of the words.

"She can't die," Callahan continued, his voice seemingly coming from every part of the high-vaulted room. "Neither can I. How can you hope to stop me?"

Again, Doyle fired two shots, the muzzle flashes briefly illuminating the belfry.

In that split second, it was Georgie who saw the outline of Callahan's form in one corner of the high room. She swung the .357 up and squeezed off three shots, the sound thunderous. As the weapon slammed back against the heel of her hand, she gripped it with all her strength, sending each of the powerful slugs into their target. She saw Callahan stumble backwards, saw blood spray up the wall behind him. She hurried forward when she saw him drop the MP5K, kicking the weapon to one side to prevent him reaching it again. He reached out with one bloodied hand, but the sub-machine gun was beyond him now. Callahan lay on his back, his body twitching slightly as he looked up at her.

Doyle hurried across to join her, looking down at his fallen adversary.

One of Georgie's bullets had caught him in the face. It had torn through his cheek, shattered several teeth and then erupted just below his ear. It hadn't done major damage, but it had caused the flesh there to flap like a sail every time

Callahan tried to move his jaw. Blood was pouring down that side of his face and, as he coughed, the remains of another tooth dropped from his open mouth.

"Where's the book?" Georgie asked, the barrel of the Ruger aimed at Callahan's head.

"It's here," Callahan grunted, his words slurred. He pointed with one shaking hand to an object close by. Georgie saw that it was the grimoire. It lay close to one of the windows, the moonlight that was seeping through the leaded glass falling upon the cover and lighting it with a cool white luminescence that made it look as if it was glowing.

Doyle raised the Beretta, aimed it at Callahan's head and prepared to fire.

"Do it," the fallen man gasped. "What good will it do? You killed me once, you can kill me a hundred times, but I'll never die."

Doyle moved closer, pushing the barrel of the automatic so close to Callahan's head it practically touched flesh.

"You wanted a world like this?" Doyle asked. "A world full of corpses?"

"I don't care about this world or anyone in it," Callahan rasped. "The only one I ever cared about is my wife. My Laura. And now we'll be together forever, despite what you try to do."

"If I destroy the book she'll die," Doyle said through clenched teeth. "And she'll feel the same pain she did when it first happened."

"'They shall suffer again the agonies they bore when death first visited,'" Georgie intoned.

"They'll all die, and they'll stay dead," snarled Doyle.

"And so will she," Callahan snapped, pointing at Georgie. He sagged to one side, barely able to support himself on one bullet-blasted arm. "'Whatever is restored by the book will cease to be when it is no more,'" he said, smiling crookedly.

Doyle pushed the 92F against Callahan's forehead, pressing so hard that the barrel cut the flesh there.

"You cunt," he hissed, his voice barely a whisper but so full of fury he could barely force the words out.

It was Georgie who fired the final two shots.

Both .357 slugs slammed into Callahan's head, almost obliterating it. The first ripped away most of the top of his head, sending a sticky mass of blood, brain and pulped bone spraying onto the wall and floor behind him. The second tore off most of his lower jaw, teeth flying in several directions as they were blasted from bloodied gums. Callahan slumped to the floor, blood spreading out around what remained of his skull. The air was thick with the smell of gunpowder, cordite and the cloying coppery odour of blood.

Georgie took a step backwards, supporting Doyle as he too backed away, his gaze still fixed on Callahan's body.

Below them, they could both hear heavy footsteps on the stairs. Figures drawing closer.

Then they heard the gunfire.

ONE HUNDRED AND TWENTY-TWO

They both realised immediately that it was bursts of automatic fire. Quick fusillades of bullets that echoed around the inside of the church.

Georgie moved towards the stairs, edging down, eyes and ears alert.

More gunfire from below them.

Doyle followed, glancing back once in the direction of Callahan's body as if he feared it would rise again at any second. Needless to say, it didn't. He followed Georgie down the stairs, the grimoire jammed under his injured arm like a newspaper he'd just bought from a corner shop.

As they reached the next landing, he halted a moment, finding it increasingly difficult to breathe. The pain from his wounds was still the only thing keeping him conscious. More than once he swayed against the wall of the stairway, fearing that unconsciousness was about to overtake him.

There was another burst of fire from below. Louder now.

Georgie paused, looking into the church itself as they reached the first landing.

Several figures were lying spread-eagled on the floor of the nave. She could see more, close to the altar, now motionless.

As they emerged from the stairs into the vestibule there were at least a dozen bodies lying there. Beyond the open doors of the church at least ten more corpses were scattered across the pathway and porch area. As Georgie emerged cautiously into the cool night air, she could see that the entire necropolis was littered with motionless, bullet riddled bodies.

Doyle joined her, his gaze also moving slowly over the bodies.

The silence was overwhelming.

Doyle put his foot under one body and flipped it over onto its back, looking at the face. The mouth gaping open and filled

439

with blood. The bullet wounds that had been stitched across the torso and legs.

"How long will they stay down?" he breathed.

"An hour," Georgie told him. "Maybe less."

"Then it all starts again," Doyle sighed.

She nodded wearily.

"And again," he murmured. "And again."

"Unless the grimoire is destroyed," Georgie reminded him.

They moved slowly away from the church, stepping over bodies here and there because they were so numerous.

"Give me the book."

The words echoed across the churchyard and Doyle turned to find their source.

Mark Granger stepped from the shadows at the side of the church, the MP5K that he carried levelled at the two agents. Behind him was the long-haired youth Doyle had seen earlier.

Doyle hesitated, eyeing Granger and the other man warily.

"Did you do this?" he asked, gesturing towards the fallen bodies around them.

Granger nodded.

"Give me the book," he repeated, the sub-machine gun still aimed at Doyle and Georgie.

"Put it down, Granger," Doyle said, nodding towards the MP5K. "We're all on the same side, remember?"

Granger smiled.

"Not quite," he murmured. "Is Callahan dead?"

"For now," Georgie said, flatly. "Him and his wife. But they won't stay dead, you know that. Just like these things here won't stay dead." She motioned at the corpses lying nearby.

"That's not my problem," Granger said.

"It will be when they get up again," Doyle reminded him.

"We'll be miles from here by then," Granger intoned. "Somewhere safe."

"There is nowhere safe any more," Georgie snapped. "Not now. Not since Callahan brought these things back to life."

"The same way he brought you back to life?" Granger

smiled. "And his wife, and Vale's father. And my son." As he spoke, he gestured towards the long-haired man beside him.

"Your son?" Georgie murmured, her gaze moving to the younger man.

"Is that why you were helping Callahan?" Doyle grunted.

Granger didn't speak.

"That's why we couldn't nail him earlier?" Doyle went on. "You were feeding him information, weren't you? Keeping him posted on our movements. He knew when we were coming, and he knew when to be prepared. Vale and I walked into a trap back at that house, didn't we?"

"It was a small price to pay for the return of my son," Granger said. "Now drop your guns before I fire."

"A small price?" Georgie snapped. "A world overrun by walking corpses? A world that will change forever? A world where the dead will overrun the living?"

"I don't care about that," hissed Granger. "I have my son back." He pulled the long-haired youth towards him. "Callahan gave me that opportunity and I wasn't about to refuse it. Drop your guns or I'll fire. I swear to God. Throw them over here."

Doyle allowed the Beretta to slip from his grasp. He raised one arm in a gesture of surrender. Georgie followed suit, the Ruger hitting the dirt with a dull thud when she threw it.

"How long have you been working with him?" Doyle wanted to know.

"Since he got back to this country," explained Granger. "It was money first and then he offered me the chance to have my son back. How could I refuse?"

"The information about him, you kept it from us," Doyle hissed. "You were stopping us from finding him."

Granger met Doyle's gaze without emotion.

"You said everyone had a price," Doyle sneered. "So that's how Callahan bought you is it?"

"Give me the book," Granger snapped. "I won't ask again." He took a step forward, the barrel of the sub-machine gun held in his unwavering grip, his finger pressing a little more firmly onto the trigger. "She might not be able to die but you can, Doyle. You're half-dead right now."

"Go to hell," Doyle rasped.

"After you," Granger smiled, and he raised the sub-machine gun so it was level with Doyle's head. He prepared to fire.

ONE HUNDRED AND TWENTY-THREE

"Come with me," Granger said, his gaze now directed at Georgie. "I'll protect the book. I'll protect my son and you too."

Doyle glared at the other man.

"As long as the book is safe then so are you, so is my boy," Granger went on, looking briefly at his son who took a step away from him. "That's all that matters to me."

He glanced again at Doyle.

"Do you want her to die?" he asked. "Do you want her to go through the pain all over again? 'They shall suffer again the agonies they bore when death first visited.'"

"I know the fucking words, Granger," Doyle snapped. "I know what they mean."

"So, what's your answer?" Granger snapped, his tone challenging. "Do you want that for her?"

Doyle shook his head almost imperceptibly.

"Then give me the book," Granger said, taking a step forward.

Doyle hesitated then moved his left arm slightly, wincing at the pain as the two ends of broken collar bone rubbed together. The grimoire dropped to the ground from beneath his arm, the loud thud echoing across the still churchyard. He took a step away from the fallen tome.

"Callahan told me how powerful it was," Granger said. "I didn't believe him at first, but now..." The words died on the night air. He smiled.

"There'll be nothing left in this world but death," Georgie said, softly, her eyes filling with tears, her gaze fixed on the grimoire.

"Not for you," Granger said. "Not for my son. You're beyond that now. You're like gods." His smiled broadened.

"You're crazier than Callahan," Georgie sneered.

"I'm offering you an alternative," Granger told her, his smile fading rapidly. "I'm the only one who can help you now." He jabbed a finger at Doyle. "He can't help you. And when he dies, he won't be coming back."

Doyle kicked the book.

"Come and get the fucking thing if you want it," he rasped, his words dissolving into a cough. Blood sprayed from his mouth and Georgie took a step towards him, fearing he might keel over at any moment.

"Don't do that," Granger snapped. He turned to the long-haired man beside him, one hand on his broad shoulders. "Get the book."

The younger man hesitated for a moment then took a couple of strides towards Doyle.

"Why did you kill yourself?" Doyle asked him. "Sick of having a father like him?" He nodded towards Granger who merely shook his head.

"Shut up, Doyle," Granger said, flatly, watching as his son retrieved the ancient tome, hefting it before him, surprised at the weight of the grimoire.

"I don't blame you," Doyle went on.

"Shut your mouth," Granger snapped.

It was then that they all heard the low roar of a car engine. It carried on the still night air, drawing nearer with each passing second.

"Let's get to the helicopter," Granger said to his son, who was still holding the grimoire. "We need to get away from here." His tone had softened considerably but there was still an edge to it. As he took a step back, he glanced down at the figure laying close by.

As he watched, the fingers flexed and then straightened several times, quivering as they extended.

Another fallen body shuddered as if hit with an electric shock, the head turning slightly to look at Granger.

"Come on," he said, anxiously, only too aware of what was happening all around him. "We've got to go." He put out a

444

hand towards his son who had also noticed several of the corpses twitching involuntarily.

The youth merely shook his lowered head, his gaze on the book. Granger frowned slightly, perplexed by the younger man's silence and demeanour. When the boy looked up there were tears in his eyes.

"We have to go," Granger repeated.

"I don't want to," the youth said, softly.

"We have to get to safety," Granger went on.

"She said there isn't anywhere safe," the boy intoned. "How could there be?"

"She doesn't know what she's talking about," Granger snapped. "Now give me the book."

The body of a young woman lying close to a stone cross reached out a hand towards Granger who stepped away from it as if he'd narrowly avoided stepping in excrement. He looked again at his son.

The youth held onto the tome, looking down at the blood-spattered cover, trailing his fingers over it.

"I can't die unless this book is destroyed?" he said, softly, his cheeks now stained with tears.

"That's right," said Granger, smiling.

The sound of an approaching engine was growing louder now. It echoed through the night. Doyle glanced down at his dropped gun, wondering if he could snatch it up while Granger was distracted.

And do what? Who are you going to shoot?

His gaze moved back and forth from Granger to his son and back again. Georgie too took a step forward, also transfixed by the two men but also aware that more and more of the bodies around them were beginning to shudder and convulse.

"No more pain, no more suffering," Granger said, his arms outstretched towards his son. "No more death."

"I wanted to die," the youth exclaimed. "You should never have brought me back." He looked accusingly at his father. "But it was what you wanted wasn't it? Everything was what you wanted. It's always been like that. You wanted me to join the CTU just like you did. You wanted me to go to uni just like you did. You wanted me to focus on a career just like you did. You wanted me to be you."

Granger shook his head.

"You never asked me what I wanted," the boy went on. "You didn't care what I wanted. You couldn't even leave me dead. You wanted me alive again because that was what you wanted, not me." He held the grimoire before him as if it was an accusation.

"You're my son, I love you," Granger told him, his own eyes filling with tears. "I won't let you suffer."

"It's not your choice," the youth roared. "Not this time."

Before the last word had left his lips, he snatched up the Ruger discarded by Georgie, thumbing back the hammer. He dropped the grimoire onto the ground close to a gravestone, levelling the .357 at the old book, steadying himself.

He fired three shots into the grimoire.

ONE HUNDRED AND TWENTY-FOUR

"No," roared Granger, lunging towards him, desperate to stop the gunfire.

The youth fired again, each heavy grain slug slamming into the tome, blasting pieces of it away, drilling through its ancient cover into the parchment like pages.

The front cover was first holed and then torn off by the lethal bullets. As the younger man kept on firing, he could see the rounds tearing right through the grimoire, blasting part of the rear cover clear too. Some of the pages, torn loose from their binding by the impacts of the bullets, began to flutter away on the gentle night-time breeze that had sprung up.

As the hammer slammed down on an empty chamber, the youth snatched the book up and managed to rip it in two, the spine shattered by the bullets that had been pumped into it. The entire tome snapped in half, the binding, already weakened by the passage of time, splitting like rotting flesh. More pages fell onto the grass and mud as the younger man gripped the remains of the book.

"No, no," Granger roared, scrambling after the pages that fluttered on the breeze. He tried to grab them, snatching some from the wet earth, gathering them up as best he could. His frantic efforts were watched soundlessly by Doyle, Georgie and the younger man who finally dropped the empty .357.

Doyle dug in his pocket and pulled out a small silver object.

"Use this," he grunted, tossing it to the younger man who caught the lighter in one hand, coaxed flame from it and then held that flickering fire to the remains of the grimoire. It went up with unexpected ease, the pages curling and twisting as the fire devoured them. Smoke rose thickly from the burning volume, rising into the night air, cinders drifting in all directions as the incinerated pages blazed.

And now a sound began to fill the air. A noise that reminded Doyle of wind rushing through some slightly open door. A high-pitched shriek that grew louder and more insistent and thrummed in the ears of those in the cemetery, rising and expanding until it sounded like one continual caterwaul of agony torn from the throats of countless sufferers. The noise swelled and expanded for interminable seconds then stopped as suddenly as it had begun.

Doyle looked slowly around, his breath rasping in his throat.

The younger man looked down at the smouldering remains of the grimoire.

"It's over," he said.

Granger glared at him and grabbed another of the pages, inspecting the large hole in the paper, tracing the outline with one index finger. His body was shaking with rage, his face pale, almost luminous in the gloom.

"He's right, Granger," Doyle offered. "It's over."

"You caused this," Granger roared, his furious gaze now fixed on Doyle. "You're to blame." He swung the MP5K up, his finger tightening on the trigger.

The first burst of fire exploded from the barrel, tearing across the wet earth, bullets missing Doyle by inches. He dropped down and snatched up the Beretta, swinging it up into position, firing once.

More by luck than judgement, the bullet hit Granger squarely between the eyes. It pulverised the bridge of his nose, driving portions of the nasal bone back into his brain as it tore through the soft matter there, erupting from the rear of the skull. Blood, shattered bone and gobbets of brain tissue spewed from the exit wound and he dropped like a stone, his eyes still open.

His son looked at him then he too staggered and fell, falling close to Granger, his own body shuddering slightly before becoming still. His head had come to rest on a scorched, bullet blasted page of the grimoire.

Doyle swayed uncertainly, his head spinning, the pain in his chest intensifying as he tried to take a breath. He looked at Georgie who moved towards him, seeing the pain on his face. But it was she who let out a gasp as she too felt a growing warmth spreading through her torso. It was as if someone had pierced her several times with a red-hot poker. She staggered and almost fell, one hand going to her chest.

When she looked at Doyle again, she had tears in her eyes. Like him, she was all too aware of what was happening to her.

Doyle moved towards her, looking on helplessly as she sagged against a headstone. He could see her face contorting with pain, her body convulsing as surely as if bullets were striking it now. Trying to ignore his own discomfort he grabbed her as she fell, holding her close to him.

"No," he murmured, shaking his head. "Not again."

She looked up at him, her eyes filled with tears.

Doyle knelt beside her, stroking her cheek gently.

"Please finish it," she whispered, her face twisted in a grimace of sheer agony. "It could take hours." As she spoke she reached for his hand. She grabbed the hand that held the Beretta and she pulled it towards her face, forcing the barrel against the underside of her chin.

Doyle shook his head.

"Please," she said, sniffing back more tears, her body jerking violently as yet another wave of agony swept through her.

Again, Doyle could only shake his head as he looked into her eyes.

"I can't," he told her, hopelessly, his voice little more than a whisper.

She gripped his hand more tightly, pushing her chin against the barrel of the automatic.

"Please, Sean," she murmured. "Stop this pain. If you love me, you'll do it." And she smiled at him.

Doyle gritted his teeth until his jaw ached.

He cradled her head on his lap, gazing into her eyes as he thumbed back the hammer of the Beretta, pushing the barrel harder against the flesh beneath her chin.

"Thank you," she whispered, squeezing his hand with as much strength as she could muster.

Tears began to roll down Doyle's cheeks as he met her imploring gaze.

He fired once.

ONE HUNDRED AND TWENTY-FIVE

Gideon Vale brought the car skidding to a halt and pushed open the door, scrambling out of the vehicle. He ran towards the churchyard, almost slipping on the wet grass that grew thickly around the gate.

As he pulled it open, he glanced across the necropolis, seeing the bodies that lay there. Vale took a breath, shocked by the sight before him. It was a moment or two before he caught sight of the one figure inside the churchyard that was moving.

Vale walked slowly towards the figure, seeing that whoever knelt there was cradling another body.

Only when he was ten feet away did he realise that the figure was Doyle.

"Jesus Christ," Vale murmured, seeing his partner. He could see the blood that drenched the older man, not all of it his. And now, as he got closer, he could see that the body Doyle was cradling was that of Georgina Willis.

"Doyle..." he began, his voice low.

The older man raised his head and looked at Vale.

"You missed the show," he murmured, a slight smile on his face.

"I'll get help," Vale said, kneeling down beside Doyle.

Doyle grabbed his wrist.

"No rush," he breathed. "It's too late anyway." He coughed.

"Callahan?" Vale wanted to know.

"Inside the church," Doyle told him. "His wife too. Georgie got him." He smiled thinly.

Vale looked down at the body Doyle was still holding.

"Granger's dead too," Doyle said, quietly. He motioned in the direction of the corpse with the barrel of the Beretta. "So is his son." He sighed. "They're all dead." He looked down at Georgie, brushing some strands of hair from her cheek. Again, he looked up at the younger man. "You took your

451

time."

"I came from the hospital where they took my father."

Doyle nodded.

"Doyle, I'm sorry..." Vale began.

"Fuck it," Doyle breathed, cutting across him, his gaze returning to Georgie. "With the grimoire destroyed, your father..."

"I understand that," Vale interrupted.

The breeze that had been blowing seemed to intensify. Several pages of the grimoire fluttered into the air, propelled across the churchyard. Vale could see the torn remnants of the book lying close by.

"What do we do with it?" he asked, gesturing towards the remains of the ancient tome.

"Take it back to the British Museum," Doyle said, smiling humourlessly. "Tell them they might need a bit of Sellotape and some staples for it." He coughed, groaning at the pain that racked him.

"I'm going to get you an ambulance," Vale grunted, reaching for his phone.

"Not yet," Doyle told him. "We've got something to do first." He struggled to his feet and began walking falteringly towards the church.

Vale followed.

ONE HUNDRED AND TWENTY-SIX

The Explorer MD900 air ambulance descended slowly into the field, landing, lights blazing brightly and illuminating the land below it.

The pilot brought it expertly to earth, landing it with a barely noticeable bump. Two of his companions scrambled out of the craft one of them grabbing a portable stretcher from a bracket on the side of the chopper, the other carrying a large box that bore a Red Cross symbol. They hurried across towards the overgrown privet hedge that separated the field from the church beyond it.

As Gideon Vale emerged from the church, he saw the two men making their way down the path that cut through the churchyard, both of them looking around in bewilderment at the dead bodies scattered across the necropolis.

When they saw him they both froze. Vale could understand why. He was spattered with blood from head to foot and, in one hand, he held a saw. Like so many other tools it had been left on the scaffolding inside the church, temporarily abandoned by the men who were working on the place of worship. Left there in the belief that no one else would be entering the church in the near future. Vale glanced down at the blade and noticed that there was still blood dripping from it. There were also several pieces of flesh attached to the gleaming steel.

He raised a hand and signalled to the advancing men, both of who hesitated before moving closer.

"I'm Gideon Vale, Counter Terrorist Unit," the younger man called. "I was the one who called you." He dropped the circular saw.

The men still loitered on the path, unsure of whether or not to go any nearer to this blood-drenched figure silhouetted in the doorway of the church.

"There's a man in here who needs help," he went on, ushering the two newcomers forward. When they continued to hesitate, Vale raised his voice. "Come on. Time's running out."

The two men stepped forward falteringly. They stepped over bodies close by the church door and Vale could see the shock and distaste on their faces as they moved deeper inside the church.

Doyle was laying on a pew close to the altar at the far end of the nave. He too was covered in blood.

Vale walked towards him, leading the way with the two men following.

"What the hell happened here?" one of them asked.

"You wouldn't believe me if I told you," Vale said, softly.

Doyle actually managed to sit up as Vale drew closer to him.

"They'll get you to hospital," the younger man said.

Doyle nodded, wincing as a fresh spasm of pain ripped through him. Even in the darkness of the church, Vale could see how pale his face was.

"More fucking hospitals," Doyle grunted.

Vale smiled thinly, watching as the men helped Doyle onto the stretcher, both of them then lifting him, transporting him from inside the building.

Vale walked alongside the stretcher as the men headed back to the waiting air ambulance.

"I wonder who I report to now," he murmured. "Now Granger's gone."

Doyle managed a weak smile.

"It's going to take a long report to describe this shit," he sighed.

Vale watched as the stretcher was loaded into the chopper. The medics hurried to hook Doyle up to a drip as the rotor blades began to spin, the sound growing louder by the second.

Vale prepared to move away from the helicopter. He felt tired. Drained of energy.

Drained of life?

"I'll come and see you in hospital," he said, squeezing Doyle's shoulder gently.

"Don't forget the grapes," the older man breathed, wincing as he felt more pain.

Vale squeezed his shoulder again and leaned close to his ear.

"They're in a better place now," he murmured. "My father. Georgie. All of them. They're at peace now."

"Do you believe that?" Doyle croaked.

"I'm not sure what I believe any more."

"Join the club."

"Doyle, what we did in the church," Vale began. "Will it work?"

"We'd better hope so," Doyle told him. "What else could we do?"

The younger man nodded slowly.

The pilot signalled to Vale, who understood and prepared to leave the chopper. As he was about to clamber out, Doyle reached out and grabbed his hand.

"Vale," he breathed, and the younger man leaned closer. "You're still a cunt."

Gideon Vale smiled.

Sean Doyle closed his eyes.

EPILOGUE

ONE HUNDRED AND TWENTY-SEVEN

The sun was shining brightly. Weather forecasters had spoken of a heatwave and as the burning orb hung in the heavens now, warming those beneath and glinting on the surface of the Thames, it certainly looked as if they might be right for once.

In most offices the air-conditioning was adjusted accordingly as temperatures rose inexorably. The offices of the Counter Terrorist Unit were the same. Employees there enjoyed the benefit of the cool air pumped into their working environment and those fortunate enough to occupy offices overlooking the Thames looked out longingly at those who walked along its banks or travelled on the waterway itself. Most were tourists admittedly but there were many inside the building who would have happily swapped places with those outside enjoying the sun.

Inside one particular room within the building it was cooler than ever.

The room was in the lower reaches of the complex. In order to get to it by lift one would need to press the button on the panel marked B -2.

But few visited this lower level. They had no need to. No need and no desire.

The figure who now stepped from the lift and strode along the corridor beyond certainly had no desire to be in this part of the building but a visit to these nether regions was periodically necessary and he was the one chosen to make this pilgrimage.

Most of the rooms in this lower level were storerooms. Everything from ammunition to phone batteries was kept down here. There was a rumour that somewhere down here was a secret passageway that connected the building to the bunker beneath the Houses of Parliament, but no one was prepared to say whether that was fact or urban myth. It would have made sense but the figure walking along the corridor had never had reason or cause to discover the validity of that particular claim.

He passed more storerooms, finally coming to another door at the far end of the corridor. By tapping a four digit code into the panel there he could gain access to what lay beyond. The code was changed every day and he paused a moment, ensuring that he was certain of the necessary numbers before pressing the first of the buttons. If the code was punched in wrongly then there were two more opportunities to get it right before the system simply locked him out, but he didn't want to take that chance. Satisfied that he had remembered the daily code correctly he pressed the first of the numbered pads.

As the last number was accepted, he saw that the small panel on the right-hand side of the door had turned bright green. The door opened a second later and the man stepped through, finding himself in another narrower corridor beyond. A few paces along this walkway took him to another door, this one too opened only by accessing another numbered panel. The man entered the required numbers here too, the door also opening for him.

The room he found himself in was about twenty feet square. Lit by the harsh white light of the banks of fluorescents in the ceiling, it was completely bare of furniture except for one metal table pushed against the far wall. It was much cooler in here too. At least ten degrees colder than the area beyond.

There were a number of storage units along this same wall which looked like a cross between a filing cabinet and the drawers one might find in a morgue. The cavities where the dead were kept. The store case for sightless eyes.

The man moved to the first of them and gently slid it open.

The human arm that lay inside had been severed at the elbow.

Two thick straps held the limb in position, supported on a

bed of white viscoelastic foam.

The man regarded the limb for a moment longer then slid the drawer closed and opened another.

This one contained a leg.

It had been severed just above the knee and also at the ankle, the stumps cauterised and sealed. Both looked bright red in the cold light. There was no sign of the foot.

The man found that in the next drawer he opened. Like the other body parts, it was secured to foam with straps.

He went through four more drawers, pulling each one out and inspecting the contents carefully before closing it once again. Another arm. Another leg. Another foot. A complete torso.

The last one he opened contained a human head.

Like the other appendages, it too had been severed from its parent body, cut free just above the lower jaw. It rested on a metal tray, held in place by strong plastic restraints that kept it upright on its stump. The man gazed at the head for a moment wondering why it had been cut off in such a way. Why not sever it below the chin and keep it complete? There was no blood beneath the stump, just a clear fluid that occasionally dribbled into the metal dish. He leaned closer, inspecting the surprisingly supple flesh.

The eyes jerked open, pinning him in an unblinking stare.

The man took a step back, surprised by the movement but he regained his composure and continued to look at the head, held in the gaze of those wide rheumy eyes. They looked him up and down then the lids closed once more.

The man pushed the drawer closed, happy to be free of that piercing look. His hands were shaking slightly as he closed the compartment, turning away to head towards the door by which he'd entered. He hoped he wouldn't have to come back in here again. He had no desire to look upon the dismembered body and severed head of David Callahan once more.

It would be someone else's turn next time and, for that he was grateful. If he never ever had to set foot inside that room again it would be fine with him.

He closed the door and headed back along the corridor, glad to be out of that room.

Behind him, wide eyes bulged in their sockets and stared furiously into the darkness, as they would for the rest of eternity.

"Confusion, all sanity is now beyond me.
Delusion, all sanity is but a memory.
My life, the war that never ends..."
Metallica